The Heart of an Artichoke

Katie Butterworth

© 2018, SAUGUS BOOKS

For this and other Saugus Books offerings go to http://facebook.com/pg/Saugus-Books
Feel free to leave a comment there, send an email to saugus.books@gmail.com. and also,
please write a review at the Amazon website.

THE HEART OF AN ARTICHOKE
ISBN-13: 9780998588018 (soft cover)

ISBN: 0998588016

Printed in the United States of America.

Acknowledgement

The editor is grateful to Cristina Ramirez for transcribing the original typescript to a digital format, to Austin Allen for creating front and back the covers, and to author Kat Argo, a Francophile, for reading the manuscript. Copy editing of the entire interior and the production of the finished book was performed by editor Francis M. Butterworth.

1

Arrival in France

"**I** tell you, Bet, I'm worried," Jim said.

"Just think—we're in France," Betty answered, refusing to listen to his blues.

"You'd better stand still, Mary dear," Jim said patiently, squinting the smoke out of his eyes. With a cigarette in his mouth, he was trying to disengage the zipper that had become caught at the back of his small daughter's dress.

They were at the Hotel du Sud in St.-Raphael, where they had arrived late the night before.

Betty was trying to find her sewing kit, not sure in which suitcase she had packed it. "To think we've been in Paris a whole week," Betty continued. "And now we're on the Mediterranean. It is so thrilling!"

"There you are, *Marie*," Jim said in the same even tone. "I guess that's what I'll have to call you from now on—*Marie*."

Mary ran to the window to exclaim over a darling donkey pulling an enormous cart. "Oh, Daddy, let's get a donkey. For Peter and me."

"My dear girls. Let's be sensible. What we really need is the New York Stock Report in the Paris *Herald Tribune*, if Peter ever comes back with it. Where is that boy anyway?"

"But Jim, we've seen the Winged Victory, Venus de Milo, and Mona Lisa. We've been up in the *Eiffel* Tower. *Notre Dame. Ste.-Chapelle.* I'll admit, I was worried, at first, too, about that French maid who stayed with the children when we went dancing at the Club Pigalle. But what fun we had! Only in France would they have those mounds of little colored celluloid balls swirling underfoot as we danced. And this nightgown you bought me. *'Parisienne at Au Printemps.'* How can we be sensible and worry about the stupid old stock market?" Betty stuck out her lower lip.

"The nightgown, darling, would have been of finer material if you had bought it at Wanamaker's in Philadelphia. And just as cheap, my dear," Jim sighed.

Their boat, the *Minnekahda*, **[See end of book.]** had landed at Le Havre at the end of October in the year 1929. They had left the United States in a golden aurora of boom times such as America had never before experienced. Money was everywhere, and while it was not yet growing on trees, nor were the streets paved with gold, still it was "easy come." People were buying anything and everything. And if you bought stocks, any stocks, a week later you had doubled your money, or so it seemed. But in the ten days it took their boat to cross the Atlantic, the money world had changed. Down, down, and away went all those golden profits. Already the French, used to their own postwar depression, were referring in their newspapers to "*Le Craque* du Wall Street," and they were rather malicious about it.

If Jim had been on the scene back home, he consoled himself, it would not have seemed so frightening, but over here, with only an expensive cable rope to take hold of, the nervous insecurity was terrific. Instead of selling some stocks and putting the actual money in the bank, both for his business and for the letter of credit for this trip, as he had originally intended to do, he had given his stocks to the bank for security and arranged to borrow more money. With the boom, he might have hoped to pay for the whole trip out of his profits. Well, some declines were to be expected. After all, he had lived through the 1921 slump, which had quickly righted itself, but in 1929 the declines had a ruthlessness that was alarming.

He had joked at first, then nervously read each day's Paris *Herald Tribune*. Today he was scared. They should have stayed in Paris. He had wanted to. He knew now he should have insisted. Nobody would even know what a stock market was in this small town.

Betty, in her way, was as determined, as stubborn. "Why, James Barton!" she had blazed at him. "We have set the date to go to St.-Raphael. I have written Mr. Glisson when we are coming, even the train, and no old stock market is going to stop us."

Bet was different somehow. Or perhaps she had been changing these last few years; it took this trip to bring it out. He couldn't follow her. It was wonderful the way she had arranged everything. He knew they would still be home if he had had the management of it. They had traveled a long way from Merchantville, New Jersey.

Fundamentally, he hated change. He hadn't realized before how much he disliked it. What a mania Bet had for everything new, everything French. It made him want to defend the familiar, the American way.

Relying on his experience during the war years in France, Jim had at first played Ambassador-at-large as they toured all the sights of Paris, and he had been entertained by Betty's effervescent energy, amazed at how she could keep it up. For the first few days, his enthusiasm had matched hers. "Bet, look at that. Bet, you must see this. But how it's changed since 1917." He found that from 1917 to 1929 was a long time. Memories of ten years shone with a glow that was out of proportion to their present value. It was like coming back to something in your childhood. How small it looked, rather worn out, shabby in spots. Or had he aged more than he realized? Certainly France had not modernized itself as rapidly as America had.

Jim admitted it would be nice to rent a place and eat some simple home-cooked food. Traveling in trains and living in hotel bedrooms and public restaurants with two children aged five and seven was not the restful vacation he had fancied. He wasn't used to his own children, he discovered. He never had experienced any of their care; there always had been a grandmother or a maid around to help out. They tired him and worried him.

"I think I'd better go down and see if Peter is all right. He's been gone more than ten minutes," Jim said, looking at his watch.

"Silly. Peter thinks he's older than you are. It would spoil all his adventure if you should follow him. You worry too much about them."

"Well, you don't worry at all. I've never seen such a woman."

Betty laughed indulgently. "It is because I have been their caretaker, their nursemaid, their guardian, ever since they were born. I know what to expect of them. And you? Their father? You've lost touch, locked up in your garage. Now you can get acquainted with them. Didn't hear you complaining about going to live in France? 'What, live in one town? Not me. We'll tour, move around.' And you'll find, too, that you won't spend as much money living here this winter. We'll save money. It will be cheaper than keeping our big house at home. Renting a house for six months, we can get a much better price. Renting for a year, we'd do even better." Betty sighed. "But I don't suppose you'd consent to that, the way things are."

"Right now, even six months is out of the question," Jim said. At the same time, he felt himself weakening, giving in to Betty again, the way he had all along on this trip. *Why didn't he say, out and out, We're not going to rent a house until we find out what the stock market is doing?* It was a though he were afraid of her.

Jim looked at his watch. "That boy's been fifteen minutes now. I'm going down to look for him."

"Here he is," Mary cried, still looking out the window. "And he has a man with him."

"With a man! What is he doing out on the street anyway? I told you we shouldn't have let him go alone." Jim looked out to see his son holding the paper in one hand, the hand of a stranger in the other. They were entering the doorway below. Jim hurried to go down, but in the hall he met them coming up.

"Daddy, this is Monsieur Glisson," Peter said proudly.

Jim was nonplussed and stood there awkwardly, What did the fellow mean by coming up to their bedroom? Why didn't he announce himself and wait downstairs in the reception room? And how had Peter got hold of him in the first place? Jim stood blocking the door.

But the Frenchman, smiling, remained where he was, as though it were quite the thing to be received in a bedroom unannounced at nine in the morning. He bowed slightly as he spoke. "My little friend"—he nodded in Peter's direction—" brought me up, so there was nothing to do but come." His English was stiff but perfect. "A coincidence. I received you letter from Paris yesterday, and just now I stopped in to make reservations as you asked, and I found not only had you already arrived but your son was asking for the newspaper. Madame at the desk was trying to tell him he would have to go down to the kiosk at the corner, so I took him myself. Monsieur Barton, it is a pleasure. As you have already guessed, it is Gilbert Glisson who presents himself." Formally, he bowed again, shifted his beret to his left hand, and held out his right hand to shake.

Jim was touched by the sight of the beret and the trenchcoat the man was wearing. Recalling war days, he was about to invite Mr. Glisson to come downstairs and have a drink.

Betty's voice came clear and bright from behind him. "Jim dear, why don't you invite *M'sieur* Glisson to come in?"

Annoyed, Jim moved aside, feeling as though he were introducing this strange Frenchman to a huge double bed and two cots, all unmade, pajamas, nightgowns, slippers, toothbrushes, unpacked bags strewn everywhere. My dear, it's perfectly impossible," he muttered.

No one but Jim seemed to mind. The two children were absorbing the Frenchman. Monsieur Glisson took two steps forward, put his heels together, and bowed low over Betty's hand. Betty, looking as pleased as a pussycat, was effusive and started using her French. "Oh, Monsieur. C'est un plaisir. My aunt, you know her. Nous sommes heureux. It is so exciting to be here."

Monsieur Glisson straightened himself but still held Betty's hand. "And I hope Madame Barton had a comfortable ride from Paris. It is a long trip." He pronounced their name each time with the French accent—Bar-tone. "And now I want to meet your little girl." He shook Mary's hand as formally as he had her mother's.

"*Oh, bien, bien, M'sieur.* Won't you sit down? If we can find a place. As you can see, we are not prepared for callers."

Jim felt enraged with his wife, with the affected half-French she was using. It was idiotic when the man spoke English.

He could have saved himself his annoyance. Monsieur Glisson was adequate to the unmade beds with a polite smile. "No, it is not possible for me to remain. Thank you, Madame. Why do you not come over to my office, in an hour perhaps, or when you wish? It is right next door. We live in the back, you know. My mother would be only too glad to look after the children, and I can take you around and show you a few houses this morning. Or is that hurrying you too fast?"

"Not at all," Jim answered, smiling with relief now that the man was not going to stay.

"We'll stop at your office in a few minutes."

After the Frenchman had left, Jim's eye caught the headline, "Stocks Rally," and he sighed with relief. Sitting on the edge of their bed, he read the details. For the moment it looked encouraging. Maybe these forebodings were a false alarm. The first drop in prices had been so sudden, there had been no warning ahead of time. To have it happen when he was over here in France, with no one to talk to, made it even worse. He kept assuring himself, *Your imagination is making it worse than it is.* If only he could be back in America, talk to his broker, or drop in at the garage to see his foreman, Joe, make a few telephone calls. Even to talk to someone on the street corner: *Well, how are things going? What do you think of prices in general?* Any one of these thing would be a consolation.

There was no use in expressing all these thoughts which kept whirling around in his mind. Betty had no sympathy for his dilemma, even though it concerned her just as deeply.

Suddenly he came to a decision with himself. *We can rent a house for a month. This Frenchman seems to think it easy. That'll give us a base, the kids can relax, it will make Betty happy. Then I can run up to Paris if things get worse in a day or so. And if it is really bad, we'll all get a boat home.*

Out loud he said, "Okay, kids. Okay, Bet. Let's take a little walk, then call on this real estate guy, Glisson."

2

Background; Betty and Jim

Betty Moon had majored in French at Smith College, and after graduation she had planned a year in France to perfect her accent and give her the polish that would be useful in teaching the language. An only child, she had been carefully brought up—private school, tennis lessons, ballet, skating, vacations in the White Mountains. Her father, a successful lawyer, was able to provide these luxuries which Betty took more or less for granted in the society of Merchantville, New Jersey. Her parents were ready to give her anything she wanted, but they were not particularly interested in a European tour for themselves, and to allow Betty to go to France alone was out of the question. They wanted her to go with a group, or at least another girl, and to be mature enough to handle any foreign situation that might occur.

All during the war, when she was growing up, she had romanticized about France, reading about visiting French generals like Joffre, who came to the United States to stimulate the war effort, and stories of *les pauvres poilus* in the trenches.

Her father had adopted a French orphan and sent fifteen dollars a month through the Red Cross to help educate the boy, whose father had been killed. In exchange, they received a picture of a thin child dressed in a black pinafore, with a letter on blue-checked paper thanking the kind American *benefacteur*. Betty had quite a correspondence with this French boy, and she asked her father to send more money the second year.

Back home two days after graduation in 1920, Betty went to the country club dance, where she met Jim Barton, also of Merchantville. Jim was five years her senior, and he was just back from an overseas assignment in France. He was a second lieutenant. They danced together the whole evening, and when they weren't dancing they were sitting away from the crowd and exchanging life histories, Jim had actually been in the trenches, he had been in Paris when the armistice was signed, and then he had spent the rest of the time as evacuation clerk in Bordeaux.

"But wasn't Bordeaux a fascinating town—on the sea, quaint old houses, picturesque marketplace, peasants coming into town?"

My dear young lady, the place was swarming with doughboys longing to get back to America. Don't forget, I worked in an office. My one idea was to sign my own release papers."

"But what about the French girls? French cuisine?"

Jim laughed out loud. "Cuisine? That's a good word for bully beef. We were fed American rations, and they were terrible. When I was on leave in Paris, I was too drunk to care what I ate. And girls? Well, you know what kind of girls collect around an army. As soldiers our chief worry was, well, not to get infected. No." he leaned over toward Betty and took her hands. "No. Give me an American girl every time."

Jim was disarming, with his dimples, his brown eyes, his smile. And what a divine dancer! The next day he came to call and met Betty's mother. She said, "What a nice young man." That evening, when Jim called to take Betty out to the movies, her father remarked, "That young man will go places. He has a head on his shoulders."

Jim Barton had always worked, beginning as a paperboy, then at odd jobs, but mostly he worked in his father's garage. He put himself through Drexel, and then, with all the war propaganda, he had enlisted. His parents were distressed but helpless, and proud too. What a relief when he came home unhurt. He began working for his father as an extra hand in the garage, wanting to build up a Packard agency.

Jim was an impatient man, and shortly the engagement of Elizabeth Moon to James Barton was announced in the papers. Wedding plans followed. The two families exchanged get- togethers—teas, showers, dinners—rather a strain on Jim's mother and father, unused to Merchantville society. In 1921, they were married, and what a handsome couple they made. James, six feet tall, carried himself well with his army training, those dimples showing as he walked down the aisle. Elizabeth's blue eyes sparkled, and her blond hair was marcelled and showing under a cloud of white tulle veil.

Betty's father gave them a brand new house for a wedding present. At first, Jim demurred.

"We can't afford it, Mr. Moon."

"But my dear young man, you can't afford not to accept it. your attitude is commendable, but isn't it sensible for my daughter to have something she needs now? Later she will inherit what she probably won't need."

"I'm not enough of a lawyer to argue the case, Mr. Moon," Jim answered. "But I promise you this. Someday I'll match your gift by way of the successful management of my father's agency."

Why don't we go to France for our honeymoon?" Betty suggested.

My dear, I'm just back from France six months. Someday, yes, but there's too much to do right here in America."

Unfortunately, two events took place in rapid succession. Without warning, Jim's father, a rugged man, hardworking, boasting he had never been ill in his life, did become ill. He developed cancer and in eight months he was dead. Jim's mother was inconsolable. She was a frail woman who had been unable to have more children after her first child, and she had centered he life on her husband and her son. Jim and Betty urged her to come live with them, but she realized more than they seemed to that their lives would be quite different from hers. She stayed on in the small old house next to the garage, with the extra bonus of Jim's daily visits. He often had lunch with her.

The other misfortune was the 1921-22 panic. Jim's father had died happy that his son had made such a successful marriage and not knowing that the new agency would soon be experiencing a financial crisis. Business was at a standstill, and the automobile industry, where an agency had to guess what the future would be, was hard hit. At that time the stock market decline was considered a corrective move; newspapers called it a money panic, a readjustment after the war. Later the papers described it as a preparation for the boom times that were to follow. Though, worried at the time and distressed by his father's death, Jim managed. He was young, and his war years gave him the tough philosophy that one had to accept what came. He used to quote from his army days, "Field improvisations, that's how we survive."

And Jim and Betty were in love, magically in love. Jim would woo her before dinner, when Betty stood with a fork testing their steak. He swept her up, fork, apron, and all, turned the gas off in passing, and carried her to the couch. She would be awakened in the middle of the night, at dawn, and Betty loved him for it, but she was slow, untrained in lovemaking. She longed for the romantic perfection of love in the magazine style. She thought she had it, but too often he was too fast for her. Too often she lay awake beside him while he slept the heavy sleep of after-love. Sometimes she thought she loved him the most when he was sleepy, lazy, satisfied. Then her embraces were allowed their own pace, slowly awaking until she too relaxed, lying in the protective warmth of his nearness. There was a wildness that would flare up within her, beyond her control. Only occasionally would it flare up in time to meet his climax. Her abandon at these times alarmed Jim rather than making them one.

As an attractive couple in their new home, they quickly expanded their social life. Betty renewed old childhood friendships, Jim met new people through business, and they were invited to join various clubs.

Betty had to keep calendar notes to remember all the invitations and meetings. Then the baby came, a boy they named Peter. The baby was brought up modern, punching his time clock for meals and sleep, no one allowed in the house with a cold, all toys disinfected, with the net result that the grandparents did as much spoiling as they could on the sly, and Betty grew thin with the anxious care of her first child. Peter was healthy, super-intelligent, and of a nervous disposition. There was a little maid, a "half-grown girl," who washed diapers, floors, and dishes in rotation, but she was not allowed to touch the baby.

And before long, there was a second child, named Mary after Jim's mother. "I wanted a girl, and here she is," said Papa Jim. He held her up, and there was no doubt, wise child or stupid, about who was her father. Brown eyes, dimples, winning smile, even the placid disposition was there. There was little fuss this time, visiting colds entered, toys were dropped on the floor, the microscopic maid metamorphosed into a broad-shouldered black woman, Lila, who grew more and more permanent. When Betty wasn't boiling bottles and milk, she was lowering the buttons on little Peter's suits. There were snow suits and galoshes in winter, woolens to be put in camphor in the spring, Jim's suits to be sent to the cleaner, the grandparents coming to dinner, the garden to be weeded, and jelly and preserves in the fall. Betty was an excellent housekeeper, and Jim was a busy bread-winner, and sometimes at dinner she would look across the table and say to herself, *Who is this man I married? I never see him anymore.*

Jim would look up at Betty, notice a thinness along her cheek line, call her "old girl," and then recount the latest news at the garage. The business took up most of his time. "We're running harder and harder just to keep up," he would say. Garages are absorbing things. When a new car was sold, Jim invited her out to dinner, leaving Lila no feed baby Mary and Peter sad and wistful, waving goodbye at the window.

If one asked Jim what was most important in his life, he would not have hesitated to say that his garage headed the list. Otherwise, he couldn't afford to have a wife, children, a house, and the social life he and Betty enjoyed. Betty, however, would have put the garage at the foot of the list. For her, the children naturally came first, but her husband, her house, and her friends were often jumbled together.

"I never see you anymore," she complained to Jim. "It's Rotary, Elks, bowling..."

"Seems to me you're pretty busy yourself. Book Club, Bridge Club, the Women's Republican Club has just invited you to join, and I think you should. They do very good work in town."

"I forgot the Army Reserve," Betty added.

"But that's awfully important, for both business and promotion. You know I've been upped to first lieutenant. If I got to be major in the reserve, on retirement I would get a very attractive pension." He laughed. "Might even get a tour of French battlefields thrown in."

"Really? Wives included? I forgot to tell you, that couple we met the other night at the country club are talking their vacation in France this year. He's the one who teaches French at La Salle College. Taking their children, too."

"Too expensive for us. Yet."

"Well, Aunt Eliza, how was France?" Jim asked, coming into the living room.

"Betty, your husband is as impossible as ever. Can't you teach him? Eight years, isn't it, or eighteen you've been married?" Aunt Eliza was smoking a Russian cigarette in a long ivory holder, looking like a mid-Victorian antimacassar resurrected by a modern dealer of antiques.

"What's the matter with the question?" Jim said, stubbornly repeating it and ignoring her last question. She knew they had been married eight years to a day, or she wouldn't have asked to begin with. He had learned this much about Betty's Aunt Eliza: she was an original. Such a pose, smoking that ridiculous cigarette, and doing it to see if she could get a rise out of him. A woman her age. "What is the matter with the question, when you've just come from France and we haven't seen you for a year and a half?"

"The matter with the question, my dear James, is that you know the answer before you ask for it. You know that France is the most wonderful place in the world. And that it is perfectly horrible to be back in the U.S.A."

"Speak for yourself, Aunt Eliza. The good old U.S.A. is good enough for me."

"Oh, Aunt Eliza, do tell Jim about that little town in the south of France you were telling me about. I know Jim would love to hear." Betty had to act as a buffer between Aunt Eliza and her husband. Her mother's only sister, a peppery New England spinster, stilted and Bostonian, enjoyed the incongruity of being both prudish and unconventional. Her views were a trial to Jim.

"St.-Raphael, my dear," Aunt Eliza prompted Betty. Then she turned again to Jim. "I was telling your wife, my dear James, all about this Mediterranean town for a purpose. I want you to take your wife and two children and go to live there for a year. It is high time Elizabeth learned about Europe. I always thought she was entitled to her year abroad before she ever married you. However, it is not too late. And it will be a terrific experience for the children, to say nothing of yourself." She straightened herself in the upright chair she had dragged from the hall into the living room (she despised overstuffed furniture) and glared at Jim. "War doesn't count," she forestalled.

As he was about to bring up one of his war experiences, he glared back. Then he laughed.

"Ridiculous. Perfectly ridiculous. A year! My eye! It is easy enough to see what France has done to you. It's put you off your rocker."

Aunt Eliza unbent enough to smile. "James, your reaction is perfect." The battle was on. The children came into the room, and she gave them kisses on both cheeks, French-style, and whispered something, intimating presents. They were her only great-niece and-nephew, Betty was her favorite niece, and she was fond of Jim, or she wouldn't have considered him worth fighting with.

It was spring of 1929, the first warm day. The windows were open, the smell of earth and Grass that rises after gentle spring rains came into the room to mix with the steam of hot asparagus, lamb chops, hot biscuits, and the tang of fresh young scallions. They were American smells, clear, distinct, none of this foreign blending of sauces. The room was distinctly American, too. When their mahogany dining-room set was bought, it had just missed the Early American influence—Betty wished she could have waited—but it was good of its kind, heavy, solid, glass knobs on the big sideboard.

The dinner conversation was all about France. Aunt Eliza talked of the Luxembourg Gardens, boats to sail, Punch and Judy shows for free. She told of steamboats on the Seine whose smokestacks were on a hinge, tipped back when the boat went under a bridge: little black pinafores the children wore over their suits and dresses, boys and girls alike, when they went to school: the advantages of living in a small town where the children could live at home and still go to school, none of those convent schools where one didn't know what was happening to one's own children; the convenient little villas to hire with electricity and gas and fine bathtubs, and so reasonable; a laundry where the bare-armed girls sang and ironed a nightgown, pleated and starched and pinned in pale blue tissue paper so it looked newly bought from the store. All done with style, a sense of form. She chose her stories to catch the ear of Mary, Peter, and Betty, and in this she succeeded. As fast as she told one story, they would ask, "Where does the smoke go without the smokestack up?" "Don't the children ever speak English?" "How much would the food be?" "Would it be possible to buy milk for the children?"

Jim alone refused to be impressed. "Why do you come home?" he taunted her. "That's a thing none of you Francophiles will deny yourselves. You always come back to the United States."

"Contrast, my dear James, contrast. Who is talking of leaving America? A separation, though, is good for one sometimes. From countries and people included. Makes you appreciate the good things of America." Aunt Eliza nodded her head over the hot biscuits.

"Oh, then you say something good about America?"

Back and forth they bickered, each pretending to be fierce, occasionally giving a dig that hurt. Betty tried to be the fair mediator, but she was exhilarated by her aunt's stories of France. How she would love to do it, go over there now with Jim and the children for a year. It would give them a new life, and they needed one. Sun and simple things. She had spent an exhausting winter. She and Jim had expended enough energy on club activities to have taken their family by prairie schooner out west and back again. How divine to be where the telephone could not interrupt every meal!

The warm weather had brought out the fact that Peter had jumped a size and a half in summer socks and underwear, and Mary had to have all new clothes. Jim had put on weight, and Betty had found a couple of gray hairs. They must snatch at youth while it was still with them. She hadn't seen Jim to talk to before one o'clock a single night this week, and tonight, their wedding anniversary, he had to go to his Rotary Club because he was on the nominating committee, and she was going to take Aunt Eliza to one of the country club evenings where there would be a benefit concert with refreshments. Everybody would be there, and she had promised Roberta to sit at her table. Jim was to join them afterward. Why were they letting life slip by? To grow more distantly acquainted each year?

That evening, one-thirty as usual, Betty was winding her watch and laying it down on her dressing table. Jim was already in bed rereading the paper.

"Jim," she said, "wouldn't you really adore it?" The thought of a year in France had not left her throughout the evening.

"Sure. It would be wonderful. Come on to bed. We have more important things to discuss."

"You don't even know what I'm talking about."

"Wedding anniversaries. But I remembered this year. Remember the year I forgot? That was pretty awful. I have it down an my calendar now. And every January second. One of Tillies's first jobs is to fill in all birthdays and anniversaries for the new year. I suppose you hate my efficiency. Why not be efficient, I say? There isn't time not to be."

"Jim darling," she said. "Not wedding anniversaries, but our trip to France." She came over with her brush and sat down beside him on the bed. Her eyes were crinkled up from laughing at him.

He could feel the warmth of her body through his pajamas and her silk things. She was nice. He buried his head in the warm softness of her lap. "You smell so good."

"But Jim, now is the time, if ever," Betty insisted, refusing to be deterred by lovemaking.

"Your business has never been better, you have a foreman you can trust, you have the office organized and a good salesman. I have some allowance money saved up from college. Now is the perfect time. Aunt Eliza tells me how cheap living in France is compared to America. You and I and the children. We can do it. tomorrow I am writing for the passport, for the boat tickets. We are going, Jim. I tell you, we are going."

Jim laughed and proceeded briskly with his affectionate attentions.

3

The town; Gilbert

St.- Raphael is situated on the Mediterranean halfway between Marseille and Nice.

Recovering from World War I, the town's working population was busy exporting bauxite, the reddish stone that goes to make aluminum, and blue porphyry, a stone used for show-front city buildings, quarried from the Esterel Hills. Cork bark was judicially cut in great slices from the cork oak forest so that the trees would continue to live and grow more bark. Sloops, either from Italy or from Marseille, would dock at the miniature port, trading olive oil for barrels of wine or the mine timber cut from forests growing ever farther back. Sardine fishing, even in those days, was a losing trade, yet boats lined the beach, and fishermen talked of better days.

In addition, businessmen wanted a real resort town, in competition with Nice, and big plans were under way. Hotels were started, villas were built on speculation, a casino was placed in the center of town, and a fine promenade to connect hotel and center followed a section of the Boulevarde du Touring Club de France, which became the famous

Corniche d'Or as one drove on to Cannes and Nice. A few English began to arrive for winter vacations, and shops sold tinned biscuits, India tea, rolls of toilet paper, but the casino never had the glamour of the big casino in Nice, and the mistral wind seemed to blow harder here than where there was more luxury and greater crowds.

The postwar depression set in, and hotels remained half finished, lots up on the hills were without houses, and the bandstand on the promenade could only afford a forlorn radio on Saturday night. There was one brilliant spot, the flower shop. The florist was a genius, and his *jeune fille*, who minced and clacked her high heels inside clumsy black wooden sabots, not for affectation but to keep her feet dry, was an artist. The shop window was large like a stage, and with the shop door open the perfumes of heaven escaped. It was a sight to make one stop. Violets, stock, pinks, roses, lilacs, primroses. Veined, passion-red anemone. Feathery yellow tufts of mimosa.

VAROOM! Suddenly, This delightful, colorful scene and floral aroma was rudely shattered by the choking smell of auto exhaust and engine sounds. The motor of a small yellow Citroen, eight years old with a bent fender, started furiously. It was beginning to rain, and, with the top down, Gilbert Glisson wanted to make for home. He had graying hair and a slight mustache, and he wore a belted trench coat and a beret on one side of his head. He looked like any Frenchman of moderate means. His dreams of becoming a famous architect in Paris had been modified by the war. He still hoped to use some of his Sorbonne training in this small town. Collecting rents was hardly inspiring. But now he was smiling because he had just collected the quarter's rent for one of Monsieur Poupai's houses in Boulouris, a summer extension of St.-Raphael, and he needed his commission. Business had been poor this year, but now, at the end of the summer season for French vacationers, he was already hopeful for the English winter visitors. Only this morning, he had had a letter from an American family who wanted to rent a place. He couldn't wait to tell his mother.

Without slowing down for the right-hand turn he had to make onto the Boulevarde du Touring Club, he missed a truck by inches. He swerved and honked his horn wildly for an old peasant stomping down the road with his back to the traffic and not stepping aside one inch for the modern donkeyless wagons that rushed past him. Gilbert shouted at him, but the old peasant would not raise his head. Two minutes later, he was in the center of town and stopped with jerk of the brakes in front of his own office. Cook's Travel was on one side, the Hotel du Sud on the other, the post office opposite. Whatever his business returns might be, it was a satisfaction to be well situated. He and his mother lived in an apartment in back, two rooms, bath, and kitchenette.

The office was empty. His mother had a janglebell attached to the door for when she was busy in back. "Hello there," Gilbert called out so that she wouldn't come through. He locked the door behind him, as it was one o'clock. "Well, and how goes it today?" He kissed her. He was devoted to his mother, particularly since the death of his father. "Not only did I get Poupai's rent, but I have a letter all the way from America, and they want a house for six months. Think of that, two big transactions in one day."

"Oh, Gilbert." Old Madame Glisson rolled out the name to its full French length. She had a Parisian accent, clear and precise, none of this sing-song guttural Provencal for her. "Tell me more, Quick, quick."

They sat opposite each other at a small table in the living room, beside a wood fire burning pleasantly. Four plates were stacked at each place, and as they finished Madame removed the soiled plate on top, leaving a fresh one for the next course. She let him finish his lamb stew with white pearl onions and capers in the gravy and placed a steaming artichoke on his clean plate before she began again. "Where in the world did they get hold of your name?"

"I feel much better." Gilbert sat back. He knew he was teasing her by making her wait, but it was good for her, he had let her become far too concerned with his affairs. He told himself this as he watched the fine wrinkles of her skin, the mottled spots that showed on her cheeks. She was beginning to show her sixty years. That illness she had last summer in the hot spell had been too much for her. "Remember that crazy American woman who came into my office when Cook's man had the flu last winter? We bought her tickets for her trip through Italy."

"Oh, that one. I'll never forget her hat. And her French! Imagine, a teacher of French. Such an accent! Surely she can't have a husband.

'Her grammar was correct, you'll have to admit. She is the aunt. It is her niece who wrote the letter. She is coming with her husband and two children. For six months. I think I shall rent her one of the Countess's little houses. She wants something reasonable."

Gilbert sighed and smiled and handed it over. His mother was right. She should have been the businessman. All French women were businessmen. Look at the way they ran the cafes and hotels. He began on his artichoke, dipping the leaves in a saucer of melted butter. "The niece has studied French in school, but she apologizes as she's forgotten much."

His mother paid no attention but read the letter over again. "If I were doing it, I would double the rents. That would give you a chance to be generous and come down as a special favor."

"You know, to listen to you, anyone would think you a tight-fisted capitalist. And it will be you who will make friends and carry over chestnut soufflé to show off your cooking or give advice when the children are sick."

His mother put out her hands in the gesture of all French women. Her smile was light and very attractive. It was true that she was vain about her chestnut soufflé, and they both laughed. Her eyes brightened as she reread the letter. "You know, this 'bringing the children over for school in France' means something more permanent than just the usual tourist. Show them places to rent, and then, as if on a sudden inspiration, take them up on the wood road. The Blacklocks' house is for sale. They would give you fifteen percent commission. With that much money, you could get through the winter. Or they could rent it with the idea of buying —I'm sure it could be arranged. They might rent a villa and buy our lot up there, and you could build the house for them. The possibilities are endless." Madame's face took on color with the growth of her enthusiasm, then her eyes came back to her son, eating his artichoke and not even looking at her. She was ready to shake him. "And I have another thing I want to talk to you about, too. The whole town is talking, so I feel quite entitled to my share."

"Eh, bien, cherie." Gilbert smiled contritely. His father had made money. As the only son, he, Gilbert, had been given luxuries. He had been at the Sorbonne, but then he was called up by the army. He had survived the war physically, but postwar conditions had led to the present hard times which were beyond anyone's control.

His mother's voice interrupted his thoughts. "I met Mademoiselle Roule this morning."

Gilbert grew busy cleaning the heart of his artichoke. "Has she gained any weight?"

"She is coming to dinner on Sunday."

"That is fine. She'll be company for you. I was planning to be out."

"I could still put you over my knee and spank you. You are going to be here, Gilbert, that is all there is to it."

Gilbert was laughing heartily. "Are you going to quiz her about her dowry? Is this to be the betrothal dinner?" His mother looked serious, but if he continued to banter he might stall off her attack. He wondered how long she had know about his affair with the young widow dressmaker.

"Do you realize how old you are, my dear son?"

"Thirty-six years. Hair beginning to turn gray, and I ought to be married." Gilbert folded his hands and smiled with his head tilted to one side.

His mother laughed, a good sign. "It is a pleasure, Gilbert, to hear it from you. But I see I don't have to remind you that Mademoiselle Roule has an excellent job as a teacher, that her papa owns kilometers of valuable woodland besides a valuable farm, that she is an only daughter not as young as she was five years ago, nor perhaps as thin. But who wants a skinny woman? She is as strong as an ox, and she has beautiful teeth and beautiful eyes, and her mind is as quick as a flash. And she is sweet on you." Madame held out her hands to embrace everything in front of her. "What more can I say? She is a jewel, I tell you. Already she talks to me like a daughter, and that is a lot in her favor." Suddenly her manner changed, and she frowned. "And you. You! Why you should waste your time, your intellect—"

"My dear mother, you confuse me talking about intellect. At any rate, such a marriage could never work."

"It can. I tell you it can." Emotion was pushing her words faster. "Look at your father and me. We adored each other. You just don't know a thing about marriage. Why don't you throw yourself out where I shall throw these artichoke leaves? That's what you are doing with this stupid little chippy. Wasting time, and your hair getting gray. It is all very well at the age of nineteen to study love on a pretty, silly face if you must, and I admit most men do. Or save her for your old age. But now!"

"Where did you hear about Suzanne anyway?" Gilbert was curious.

"Where did I hear about her? With your yellow car in front of her house at any hour. Do you think I am blind? My hair is grayer than yours, but any brain underneath it is wiser." Again her manner changed. Her voice grew low. "You father died, and we took everything and came down here. Paris was too big for a young man starting out. Monsieur Edouard gave you the new branch office down here, they'd bought the land. Everyone expected a real estate boom after the war. I had such hopes you would be a great success, with a good job, and expecting you to marry well. And look at us! The last three years have been disastrous. But if you were to marry Aurelie Roule, you would be a great success."

"But what is there to do?" He became impatient when she reviewed facts he knew as well as she. "Here we are. It is the times, my mother, and they'll grow worse. What can you expect with the franc the way it is? Look at politics. France can't pay its debts. Nor can any other European country. We're in for Bolsheviks and revolutions. You're as bad as the Americans, expecting to make a fortune with the world going to smash. I don't want to marry. It is just another permanent tie—or rather it tries to be permanent. I'll look after you, *cherie*, whatever I do with my own personal life."

"You talk like a Russian. No sense." His mother sighed, cleared the plates, and brought the salad. She sat down to mix the dressing, measuring it carefully in a big wooden spoon held over the bowl, one of vinegar, four of oil, then stirring it over and over. She still had pretty hands, and she still wore the several rings her husband had put on her fingers. *They'll be the last things I'll give up,* she would shout at Gilbert when they were hot in one of these arguments. He was expecting her to say it now.

"You are right about these Americans. I must be firm, but I don't want to scare them away. I've always liked Americans. I knew many during the war. I'm not too bad at business. You were ready to laugh at the aunt, but aren't you glad I was so gracious to her? Bread upon the waters."

"Gilbert, you are wonderful." His mother gave him an affectionate smile. "That smile of yours will win you anything. If it doesn't ruin you. You'd far better be wondering what the husband is like. American men carry their own pocketbooks. It is the men who run business there. But I wish I spoke English as well as you do. It is so hard for me to follow it, and the ones with the money never speak French. Oh, I would lift your business—office, car, and all—right out of your hands. I need to be thirty years old again." She reached across the table and patted his hand. Underneath she was the proudest of mothers.

Gilbert smiled. "How about celebrating? I'll take you to the casino tonight. The movie, I understand, is very good. Let's go." He decided to be magnanimous. "I have it! We'll wait until next week. Take along Mademoiselle Roule. We'll go to the cinema after dinner, the three of us. How will that be?"

His mother seemed very pleased with the idea. "I'll tell her tomorrow. I think we should dress up. I'll wear my black velvet." Then she began again. "You talk about bread upon the waters. Aurelie Roule would repay you a thousand times. You only have to give her a little love. Her heart is big. I know. She does not tell me, but I know. You would marry, all the fuss that goes with it, the new things, the new house, you would be busy. She is a wonderful cook, you know that. The time would pass. If you must, in five years, something, she would not mind if you had to find some pretty little thing, as long as you did it nicely, on the side, and didn't let people know about it. I tell you, she is big and generous, and she would give, give, give."

"She is big, all right," Gilbert interrupted. Anything to stop his mother's voice. She was repeating her constant dream. Maybe the Aurelie girl was nice, but she would stop teaching as soon as she got married, they all did that, and how did one know what the father would give for a dowry? She wasn't living at home. He knew the farm type of people she came from, hard as nails, and close. He found the girl herself tiring, she talked all over the place. She and his mother would be thick as thieves, but where would he come in? Now he was free to do exactly what he wanted. He didn't like her taste; her little apartment up on the hill was the maddest place he had ever been in. Evidently her childhood had been a long denial, and with her teaching job and her own money she bought everything she saw. There was nothing she stopped at; she bought out the department stores, rococo fake modern at its worst, purple grapes the size of oranges on the wallpaper, chairs, structures of glass and metal, with Empire lamps. And the glimpse he had had of her bedroom was a mound of lace and ribbons and little satin pillows. Whereas her parents' home, no doubt, was filled with genuine antiques. No, Aurelie was all right to call on for tea for his mother's sake, but he couldn't see marrying her. In fact, the more he thought about it, the more sure he was that his mother had overbid herself regarding the dowry. It was a delicate question. You couldn't say, *My price is so-and-so, cash on delivery.* Not that he doubted his mother's ability as matched against old man Roule. One thing against his mother was that she was too anxious for the marriage. He pictured himself supporting not only his mother but the girl, too. He would be forced to hustle in earnest. And children. Children! His fancy was checked short. He had better take the bull by the horns.

Abruptly, he spoke. "Have you ever seen Suzanne?"

"No. I never intend to. I suppose you're inviting *her* for dinner." Her voice grew hysterical.

"Are you trying to insult me? Or Aurelie Roule? Have I ever seen her! I wouldn't look at her if I met her face to face. I tell you, Gilbert, you may be thirty-six, but I demand that you stop going to see her. Everyone I meet tells me about it or implies that they know about it. The doctor's wife said she saw you on the promenade last Sunday, and that you bowed to her, with that creature on your arm. You have to stop it. How can you keep on seeing her?"

"My dearest Mother, you're ridiculous. At least laugh about it. I don't suppose the doctor's wife admitted that it was she, in a way, who introduced us. I offered her a lift in the auto one day. She was carrying a bundle. She asked me to take her to the dressmaker's, and I carried the bundle to the door for her. Suzanne answered. She helps her older sister, they live together. And then the next day I stopped at a café in the neighborhood, and Suzanne was sitting there drinking coffee. It was all as casual as that. And she is as pretty and as delicate as Aurelie Roule is a big peasant; she comes to my shoulder. She is a widow, and only twenty. Her husband was a sailor, they were married six months, and he was killed two years ago by some fool thing exploding in the engine room. And she gets a pension; not enough to live on, but it helps."

His mother had been listening in spite of herself. "Stop it, Gilbert, I can't stand it. You've had girls, lots of them, but I feel this isn't as casual as you make out. Or else I'm getting old. That spell last summer. I want to know you are settled, looked after, if anything should happen to me."

Gilbert jumped up. Going over to his mother, he put his arm around her, sitting on the arm of her chair. It annoyed him that she could touch him so easily, that she should play upon his sentiment when it was a matter of her getting her own way against him getting his. She wasn't playing fair. It was this that made him retaliate and say what he did. "Oh, well, *cherie*, if you insist on my marrying, why don't you make me marry Suzanne? She is going to have a baby." As soon as he said it, he knew how brutal he had been.

His mother sprang up from the chair, nearly knocking it over. He stumbled to recover his balance. She screamed, "Gilbert Glisson! What are you trying to tell me?"

"My dear Mother, my dear Mother." He went over to her and tried to take her hands, but she pushed him away.

"You can stand there and talk to me like this! Better that I should be dead." She had reached his chair at the other side of the table. Supporting herself with the back of it, she glared at him. Anger made her face red.

He was a clumsy idiot, that was all. "Mother, Mother. The devil has got into me. I have as much intention of marrying Suzanne as nothing at all. It is enough of a mess as it is. Your poor, poor heart. You have been goading me, but I have no excuse. I'm a fool. Listen, sit down on the couch. So. Here, take a sip of wine. I never should have told you, ever. The thing has become so involved. But nothing matters, really it does not. I shall always be with you, *cherie*. So. Now you feel better."

His mother sat quietly. "Let me hear the whole story." She pressed her hands together in her lap. "Get it over with."

"You really want it?" He took out his handkerchief and wiped her eyes for her. She nodded her head. "I've only know myself a couple of months. It's been hell. Honestly it has. Suzanne never would have done it if her sister hadn't put her up to it, of that I'm sure. She won't say so in so many words, but she is too innocent, and too dumb." He looked at his mother, but she kept looking down at her hands. "The sister thought I'd make a safe husband. I guess Suzanne's reputation is none too good. So she tried this trick, saying that after she was pregnant she tried everything. She and her sister together, they tried everything, but she was afraid to tell me. Very carefully, she waited until she was five months along before she breathed a word to me. That was her sister's doing. I began to notice things myself then. I nearly went insane. I took her to Dr. Bohme. He said it would be a major operation. Too dangerous. She would die if it wasn't done in a hospital, and he couldn't do anything. It was not his specialty. Too much was at stake for him. We went to a midwife, and she, too, was afraid. She advised Suzanne to have the baby and put it out for adoption. Well, there you are. I will not marry Suzanne. I told her I'm too old to be her husband. I'm perfect as her good friend. She'll have to go through with it. It has happened in this world before, and the world keeps on going."

Suddenly, his mother began to cry. She cried into her hands, and then she let him put his arm around her, and she cried on his shoulder. He gave her his handkerchief. "Have you ever known such an ass? I've put in two terrible months. I've tried everything. I've thought of everything any man could think of. But I refuse to marry on a trick like that. Suzanne is resigned to it. After all, she has been married, she is a recent widow, and who will know the dates a few years from now if she wants to keep the baby? She's not a native of St.-Raphael. I'll pay the hospital and doctor, and I'll help out afterward. I'll give her an allowance for the baby."

His mother began to speak slowly. "To think that a son of mine should get himself tied up in such a fashion."

"You'd think, wouldn't you, that I was an innocent boy. Never seen a girl before." Gilbert wanted to laugh but thought he had better not, his mother wasn't yet ready. "The sister knows that she is helpless, but she likes to bluster. Suzanne is surprisingly nice about it. Her sister upsets her more than anything else. She is even making a little layette and talks about a name. She wants a girl. I never dreamed she could be so maternal."

"She is clever. Cleverer than I thought." His mother hardly parted her lips to let the words come out. She twisted the handkerchief around her fingers; it had a big G, one of the ones she had embroidered for his birthday, "She knows you are like the traveler; the wind may bluster and blow, but the warm sun will make you take off your coat. She is a smart one, I can see."

"Now listen *cherie*, you are taking this far too solemnly. Not that I blame you when you find your one and only son is an idiot. But, now look at me." He held her chin and turned her face to his. "I shall never, never, never, I swear this on all my love for you, I shall never marry the girl. You understand, I give you my word. The rest of the thing, bad as it is, will in time blow over. The next two months will be a strain. I can't desert the girl until the child is born. I have talked with Dr. Bohme and he has been kindness itself. He's promised not to tell even his wife—he knows as well as anyone what a gossip she is. By the way, that is why she is sounding you out to find what you know about it. She has seen me over there several times. And he's doing it for practically nothing. He's got Suzanne an endowed bed in the hospital because she is a sailor's widow. I have given two hundred fifty francs to the sisters toward their new chapel. They are delighted and will do anything for me, and I'll donate another two-fifty when she is in the hospital. It won't be so bad. Once the baby is born, that will be behind us, and then we can think of what to do next. I am over my first anger, and I can think out all kinds of solutions, and that is what I want you to do. The first couple of years Suzanne will make all its clothes. A few presents, oh, it is easy. I've even thought of marrying Suzanne off to some nice young man, one in her line. I might begin on the bicycle man. I've spent hours explaining to her that I may be upper-class but I have no money. I tell her how you'll never let her in the house—"

"Well, I won't. Ever!"

"I know, I know. And I tell her how extravagant you are. Now, now, that is just what I tell her! I've made her terrified of you. And how I have to support you, how I never could afford to manage two houses, and then—this is where I really have her—if she marries me, her widow's pension will stop. And you will see to it that we are soon divorced, and then where will she be? Far, far worse off than now. She and her sister have worked up a very nice little business. I told you that Madame Bohme went to them. Now, do you feel more reconciled? It might be much worse. And you are going to be a grandma and didn't even know it."

Gilbert watched her carefully to see how she would take his first joke. The corner of her mouth twitched, but quickly she pulled it down. She spread out the corner of his handkerchief and ran her finger over the initial. She was coming around, and he sighed heavily and reached for his cigarettes, a yellow package, the cheapest the government offered. He hunted for his lighter and saw it over on the desk. He came back and sat down beside her again. He needed a smoke after this ordeal, but it made him feel wonderful to think the confrontation was over and done with. He was still something of a little boy scared of his mother.

He put his arm around her and squeezed her shoulders. They sat there in silence, he smoking, flipping the ashes in the direction of the fireplace and missing by a foot. "we might even adopt the child. How would you like that? And me a proud papa."

"Gilbert, I can joke tomorrow. Today I am too exhausted. Go get the coffee and fruit. The Coffee is all made. There's a good boy."

Gladly he worked, and whistled.

4

Renting the house

The door was unlatched. The bell jangled; they walked in. It was a small, neat room. A vase of dried grasses with a few unusual sea shells sat on a table in the corner. There was a loveseat upholstered in worn brocade, a couple of chairs, and a huge desk with surveyor's maps on the wall behind it.

"Makes me think of old Doc Powell's office when I was a kid," Jim said. "Vintage 1910."

"But so charming, and so French," Betty said. "I think his mother arranged it."

"And so she did." The door in back opened, and Monsieur Glisson was smiling. "You are prompt, but they say that is typical of Americans. By the way I engaged a hotel room for you, a day late, is typically French. But come in. I want you to meet my mother."

Madame Glisson beamed upon Betty, then Jim, shook hands with everybody, and put an arm around each child. "My English is so poor." She shrugged her shoulders. She led Jim to a chair near the couch, and, with a child on each side, she sat opposite.

Betty walked around, taking in the room, lovely with a dark oak armoire, big oak chairs, and a massive table. Bookcases filled with leather-bound volumes, yellow French paperbacks, some English novels. Pillows on the couch of Persian blues, dull reds. The whole effect was warm and homelike, with a big cheerful fire blazing. "How good your fire feels," Betty said, walking over to it. "Oh, look at the pine cones. Aren't they artistic?"

Monsieur Glisson followed her. "More useful than artistic. They are essential to start a fire. Our wood is green and, if wet, impossible."

"Still, I think it is very romantic to use pine cones for kindling wood." She turned her face up to look at him and found his eyes a shade too intimate. She called to her husband, "Jim! Look at the pine cones for kindling wood."

Jim did not hear her. He was talking to Madame Glisson. She was on the couch with the children. Betty wanted to laugh, for Jim with his primitive French was explaining to the old lady the name of each child, their respective ages, what train they came on last night, what his job was in America, that he didn't think much of prohibition, that he had fought in the World War and been to Paris but this was his wife's first trip, and that robbers and murderers did not run loose in the streets of the United States like wild Indians, nor in fact were there many Indians left. Jim was using his slow, loud English with an occasional French word, and Madame would toss off a stream of French and add an English word, but amazingly they seemed to follow each other.

Jim looked at his wristwatch. It was Peter who spoke for him. The two children had been as quiet as proverbial mice. "What I want to know is, when do we go to look for our house?" Peter's voice was clear and made everyone's face turn to the children and soften in smiles.

"Peter, my boy, you said it. Let's get started. Your mother will chatter all day."

"The trouble is, I have only room for half of us in the car. I had thought we might leave the children with my mother." Both children looked at him in disappointment, and Monsieur Glisson could never withstand the sorrow of children. On an impulse, he said, "I tell you what I'll do. We'll all go. I'll take the company car, even though I haven't paid the license fee for this quarter. I'll risk it."

"You don't mean to tell me you get a license by the quarter," Jim said, astonished.

"Of course. You save a lot that way. You don't need it for a couple of months, and you do not take out a license. It is very economical."

"Oh, I think it very sensible," Betty said. "We Americans don't know how to save."

Jim, in disgust, said nothing. Of all the "frog" systems, this one took the cake. Not only for the few pennies one saved, but even the time one spent getting a license, once a year was too often. And they called Americans dollar chasers; these French haggled over sous.

"Well, let's get started," Jim said. He was restless sitting around like this. For the first time since they had started on this crazy trip of Betty's, he was realizing that he could no longer say, "Got to dash, dear," and merely drive to the garage on go to his business haunts in Merchantville. His business world was his tonic, his stimulant. "I'll go with you", he said as Monsieur Glisson was going out the door.

"Want to come along?" he said to Peter. He felt that action would save him over here, action and the company of men. His security returned to him as he waved to Betty. He was leaving the women behind. "What make of car is it?" he asked Monsieur Glisson.

"Chenard-Walcker."

Jim was impressed. He had never heard of it.

Madame explained to Betty. "It would be much better if I stayed here with the children. I am sure Gilbert will be fine. They are very strict, but no, Gilbert must always take risks. If he had the license to the big car, then he would not think to use it. Ah, these man. Your husband, is he like that?"

"I'm afraid he isn't. He plays safe, he is careful. It is I who take the risks in our family."

"So?" Madame looked Betty up and down, a trifle more coldly, Betty thought, than was necessary. But at once the old lady smiled freely. The lines of her face were as fine as the handmade tucks on Betty's new

French nightgown. "Tell me why you come to France. You and your husband are not happy at home? You need adventure? You are bored?"

"I think it is wonderful to travel. It broadens one, gives one a new point of view. Americans are restless, you know. Did you notice how my husband could not sit still? He had to go running off with your son. That is one reason I brought him over here. So he could learn how to relax, so we could sit with nothing to do, to find out about ourselves and each other. He is so busy at home that he hardly sees his children more than to say hello at suppertime."

"It seems a queer way, it is a paradox. To travel thousands of miles to learn how to sit still." Madame laughed gaily. She looked down at little Mary sitting beside her. "Eh, what, petite Marie. What do you think?"

"Is Monsieur Glisson your little boy?"

"Yes, Marie, he is my little boy. But he is a big little boy, eh?"

"Doesn't he have a little boy or a little girl?"

"No, he doesn't, Marie." Old Madame sighed to be reminded of the dressmaker. "Someday maybe."

Betty laughed. "It takes the children. I've been dying to ask if Monsieur Glisson were married. He seems so attractive. Doesn't he like the ladies?"

Madame Glisson nodded her head. "Too well. He likes the ladies. I want him to marry, for a long time. I have a wife all chosen."

"How exciting. We'll have to see what we can do. I'm a wonderful matchmaker. What is the trouble, won't she marry him?" Betty considered it could be only the woman who would refuse.

"Ah, Madame Barton. If only it were as simple as that."

The sun had finally come out.

The car was a seven-passenger limousine, with two drop-down seats. It had many features of the best American cars, but its performance was sluggish. Monsieur Glisson drove with a swagger that made Jim feel certain he would land them in the ditch. He was seated in front beside Monsieur Glisson, while Madame and Betty made French exclamations on the backseat over the heads of the children.

Jim recalled the French attitude toward machinery during the war. Their airplanes seemed tied together with wire and bobby pins. They made up for the deficiencies by daredevil flying. This Glisson had the same stunt recklessness to his driving. Jim sat ready to grab the wheel or try to reach for the brake if the need came.

It's as though they show no respect for machinery, Jim continued thinking to himself. He worshiped his own cars, lavishing the care of a proud father on them, turning on the motor and listening, adjusting a screw here, fiddling with another part, until the whole engine sang in tune.

If only he had explained all this to Monsieur Glisson instead of sitting beside him in sulky annoyance which the Frenchman could not fail to detect.

Monsieur Glisson, his hands lightly touching the wheel and now and then gesticulating with both hands up in the air, made Jim's blood run cold. He let his hands clench the wheel, at which Jim gave an audible sigh of relief. At once Monsieur Glisson turned to him, taking his eyes off the road, and with the car moving full speed ahead, he asked, "What is the trouble? Do you have indigestion?"

"I soon will have. Drive, man, drive. Don't bother about my digestion."

Poor Monsieur Glisson was troubled. He looked back at the road for a moment, swerved for a man on a bicycle, honking his horn wildly to cover up the fact that he had almost missed seeing the man, and then cut in too short in front of the man to Jim's way of thinking.

"My God," Jim could not help exclaiming.

"Oh, that's nothing, nothing." Monsieur Glisson said amiably. "These peasants hate the auto. They call it an invention of the devil. But, as I was saying, I don't think you'll like this house. It isn't large enough. Americans always like lots of rooms, I know from experience. This is just an *aperitif*, so to speak, and then I'll show you something that is really good, up on the hill, beautiful grounds, something handsome."

"Oh, I don't know," Jim said. "We want it pretty simple—not too expensive."

"Don't worry. We have all kinds," Monsieur Glisson said grandly. "My mother even wants to show you some charming wood lots where you could build--."

"Build!" Jim exclaimed in horror. "Heaven forbid."

Monsieur Glisson saw he had gone too far. He should let his mother handle everything. When he got going, he forgot himself and talked too much. He never did like American men anyway. They always had the know-it-all attitude without any fun in it. They never thought anything was funny that he did, and they laughed at things he found dull. Give him a woman, any woman, and he could have her giggling in five minutes. He wished he'd arranged for Madame Barton to sit with him—with one of the children beside her, the little girls, it would have been quite *comme il faut*.

He turned up for the Villa Sans Souci, and with a sharp right he drove the car full speed through the gate which was very narrow, and in a cloud of dust he stopped in front of the steps in the stone wall. The American beside him gave another great sigh.

"Oh," Betty exclaimed before anyone got out of the car. "I think the house is the Frenchest thing I have ever seen. I adore it. We'll rent it at once." She smiled around her. This French vacation was going to her head; she wanted to act without forethought.

The house stood before them, a pale blue with yellow blinds drawn, the usual red tile roof with a modernistic angle, and the railing of the front porch a descending series of squares. A line of eucalyptus trees marked one boundary of the yard, a stone wall the other. There was no lawn, just gravel beds and stepping stones. The ground sloped off at their feet, banked with a cactus growth of fleshy blunt spikes which were dotted with flowers and had the startling contrast all the cacti family produce between their unrelenting leaves and the frail explosion of bloom. A parasol pine was growing at one side, tilted like a beach umbrella. The walk up to the house was bordered with orange calendulas and sweet-smelling English stock.

"What is that up against the house?" Betty asked. "It looks like corn in tassel."

"It is, Madame. For ornament."

"Don't you eat it?" the children asked together.

"We plant it to look pretty." Monsieur Glisson seemed amused. "I understand you have some strange way of using it as a food?"

Monsieur Glisson smiled faintly. What really interested him was to see if the American lady was as good as her word. He knew his mother would tell the story for years to come—the crazy Americans renting a house because the wife liked the outside, and the husband letting her do it. If he did, his estimation of the man would go up. But he was too dull, he was sure.

"Quite a little section here," Jim said, noting the houses through the trees and over the stone wall. "Not too close, restricted suburban, if you could call St.-Raphael a city." He was stalling for time, watching Betty out the corner of his eye.

Madame Glisson was the first to get of the car. "Come with me, Monsieur Barton. You and I will look inside, check on the cooking stove, the bedrooms, the heating systems. We have the cold days, the rains over here, and you will find everything very cheap in France compared to America. Oh, everyone who comes says that."

Jim let himself be led. Yes, the old lady knew her line, and he was delighted to see himself being given a salesman line.

Betty hesitated, shrugged her shoulders, and looked at the Frenchman. "Are you coming?" she said.

How she would have loved to sit down on the stone steps and wave to Jim. *We'll take it, darling. No use your going in, I'm signing the lease now.* Jim knew her too well. She liked to play the little rebel for him, but her daredevil stunts were never any more serious than Peter's or Mary's, and seldom could she ruffle the surface of Jim's calm.

"Come on, kids," she called to Peter and Mary. "We'll have to see what our new house looks like." The children raced ahead.

Monsieur Glisson was at her elbow. "Oh, Madame Barton. I had so hoped you would be the *grande dame*. Snap your fingers. Take a house without a look."

Betty smiled up at him. It was nice to be appreciated. "Oh, I am too curious not to look."

Inside, there were red tile floors to match the roof. Betty said. "They are lovely to look at, but I wish the floors didn't make so much noise."

"Oh, you wear felt slippers in the house—that is, if you want to be French."

"Oh, I do. That is why I want to live here. To wear felt slippers in the house and clogs on muddy days and all the rest of it. My husband thinks I am crazy."

"It is nice to be crazy some of the time. But I still can't understand why you come to a dull little town like St.-Raphael. Why don't you go to Paris? Now, you get a wonderful view of the sea from this front bedroom. I imagine this is the bedroom you and Monsieur Barton would use. Come, let me show it to you."

He hurriedly pushed her out one door and would not let her explain about the difficulty of children in a big city. Jim and the mother entered by the other. Betty was intrigued. She only wished Merchantville were watching. "Oh, this is a nice room," she said, giving the Frenchman a dimpling smile. "But the Mediterranean isn't as blue as I had hoped it would be."

"It never is on this shore. You have to go to Nice to get that glorious aquamarine. You had better change your mind before it is too late and move farther down the coast toward Cannes."

"Why do you keep urging us to go away and telling us what a dull town this is? I should think you would try your best to rent us one of your houses," Betty looked at him with her clear, frank eyes.

Monsieur Glisson laughed, delighted, leaning one hand on the handle of the window. "Ah, Madame, the practical female. I always tell my mother it is the women who are built to conduct the business of this world. We poor males should be allowed to sit in our cafés and philosophize."

"I wish you'd tell that to my husband. All the men I have ever known only know how to talk business, until I could throw them out the window."

Monsieur Glisson swung open the window for her and made her a mock bow. "Go ahead, Madame. This is an excellent window to begin on. Nothing could be easier. But really, I am quite serious. It is the women who should conduct all business."

"But you are not logical. If women should conduct business, then you should have left me with your mother instead of my husband."

"Oh. I had much rather talk to you than to your husband." Monsieur Glisson smiled,

"That's just making pretty speeches."

"Besides, Americans are different. It is the men who conduct the business, and the women are ornamental, like flowers, birds in gilded cages."

"Oh, is that so? I wish I could give you a picture of my life at home. All the roles I play; chauffeur, gardener, maid of all work, clubwoman, etcetera. Whose garden is this?"

"That is the Countess's. You see, this house is the largest cottage on her estate. Since the war, she rents them out, and that is her kitchen garden."

"A countess! Goodness, how impressive. I thought you and your mother owned this house."

"Oh, good heavens, no. I am just the renting agent. For a commission. I earn a bit of change to keep Mother and me between my architectural jobs. And the Countess is a fat little old lady who is infatuated with the Protestant church. Her artichokes are doing nicely in the garden, aren't they?"

"Artichoke! How thrilling. I have never seen them growing. At least you will let me get excited about artichokes, if you disillusion me about everything else, including your countess."

Monsieur Glisson smiled on her indulgently. "Lean out, and you can see the artichokes growing. They are the finest artichokes in St.-Raphael, perhaps the finest you will see in France."

Betty leaned out gingerly. The window was too narrow for her not to be conscious of the bodily presence of the Frenchman, but he seemed to have forgotten his flirtatious attitude of a moment ago, "See," he said. "Right there, where those tall stalks are rising above the green leaves. Those will be big fat artichokes in a few weeks. And if you are very polite and friendly with Jacques, the gardener, when he comes to cultivate he will give you some. He likes to eat his lunch sometimes under your parasol pines or get a drink of water in the kitchen."

"Oh, I shall bring him out a table and chair and give him coffee," Betty said happily. She drew in her head quickly as she heard the approaching voices of Jim and Madame Glisson.

"Well," Betty said as Jim approached. "Have you settled everything? I think we might as well take this house as any, don't you?"

"It is for you to decide, my dear," Jim said evenly.

"How much are you asking for it?" Betty said, turning toward Madame Glisson.

Madame looked alarmed. She looked at Gilbert to read from his face what he had been saying to the wife. She had not reached the matter of price with the husband, although she was leading up to it and had hoped to bring it to a head in this room if Gilbert would give her the lead. She had found out that the husband was undecided whether to rent a house at all and that he was very concerned with his business affairs at home. Only a slight intimation of the Wall Street affair had as yet leaked through into the French papers, which were only interested in some lurid stories about bootleggers.

"Bien," Madame said after a long pause. "It is, of course, not possible to say definitely—the Countess is very erratic, the house has just been painted—but as friends of ours—and in a way you are friends, for we knew your aunt when she was wintering here, and what a charming old lady, although somewhat eccentric but with friends whom we know— I think we could get the house for you for nine hundred fifty francs." Madame gave a tiny sigh and smiled sweetly.

Gilbert was horrified. He only hoped his face didn't show what his mind was thinking. His mother had made the price one hundred fifty francs more than the Countess's top price, and she had told him he could go down another hundred francs as she needed the money. Oh well, the Americans could stand it, and it probably wasn't too dear for them.

"Cheap enough," Betty said. "We'll take it as is. Everything looks so clean, why can't we move our bags over this afternoon?"

Gilbert interrupted. "When the countess sees your delightful children, I think she will make you an adjustment just out of goodwill."

Madame was scandalized. "Madame. Madame Barton. C'est impossible." She threw up her hands. "The gas. The electricity. The water. The lease itself. The Countess has just left for Paris. It will take at least a week. And that would be rushing matters. And you cannot take the first house you see. That would be folly."

Betty was crushed. "Why couldn't we sleep here?" she said, appealing to the Frenchman and including Jim in her look. This was the house she wanted. If they hunted a month, they wouldn't find a better one for their needs. Living in the hotel would cost them a lot.

It was Madame who forced them to visit another house and waste the morning. Betty insisted that she liked the first house the best . "Oh, I am sure you could make it possible for us to move in by nighttime, Monsieur Gilbert," Betty pleaded with him.

He knew that his mother did not approve of giving the American lady her own way too much, but for himself he rather liked Madame Barton. He could see that she was much more anxious to rent than the husband, and so he compromised and said, "Well, perhaps by tomorrow or, if not then, at least the next day."

To his surprise, Monsieur Barton answered, "But I still cannot see why it is impossible to do it today. Well send a telegram to the owner. I will give you a month's deposit. And if I drive around with you, I best I can make all gas, electricity, and water men act fast. It will only take them a minute to make the connections. We'll tell them about the children. We'll get in some things to eat. And the thing is done."

The Glissons felt helpless before this energy. And Monsieur Barton had appeared to be a lazy, slow-moving man. "But the inventory!" Madame Glisson exclaimed.

"Oh, we'll do that, too," Monsieur Barton said. "We'll check it tomorrow."

It was Jim's energy that pushed the thing through. Betty had to grant him that. And it was for her that he was doing it. They were here, they had to have a place to stay, and with the children hotels were exhausting places. Therefore, with the facts before him, Jim was characteristically ready to go ahead and settle. He wouldn't even let the Frenchman enjoy his usual two-hour lunch, which was often extended to three if nothing came to interrupt. Jim's French might be more gestures than words, but with a small tip the gas man was overjoyed to help him out, and the others were quick to follow.

Monsieur Glisson was amused. He had heard about crazy Americans who blew so hard they made the windmills turn backward, but he had never seen one in action. He found entertainment in the new, unlike his mother, who expected certain things out of people and had no use for them when they fell short of her expectation. He let the Americans whirl him back and forth between villa and town a dozen trips, he helped them to buy groceries, and by four o'clock the house was taking on the personality of the Americans family. Betty had unpacked her sewing basket and stood her traveling clock on the mantelpiece.

"And now for the inventory," Monsieur Glisson said, taking out a bunch of papers.

"You're not really going to make us count all the spoons and plates, are you?" Jim said, bringing down an armful of coats to hang in the hall.

"It is customary," Monsieur Glisson sighed.

"Well, let's forget it," Jim said. He had been getting his own way with American push, and he had begun to expect it.

"I am so sorry when you are so tired, but it will have to be done." Monsieur Glisson spoke mildly.

"Out of the question," Jim said arrogantly, offering an expensive Camel cigarette for the fourth time and having it accepted. He'd give the man one of his best cigars if he continued to resist.

"But you see, it is essential," Monsieur Glisson repeated in the same mild voice.

"But I don't care to do it," Jim said, and the way he said it was rude.

"Oh, that is quite all right." Monsieur Glisson let the smoke trail out of his nose in a luxury of fragrance. "But you see you shall have to do it."

Jim would give this Glisson something, but he'd be damned if he'd waste his energy on taking an inventory. It was just one of those stupid

French customs. Any sane person would include the profit and loss of a broken dish or two in the rent and let it go at that. But not a Frenchman. God how petty they were. It was like making you pay extra for a program at the theater and then having to pay the woman who ushered you to your seat. Why, a woman couldn't even go to the toilet without having to pay, and if that wasn't discrimination against women, he'd like to know what they called it.

Jim was just wondering how much dough would call off the inventory when Betty came into the living room with a Heath's French dictionary and three Baedeckers of England, Paris, and southern France under her arm, along with a small electric iron she had ordered from Abercrombie and Fitch with direct current. "What's all this about an inventory?" she said, eyeing her husband and wondering what made him look so ruffled. Monsieur Glisson appeared calm enough. "Shall we begin taking it now? I think an inventory would be such fun, and it is so French. It will be a great vocabulary lesson for the children."

"Very good," Monsieur Glisson said quietly, showing not a particle of satisfaction that the wife was siding with him. "It would be simpler, I believe, to follow the inventory list which starts with the kitchen. That will do away with the most difficult part of the task."

Betty said, "Come on, Peter, Mary," and she walked out of the room without a backward look at her scowling husband.

With a little bow and an unreproachful "*Pardon, Monsieur,*" Monsieur Glisson followed.

Jim could hear them all chattering together, and they seemed to be having a very good time counting—"*Couteaux, onze ; couteau a decouper, un ;four-chettes, quinze ; couilleres, vingt ; coillers a soupe, six ; couiller a ragout*"—the list seemed to go on like a song. There was a great deal of laughing when Betty didn't know the name for some common article.

It was a curious feeling Jim had standing there alone in this foreign room which was to be his living room, with its red-tile floor and its long French windows, listening to his wife jabbering in French and the clear voices of Peter and Mary repeating, "Knife, *couteaux* ; fork, *four-chette.*" No one seemed to have a thought that he existed. Jim was not given to reflection, and yet, as he paused, undecided whether to be magnanimous and lend a hand with the inventory or stay annoyed, he suddenly wondered what it would be like if he should have to go home alone. Would his family chatter and laugh and go about their ways as though nothing had happened? Wouldn't his going away make any difference to them? It gave him a queer feeling.

Then he laughed at himself for having such doleful thoughts while his wife and children sounded so happy, and he strode into the kitchen. He wasn't going to let that Frenchman, with his sly, quiet looks, think he could have everything his own way.

"You people are nuts," he said as he entered. "But if you insist on being nutty, let me help to get it over with the quickest way."

5

First impression of the French

They woke up in the morning to the sound of the eucalyptus trees rattling in the wind outside the window. Betty was feeling contrite. "Jim, darling, have I made you take this house against your better judgment?"

Jim was rested for the first time since they had left home. Sleep on the boat had been a nightmare, the four of them layered off like bodies in a morgue. And when the children weren't asleep, he was in a torment lest they fall overboard. And in the hotels he had been worried almost as much. What was most annoying was that Betty never appeared to be concerned about them. Mother love? It was Daddy love that snatched them out from under Parisian taxicabs, worried about their diets, and made sure that they were getting boiled milk to drink. Last night the milk was boiled because he had boiled it himself—all over the gas stove. They had eaten their first private meal, in where the kids could yell and run around the room without being shushed. And they had been put to bed in their own beds and their own rooms, just the way they had always been put at home.

Jim stretched again just for the pleasure of it and rolled over to give Bet another kiss. "My dear Bet, to rent a house in France is the solution to everything. Let's go and rent another today. Although for the time, one is enough. Stock market down or up, I feel I've really had some sleep. Let's have bacon and eggs, griddle cakes, maple syrup, sausages, fish cakes, grapefruit, hot oatmeal, cold dry cereal with bananas and cream, and...and pie. I must have a pie for breakfast."

It was grand to have Jim in such good spirits. "I'll bake you a pie for supper. But I'm afraid we haven't any one of the things you want for breakfast, sir. Won't bread and coffee do you just one more? I'll scour the town for food today."

The children were a pleasure to manage that morning. They didn't demand any managing, with the space they had to run in. Climbing a tree, in and out of the house a hundred times before breakfast. The road came to a dead end one hundred feet beyond the house. "At least we don't have to worry about crazy drivers." Jim could not resist his usual comment, but he didn't say "crazy French drivers" in deference to Betty's sensitivity. The children swung on the gate, and no one shouted not to. Betty opened a trunk and brought out a lot of toys. They had had to be small ones for the traveling, but after having been put away so long, the old shovels and pail and the twenty- five-cent trucks looked as big as their most expensive toys back home.

"Let's leave everything and take a walk together around the port," Jim shouted, coming in out of the sunshine.

Betty threw off her apron at once and ran upstairs to powder her nose.

There were not many people along the promenade so early in the morning. They crossed the road and peered through some of the walls, but the shrubbery was so arranged that if was hard to see what the big places really looked like. Betty wanted to go through the shopping section of town, but Jim steered her around a side streets in back of the casino which brought them out in the port section. Here it seemed alive. Women came out with big tin pitchers to fill at the sidewalk pump. Evidently, having running water in the houses was not universal An old woman was sitting in the square, picking a hair mattress to pieces, cleaning it in the sun. Three boys walked ahead of them in caps, mufflers, and clogs. They were aware of the foreigners but in a polite way. Men and women and even the children wore black. Betty became self-conscious of her silk stockings and the bright colors of her clothes and the children's. Even Jim's necktie looked too bright, colors that at home were conservative. And yet there was a friendliness that held in the air. Everyone was pleased to see the children. And now Jim was as smiling and friendly as he was at home. At home he could meet the garbage man and put him at his ease; he was naturally a diplomat. He had developed that talent growing up in the garage. It was a fine quality, one that Betty much admired, and now it was showing up here.

The harbor was built with a protecting breakwater arm on the harbor side. It was paved and served as a wharf, and they stopped to watch a stubby, thirty-foot, gaff-rigged wooden sloop unload kegs of wine. The boat was tied, but it looked as though it were held only by a gangplank which was in truth nothing more than a long plank that touched the pier at one end the boat at the other and bent low with the weight of the men going back and forth on it. They were barefoot, and with wonderful ease they swung up a keg, balanced it on their shoulders, and went fast over the plank to shore. It was like tightrope walking, and their queer stocking caps flew out from their heads. The three boys stopped, too. Jim, with an eyebrow, questioned them, and they nodded and said, "Italiano."

Together they read the sign: "*Ici Napoleon Bonaparte après avoir conquis Egypte debarqua le 9 Octobre 1799 et s'embarqua le 28 Avril 1814 pour l'Ile d'Elbe,*" It gave them an extraordinary sensation to think Napoleon had stood where they were standing and that he, too, had looked about this simple harbor. *What must have been his thoughts as he looked at the boat that was to carry him into exile* ?

Farther on, men were mending their fishing nets. A gypsy family was camping and cooking a stew in a pot swung over a fire on the shore. A half-dozen fishing boats with carved figureheads resembling phallic symbols on the prow were pulled up on the stony beach. It was quaint and foreign. But not to be too quaint, a neat hydroplane was anchored out among some sailing catboats and bobbed up and down in a matter-of-fact way.

"Oh," Betty sighed, speaking for the first time. "How sweet it is. And simple. It is plain and easy to live like this. A mattress woman in the sun. or an old man mending his nets. His wife comes out and fills her pitcher. One change of clothes, the children one toy. Just wrap a muffler 'round your neck when you're cold. No summer curtains and grass rugs, no winter hangings and fur coats, cloth coats, raincoats, evening coats. We are glutted with things. With no meaning. And worried sick about the economical health of a thing like Bethlehem Steel or General Motors. What have they got to do with our lives, yours and mine and our children's? I want to get out of it, I want to go simple, live in one room with a boat and a fish net, and have nothing else in the world." She looked at him, wanting him too agree, to say, *Yes, you and I are all that matters, you and I in a fishing village.*

He patted her arm. "Bet, you are impractical. How do you suppose we got here but on profits from the stock market? And how shall we stay, now that the profits are vanishing?"

"Why didn't you sell? Sell everything and put it in a stocking," she cried at him. "Then we wouldn't have to worry now."

He frowned at her. "You talk hindsight, not foresight." He kicked some stones with his shoe. "You women are all alike. You pretend to know everything. But *after* it has happened. Anybody can talk about it afterward."

"Monsieur Glisson predicted it the first day we met him," she flared back.

Jim was furious. He went red with anger. "What has that frog—what has that stupid Frenchman got to do with my business, our business? You talk hindsight. He talks crazy. And you listen to him." Jim was shouting, and the children, who had run down to the edge of the water, both turned their heads to see what was the trouble.

"I was only saying..." Betty was sorry and would have given anything to unsay what she had. She knew that Jim believed in the fundamental wealth of his country more devoutly than in God, that all this talk of the Frenchman was so much froth. And it was her place to stand by her husband's beliefs. She would have to if she wanted a closer understanding to grow between her and Jim during their stay in France. She had counted on so many things to happen between them, a new love to bud and grow. She held her mouth in a firmer line. Timidly, she moved her hand and slipped it into his. "Jim, dear Jim, I love you," she whispered.

His reaction was colder than he felt. He looked down at her glistening eyes and he felt that women always cried at the wrong time. He was reminded of his mother, who was always ready to cry in a crisis. He squeezed Betty's hand. It was small and warm inside his big one, but he let go immediately. He was worried, more deeply alarmed at the relentless downward plunge the market was taking than he could express in words. The responsibility was on his shoulders, not only for his wife and children but also for all men working under him in the garage at home. It did not stop because he was off enjoying himself on vacation.

Looking out to the Italian boat unloading kegs of wine, he could see far and beyond to his own country. He could feel the whole country at home vibrating in one sympathetic chord over this crisis. There would be extras out every hour or so. How the garage would be buzzing. All the men would have a warm, close excitement about it. there wasn't a man at home who didn't have some money invested in something, if it was no more than fifty dollars in Canadian gold mines. There would be plenty of differing opinions, and after listening to them you could have some idea of the course things were taking. You would realize some of the causes for this disturbance and be able to form your own judgment. He had grown proud of his conclusions in the last five years. He had recommended stocks to some of the boys who were starting out, wanting to get married, and he had watched their profits grow along with his own, and this had given him a fatherly satisfaction. Now he felt responsible for them, now that things were going the other way. He had heard the occasional prophecies of a terrible crash after the phenomenal rise, but the market had gone up and up, it must keep going up more.

Betty saw his eyes turn away, she felt his hand relax, and from the frown she knew that he was back with money affairs at home. For the first time, she felt an inertia overcome her. She could no more change Jim than she could move a mountain. "Come on, Jim," she said. "Let's go out on the breakwater." The children, pleased, ran ahead of them.

They wandered out to the end of the wharf. One side was a high stone wall of enormous rocks against which the waves beat. They looked back to the shore and across the little harbor. A man with a shotgun was shooting at two diving ducks that were swimming rapidly and diving among the boats in the harbor. The man would take aim, but before he could pull the trigger the ducks would dive and the place they had been would be ruffled by a spray of shot. The ducks seemed to enjoy the game. They would bob up to the surface fifty feet away and dive again. The man never came anywhere near getting his shots off before the ducks disappeared. The sportsmanship was ridiculous. With the harbor so alive with boats going about, it seemed foolhardy.

"What the hell is that man doing?" Jim exclaimed in irritation. "He must be insane." The man was now pointing his gun directly in toward shore, and there were half a dozen children playing at the edge of the beach.

Betty was curious herself about the man's actions. She said in her best French, "Pardon me, sir, but what is it that you are doing with your gun?"

The man immediately lowered his gun, beamed on Betty, nodded to Jim and the children, and exclaimed, "But you are Americans." He then took out his cigarettes, lit one, offered the package to Jim, who curtly shook his head, and after removing his cigarette from his mouth, he said, "Well, I will tell you, Madame. It is for the sport. For the sport of the thing." And he beamed on them all again as though he had explained everything. "Would Monsieur like a shot perhaps?"

Jim backed away, furious. "Tell the man he's cracked," he shouted at Betty. "Come away from him." He jerked Peter's arm and called back over his shoulder, "Tell him to kill off a few children while he's at it."

The man could see Jim was angry over something, and he stopped smiling. He probably thinks Jim is insulting him because he is such a poor shot, Betty thought, and out loud she said, "Many thanks, sir. My husband is in a hurry." She left, feeling very silly to have spoken at all, and had to run to catch up with the others.

"That's your Frenchman for you," Jim began at once. "Of all the goddamn fool things I've seen. 'For the sport of the thing!' The whole country's cracked, and they can shoot each other for all I care."

Betty was too angry to argue back. Who could argue with anyone who took the stupid action of one person and made it stand for a whole nation? She could find plenty of single American stupidities that she would never dream of calling representative of America. She had left the house this morning feeling she could conquer the world, serene in the unity of her own little world, her own family. It was hopeless. Every experience was a crisis. Betty trotted obediently beside him, feeling anything but obedient within.

"Have you noticed that everyone has bobbed hair over here?" she said.

"It's the same style at home," Jim said, still sulky.

"I'd love to bob mine, if only for the fun of the change."

"Say, what's got into you, Bet?"

"I don't think one ought to get set. I feel as though both of us were hardening in a cement mold. It scares me. Now, if I bobbed my hair I might change my whole personality."

"Well, all I can say is, if you bob you hair you can find another husband. I detest it."

"You're just challenging me to do it when you talk like that," Betty said defiantly.

It was four days before Jim said, "I think I'll take a run down to Nice."

"I should think it was about time," Betty said.

"Why do you say that?" he said, wondering.

She started to say, *Monsieur Glisson has been advising you to go to Nice, not to Paris*, but she thought better of it. it would only stir things up, and she hated these fights in front of the children. The time had been impossible. It was nothing but one angry scene after another, Jim criticizing her, she snapping back. Jim was unbearable company, and he was ruining their first days in the new house. He would begin at breakfast on the stock market and fly off to buy his newspaper, spending the rest of the day bewailing how old the news was. Each day there was a new low, with a gloomy write-up about the general trend. A prominent American banker had fallen out of a fifteenth-story window for no good reason except that he had lost all his money. The causes and details of his death were their sauce for dinner.

Jim covered sheets of paper with figures on how much money he had already lost and how much he might lose. He was in a constant stew. Should he sell everything and come out with a neatly balanced zero? Should he hang on for a rise? Surely things could not go lower. Surely there would be some rebound. He was worrying like an old woman. And merrily the market toboggan kept on going downhill.

"I still can't see why you didn't sell when you knew everything was high," Betty said.

Jim went white with the violence of his reaction.

"Sell now," Betty taunted him. "Get it over with. You're like a spoiled child. What if we do lose a little money? Be a sport. *Pour le sport*," she concluded, knowing how to incite him further with this common French phrase.

He had started to cable a dozen times to sell everything, and as many times he had held back. He was like a kid, afraid to dive in, standing out on the diving board and shivering.

Indeed, everyone he met seemed to find a malicious pleasure in the American calamity. The paper woman nodded her head and smiled. "Le craque du Wall Street. It is good for Americans. They talk debts too much." A man with whom he had no more dealing than to buy his cigarettes took a vindictive delight in finding that Americans were losing money. "They talk big, everything about them is big, and now they lose big money. In a big way." Americans were sentimental enough about France, but now that America was in a financial bind, the French enjoyed their discomfort.

At first, Jim was going to Nice for the day; it was only a two-hour run by train. But Monsieur Glisson advised him to stay overnight. "You will have the time element, six hours' difference. You'll want an answer to your cable. In fact, you may want to stay two nights. I can give you the name of a reasonably priced hotel."

Madame Glisson was all consideration. "You must not worry, Monsieur. We shall check on the welfare of your wife and children."

6

Jim must go back to the United States

For the two and a half days Jim was in Nice, Betty kept imagining what it would be like to remain in France alone with the children. There would be many problems, but she hoped that somehow she could manage. The Glissons were kindness itself. Madame introduced her to the Masse family, who ran the best grocery store. Monsieur Masse had a short, square-cut figure, smiling behind his enormous black mustache, while his wife was thin and wiry and always complaining. Their daughter, whom they called La Petite, was built like her father, short and broad, with black hair and red cheeks, a happy, good natured girl. The great convenience in dealing with the Masse shop was that not only were they delighted to buy her anything they didn't have in their store, but Monsieur Masse would also deliver everything to the house by bicycle.

Betty particularly disliked the meat shop, which was painted red to match the great carcasses hanging on hooks from the ceiling. There were string curtains to cut down the flies, but the windows and door were open for air to circulate. Monsieur Masse could buy her meat as well as groceries, fruits, and vegetables and seem to save money into the bargain.

The Glissons could also arrange about school for the children. They thought she should wait a few weeks until Peter and Mary knew a little more French. Right after breakfast, Betty would sit down and give the children a short lesson. It amazed her how quickly they seemed to pick up the language and remember French phrases. She wished other children lived near for them to play with, but many houses were vacant or occupied by elderly couples. All the children seemed to live in the old section of the town, near the shops. After their lesson, Betty and the children walked into town. They met Monsieur Glisson.

"Ah, how goes it?" He was all smiles. "I take it your husband has not yet returned. My mother and I hope for good news, that you will be here to spend the winter."

Betty had not yet voiced it out loud, but now she blurted, "I have made up my mind to stay on with the children, even if my husband insists on returning to America."

"Well, good. On that, let me invite you in to the café to celebrate. How about it, Peter, Mary? Hot chocolate for you? Your mother and I will have hot tea and rum on this cold windy day."

"Oh yes," the children answered, smiling at the thought.

Betty hesitated, feeling a sense of guilt at accepting an invitation from any man other than her husband. yet how absurd, particularly with the children along. As they walked down the block toward the café, they passed a beauty parlor with a picture of a woman with bobbed hair in the window. "I've always wanted to bob my hair," Betty said impulsively.

"Then why on earth don't you? I should think it would be most becoming."

"My husband objects."

"But it's not like cutting off your head, you know. It will grow in fast. Your husband might find it very attractive."

While they drank their hot chocolate and tea, Betty listened to the chatter of the children and Monsieur Glisson's amused banter, and she kept thinking about getting her hair cut. Outside it was as though he had read her mind. "I'll take the children for a walk to the beach," he said. "We'll be back in half an hour."

Inside the shop, there was no escape, much as she wanted to run out again. The coiffeur wrapped her in a sheet, indicated the length by placing his long shears by her ear lobe, and after the first cut there was no turning back. He worked fast, trimmed a bit, then curled the ends with a hot curling iron. "So." He smiled. "Next week, come back, we shape it better. Madame will like very much."

Betty shook her head, not to say no but to feel the lightness. She had signed up for independence.

The following day, Jim walked in the door, calling out cheerfully, "Where's everybody? How's tricks?" He dropped his suitcase by the couch, his coat on one chair, his hat on another, and his dominant maleness seemed to fill the house.

Hearing his voice, Betty could hear the voices of all their Merchantville friends echo in her Mind. *Oh, what a shame you had to come home so soon. Bet's back, but I knew it wouldn't work. Such a crazy idea, Jim never did want to go, and for six months. Six weeks is the most the rest of us can afford. With all her French airs, her poor husband is too good to her.* Betty came out of the kitchen, her mind firm. She would not give in.

"Well, my dear. All set. I'm giving us three days to get out of here. I ordered the tickets from Cook's, and we can pick them up and play for them right here in St-Raphael. They have a very efficient system. Our boat sails from Naples in ten days. As long as we're over here, I thought you'd enjoy a little extra sightseeing. Cook's will plan the places in Italy you want to see, make reservations."

I'm not going back with you," Betty said deliberately.

Jim paid no attention to her statement, or was it that he didn't want to hear what she said? He continued, "You know, Bet, those two Americans were wonderful guys. I don't know what I would would have done without them." Jim stopped to light a cigarette. "Of course, we were all in the same boat. One of them was from St. Louis, Mr. Wentworth Harding. He was over here for the winter, just like us, had his wife along and a daughter studying music, staying at Nice. He's an older man, about fifty. The other fellow was from New York, a buyer from Altman's rug department. He came up from Constantinople—breezy fellow but very fine. Both of them are just about wiped out. The St. Louis man had a letter of credit, the bank holding stocks, the way we did; the other fellow had a lot of stuff on margin. It was wonderful, though, having someone to talk it over with. We saw the closing prices in the broker's office. They don't list all of them by any means. Then we went into conference, talked it over half the night. I cabled the bank this morning to sell. The others did the same. The market had taken a terrible licking the past twenty-four hours."

Betty had entirely stopped listening to him. She was wondering if there was enough bread for lunch and dinner too. She closed her ears until she heard him saying, "I didn't meet the wife of the St. Louis man, Harding, but I wanted to wait until you were along. They're planning some kind of a shindig Saturday night if we can make it. We can park the kids with a maid in the hotel. This house and all, I told him, might take time to settle. Say! Where are the kids, anyway? The house seems awfully quiet. Where are they?"

Betty let him listen to the silence of the cold house for half a minute, then she said, "Mr. Glisson has them with him. He took them for a ride."

"Oh, so he's still around, is he?" Jim spoke as though Monsieur Glisson were some annoying old busybody.

"Yes. He is still around. If you can call it 'still around' when you have met a very charming, kind, friendly, helpful person nine days ago."

"Nine days! Don't tell me we came here nine days ago. It seems like ninety years. What I've been through!"

"And what you still have to go through." Her voice was slow and cold. "You have signed your name to a six-month agreement."

Jim cocked his eye at Betty. *So that was the way she felt.* He threw his lighted cigarette into the fireplace, and it burned, the smoke rising like a microscopic fire with no warmth to it. "They can't hold us when we haven't any money. I suppose you think they'll just love having us stay here for six months without paying any rent."

'I shall pay rent," Betty said in the same even voice. "And for six months. For a year, if I like."

"Listen, Bet." Jim made his voice friendly, conversational. "You simply don't know what you're talking about. My dear girl, you're never been interested in money. Why try to be now? I'm running this little party. We'll be polite, of course. You don't seem to realize we have no money. We have just enough to get home on. That's all. Don't forget, I have ordered new cars, if you are talking about a commitment. I can tell you I've been through a time. I bet I've lost ten pounds. Now that I've made the decisions, now that our debt to the bank is cleared, I can take a new breath. I feel as though the worst were over, as though we can go home, begin to work again. You don't seem to have any conceptions of what this means to me, all the years I've worked. All my profits! You act as though it were about somebody else you'd never seen before."

"Sometimes I wonder," Betty said in a low, theatrical voice. She raised it a little. "And as for me? You don't even know who I am."

"Bet, for God's sake." Jim began to bite the cuticle of his thumbnail. Abruptly, he stopped and pushed both hands into his pockets. "Listen" he didn't look at her but noted the smoke from his cigarette, which was still pointing a wavering finger up the chimney.

Betty watched him all the time, every gesture. Her eyes were extra bright, and she watched his eyes to see if he were going to look at her. She was ready for him. "Well, I'm listening."

Jim sighed heavily. "Listen to me. We have two children for whom we're responsible, their education..."

"Oh, as for education—" Her voice was very light as it interrupted his. "Madame Glisson is taking me to the kindergarten teacher in a day or so. It's all arranged. Peter's school, too. The Glisson can do anything. We meet the mayor and sign something and pay a very small amount." She smiled at him, but he would not look at her to see her smile.

"Bet! We have no money. I've told you that ten times over. We have no money." Then he looked at her for the first time and cried out, "My God, you've bobbed your hair."

Yes, I've bobbed my hair." Her words came fast. "I can and I am going to live here in France for six months. That is the agreement, and I shall live up to my side. I happen to have a few principles of my own, whatever you may consider doing. I also happen to have two thousand dollars in the savings bank in my own name at home, saved from birthday presents and what Daddy's given me. "I'll cable the bank to make it over into a letter of credit, or however it is done. I'll find out. I shall keep the children here with me. I shall live up to the lease which you signed for this house. I shall live, too, live here, find out a lot of things about another world than the world of Main Streets, U.S.A., which after all is pretty small place. If I run out of money, I'll scrub floors. You don't have to worry about a thing. I'll tend to everything." Her voice was getting hysterical. "And if you will stay—oh, Jim, if you will stay, I want you to, I shall love to have you." Her voice was husky.

"There. That is my ultimatum."

Jim was angry. "Bet, you're the damnedest fool I ever knew. Why, the whole thing is preposterous. If you think... And my children! You are absurd. Can't you listen to reason? You with your bobbed hair. A woman who bobs her hair has not any brains left, she—"

Betty walked up to him and slapped his face as hard as she could with her right hand.

Jim was shocked. He was shocked cold. He was shocked as though he had walked into an insane asylum and seen his wife an occupant. He could not believe that this was his wife. Then his own anger began to rise in a healthy wave. Words didn't come, but anger, rage. What right had this woman, what right did she have to strike him? He would show her her place. He made a step toward her. What was he doing?

At that moment they both heard a car turn in the drive. And from the knock of its engine and the squeak of its brakes, they knew it to be the little Citroen of Monsieur Glisson. In minute, they heard the children on the porch. To Betty it was a relief. She had had the last word, and she felt Monsieur Glisson would be a prop to her cause. But Jim was disgusted. Here came the Frenchman at the usual wrong time. The man never had the sense to see that he was intruding, and as though the thought put the man into action, his slower steps followed those of the children. Jim saw his wife turn away from him and hurry to open the door.

The children came in running. When they saw their father, they both cried, "Oh, Daddy is home! Presents, presents. What did you bring us?"

Jim opened his arms to them, saying to himself, My own children, and all they think of is presents.

Monsieur Glisson followed, holding his beret in his two hands and bowing a little from the waist. He inclined his head toward Jim. "Ah, Monsieur Barton, it is good to see you back. I can only hope you bring good news of your stocks." He extended his hand. What Frenchman can ever meet or leave another without shaking hands? He replaced his hand on his beret as Jim made no move to take it. Evidently, he had arrived at an inopportune moment. "Madame," he said, turning to Betty. "I returned your children safe, and now I must take my leave." He bowed low over her hand, and again to Jim he added, "Au revoir, Monsieur. Until tomorrow." He had no intention of being trapped in a family quarrel—he had plenty of his own to contend with—and he was going to leave as rapidly as he could make his exit.

Betty, however, found in him another straw in her stack of reasons for remaining in France. It was nothing personal; he stood for the France she wanted—foreign, bright, gay, intellectual, artistic, a talking argument, and a buffer between her and her husband. She put her hand on his coat sleeve to stay him, anything to ward off Jim's stupid, dull anger. "Ah, Monsieur Glisson, you are too kind to us. Isn't that so, Jim?"

"Betty," Jim glared at her. "This has to be settled now. We are leaving for America in three days, Glisson. We sail from Naples. Our money is wiped out—"

"But," Betty interrupted, "it is only my husband who must return. The children and I are staying on as planned for the winter. My husband will return at Christmas."

Gilbert Glisson, bewildered, looked at the angry husband and wife. "You must pardon me, Monsieur, Madame. Tomorrow you can come to my office. Right now I have an appointment." And with another bow he fled.

It was Madame Glisson who was the most understanding. She could sympathize perfectly with Monsieur Barton's dilemma. Losing money could change any situation overnight. He should go home and take his family with him. But Betty's decision to stay on without him was beyond her comprehension.

"I've got to go home. There is no other possible way to handle it." Jim spoke with feeling. his eyes had dark circles from lack of sleep. "And I can't leave my wife and children here alone. She just can't manage alone," he repeated for the fortieth time. "Suppose the children get sick. What will she do in that house alone? Or worse, suppose she gets sick?"

"Monsieur, I have a suggestion. I know a woman who is very trustworthy. She is out of work. She would stay at the house for her room and her food, for very small wages. She is a hard worker, she could clean, help take care of the children. Let me bring her over tomorrow and let her talk to you."

— ~ —

Caterina looked very foreign, a product of Spain, Italy, and southern France, with sly black eyes, black hair, artificially red cheeks, and too-white teeth.

"You promise we can trust her," Jim said to Madame Glisson when Betty had taken Caterina out to inspect the kitchen.

"My dear Monsieur Barton, I've known her for years. She is as good as she is honest. She'll become a member of the family and try to run your lives for you."

"Maybe she can do it better than my wife and I seem to" was Jim's answer.

It amused Jim that from the moment Caterina moved in, she would do nothing without his approval. He wasn't sure whether she realized that he was leaving for America in a few days, but his slighted wish was her law. She soon found his favorite dishes, and these were served at dinner. She asked if she could do the buying of the food, and when Betty demurred, she said, "But I can do it so much cheaper. I know Monsieur Masse. I can do better with the meat. We'll have *lotte*, which is cheaper than most fish. All this if Monsieur Jim will want it that way."

"But it is my house," Betty cried out, "and Caterina is trying to do everything. She never asks my opinion. She only wants your OK."

"I know, my dear, but I'll be leaving soon. Then you can take over."

"But Monsieur Jim, he doesn't look well today. We must fatten him up. We must make him more happy. Poor Monsieur Jim, he is so beautiful, so handsome."

There was armed neutrality between Betty and Jim, but Caterina's excessive concern with Jim struck them both as funny. And when Caterina found he was leaving soon, her solicitation increased.

"You must take good care of my wife and the two children. Caterina," Jim told her.

"Monsieur Jim, they will be my only thought, for your sake," Caterina vowed.

Caterina's extravagant interest made it easier for everyone. Jim's plans for the trip to Italy Were canceled, and Cook's booked him by way of Paris and Le Havre. There was a North German Lloyd boat in five days.

7

Betty adjusts alone; children's school

Betty and Madame Glisson were in the old section of town, on the other side the railroad. It was picturesque but quite the opposite of the gypsy poverty of the port section or the elegance where Betty lived. Here was a middle-class reserve. People looked subdued walking between the high straight sides of the houses, intent on what they were doing; with the number of bicycle riders and donkey carts, they had to be watchful, to avoid a collision.

When they were finally able to walk abreast, Betty found Madame Glissson was still muttering, "That son of mine, why can't he do what I ask? Business! You and I have more business to attend to than he does. Bah!"

Betty was very amused. It had been Monsieur Gilbert's idea in the first place that he and his mother make arrangements for the children through the kindergarten teacher, a friend of theirs. But when the time was set, he excused himself on the plea of business. Obviously, he had not wanted to call on the teacher, and just as obviously his mother had wanted him to come.

"Still, you can't expect your son to do everything you tell him—at his age," Betty said.

"My son could do well if he followed the old French custom and let his mother marry him off. By now I should have for him a fine rich wife and an armful of children. At thirty-six he'll never marry."

"Marriage isn't the perfection of happiness," Betty said petulantly. "Look at me. I married young, have children, and where is my husband?"

Madame only raised her eyebrows. She did not approve of Betty's staying and letting her husband return to America alone, and she made no bones about saying what she thought.

"I always like to watch the men tidying up the trees," Madame Glisson said when they came to the public square bordered by sycamore trees. "It makes me feel some tidiness and order is left. But, as for your marrying young, my dear Madame Barton, you are foolish. No girls can marry young enough to my way of thinking. Before we visit Mademoiselle Roule, I want to stop off at an old friend of mine who lives in this neighborhood. Do you mind?"

"I should enjoy it."

"Madame Cousin lives alone with her cats. You may find her queer, but she was born a Prevost. We went to school together as girls in Paris. She has lost all her money now and lives on memories and gossip. We shall be only a minute."

They pushed open an old wrought-iron gate. The shrubs were overgrown, there was grass between the bricks, and most of the blinds on the windows were shut. A musty old lady answered the door, and she looked as badly in need of repair as the house. Betty thought she was the housekeeper, but it was Madame Cousin herself. The rooms through which they were led were dated by each generation that had lived in them; no one had bothered to remove a thing. The confusion was beyond belief. After half a dozen of these rooms, they stopped in one that had the advantage of being warmed by a large porcelain stove.

Madame Cousin paid little attention to Betty. She put up a lorgnette when she heard the word *Americaine*, murmured, "*Jolie*,' and showed Betty where the cats were, a whole family of new kittens in a box behind a big painted screen. She left her there to play as though she were a child. Madame Glisson nodded and said again, "Only a minute, Madame Barton, you will pardon me," and the two women rattled off in a whirlwind of French. Betty tried to be polite and listen, and then she decided it was more polite not to listen and to go back and play with the cats. Evidently, the women had something to talk over between them which they felt did not concern her. Idly, Betty amused herself with the kittens until she caught the words Gilbert and *enfant* repeated several times. It brought to her mind a remark Mary had made only that morning that Monsieur Gilbert had told her and Peter all about his, Monsieur Gilbert's, son, a new baby. "But Mary, that is impossible. Monsieur Gilbert cannot have a son. He is not married." Mary, when contradicted, grew sulky, and Betty had let it pass as another one of Mary's flights of imagination. Odd that these two women should keep repeating the *enfant* and then speak of *Gilbert, mon fils*. But when they had taken their leave and were once more on their way to Mademoiselle Roule's, Betty forgot all about it.

"Ah, you will like Mademoiselle Roule so much," Madame Glisson was saying as they climbed the hill. "She lives in St.-Raphael's only apartment house, very modern—a sample of the real estate boom that never got started—but with only one wing finished it is a good address. *Mamselle* comes from a farm in the hill country beyond Draguignan. Her father is a rich farmer owning many woodlands. I can imagine her dowry would be great. Instead of remaining at home and marrying, Mamselle preferred an education. She has only had her appointment here in the school three years. She is very bright, everyone in town thinks so much of her. She is one of our moderns, preferring this independent life, but she is charming. I tell Gilbert she is one in a million. It is the wish of my life that Gilbert marry Aurelie Roule. Ah, yes." Madame Glisson sighed heavily.

"Really," Betty said, astonished. "I had no idea. She sounds as though she would make a fine wife. To what does Monsieur Glisson object?"

"That she is fat, but that is not a reason. Women are fat because men like them that way."

They rang, and the door was opened at once as though they had been seen from the window. Mademoiselle Roule kissed Madame Glisson and shook Betty's hand, exclaiming. "Ah, Madame Barton, Madame Glisson has told me so much about you. It will be my great pleasure to do what I can for you. Come in. What pleasure I have." Betty was overwhelmed.

They were led into a large living room with modernistic colors of purple grapes hanging on cerise-striped wallpaper, modern furniture, Empire lamps, lemon, cerise, and rose draperies. The whole room jumped at one with its color and lines. Before she could get her breath, Betty was urged into a low chair with a baby blue slipcover and lemon satin pillows at her back She had to make a great effort to follow Mamselle's French, which was more Provencal than Caterina's accenting all the final 'e's as though she were reciting poetry.

Mademoiselle Roule was herself worth taking in, a dark-complexioned young woman with healthy pink-brown skin, black eyes, kinky black hair which grew low and thick on her forehead, full lips, a tower of a neck. Her whole figure was short, powerful, front a long line of Roman legionnaires or women built for labor in the fields. There was action connected with her, something robust, a Renoir with powerful thighs. She had manicured her fingernails, dressed herself a la mode, and wore high heels.

Madame Glisson was saying with exaggerated politeness, "Ah, dear, dear Mamselle. Gilbert sent his deepest regrets. A client. And he had counted on coming to see you. Unavoidable. You know these people who demand instant attention."

"Ah, yes." Mamselle knew only too well.

"But"—and Madame Glisson rolled her eyes to Betty to second the truth of her statements—

"Gilbert sent his best regards to you. And even so, he may be able to dispose of this annoying client."

"And now, tell me of your children, Madame," Mademoiselle Roule said. "Their ages. Why didn't you bring them along?"

Betty tried to collect herself and think of her grammatical phrases. She was looking at an oblong mirror etched at the top with ferns and the nude figure of a woman leaping forth. She went on to tell about Peter and Mary, their ages, and what each could do and had learned. After many more questions, Mamselle decided that Peter should be ready to enter Monsieur Bonnet's classes but that Mary was for her, Mademoiselle Roule, and she would give her special attention in perfecting her French. "For, after all, what would I not do for a client of my dear, dear Monsieur and Madame Glisson. It was only the other day I met Monsieur on the street, and he was so kind." Each Frenchwoman was outdoing the other in compliments.

"But tell me why you are here, Madame? It seems so strange for you to come all this distance just to put your children in school."

"Why shouldn't I come? I want to see the world, to see how the French do things. If there were more money, I should travel more. As it is, I hope to learn a great deal right here. would you not like to travel? You must come to America sometimes."

"Oh, no. never. I could never cross the great ocean. It gives me fear."

"Oh, that is foolishness," Betty said kindly.

'Why, my family thinks I am foolish to come here to St.-Raphael to live. So faraway from home. I have not yet been to Paris, only Marseille."

"Oh," Betty laughed. "You French are too set. We Americans are used to travel and think nothing of an ocean. I suppose it is because we have always had to travel, ever since the founding of America. It is in our blood. But isn't your home very near here?"

"Yes. And yet it is in another world. The house is dark and old and heavy, and we can only do as my father says. My mother never has new clothes, and she works as though there were the need. I must do this and that when I am home. Here I am my own mistress; I buy and do what I like. Come, let me show you the bedroom. Oh, how I love it here." she led Betty into her bedroom, and the living room was dull in contrast. It seemed as though Mamselle had composed it from the summation of all the bedroom scenes of yellow-backed novels and American movies. The room dripped with boudoir laces and ribbons. There was a mound of little heart-shaped down pillows on the bed, two apple-green long-legged dolls lay with their arms clasped together, and there was pale lavender silk showing through the lace bedspread. The dressing table was all bows and ruffles. It was the more extraordinary to look at when one regarded Mademoiselle Roule's stocky figure.

"Isn't it lovely? Isn't it too sweet?" Madame Glisson was cooing behind them.

There was a ring at the doorbell, which was a relief and allowed Betty to escape from saying what ought to be said. Mademoiselle Roule opened the door, and there was none other than Monsieur Gilbert himself, bowing and smiling, and he had brought Peter and Mary. Where was his mother's story about the pressing needs of business and clients?

"And what have you women been gossiping about all this time?" Monsieur Gilbert asked when they were all seated back in the living room.

"Nothing and everything," said Madame Glisson. She added, "I hope you attended to your client. You must have finished earlier than you expected to take the American children out for a ride."

"What foolishness," he said. "There days clients never keep their rendezvous."

"Oh, you are dears," Mademoiselle Roule was saying, smoothing Mary's hair. "I so adore the children," she said to Betty.

"French people love children," Betty said to help her out.

"Yes, yes, that is true." Mary looked like a little angel standing beside Mamselle's chair, looking up into her face.

"Do you know what Mary said?" Peter announced, coming over to his mother. "Monsieur Gilbert asked her who made the ocean, and she said God did, that he made a big pee-pee."

"Why, Mary! Peter!" Betty was startled as one always is by the revelations of one's own children. "You should not talk that way."

Mary, who did not enjoy being told on, called across the room, "Well, I don't care. Maybe he did do it. Anyway, I think my daddy made the ocean. The ocean tastes salty and smells." Mary seemed more alarmed at misstating her facts than shocking the sensitivities of the grown-ups.

With Mary's year in nursery school she had been trained in natural-ness, which was liable to break out at most inappropriate times. Betty considered herself modern, and yet her own childhood had had all its bathroom doors closed, nudity was frowned upon, and she could not eliminate her modest reactions when naturalness was exhibited before strangers.

The three French people were delighted. "Oh, that is funny, very funny." Monsieur Gilbert turned to Mademoiselle Roule and trans-lated. "Or you think Papa may have done it, Marie, eh? To make the sea, that would be a big, big pee-pee for him, what?" This set the three French people roaring with laughter. And then Betty laughed, too. How could she help it?

"Ah, how wonderful are the children," Monsieur Gilbert contin-ued. "Perhaps Papa, he made the sea. That is faith. Raising common man to the sublimity of God. I should like that. To be made into a god. And are you, too, holy, Madame Betty?"

"I haven't any idea where Mary could have found such an idea," Betty said. "She knows better than to make such statements."

"But Madame, you are wrong. In its way, it is the truth. The per-sonification of God, our father, translating him into the form of one's own father. It is universal. A wonderful illustration of the origin of religion. Marie should be encouraged in such remarks, not frowned upon by the prudery of her mother."

Betty shrugged her shoulders and spread her hands to cover her embarrassment.

"Don't you think, Mamselle, that the state of fatherhood is a very wonderful thing?"

Mademoiselle Roule cried in affection, "Oh, indeed, yes, Monsieur Gilbert. To my mind, to marry and have children is the ultimate goal of us all. For same, it is more difficult."

"Well, well, I had not meant exactly that," he answered.

"Oh, Gilbert." His mother spoke. "I have just asked Mademoiselle Roule for dinner next week. Will Tuesday suit you?" She smiled, daring him to try to avoid the appointment.

"Yes, yes, I suppose so. And what about you, Madame Betty?" he said, turning to Betty.

"Will that suit you, too?"

As no mention had been made of a dinner, Betty hesitated, looking to Madame Glisson to seek her answer.

"Of course, you did invite Madame Betty?" Gilbert returned to his mother, speaking, Betty thought, with more sharpness than was called for. Madame Glisson looked exasperated.

"You must not tease your mother, Monsieur," Mademoiselle Roule said.

"Indeeed, Mademoiselle Aurelie, mothers are made to be teased. They never love their children as much as when the children torment them."

Mademoiselle Roule beamed on Monsieur Gilbert, not listening to his words. He had called her Aurelie.

"And I am the dutiful son," Gilbert continued, "acting always the way my mother likes best to see me act. Dutifully I torment her, and this makes the gossip fly. Tell me, Mademoiselle Aurelie." He paused to catch her eye. "Tell me, have you heard a lot of gossip around town about me?"

She looked her discomfort. "What—what—gossip?" she said. Then, feeling she was laying herself open to further attack by the question in her voice, she blushed.

Skillfully, Madame Glisson's voice rose to fill the gap. "I stopped in to see Madame Cousin on the way up here, and she was telling me her gardener fell out a fruit tree, and she doubts if she'll get her garden properly done this year."

"The poor gardener," Mademoiselle Roule said, relieved that the current of the conversation had been safely turned.

"You didn't tell me you were going to take Madame Betty to see Madame Cousin, *ma mere*," Gilbert said. "What did they talk about, Madame Betty? But no matter. My God, I can well imagine."

"Oh, the cats were wonderful. I played with them. I couldn't follow the speed of that French conversation, Madame Cousin certainly is an odd old lady. Although I don't think much of the way she treats her gardeners."

"Well, I only wish I could feel the way she does about life. But no one can in these modern times and not be affected about it. It's a pose on her part to show off the dates on her tree. She'll allow no gardener to climb that, if she has to go up after him and tumble him out of it herself. One has to admire her for that."

"I'm too democratically American to admire anyone with such high-handed ways," Betty said.

"You only permit the high-handedness of robber barons and Standard Oil kings in your country," Monsieur Glisson jeered. "Otherwise your society is perfect."

"I wouldn't say that," Betty said, and then she laughed. For Monsieur Glisson was laughing too. She enjoyed his banter. She caught Madame Glisson watching her and thought, My goodness, I hope she doesn't think I have any designs on her precious son, "Oh, Peter, Mary, we must be going. We have long outstayed our welcome."

"Oh, but first you must have some tea. I have it all ready out in my little kitchen," Mademoiselle Roule insisted. "I could not let you go without eating . And the English always have tea." In her mind, she considered English and Americans as the same sort of queer people.

A queerer tea Betty had never tasted. Their hostess had it ready on huge trays. They all helped to bring it in. But tea was a mere excuse for the rest of the things. The tea was made with a half-teaspoonful of leaves and the water boiling on the back of the stove. "It must be weak, or it might hurt the children," she explained. But the rest was like a pastry cook's dream. Two dishes of liquid custard, one chocolate and one vanilla. These were ladled out onto flat plates to be sopped up and eaten like gravy by means of sponge cake lady fingers. Betty could hardly eat her own for watching the children to see that none spilled on the satin pillows and slipcovers. There was stiff chestnut soufflé which was so sweet it hurt. There were chocolate éclairs and puff pastry with jam between the layers, and there were green, violet, and pink frosted cakes.

Betty marveled at the excesses to which this French girl went in the way of house furnishings and sweet food. She must be starved in some other way and trying to make up for it. The Glissons ate sparingly, Betty noticed. A second time Betty rose to take her leave. She was afraid if they stayed much longer her two children would make themselves sick. "Oh, just one little taste more," Mademoiselle Roule kept urging everyone

"Would it not be a good idea, Gilbert, *mon cher*, to drive Madame Barton and the children to their villa and then return for me?" Madame Glisson said.

"Oh no," Betty hurried to say. " The walk will do us good."

"But that is an excellent idea, *cherie*, Gilbert said easily. "Too crowded in the small car. Also, it will give you a little more time to talk to dear Mademoiselle Aurelie."

Betty agreed, feeling that Madame Glisson would not have spoken with such emphasis if she did not have good reason.

"Whew!" Monsieur Glisson said when they were in the car and he was shifting brakes.

"*Quelle vie*." He laughed as he said it, his white teeth showing. "Let's take a little drive. Where shall it be, Marie?"

"Oh, *sur le plage*. *Je l'aime le plage*," Mary said, looking confident that Monsieur Gilbert would go where she wanted. She was squezzed in between the two grown-ups, and Peter had been made to sit on the floor, his feet on the running board, holding the door of the car for protection. Betty protested that Peter should sit between them and she would hold Mary on her lap, but Monsieur Glisson wanted it this way.

"I shall drive carefully, and your son will not fall out," he had said. Betty doubted if a Frenchman could drive a car carefully, but as Peter enjoyed the novelty and Mary had refused such babiness as to sit in her mother's lap, Betty had given in.

"I don't think we should take any drive," Betty said, protesting again. "Your mother will be expecting you right back." Her tone sounded weak, for she really wanted to go and breathe some of the fresh sea air on the beach. They all needed in after that cloying food.

"How is your baby?" Mary said suddenly. "Any teeth yet?"

"Oh, the baby is fine," Monsieur Gilbert said. "But babies don't get teeth, you know, until they are six or eight months old. Little Gilbert is only two weeks old today." He looked over Mary's head to Betty. "How do you like all this gossip running around town about me? I guess you heard plenty when my mother and Madame Cousin got going. Now she is going to tell Mademoiselle Aurelie all about it, but carefully painting the thing in the light in which she wants her to see it. I thought I would give her plenty of time to tell her story."

Betty sat transfixed. She did not have any idea what she was expected to say. That her own child should know all about it flabbergasted her. What was she supposed to do, congratulate him on the birth of the son? Actually, she knew none of the details, and she was embarrassed to ask. Should she pretend she knew all about it and let the subject slide like that? Caterina would tell her the story tonight. That was the best way, to pretend she knew all about it. It was hard work to remain composed. "You had better look to your driving," she said as Gilbert swerved to avoid a man on a bicycle.

Monsieur Gilbert stopped the car short in the dust by a bathing pavilion which was closed for the season. One attendant was left as watchman, and he tipped his hat as they went by. The place looked as though it were falling to pieces—Betty could just hear Jim's sarcasm—but Monsieur Gilbert assured her it was one of the smartest places on the beach. The children raced ahead to get near the water. Without them as a prop, Betty felt even more uncomfortable.

"Tell me what you think of it all," Gilbert said, idling along. He looked off to the two islands which were merely picturesque rocks rising out of the sea, Lion de Terre and Lion de Mer. He asked his question more as though he were speaking his thoughts aloud than wanting an answer. He lit a cigarette. "I really don't care what you think, or anyone else, for the matter. Tell me one thing. Was your husband terribly excited when Peter was born, and did you remain somewhat cold? Suzanne just won't get excited over anything. It must be the physical reaction of the body, keeping calm to let the tissues mend..."

"Suzanne!" Betty exclaimed, paying no attention to what else he was saying. "Suzanne! When did you marry her? Why didn't you tell—" And then, bewildered by all the pieces of the puzzle she had been handed during the day, she stopped short. "You must tell me the whole story. Even Mary knows more than I do. And yet everyone seems to think I know all about it."

"But I thought you were being polite, saying you had not understood my mother and Madame Cousin. Didn't your children say anything?"

"Mary had some story. I told her it was quite impossible. I put it down to her child's imagination. Why, only today, your mother was telling me she would like to see you married. She meant, I can see now, to the right girl."

"You are right. I am not married to Suzanne. Does it shock you? It upsets most people. My mother turns herself inside out to explain it. What everyone seems to mind the most is not that Suzanne has had a child but that I am recognizing little Gilbert as my son. You see, I have every intention of adopting him. Therein lies the crime, the social crime."

"But I think it is a crime that you don't protect Suzanne and marry her. Surely you intend to," Betty said, trying to assimilate the facts. She could not deny she was shocked.

"My dear Madame Betty, you are a typical reformer. Knowing half the facts, you jump to conclusions. I certainly shall not marry Suzanne, and my reasons are excellent. On the other hand, I adore this child. I adore him as I have loved few other human beings, perhaps because he is the reflection of my own image in miniature. He stirs within me sentiments that I did not dream I could possess." Monsieur Gilbert smiled, extending his hands.

"I wish you'd tell me why you can't marry Suzanne," Betty persisted.

He laughed. "I must send you to my mother. She would give you enough reasons. Let me limit mine. Suzanne is charming, she is inconstant, she is uneducated, delightful for a moment but hardly one to tie oneself to for life. She doesn't want to get married to anyone. As a matter of fact, it was never my intention to complicate the affair with a child, but there is no need to go into that. Suzanne was married to a sailor, he was killed in an accident on duty, and his widow receives a pension while she remains a widow. My own financial state is nothing to boast of. I must take care of my mother. My mother would not permit Suzanne to enter the house. Suzanne would come without a dowry, without a brain in her pretty head, her pension would stop. For me to pay for two *menages* would be more than my pocketbook could support. In short, I could continue my reasons ad infinitum not to marry Suzanne. It would be folly. But the child, he shall have a legal name for which he may bless or curse me as he likes when he grows up. One look at him and there is no doubt about his papa. My mother will not acknowledge his existence."

Betty sighed. "You are the most convincing of persuaders. But my prejudices are still as strong for the marriage as those of your mother's are against it. I can see your dilemma. But I feel sure—positive—that after you were married to Suzanne all these difficulties would smooth themselves out. I feel sure. I can even see your mother capitulating. To me it is very simple. Suzanne would make as sweet a wife as she is pretty."

Monsieur Gilbert only laughed at her and lit another cigarette. "I adore your American romantic puritanism. It fascinates me. Faith! That is all we need. Faith and the happy ending."

"You can make fun of me all you want. You will marry her yet," Betty said. She was hurt by his joking. "It is late. You've got to take us home at once, or your mother will be blaming me."

8

Pierre de la Fée

"Let us go to Draguignan."

"Oh, let's go to Draguignan."

"Is there a dragon there?"

"No, there is a fairy stone. Pierre de la Fée. We'll eat our lunch under it, and maybe a dragon will come out."

"And what is this about dragons and *draguignans*? Is a *draguignan* a baby dragon?" Betty came out on the porch to find Monsieur Gilbert sitting on the steps in the sun with her two children. They were more like three children. The brilliance of the sun showed the spot where his hair was going thin and a slight sagging to his cheek line, but is was his eyes that were important. They were gay, young, flirtatious. *How amusing he can make the slightest thing, Betty thought. Why should I laugh about dragons as though I, too, were the age of my children? But his gaiety is infectious, and a minute ago I was ready to cry. If only I could read him Jim's letter.* She had received her first letter.

"It is such beautiful weather, Madame," Monsieur Gilbert said, standing up. "How would you like to go on a peek-a-neek?"

"A picnic!" Betty exclaimed.

"But why not? So beautiful a day. We may lose it tomorrow. Now, do say *yes*, for it is all up to you. Your children will die of disappointment. And so will my mother and Mademoiselle Roule. But most of all, shall I. " He rolled his eyes at her.

"But when do you want to go? At once?" She meant to sound incredulous.

"But of course. The train leaves in an hour. For Draguignan, where there are no dragons but a fine dolmen, an old town, a museum. My mother already packs a lunch. Mademoiselle Roule, too. You can bring a little fruit, if you like, but with the children my mother said for you not to incommode yourself."

"But look at me." Betty was unprepared for a sudden excursion. She was wearing her French felt slippers and an old dress. "The children, too. How can I get ready? Why didn't you let me know before?"

"Ah, Madame, it is all my fault," he said humbly. "And a little my mother's. We quarreled again last night. As usual. And this morning I felt very contrite. And with such fine weather, I suggested a picnic, and on a Thursday, and I was magnanimous about Mademoiselle Roule. Ah, you will come. Voila! It is all settled."

He gave her his most disarming smile. "Why don't I take the children now, to get them out of your way and allow you to dress, and we shall call for you in half an hour?" Monsieur had the high-handedness of all men when he found he was going to get his own way.

"You'll do nothing of the sort. Peter! Mary! Into the house this minute. Look at those faces and hands. Caterina! Caterina! *Vite. Vite. Dépêche-toi.* Quick, quick, hurry."

Betty never knew how all the things were done that had to be done, but she was ready when Monsieur Gilbert called, and they drove up to the station five minutes ahead of train time and waved to Madame Glisson and Mademoiselle Roule, who were standing waiting. There were smiles and exclamations of pleasure and the usual round of handshakes.

Last week the children had started school, and this was their first Thursday holiday. It was hard to adapt oneself to the idea that the children would be in school on a Saturday. Perhaps it was a good thing, dividing the week into two parts. Others were also taking advantage of the holiday and the beautiful weather, for the platform was crowded. It was Betty's and the children's first taste of backcountry travel. This was a branch line. The station was tiny, even the track was narrower, and the people waiting looked different. There were so many English and foreigners coming and going to the big watering place of Nice that the main station was very cosmopolitan, but here their own party was conspicuous. The women wore full-gathered skirts and shawls, and some of them had on black straw hats that looked older than the sun wrinkles on their cheeks. The men wore the interminable muffler and cap. It was the grown-ups who acted as though it were a free holiday, while the children clung to parental clothes, as solemn as little owls. Three men were going fishing, and the way the women shrieked with laughter, there must have been some spicy joke. Betty tried to follow, but Provencal was too much for her. Even Monsieur Gilbert could understand little. Mademoiselle Roule was the one to translate, but she turned her back on the peasants and made serious conversation. She was dressed modishly, but Betty felt that given a shawl she would have been at home.

"Madame, you will find our countryside filled with antiquities. You will not need to travel to Rome to see an arena. We have a beautiful one next door in Frejus and-"

"Not a real Roman arena?" Betty exclaimed.

"Yes indeed," Mademoiselle Aurelie continued. "A very good one, too. We have many Roman ruins around us. Frejus used to be a seaport, but over the centuries it filled in with alluvial deposits, and the sea is three kilometers away. Augustus used it at one time to harbor Roman galleys. Gallus, a Roman poet, was born in Frejus, also Agricola, a general. Oh, yes, we have our own crumbs of fame with which to feed our pride. And Draguignan boasts the finest dolmen outside of Brittany."

The train arrived to interrupt her discourse. There was too much commotion getting settled to do much talking for a few minutes. There was much pushing and shoving, and Mamselle looked ready to fight a number of her compatriots. Betty, however, thought it was wonderful, for while people shoved her, they did it with such good nature. It made her one of them. She, too, was going with her children and her friends on a peek-a-neck, lunch baskets, string bags, and all. The cars were open as on American trains, and she could continue to watch the joshing men and women.

"Frejus looks very fine from here," Mamselle said, pointing out the rising arc with the ancient church at the summit. "And there is the Lanterne d'Auguste. It was a sort of lighthouse. And on the road under the old gate, one can see the grooves made by the chariot wheels." From her casual reference to Roman chariot wheels, she might be talking about some ordinary carriage ruts.

The train was going through real country. No more villas and seaside resort artificialities. Dirt roads and long lines of poplars that looked like the painting of Jongkind—farms, fields, gardens neatly lined and squared—and then they flashed by a shepherd who stood looking up with an expression as if it were his first view of a train. He wore a cloak and actually carried a crook, and his sheep moved round about him. Betty cried out for the children to look, but they and the others accepted him as nothing more than what they saw, an old man with some sheep. They could not see the significance of the shepherd as living history which she had thought was dead. She could see world after world, circling back into history, but held alive in this old country by marking of chariot wheels and shepherds with their cloaks and crooks. She leaned her hot face on the window pane.

She reviewed in her mind Jim's letter telling her that she must come home at once. "The bank didn't sell when I cabled, and I now have a safety deposit box full of stocks worth half what we paid for them, a huge debts to the bank, and as far as I can see no business except garage work. Who will ever buy a car when they have no money even to make a down payment for it? Things are worse than I had dreamed possible. The best thing for you is to get a boat at once and be with me for Christmas. You can, of course, stay on in France for a while if you want, as you so pointedly said when we parted. You have a bank account of two thousand dollars in your own name, and unless the bank goes up you have that to draw on. Your father is very depressed. He says he can't help us.

"As you wanted, I am making your money available through the bank. You'll get the necessary papers to sign probably in the mail following this.

"But honestly, Bet [this was what disturbed her so much], I can't see what you are going to get out of staying on in France. Come on home and show a little sense. I haven't told anyone about the tiff we had. I am just acting as though it were a temporary arrangement when I talk to anyone around town. Everyone asks about the children, and I find it hard to answer. I say as little as possible. But come home, Bet. Come home. Your lover, Jim."

She wanted so much to talk to someone, but whom? Was she doing the right thing? With Jim present she had something to take hold of, to answer back. But letters were so remote. She felt great guilt, deserting her husband. She wanted to ask the advice of someone who would agree with her, which is the reason why most people ask for advice.

It made he laugh at herself. How weak she was growing in her stand to remain in France. Monsieur Gilbert had helped her out before, maybe he could again. She did not know his mother or Mademoiselle Roule well enough to ask their advice.

— —

"How old," said Betty as she looked up at the cobbled, gray stoniness of Draguignan. She thought of new wooden American developments that sprang up a whole street at a time. Two worlds. Was it possible for people to be living in these houses, washing out their kitchen sinks, telling the bread man to leave an extra loaf today, shaking a rug out of a bedroom window? Was it possible to clean and eat and sleep in these ancient houses? They might be the backdrop for a stage setting of a historical drama of the Middle Ages.

"It's the judges," said Monsieur Gilbert. "They're all of them too old. This is the county Courthouse seat, you know."

"I think we should go to the museum at once," Madame Glisson was saying. "Monsieur Poupe is apt to go out early."

"Monsieur Poupe? But that means a doll," Mary cried out. Mary was proud to recognize a French word for herself.

"Right you are, Mary," Monsieur Gilbert laughed. "Monsieur Poupe is a doll. I can imagine the boys, when he was the age of you and Peter, twitting him on his name. Monsieur Poupe is the learned doll now, head doll of the museum, professor doll of this, and doctor doll of that."

"Professor Poupe is a very wonderful man, Gilbert. I don't like to hear your flip tone. He is one of the foremost antiquarians around here," Madame Glisson explained to Betty. "We are very proud of him."

"Professor Poupe's specialty is the Romans," Mademoiselle Roule continued. "Our families have known each other."

The museum was up on a hill, a climb over cobblestones, and they had to watch out not to turn an ankle. When they finally reached the museum, the caretaker said Monsieur Poupe had just gone out, and unwillingly he turned on a few lights. Betty had pictured a gem hidden in this remote town and herself as its discoverer for other Americans to follow. Instead, it was dull. Such a conglomeration of dark pictures, bits of Roman pottery, mostly in fragments. There were casts of famous statues, and mixed in with the Roman antiquities were old costumes donated to the museum by someone who didn't know what to do with them, all covered with dust. Mademoiselle Roule pointed out a collection of coins, but they were poorly marked. Guns and muskets were stacked in a corner, heaven knew from what period. It was a disappointment. It was obvious that anything good had been requested for the Paris museums.

Monsieur Gilbert pointed out the picture of a crucified Christ which had been painted with such anatomical detail that it suggested a chart for medical students. It had no date or signature. "I would like to steal it," he laughed, "and send it up to a Surrealist exhibition in Paris. They would think it a dream come true."

The three ladies shuddered. "It is horrible," they all agreed. Just as they were leaving, Professor Poupe came in. He looked the part, Betty thought, white hair in a pompadour, white waxed mustache, an antique black suit with a little red ribbon in his buttonhole. He begged them to stay so he could go over the antiquities with them again, and Madame

Glisson and Mademoiselle Roule would have let him, but Monsieur
Gilbert was firm. "We must leave at once, or it will be too late for the
dolmen and to catch the train back." For this, Betty and the children
were grateful.

They left the ankle-turning cobblestone of the town and were on a
dirt road. It was lovely out, a pale sky with a soft, warm wind, touches of
green in the fields, but the vineyards were brown, the fruit trees bare.
Tomorrow there might be November rains and the mistral blowing.
The children ran in the fields, and Mary came back with some plants
she had picked. Betty was about to scold her, but Mademoiselle Roule
said, "Let's see what you have, Marie. Ah, romarin and lavender. In the
spring you'll find the blossoms, but the leaves smell delicious. Crush
them. We use the oil in perfume. The famous honey from Narbonne is
flavored with romarin. Let's see if we can find any thyme."

"You mean the kind we use in cooking, for chicken stuffing?"

"Exactly, I always pick my own and dry it. There's an excellent book
on the flora of the Cote d'Azur by Marret, if you like flowers, Madame
Betty. In the spring you should see the hillsides. These bare hills are a
beautiful sight."

Up ahead, they could see the Druid stones outlined against the sky.
From the distance they looked like a child's building blocks, two upright,
one across, a gate, and not very impressive. But as you came nearer, you
began to realize how enormous they were. Strangely, they were on a private farm, at the beginning of a long lane leading to the house. "I should
think the town would buy the land," Betty said, picking her way in the
ruts. "Or at least there would be a sign explaining what they were."

"They explain themselves," Monsieur Gilbert said. "And what could
one say? Really, we Know nothing of why they are here."

"In America, there'd be signboards, with full explanation of their
origin."

As they stood under the dolmen, the great moss of the stone was
threatening. The stones were gigantic. How queer, Betty thought.
Queer was not the word. Uncanny. Extraordinary. They all grew silent. The stone loomed high up over their heads, not as three blocks

of stone but as One Thing. It was supported on one end by two stones; on the other end there were also two stones, but only one supported the capstone. Awesome. Fearful. Who had been able to build it, balancing that roofstone almost as high as a second story and with its mighty weight? Men and women must have trembled before its presence in ages past.

It was a relief to hear Madame Glisson's prosaic voice saying, "Remember, Gilbert, when we came here long ago?"

As Gilbert moved toward the house, an old man leaning on a cane came out the side door. Gilbert took off his hat and asked permission to eat lunch.

The old man stared at them. "Too cold," he said in a high old voice. "Too cold for that. Should come out in the summertime. I'd ask you inside—I get lonely out here—but my daughter won't allow it. You never know who they are, she says. She's away now with her husband."

"Perhaps you would let us move a couple of those boards over and lay them across the doorstep," Monsieur Gilbert suggested.

"Yes, yes, do what you like. Only you can't come in the house," the old man said. His eyes were as black as a dressmaker's pins and his skin lifeless like leather. He watched Monsieur Gilbert, who had asked the aid of the children to help him arrange the boards. They balanced them on some stones, making two benches with the stone doorsteps for a table.

"How does that suit you, *mesdames*?" They all agreed that it was very nice.

The old man, watching Monsieur Gilbert all this time at work, suddenly piped up. "Say, young fellow, I remember you. Why, you were out here not so long ago with your wife"—here he looked at Betty as though he identified her, too—" and we talked about the war together."

"Yes, that was so," Monsieur Gilbert mumbled. Out the corner of his eye, he could see his mother beginning to look suspicious.

"Oo-lala," the old man said, smiling slyly at Betty. "Tell me, which was it, a boy or a girl? You get about quickly, Madame. It shows the fine peasant stock is still strong."

Betty blushed so that her whole face and neck were colored red. She looked hopelessly from Monsieur Gilbert to Madame and Mamselle.

Monsieur Gilbert thought it was terribly funny, the old man's confusion of Madame Betty and Suzanne. Also, he was amused at his mother's rage and Mademoiselle Aurelie's slow awakening to what was being said. As long as the fish were spilled, he thought he might as well enjoy it.

The old man was still peering from face to face to see why someone didn't speak up. It was Mary who stepped forward, and in her shrill child French, she said simply, "It is a boy, but you're Wrong. It was another woman. This is my mother,"

"Oho," the old man said, pursing his lips and nodding his head. "*C'est ca.*" His mind was not as slow as his body implied. He could see that there were complications, with two ladies involved and children in each case, and gazing at Betty's blushing red face he saw he had put his foot in it, as his daughter would have scolded him.

Gilbert was by this time grinning broadly.

Madame Glisson briskly stepped forward. "It is all right, my good man," she said familiarly to the old man. "This will do very nicely. We can eat our lunch here in the sunshine. You say, though, that *monsieur mon fils* and you exchanged your war experiences. Surely you were not in the last war."

"No, no. The war of 1870, I am an old, old man, you see. But I was young then, with no hair on my chest. But I knew it all, and proud to get in the fight, until they hit me in the leg. Everyone said I would not live. But I came home again and found my wife had borne a boy while I was gone. We never know what life will bring to us, do we? And that baby was killed in 1915. And here am I still living. You never know. You never know. My wife dead. My son dead. My daughter's husband running the farm. And I'm an old, old man, almost dead, too." He looked up at the giant stones with their grim blackened sides. He waved his cane at them. "But I'm not as old as they are. I used to scramble up on those as a boy. They've always been here, and they'll be here a long time when I'm dead and gone. There is a little hole in the top one, and they say that is where the blood used to run through when they sacrificed the animals. *Pierre de la Fée.* Yes, yes, my father knew them, and his father, and his father before him. Nobody knows how old they are. People come for miles to see them. Yes, you never know, you never know." He turned to looked at them sharply. His mind was wandering, and he searched each face again. His voice rose higher.

"And there'll be another war, too. The sons will be in that one." He pointed his cane to Peter. "But I won't see it," he added, his voice sinking. "I'm too old, too old. My son-in-law laughs at me when I tell him there'll be another war. But there will be. The stones will see it. The stones see all the wars. Too cold, too cold out here. He shuffled his feet, preparing to go back into the house. He had grown tired with his long speech. Monsieur Gilbert hurried to help him, but the old man pushed him off. "I can still make it," he said, laughing. He patted Monsieur Gilbert's hand. "I'm glad it was a boy, war or no war," he said. His mind evidently had streaks of quick insight.

"So am I, sir," Monsieur Gilbert said, laughing. "Thank you for letting us stay here."

They all watched the old man make his way back into the house by the side door. No one had been prepared for such an oration.

Madame Glisson was the first to break the silence. "Well, well. We must get our lunch ready."

"What an extraordinary old man," Betty said, still under the spell of his birdlike voice.

"Oh, one often finds characters like that in the backcountry," Mademoiselle Aurelie said easily. "They are all philosophers in their simple way. He probably hasn't had anyone to talk to since the last time you were out here, Monsieur Gilbert." She laughed.

Betty hoped they would let the subject drop. It seemed the least embarrassing thing to do. And she had expected Mamselle would be too modest or too annoyed with Gilbert to even admit she had understood what the old man was talking about. Instead, she laughed at Gilbert as though he had been caught stealing jam and as though the joke were on him.

Turning to Betty, she said, her eyes still crinkled with laughing, "The old man was determined to make you into a French wife, was he not? You do begin to look a little French, come to think of it."

"Oh, do you think so?" Madame said, looking Betty over as though she were discussing some character in a book rather than a living person. "I had thought of her as typically American."

"At least the old man thought her French, and a legal wife, too," Mademoiselle said pointedly.

Monsieur Gilbert was amused at Betty, who blushed more than ever. "Do not mind our banter," he said kindly. "And as far as that goes, I would not mind having you for a wife at all. In fact, I think the idea is an entertaining one. What do you say, Mama? Would you like an American daughter-in-law?"

"I think we have all gone quite far enough. And from my remembrance of Madame Barton's very nice husband, I should say you had small chance, my dear Gilbert. You have complicated your life quite enough as it is." And with this little rap at her son, Madame launched the conversation into an impersonal eulogy on Pierre de la Fée and Druid stones in general.

9

Trip to Frejus

It was Tuesday, the day of the archaeology meeting at Frejus that they had promised Professor Poupe they would attend. Of course, Mademoiselle Roule and the children were in school, but the Glissons were to pick Betty up at quarter of two, and already it was two-fifteen.

"I'll wait out front, it is so late," Betty told Caterina. She wore her Paris taffeta hat and suede slippers for the lectures, but she carried an umbrella. It was an overcast day. She was through the gate when the yellow Citroen turned the corner. Monsieur Glisson was alone.

As she climbed in, he said, "I do like your hat. Isn't it new?"

"Oh, I bought it in Paris. But I haven't had occasion to wear it down here. Where is your mother?"

"She has a headache."

"You know," she said, "I don't think I ought to go with you. Alone. It doesn't look right somehow. And don't try to tell me it is all right because I am married," she went on quickly, not giving him time to smile. "Stop for your mother. I'm sure I can make her change her mind."

"You can't. besides, I enjoy taking you."

"That's rubbish. The more I think of it, the less I think I ought to go. Drop me off in town. I have to buy some thread at the Bon Marché."

"Now who is being absurd? Whoever heard of buying thread in her best hat and slippers?"

"Oh, you're impossible," Betty said, and she tried to look put out. There was no use denying that wherever you went with Monsieur Gilbert, you had a good time.

He attended to his driving. They had reached the main road, and there was a good deal of traffic. Betty was just as glad, for she never felt the safety she always had with Jim. They could say all they wanted about the high speed of American driving, but give her an American at the wheel every time. She recalled how Jim made fun of the French with their constant honking of the horn. Monsieur Gilbert twisted the auto around by the casino, drove fast by his office, and again on the long smooth road to Frejus that ran along the *plage*.

"Goodness, I wish you wouldn't drive so fast," Betty said, holding her hat. She didn't have the heart to tell him that she didn't admire his driving, for she knew he was proud of it. "And also you didn't make the slightest effort to stop for your mother."

"Wait until we get into Frejus if you want to see some fancy driving," he said, putting on the brakes and coming to a stop. "But first let me have a cigarette, and I'll explain everything to you if you promise not to get out and run away from me."

"I'll promise that easily with the sand and dust and a long walk to town." She smiled. "In my best slippers."

"You shouldn't have worn them, you know, on this trip. I should have warned you there'll be a tour as well as lectures. I was too busy thinking about my mother."

"Oh? What is it now?"

"It is you."

"Me? What in the world have I done?'

"Mother thinks you are just a touch too attractive. That I am just a touch too interested in you. She felt that on the picnic."

"Why, I never heard of anything so absurd in my life."

"Isn't it?"

"And you ... practically married to Suzanne. Or you ought to be. I still feel that is the only solution."

Monsieur Gilbert made a grimace at her. "Please, please," he wailed. But it is a good antidote to my mother's arguments which I listen to all day. I have just arranged the papers for the formal adoption of my little son."

"But I still don't see how I enter into the picture. Me married and with two children."

"A married woman's privileges, you know. They have no limit here in France."

"You are just trying to tease me, I am sure. But if your mother is so troubled that we go out together, take me home. I insist."

"And I insist on taking you. If you want a picture of French life, you should not miss these fusty old archaeologists, and it is very good business for me to be present. And with you, I won't be bored to death. See how easy it is? And pleasant for everyone." He waved his cigarette grandly.

"You make it sound easy, Monsieur Gilbert. But I feel positive it isn't. Take me home while there is time."

"Never," he said, starting the car. "And the real reason my mother wouldn't come today is because she thought if she didn't come, you wouldn't come, but you see I have fooled both her and you."

"I do wish you'd turn around," Betty cried, but already they were climbing the hill into Frejus.

Frejus was one of those towns that was never intended for modern traffic. Ingrown for a thousand years, it was squeezed together on one small rise of ground, capped by an ancient church whose steeple looked indecently pagan.

A car could not penetrate the twisted heart of the town. Succeeding generations had added wider but equally tortuous streets, and with the sharp hill that led into town, the one traffic policeman had to expend all his ingenuity to see that the populace on wheels didn't destroy itself. He spent his days disentangling donkeys from bicycles, and when as auto was included, the damage was serious. People on foot at least had the chance of escape by running into some deep-cut doorway. Betty longed to walk, as Gilbert flung them around the corners.

Today Frejus found itself entertaining a set of antiquarians who made the most novelty- accustomed inhabitant smile. There were white-haired professors, with red rosettes in the buttonholes of their cutaway coats, as true to type as a comic-strip artist might have painted them. Professor Poupe led this group. And Nice had chartered a mammoth bus but had been able to find only a few learned gentlemen. Undaunted, someone had collected two dozen English ladies who could not understand a word of French and were rather hazy about what the trip had meant to begin with. It was their money, however, that paid for the bus, so no one could poke too much fun at them. There was an artist who might have walked out of the novel *Trilby*, with his flowing hair and artist tie. There was a military gentleman whom Gilbert recognized and pointed out to Betty as an Alpine skier on leave from the Italian border. And "Betty Americana" stood in her high-heeled American shoes accompanied by wax-mustached Monsieur Gilbert, who was the most cosmopolitan-looking Frenchman present.

The group had finished a tour of St.-Etienne, the old church, and a monsignor in full-red regalia stepped out of a doorway to give his blessing. Several shawl-headed townswomen appeared from out of nowhere, knelt in front of him, and kissed his ring.

This act caused a flutter among the English women. Should they kneel? Should they kiss the ring? Or should they be rude and defy the papacy, the church of Rome, like Henry VIII, but mildly, and assert their independence? Half of them attempted the act and looked awkward and foolish.

Betty, watching them, felt it a salve to her American nationalism to see the English embarrassed over protocol. Alone, Betty would have felt in a quandary herself, but beside her Monsieur Gilbert remained standing easily, his head bare, watching the ceremony. When the monsignor passed in front of him, he bowed his head a moment, and Betty followed his lead. The monsignor paused to speak to various professors and then disappeared inside the church.

Professor Poupe hurried forward to greet them. He was in his element today and looked very impressive with his Legion of Honor rosette, his suit smelling of the cleaners, the tails flying out behind, and his hair, which had been neatly brushed, beginning to stand on end as, in his excitement, he kept pushing it up. He grasped both of Betty's hands and all but embraced her. "Ah, Madame L'Americaine, it is a pleasure. A great pleasure for all of us. I must have you meet my many illustrious colleagues. And Monsieur Gilbert Glisson! Where, where is your wonderful mama? What? A headache. But that is terrible. A calamity. My deep solicitations to her. Ah, I am desolate. How well I remember your dear papa. A wonderful and deep intellect. We all loved him as a brother. Yes, and now you must march into his great art. We all look for great things from you. Yes, yes, now you must meet my dear and estimable friend, Professor Durande."

Professor D. Durande's enthusiasm equaled if not excelled Professor Poupe's. And Betty felt that Monsieur Gilbert was losing his cynicism and warming to the general extravagant remarks. The other professor also seemed to know Monsieur Gilbert's father, and they exchanged pleasantries on friendship and the present gathering.

"And we are delighted to have an American with us also today," the professor said, turning to Betty. "And to have such a pretty, chic American. You are wintering on the Mediterranean?" he said by way of finding out more about her.

"Yes, yes. Madame Barton is here with her two charming children," Monsieur Gilbert said.

"Ah, charming and more charming. And Monsieur Barton? Is he here also? Ah, you say he is in America. These trusting American husbands. They are the world's marvel."

Betty felt furious. Always praise for husbands and distrust for wives. Why did husbands have to get all the credit for everything? The Frenchman was, of course, merely cataloguing her as American grass widow, pretty, spoiled, but when she found her individuality being tucked neatly into a pigeonhole, she resented it. Smiling, she said, "There are exceptions, even in America. But really, my husband is forced to stay in America. The Wall Street crash, you know."

"Ah, *le craque du* Wall Street," the professor exclaimed, his face lighting up with positive pleasure. Others were tasting France's misfortune. "But it can't be so very bad if your husband can afford to keep you over here."

"I am not kept," she said too sharply, then laughed to cover her embarrassment. She was sure the Frenchman had not intended the meaning as she had interpreted it. "I mean that I am paying for the rest of my stay here with my own money." And again she stopped short. Why should she explain herself to this Frenchman, justifying her actions? Either she should explain more fully or else, and far better, she should have said nothing at all. It was the straining after moonbeams which Monsieur Gilbert had said was so characteristic of Americans. She turned to look at Monsieur Gilbert, who had been silent, and found him smiling his amusement.

"Ah, the American heiress," the professor said. It was true she had given him just that impression.

"All the others have gone on to the museum," Monsieur Gilbert said. "We had better hurry." Bowing profusely to Professor Durande to end the conversation, he guided Betty away in the wake of the English ladies.

"Oh dear," Betty said, surprised to feel relief when she turned to Monsieur Gilbert. "I didn't mean to say any of the things I did. Why didn't you stop me?"

"What does it matter what you said?" Monsieur Gilbert said comfortably. "Come on and enjoy what the museum has to offer, although I'll admit it isn't much. There is a handsome head of Jupiter which is the real thing, and that is about all there is to look at."

"Oh dear again," Betty sighed. "You seem to know just what to look for and what to pass over. Now, I—"

"But Madame Betty, you are getting positively psychopathic. Don't you realize I've lived in France all my life, that my father taught me more about those things than the ordinary Frenchman? Now, in America, I should be helpless before your modern skyscrapers."

"Oh, America. There is nothing to see in America anyway."

Monsieur Gilbert raised his eyebrows. "Tell me, when did you last hear from your husband? Recently, I'll wager."

"Yesterday. Three letters at once. And such letters. He is demanding I sail home on the next boat. It hasn't yet entered his head that I am almost ready for a divorce."

"You are too impetuous."

"Yes. Let's forget me and my husband. Is this the head of Jupiter?"

"No, it isn't. It's a faun. And not an authentic one. I'm sure it was made in an Italian cellar the year before it was bought. You complain of the innocence of Americans, but we're just as gullible where Italians are concerned. Here's our Jupiter. Now, isn't that a fine thing?"

Betty was very impressed and tried to take it in from all sides. What a help Monsieur Gilbert would have been in Paris. All she and Jim had known was enough to look for were things like the Mona Lisa or the Venus de Milo, and while it was exciting to see the actual, it was disappointing, too. Having been fed reproductions all one's life, the real thing ceased to make an impression. One could almost have set up a series of postcards and been just as satisfied. She thought of herself visiting the Louvre with both Monsieur Gilbert and Jim, and she couldn't help but smile at Jim's annoyance, even though it was only a fantasy. And then she imagined a "fling" in Paris with Gilbert Glisson, alone, but she shied away from that thought like a bird from a snake. It made her feel very guilty to have even thought of it. Monsieur Gilbert was standing beside her, inspecting the head of Jupiter, as cool and impervious himself as another polished and quite authentic statue. Madam Glisson's suspicions were justified if she were going to have thoughts like that. Studiously, she concentrated on Jupiter. He was a lofty subject and ought to help produce lofty thoughts.

"Ah, Gilbert, how is time passing with you?" The young man Gilbert had pointed out to her as the Alpine skier stopped beside them. He had a long, dark-toned face with an aquiline nose and a big pompadour of hair. He looked more poet than soldier on skis.

"Monsieur La Cour! I saw you in the distance but was unable to catch your attention. It's a pleasure to see you." Monsieur Gilbert introduced Betty. "You are here on leave? And how goes it at the frontier?" he added.

"If the actions of the Italian skiers and ours mean anything, we'll be at war in a month. I am only allowed three days' leave."

"But that is absurd," Betty exclaimed. "It is impossible to have war. There couldn't be another war after that last one."

"*Couldn't* is a big word," Monsieur La Cour said, smiling. "Oh, there'll be war all right. The question is, will it come this summer? If you read the papers at all, Madame, in the south here, you will find how hot the feeling is against Italy. Only the other day we were out reconnoitering along our frontier. There was a snowstorm, and it was hard to see, but we passed a group of Italian skiers, and there were a couple of shots exchanged—no one was hurt—but we handed in our report. The Italians fired the first shot, although they had sneaked onto French territory. The report will be handed up to Paris, and lost, the way it always is, but it shows the sentiment."

"Why, it is fantastic," Batty said, looking from on to the other to make sure they were not trying to pull her leg. "Things like that don't happen today. And how could two civilized countries like France and Italy even think of war?"

"You know, I've heard that Americans feel that way," Monsieur La Cour said to Monsieur Gilbert. "In a way, it explains poor Woodrow Wilson's arrival and departure over here. Such high ideals and such a lack of practical facts. No logic. No logic." He looked at Betty.

"But the last war was to end all wars," Betty said, indignant and unaware of her platitude.

"Madame's sentiment is charming," Monsieur La Cour said.

"I feel sure there'll be no war this summer," Monsieur Gilbert said. They would be left behind if they didn't hurry. He grew bored with

Monsieur La Cour's argument for war. The man was too close to the sources, but you couldn't tell him that.

Their visit to the museum was brief, as Monsieur Poupe began to explain in an authoritative voice that "there was much to see of the antiquities in and around Frejus." How often the French repeated that word, *antiquity*, and how dearly they loved to roll it off their tongues. They returned to their autos and motorbus, Monsieur La Cour accompanying Gilbert and Betty (he had come on his bicycle), and followed Professor Poupe, who led the procession in a long, handsome touring car belonging to one of Frejus's important citizens. They visited Roman ramparts and towers and were given a technical lecture about how, when, and why they were built. There was the Butte St.Antoine and the Citadelle du Couchant, standing like sentinels to guard the old seaport city. The Porte Dorée, an ancient arch, restored and probably part of a colonnade. The turret of the Lanterne d'Auguste. They visited the ancient theater and the remains of the aqueduct with the Citadelle du Levant, another fortification. Betty enjoyed it all.

The arena was a short ride outside of town, and with a little repair one felt it could be put in working condition in no time. 'Not that I would ever want to see it put to use again." Betty said to Monsieur La Cour in an undertone while the lecture was going on. "I am squeamish. Imagine lions coming out from the archway, and the poor Christian martyrs."

"What you need to see, while you are here, is a good bullfight. Most of them are held at Nantes, in the old arena, although there are occasional itinerant ones. France as a whole doesn't sanction them."

"A real live bullfight?" Betty said, horrified. "I never could stand the cruelty."

"You are merely ignorant. There is poetry in bullfights. You must learn to understand them. Read Henry de Montherlant. He's written a wonderful book, *Les Bestiaires*."

It is more cult than poetry." Monsieur Gilbert mocked.

"Oh, that's the way you feel, is it?" Monsieur La Cour looked indignant.

"I could read a hundred books and still think bullfighting horrible. Those poor horses! Cornering an animal like that. Do you really like them?" Betty appealed to Monsieur Gilbert.

"I'll whisper you a secret," he answered, smiling. "I despise bullfights. At the same time, I admire Montherlant's book, which is most impressive. But I wouldn't admit it to a Midian like La Cour for anything in the world."

"Mon Dieu. Another fool," La Cour said hotly. "That is Parisian weakness and stupidity for you. Sitting in the middle of the fence. I tell you, Madame, bullfighting is beauty. It is a religion, if you will, dating back to the warm, health-giving, red-flowing worship of the sun. You're only thinking of your own silly physical reaction to the intestines of some old boneyard. You talk about cruelty, and you eat meat that has been slaughtered in the most degrading fashion."

"Convincing, isn't he?" Monsieur Gilbert said.

Betty was not sure which man was in earnest, if either.

"This arena, as you can see, was built in the shape of an egg," boomed the classroom voice of Professor Poupe, "holding nine thousand spectators, almost large enough for the present population of Frejus. The pillars and part of the gallery are still preserved..."

His voice trailed on while the English ladies scrambled up the broken stone seats and got their shoes muddy.

"I told you not to wear your best slippers," Monsieur Gilbert said at their next stop.

"Here is where the Roman matrons did their wash," Professor Poupe said. There was an arch through which one had to pick one's way. It was part of a long brick wall. Remnants of the famous Roman aqueduct were on one side. The bricks looked so like ordinary bricks that it was difficult to imagine their age. Inside the arch was a long vaulted space, dark and clammy. The tubs had been cut in the stone floor and even now were filled with an opaque green water. "Here the Roman ladies knelt and swished and paddled their clothes just the way women do today down in our public wash troughs, but with one difference. Roman women did not have soap. Their anger was intense if they saw a man standing nearby to relieve himself." At this point, Professor Poupe's French grew rapid, and his sentence ended in a gust of laughter which passed from one set of whiskers to another until Betty watched them in bewilderment. The stiff English ladies also missed the point, and this seemed to strike the gentlemen as even funniest, for their laughter echoed on the walls and arches overhead.

"I'm awfully stupid," Betty whispered to Gilbert.

"He didn't have to explain fully because everyone else here knows about it. But the Romans used a mixture of ashes and urine to whiten and clean clothes. So if the lady saw a man urinating against a wall, she considered it a great waste and scolded him for not going to the laundry and using the large jar there. That is our French idea of a beautiful joke." Gilbert smiled at her sweetly.

"I didn't dream these fine-looking old gentlemen could tell jokes like that. And in front of Such proper old ladies."

"You don't know old gentlemen." Monsieur Gilbert laughed.

The gathering was now breaking up. Most of them were going back to the museum to hear lectures by various professors of archaeology on their pet subjects.

"Nobody wants to listen to that tripe," Monsieur La Cour said. "But we can't break up like this. Why don't we have a glass of beer and then take Madame down to the Indochinese temple and show her how we French prepare for war?" He was very jocular and friendly and seemed to find great pleasure in making Betty argue with him.

Betty was beginning to be rather repulsed by him, but she felt she must be polite. Before she could answer, however, Monsieur Gilbert said, "No, no. It is far too late. Madame must be taken back to her children, and I go to work. Sorry, La Cour, we can't strap your bicycle on and take you with us, but the auto is too small." Fussily, he made it evident that he tired of having Monsieur La Cour remain with them. They all said an elaborate good-bye, and Betty and Gilbert watched La Cour find his bicycle and ride off. He lived back on the hills of St-Raphael.

"We got rid of him." Monsieur Gilbert smiled.

"But I thought he was one of your special friends."

"I don't have any friends. And this war talk bores me to death. As a matter of fact, I myself was planning to take you home on the back road and visit the Indochinese temple. So why drag him along? If we give him half a chance, he'll be on his favorite subject. He's a royalist and wants a king. He feels that France should be the master of Europe. We French are only forty million, but he counts our sixty million colonials as making us greater in number than England, Germany, and Italy—and so easily capable of being a people of destiny. He's quite cracked on the subject. He goes around lecturing. For every two Frenchmen, there are three slaves. France can save Europe from bolshevism, from another war. He collects information from the Italian press about their plans to dominate us and be once more the Mediterranean basin. The Italians call it Mare Nostrum, 'our sea.' He's quite a fire eater."

"And the French colonials, the slaves, will help the French?"

"He insists they will tie their destinies to that of France because they are now citizens of France."

"And you French have a king?"

"There are always a lot of ex-kings lurking in the wings."

They drove down one of the straight poplar-lined roads that inevitably lead into the French countryside. It was a couple of miles to the temple, and of all the strange sights in the center of soft green French farmland, this was the strangest. Here stood the Orient itself at the top of a hill. A tile roof colored red, green, blue, and gold stood out like a garish Oriental print. They stopped at the foot of a long, winding flight of stairs on whose posts were mounted a blue horse on one side and an orange and black tiger on the other. They were Oriental but fat and distorted and about the size Mary would like to play with. An Indochinese soldier appeared and walked slowly down the stairway.

"What in the world are they doing here?" she repeated. "I've never seen anything so extraordinary. I don't see how you can let anything so Buddhist dominate your Christian landscape."

The figure of the soldier disappeared in the curve of the stairs to suddenly reappear at their elbow. He looked at them and through them, as though they were part of the stone wall. When he vanished, Betty continued, "I never should want him to be my ally in case of war. Who knows what magic he had been conjuring up there in that temple of his?"

"He gets paid, doesn't he? People will do anything you ask them to do for a little money. Besides, where would we get our rubber and rice? Let's go up and see what it looks like."

"Goodness, you're cynical."

"It is good to be cynical. It saves future bumps. As a sentimental American, you'd do well to learn from me."

"Maybe I will, later on," Betty said.

They climbed the long flight of stairs, and as they approached, the temple looked smaller than Betty had expected. They entered a doorway, just an oblong opening in the side, and were met by a blank wall which proved to be the side of a temple within a temple. It was as though a square box had been built inside another square box, but with the opening of the inner box turned a quarter, obliging one to walk around the corner to enter the real interior. They were met by another soldier standing before a large figure of Buddha, but whether to protect or to worship the idol it was hard to say. He, too, ignored them, but they felt his back was aware of their intruding Occidental [cppd?] presence. The inner shrine was brilliant, with hundreds of gay-colored streamers hanging from the ceiling, mostly gold and red. Each was a prayer. It made the stiff little men grow soft and human for Betty as she pictured each one of these prayers portraying a wish fulfillment—protect my honorable mother, give me health, care for my wife and child, bring me and my faraway family good luck for the New Year. The prayers hung fluttering before the unmoving eyes of the most God of Wisdom. Surely one of these prayers would be answered by the serene Buddha.

"Don't take it too seriously," Monsieur Gilbert whispered at he shoulder. "Let's go outside where we can talk."

"You make fun of everything, but underneath you do respect the serious things of life," Betty said when they were out again in the fresh air.

"Never," he cried, mocking.

"Yes, you do."

"Here's a sight you can take seriously," he said, and he led her behind the temple where they could see down the other side of the hill. The camp for the soldiers lay before them, a set of low whitewashed barracks in double rows. What took the eye long before it came to the houses was a tremendous graveyard of white wood crosses planted as in some fearful garden. "They died for France. Their France," Gilbert said.

The crosses stood like living plants representing the dead, rows that numbered into hundreds, undulating with the rise and fall of black earth. "Indochina's sacrifice for the motherland." He laughed. "We have no color prejudice in France."

"Oh," Betty cried," will you mock them? The living beside the dead. The poor devils, dying so far from home."

"French realism," Gilbert said dryly. "They run more of a chance of death at home from famine or plague. They really prefer it here. They go home rich men—if they go home," he ended cryptically.

"I will say this much," Betty conceded. "You've given them a beautiful temple. That must be some consolation to the poor things. Are you a Catholic?"

"Naturally."

"I suppose it is natural in France."

"Not that I ever go to church." Monsieur Gilbert smiled. "I usually go to midnight mass on Christmas Eve. There is nothing more handsome and moving if you're drunk enough to get the full effect."

"But I thought you had to go, that you were forced to. At home it is a sin for a Catholic to miss a Sunday."

"Having to go and going are two different things. I doubt if it is any different in America. I'm sure I could find millions of nonchurchgoers for you. I always attract them. You Protestants are forced to go to church in the same way, aren't you?"

"No indeed. We go of our own free will. It is an individual thing, from the heart."

"Ah, from the heart. How charming. Love is the only thing that comes from the heart anymore, and that very seldom. Religion and the heart parted company in the Middle Ages, after Giotto and the Bellinis and Mantegna. Michelangelo and Leonardo were too sophisticated. And Today we know far too much to be simple and religious. There are a couple of fossils who cling to the fantasy of Adam and Eve as a true story, but they aren't playing fair. They know as well as you and I that it is a beautiful story, and the true believers artfully cling to traditions. No one can be religious today and sincerely be in his right mind. We are a world of sensualists."

Betty listened to him, leaning her elbows on the stone wall and looking over at the grim little wood crosses. "I can understand everything you say, and as you say it I feel it is true. But I'm glad my dear father cannot hear you, for it would hurt him so much. He believes in God with simplicity. And yet he can put his religion in a compartment when it is time to eat breakfast and go to business. I believe in him. But I know what you say is all true." She looked at Monsieur Gilbert with a shy smile.

"My dear Madame. You frighten me. To take all that I say so literally. I am just talking for fun." He shrugged his shoulders. "here we are serious again. What is it in you that makes me so? I am not a serious type." He laughed. "Your hat is most becoming, Madame, and that really is far more important."

"I like the way you change from the serious to the gay. You always do, don't you? It is as though you hate to be caught being serious. You know, I remember so well that first day when we came to St.-Raphael—it is impossible to believe it was only two months ago—and you took us around in the car. You and I were leaning on a wall—no, it was a windowsill—but just the way we are now, and talking, and looking over the garden. What was it we were looking at?"

"Artichokes, Madame."

"Of course. How stupid of me to forget. And artichokes are much more pleasant than wooden crosses. I do hope they will be ripe soon, for I have never eaten them fresh out of the garden. They are very expensive in America, you know, and uncommon. They symbolize for me the foreign and exotic. I always associate them in my mind with you."

"My dear Madame, you don't flatter me. For not only are they a very ordinary vegetable here, but we have a saying about them: *Il a le Coeur d'un artichaut.*"

And what does that means? It sounds very good. 'You have the heart of an artichoke."

"Quite the contrary. It is not at all complimentary. To say of a person *'Il a le Coeur d'un artichaut'* means that he is, how do you say, fickle. That is the word, fickle. That he is not to be depended on with women. That he gives away a leaf of his heart to every lady he meets, and when he is finished, he has little heart left. Artichokes are nothing but leaves, and when you take them all away, the heart, the core, is merely a mouthful. The funny thing is, *ma mere* always is saying. *'Mon fils, il a le coeur d'un artichaut'* also. And now you. It is not at all polite to think that of me. You know, we also say it about women."

"But I don't. I don't." Betty hurried to defend her opinion of him. "I think just the opposite. That your heart is very big and that you are very kind and generous with it. You are so kind and generous to me with your heart, and it has meant so much to me over here all alone. Far more than you can ever realize." Betty found herself over enthusiastic in defending Monsieur Gilbert's heart. They were speaking in French, *and when Americans speak in French they can be much more irresponsible with words than they would be in using English.* She changed the subject back to the archaeologists and how she had enjoyed seeing the various French types. "To me they were fascinating. And so utterly different from the ordinary run of Americans. Even Professor Poupe was not at all boring today, and that elegant Professor Durande and Monsieur La Cour with his crazy ideas about war. Of course, the one I liked best—" And then that eternal blushing of hers brought her up short.

Monsieur Gilbert was very much amused, and he thought her blushing rather charming. This American lady had some of the innocence of a young girl. "It is, of course, naturally impossible to guess the one you mean! But Madame, I still resent your classifying me as a type. I always feel that when one classifies a person as a type, then he is not yet a friend. Once he is a true friend, then all classification disappears."

"Oh, but you are a friend. A very dear friend. On whom I depend so much." And again Betty blushed at showing her fervor.

And again Monsieur Gilbert ridiculed her. "Madame, you take it all far too seriously, these types and these friends. That is your chief fault, if you do not mind my being so personal as to say so. You take far too seriously all these things that do not matter, and yet where your husband is concerned, you do not take him seriously enough."

"But how do you mean?" Betty was at once on the defensive.

"I am talking too much as usual," Monsieur Gilbert said lightly.

"No, please go on. At least finish what you were going to say."

"I merely meant that for a woman a husband is the most important thing in her life."

"But you advised me to leave mine, to let him go home alone."

"Not to leave him, but to let him leave you. For it is just temporary. It is to teach you how important he is."

"Oh, you are just talking again," Betty said.

"Fine. Fine. That is the way I like to hear you talk. Argue, fight back."

Betty laughed. "What a lovely picture you paint of the fighting American woman in France. I shall get a reputation like Carpentier or Dempsey. And so you want me to go back to my husband now that we are separated?"

"But don't be too hurried about it."

"I think you are an absurdly exacting person, and I shall do just as I please, and neither you nor my husband shall dictate to me."

"Bravo." Monsieur Gilbert swept off his hat. "Only stick to your guns. The unfortunate thing is, women never do. Sooner or later, they begin to droop, and then a husband comes along—or a lover, it doesn't make much difference which—and the woman turns to water and does whatever the man says. It always works out so."

"You are insulting."

"Never intentionally."

"Oh, yes, you are. You are over polite, and the same time you are very scornful of women and would insult them all without a scruple."

"And where is this good heart of mine that you were telling me about a minute ago?"

"That is the worst of it," Betty had to add. "You are a mixture like a marble cake, of mocking insults and deep kindness."

"Well, well. We must go into this further. You seem to know all about me. Do you read palms? Or are you a psychoanalyst? I shall have to begin telling you my dreams."

A troop of men had marched into the grounds and were scattering to their various barracks, some disappearing in the doorways, others relaxing on a bench, lighting up a cigarette. From their stone wall, they could look down on the scene like gods from the temple.

"Poor devils," Betty said with compassion. "I should feel much better if they were back home in Indochina. They are like American blacks—not slaves, but neither are they free. Hungry or working themselves to death, they would at least have the consolation of their families and the familiar setting of their own country. I feel unhappy just to look at then."

"What about yourself? Sounds to me as though you and they were in the same category. You, too, are torn away from your husband and your skyscrapers."

"At least I can be with my children right here. Look how late it is. I had no idea."

"I'll take you home, don't fear."

They walked down the long flight of stairs, with the sun hidden behind the line of clouds which always seemed to gather along the edge of the sky in the late afternoon. They climbed into the Citroen without further conversation. Betty went over the various things they had talked about as she sat beside the Frenchman driving along the country roads, and she found a relaxation in the silence between them, the kind one has with an old friend. It was odd to consider Monsieur Gilbert as an old friend, and yet she felt she knew him already better than many people in Merchantville whom she had known all her life. She trusted him, and she surprised herself with this trust, in view of the way he was treating Suzanne. His own mother accused him of being fickle with women. Betty could not hope to believe that she would be any exception. She wasn't looking for any axe to grind. All she wanted was a human being on whose advise she could depend, and if the person were outside the family, his opinion would be unbiased. She turned to watch his profile, and she discovered she was familiar with the lines of it.

Hurriedly, she began talking, and she told him about Merchantville, about growing up there, her parents, her house, her school, how she met her husband, how they had married, Peter's birth, and their house which her father had given them, what it looked like, and how pretty the garden was in back and the green grass in front, and the line of maple trees. She jumped to the relationship between herself and her husband, how they were outwardly such an ideal couple, and how fond she was of Jim, and yet how lacking she found him, and her longing for wider fields and rebuilding their married life. "But Jim never seems to understand what I want. He seems to think I should be satisfied without perfect married bliss like some magazine-story girl and live happily ever after without a question. I suppose I should." Lamely, she ended, dumping all her troubles in the Frenchman's lap, hoping to have him assemble the parts like an automobile and make them run smoothly for her.

Monsieur Gilbert cleared his throat, for he had not said a word for a long time. "Madame," he said slowly, "how on earth can I help you? It is you who run your own life, and it is you who must find out what to do about it. But talking will do you good, clear your mind. Maybe life in St.-Raphael will perform the miracle."

She did not think he was being sarcastic. She did note, however, that he had taken a back road and that to reach her villa it would not be necessary to drive past his office.

10

Picnic with Marquis the donkey

They planned the day for the children. It was arranged with intrigue and with an innocent casualness that could not possibly have any hidden motives behind it.

"Hush," said Gilbert to Betty, Mary, and Peter. "Now, when we go through the town past my office, you must all duck your heads so my mother won't see you."

"But that is absolutely absurd," Betty cried. "and I don't approve of the deceit. What if your mother does see us? Someone else is sure to, anyway, and will tell her about it."

"Ah," said Gilbert mysteriously, and he wagged his finger. "Now then, duck." And Betty ducked, too, along with the round-eyed children. "The point is," Gilbert went on when they were safely down Rue Brey and turning under the bridge, "if she should see you with her actual eyes, then I would be stuck, because, you see, I'm supposed to be working, taking prospects around, that is what I have told her. But if someone else sees you, then I can say, 'Oh, of course, I was just going out and met the Americans and they were going for a walk, and I gave them a lift.' You see how easy it is to explain, and besides, we have this wonderful day. Why, we may not have another day like this for weeks. It was absolutely born for our special purpose, and a Thursday! Nothing could be more perfect. And then my mother just might pop her head out and cry, 'Stop! If you're going on a trip with that American and her children, you'll have to take Mademoiselle Roule and me!'"

"I adore Mamselle," Mary said in French, clasping her hands. "She is so beautiful. I adore her all the time."

"Well, Marie, when did this infatuation start?" said Gilbert, cocking an eye at her.

"Always I have adored her," Mary said solemnly. "We should have her here with us today. And then my happiness would be complete."

"Where would we put her?" asked Peter. "It's a squash as it is." The four of them were sitting in the little Citroen, Mary in Betty's lap, Peter between Gilbert and his mother, his legs twined to avoid the gear shift.

"Yes, where would we put her?" Gilbert said in sarcasm. "she's as big as an elephant."

"You know, I am next to the head of my class," Mary went on, avoiding the practical placing of Mademoiselle, "in my alphabet. Mamselle told me yesterday that I am very bright. When she called me up before all others, I thought my heart would burst. Jean-Jacques is first, and I am second. And did you know, ma mere, that Mamselle says we shall be writing in ink before the end of the year? Imagine, in ink."

"Wonderful," Betty said.

"Ink is nothing," Peter said. "We use it every day," as his fingers testified. His career at school was not as full of charm and sweetness as Mary's, and his standing was far nearer the second from the foot. "Tell us more about this postman, Gilbert." Peter wanted to forget school, as was his holiday right.

"Well, I'll tell you. Monsieur Papillon is a very dear friend of mine and is great fun. You'll like him a lot." In an aside to Betty, he added, "He is a wonderful old character. Not only is he a postman who rides a bicycle all over the countryside, but he likes to fish, and he has a wonderful philosophy of life, and he owns a donkey. That's what we're going to see today."

"Can we pat him?" This from Mary.

"Monsieur Papillon loves children—perhaps that is the bond of our friendship—and you can pat the donkey. It is going to be very exciting."

"But what is it?" Peter cried. "You've been having secrets all morning, you and Mother, and you won't really tell us what is so exciting about a donkey."

"We're going on a picnic. Isn't that enough?"

"It is more than that, I can tell," Peter said.

"And the donkey's name is Marquis," Gilbert said.

"Marquis?" Mary repeated. "Does he bite?"

"You shall see for yourself." Gilbert turned the car in at an old farmhouse. It was of gray cement with a red-tile roof, girofleurs growing bright-colored by the big stone doorstep. These were no distinguishing features, but there was about everything a clean, brisk precision that was not common among these little southern farms. Betty recalled the farms on that dirt road beyond Draguignan, dull, hopeless mud, black dresses, hard faces, and the high, thick stone walls that tried to shut out intrusion. The stone wall here was low, with an iron grill set on the top in cement. The grill was freshly painted black. There was a small barn, a vegetable garden, chickens running about, and gravel walks lined with flower beds. And there were low, beautifully pruned fruit trees set out among the vegetables and a row of them trained against the back stone wall.

"This is my idea of a French farm," Betty said, getting out. "How cheerful it is. That is the word for it, cheerful. I had pictured southern France as one long, brilliant vineyard with fruit trees trained against a wall and all the peasants singing and dancing in wooden shoes."

"Money oils the wheels of life, in southern France as well as in America. Anyone can have fruit trees and paint their iron fences and sign, too, if he has the money," Gilbert answered her.

"This place would be just half, less than half, as attractive as it is on a postman's salary. A French postman's salary is enough to eat and have a roof over his head, no more. Madame Papillon teaches school in Agay, and that's where the extra money lies. They have no children, which spells tragedy for Monsieur, and so he urges nature to flower and fruit on his land in between his trips for the post. He was educated for better things than to be a postman, but the war ruined his chances."

The side door was thrown open violently, and out popped a short, fat man with a round red face. "Ah, Monsieur Gilbert, *mon brave* Monsieur Gilbert, *mon ami brave et beau, comment ca va*?' He ran down the walk, and holding out his arms, he unaffectedly embraced Gilbert and kisses him on each cheek. Gilbert was not at all embarrassed, he returned the embrace, and they both shouted and laughed. "How goes it?" "How have you been taking care of yourself?" "Why do you never come to see me?" "How does your mother do?" "How does your wife hold herself?" "I have heard very wonderful news about you." "You are the first person who has called it wonderful."

"Oh, but it is the most wonderful." "But it isn't conventional." "Nothing is wonderful and conventional at the same time, that is, for you and me, my friend, for you and me. We cannot be conventional, is that not so?"

"You are more than kind, Monsieur Papillon," Gilbert said. "But let me introduce you to some friends of mine, Americans, Madame Barton, Marie Barton, Pierre Barton—and they are all very dear, and you will like them very much."

"But I should like anyone who is your friend, *mon* Gilbert." Monsieur Papillon, with his funny red face, bent low and whispered to Peter and Mary, "And the only reason you have come to see me is that you want to see my donkey, Marquis, what? Is that not so?" He shouted it so loud that he made both children jump, and then he went off into paroxysms of laughter, slapping his thighs. The two children looked from their mother to Gilbert, not knowing what they were supposed to do. Monsieur Papillon went on without pause, in a normal tone of voice. "And you shall see Marquis, for Marquis is a very wonderful little person, and you will learn to love him as much as I do, and he will learn to love you very much as he loves all the children." Monsieur Papillon put a hand around each child's shoulder, and in a very earnest voice he asked, "Did you bring any dry bread?"

"Dry bread!" Peter said in amazement. Mary had lost her tongue in wonder.

"Of course I brought dry bread," Gilbert said gaily. "A big bag of it. You don't suppose I would come without dry bread. They are new and American, that is why they did not know."

"Marquis will forgive them. I think I'll pull a carrot, too. This is a holiday with your arrival." He stepped over into the garden, ran his hands along the carrot tops, selected and pulled a long orange one, brushing off the dirt. "My wife," he said, looking apprehensively toward the house, "is very busy cleaning. She has a young girl, and they are waxing and scouring until I shall not be able to find a single belonging. She told me to tell you, mon Gilbert, she did not have time to stop to talk today. Thursday, you know, is her cleaning day, and she does it with such a vengeance..."

"Oh, that is quite all right, Monsieur Papillon. I quite understand that she does not approve of my recent misbehavior. But she'll get over it."

Monsieur Papillon smiled and nodded his head. "Ah yes, ah yes." Then, looking at the carrot in his hand, he cried, "But here, here. Come, my children. What nice names, Marie and Pierre. You know, Marquis used to belong to a man who was not kind, he beat Marquis, beat him until Marquis could hardly stand up, and I saw it, and Marquis looked at me, and so I bought him. Of course, I cannot use Marquis in my job because he is too slow and too uncertain, but even though I have a bicycle, I bought him anyway, and he earns his keep in the garden. He helps me cultivate, he runs us errands, he takes Madame out in the country, and we try to make him forget his sorry past. Sometimes Madame Papillon thinks I spoil Marquis, but she is a woman and she does not fully understand." He ducked his head toward Betty. "Pardon me, Madame, but you are an exception," he said, which made Betty laugh. Before she could give him an answer, he had let the children into the barn, and he was talking to them. "Now, Pierre and Marie, the only thing to remember is that Marquis used to be whipped too much, and so when you come on him from behind, the way we are doing now, you must look for his heels. Look out!"

As he spoke, the back feet of Marquis flew out with a startling abandon. "He knows I am not alone," Monsieur Papillon continued. "He would never do that if I were alone. You two wait here." Holding the bright carrot way out in front, he sidled around the edge of the stall until Marquis, turning his gray fuzzy head, saw the carrot, and then everything was fine. Marquis allowed himself to be led forth.

He was the most donkeyish little donkey any of them had ever seen, and once out of the stall he would let any of them pat his head, rub his nose, or put an arm around his neck. He liked his ears scratched particularly, turning his head like a cat to get the full effect, and when Gilbert offered him a piece of hard bread, he bared his teeth in pleasure.

"I assure you, Madame, it is for pleasure." Monsieur Papillon calmed Betty. "Marquis may kick, but he never, never bites."

Marquis was curried until his thick gray fur curled and glistened, and his ears and nose were like gray plush velvet.

"Look at the cart. Oh, Mother, look at the darling cart!" Mary cried. Monsieur Papillon dragged out a square wood two-wheeled one about the size of an American pony basket wagon, painted a delightful yellow and red. The two men harnessed him up, and Marquis did his share, backing when he should, bending his head for the bit and head gear, all until it was time to fasten the girth belt.

"This is Marquis's game," Monsieur Papillon explained as he braced a heel on Marquis's fat side. Marquis drew in a big breath and swelled his belly up like a balloon, and hard as his master pulled, Marquis held himself rigid. Monsieur Papillon's patience wore out before the donkey's, he fastened the buckle, and at once Marquis heaved a sigh and the belt hung two inches loose around him. Monsieur Papillon tried again, pretending to pull and then giving a sudden yank. Then Gilbert had a try and after the fourth pulling and fastening, Marquis finally nodded his head to shake off a fly and docilely let them fasten his belt properly.

"It's as though he were alive," Mary said, and they all laughed at her French mistake. She frowned. "I mean, as though he talked."

"Who will ride?" asked Peter, looking in the wagon which was not much larger than a packing box.

"Why, all of you," Monsieur Papillon said. He laid a board across the front. "Here is a seat for Monsieur and Madame. Lunch underneath your feet, Madame. And you children can ride on the floor in the back. *Voilà. Voilà.* And you shall have a wonderful picnic. Marquis will manage everything."

Betty began to object. Marquis did not look much bigger than an average human being standing on four legs. "We're too much for him to pull. Why don't you and I walk alongside and let the children ride? I think it is cruel to work that poor little donkey so hard."

"But Marquis is strong as a horse. This is a light pleasure trip for him. Jump in, Madame, and you will see. You should see the stones he drags and the hay."

They all climbed in, Gilbert holding the reins. With ease, Marquis pulled them out of the yard, walking along as though the wagon were empty behind him. Monsieur Papillon waved his hat, and they all waved back. "Out into the world to seek adventure," shouted Monsieur Papillon.

"We shall find the pot of gold," Gilbert shouted back to him.

"We won't forget to come back," Betty said, smiling.

"We've got the dry bread," Peter and Mary cried, not wanting to be left out, and they waved the bag between them.

They rattled down the white clay road and out of sight of Monsieur Papillon, who stood waving his hat until the last. There were no other people in sight, and the fields they passed on either side, the poppies, the light blue morning sky overhead, the fine white dust that stood behind them like a halo, the wheel ruts and the stones in the road, and the beautiful warmth of the sun that lay upon them, each and all of these things used Marquis and the four people in the donkey cart as a focal point. They all met in converging lines at the exact spot where the cart happened to be, and as the cart moved forward the center of the converging lines of all these surrounding things moved too, at a duplicate rate of speed. Any new object that came into their line of vision simply added another converging line: the bridge built on a rise up which they toiled and, after reaching the peak, down from which they clattered, hooves slipping, brakes squeaking, dust six inches deep; the yellow-green flat disks of the euphorbia plants growing out of the dust like ragweed at home; yellow hyoseris growing like small dandelions; all these giving way to no flowers at all, no grass, but stones and vineyards. The trees would make a new formation, a cloud would come in the pale sky, until it seemed to Betty that she and Gilbert and her children were the center not only of these converging lines of things that came within their vision but also of the entire universe.

Out of nowhere came two Englishmen, it was as though the ground had cracked and two men had stepped forth newborn. They wore English navy officers' blue coats, but one really knew they were Englishmen by the way they stood, their tall bodies, their clear faces.

"Look at those two Englishmen," Gilbert said.

"Now, how do we know they are English?" Betty aked. "Without the uniform, I'd be sure they were English, but what makes us think so?"

"Who else but an Englishman would be walking alone, out here, bare-headed," Gilbert answered. "A Frenchman would be working, or he'd be wearing a beret, and an American wouldn't have a cane, and a German would carry a knapsack."

The men watched their approach, standing back in the grass, and the children and Gilbert and Betty watched the men as Marquis rattled them nearer. Opposite, one of the Englishmen made a move forward with his foot, preparatory to speech, and Gilbert reined in Marquis, for one could hear nothing above the rattling noise of the cart.

"Pardon me, Monsieur, do you have the time?" the man said in very poor French but with a good Oxford accent. Both men stared as though they had never seen anything as extraordinary in their lives as Gilbert and Betty perched high on the wooden plank and the heads of Peter and Mary peeking out from in back of them.

Betty could not help but laugh at their frank curiosity. Looking at her wristwatch, she answered easily in English, "It's just eight minutes after ten."

"You don't say," both the Englishmen exclaimed together.

Betty laughed again immoderately, but before she could explain that her laughter was caused by the incongruity of their bad French, their perfect Oxford, and her American accent, by their solemn surprise to hear a French peasant woman answering them in English, or by their actual existence at all in this otherwise unpeopled landscape, Marquis took it into his donkey head to trot away and leave the Englishmen to themselves. Again the wheels banged over the stones, drowning out all other sound, the dust rose, and the Englishmen faded into an English state without another word or movement of laughter until they might as well have been two English oaks growing by the roadside.

Betty was still laughing. Gilbert looked at her, amused. "I can't help it." she gasped between the bumps. "as a Frenchman, you are downright cruel at the expense of the English. We Americans, with our English inheritance, get much more fun out of the English. We're too much in awe of them to be cruel, but we can find subtler distinctions."

"Perhaps."

"What do you mean, perhaps?"

Gilbert laughed himself. "Just that. Perhaps. It is too hard to generalize about nationality from one person, although it is the way we usually do it. But what I do like about your sweeping conclusions is that you make them at all. When you first came here, you seemed to be afraid to commit yourself, as though what you said would be held against you. Generalities never are."

"I say we have lunch and stop talking about generals," Peter cried out.

Marquis must have heard the word lunch, for he stopped short, almost throwing them all out, and began trying to eat grass, nor would he move on, however much Gilbert slapped the reins.

"We might as well have something to eat now," Betty said, "It is a nice place." The fields had turned into an uncultivated spot with low twisted oaks, a parasol pine, some rocks, and the tough, low cistus bushes. The sunshine had brought out a couple of cistus flowers which resemble the American wild rose. These were white-petaled with gold centers.

"Oh, I must pick some," cried Mary. "To take to my Mademoiselle Roule. She has asked us to bring in flowers, and no one has brought these."

"A good reason why," Gilbert said. " The petals falloff as soon as they are picked. Another name is Spanish money—they slip through the fingers—but they are pretty, aren't they?" Gilbert climbed down and loosened Marquis's strap so that he could eat some grass. "Queer about so many of the field flowers. They won't stand picking. They look so handsome growing, but as soon as they are picked, they either fade or lose their rich color. They must be massed, in their own setting. They are an effect and can't bear too close inspection, like some people's theories." He laughed, helping Betty down off her perch.

"What about some of your own theories?"

"Oh, that goes without saying. Mine I leave quite alone, just admire their beauty from a safe distance."

"I don't believe you," she said. "What are you children doing? Now, let me sort out the lunch. You're eating your dessert first." Each child had a tangerine. " Here is a cheese sandwich, two cookies, and another tangerine. Why don't you take them up on those rocks to eat?"

"What about Marquis?" Mary asked. Marquis did not seem to think much of the grass but turned his head as though he, too, wanted lunch to eat up on the rocks. "Poor Marquis." They crowded around, patting him. They fed him some dry bread, and he certainly did enjoy it, putting back his ears and crunching the hard pieces. He had been made into such a pet it almost seemed as though he were talking to them, too. They threw his reins in front of his feet so that he wouldn't run away. The children climbed up and jumped from rock to rock, Peter doing it more expertly than Mary and obviously proud of it. "We'll sit here," Peter called back, knowing his mother was watching them.

"And we'll eat down here," Gilbert called back.

"Isn't it a breathtaking day," Betty said, laying down half a sandwich. "I think you must have all this rain and fog and wind on purpose in order to appreciate the perfect weather. Is it this way all through France?"

"I think so. Although in Paris, such a day is rarer than here at this time of year. I can remember as a little boy, when my *bonne* took me to the Luxembourg, we always had a bag for the rubbers and a umbrella strung on the perambulator. French children even when they are quite big, still travel to and from the gardens in a carriage pushed by the nurse. I suppose it is to conserve their energy for play, even on the nice days. And one day, just such a day as this"—Gilbert shaded his eyes, he was lying on the ground, in the sun, at her feet, and she was propped up against an oak—" I can remember it as vividly as yesterday. My *bonne* led me into a wood. It must have been prearranged with my mother. Of course, I knew nothing about it, but she took my hand and led me into this wood. We paid some money, and she sat me down on a little chair in front, and there were a lot of another children around me, and she had to go in back where the grown-up chairs were. I looked back to see her and was very worried, but then suddenly the Punch and Judy curtain went up and the show began. I forgot my nurse, the strange children around me, everything in the startled wonder of that show. The puppets were alive as though I were among them. I can't remember which nurse it was who took me, how old I was, where we were living at the time. But the brilliance of the sky, the dark woods, I can picture the face of the woman who took our tickets, every little detail. A bright sky and dark woods even now stir my blood." He looked up at her to smile. "Do you suppose I shall be able to give my son a remembrance like that? How I should like to give him one just like mine. I must try to." He sighed heavily.

Betty felt herself yearn to comfort him. She knew, as though it were a fact that had occurred instead of a future possibility, that he would never be able to take his son to a Punch and Judy show in the Luxembourg Gardens. His mother, the child's mother, the financial state of things, all revealed to her how hard it would be for him to have much say in his son's life. But more, she saw something within this Frenchman's character that had allowed the circumstances to shape themselves the way they had. He seemed so wise, and yet he let these things around him become twisted. Just as she had permitted the relationship between herself and Jim to grow twisted and out of harmony. Even on this perfect day, she held the trouble about herself and her husband within her, nor could she rid herself of it. and in this flash of her judgment, she could see the Frenchman, Gilbert Glisson, harboring his troubles deep down out of sight of other people. It made her feel she understood him, all in a moment.

Gilbert looked up at her and smiled lazily. He reached into the paper bag beside her, found a tangerine, and began to peel it slowly. The smell of the broken rind was sharp to her nostrils. "I think you and I have given such a day to Peter and Mary, surprising them the way we did with Marquis. Do you suppose Mary, say, will look back, when she is as old as you are and married and has children, and suddenly recall this sky and these woods and Marquis? But will she be unable to remember whether it was her mother or father who was with her, or, better still, she'll think it was both of you and not me. She'll never remember me. Or know that I existed at all."

"You know, I think you are right," Betty said abruptly. "My husband threatens to divorce me if I don't come back at once!"

"But I spoke as a joke. I was teasing."

"The thought of Mary's remembering this day and that she might never be able to remember her father. It shocks me."

Gilbert was laughing. "And don't you want her to ever remember me?"

"More than you'd think."

"Oh my. And what am I supposed to say to that?"

"Nothing. I'm very mixed up, and I wish I knew what I thought about everything. I think most men know what they want much more than women do."

"It's the way they're trained. Or the way they think they're trained. They don't know their own minds any more than women. Take my mother. If anyone knows her own mind, it is she."

"But did she where her husband was concerned?"

"Oh, well, she was crazy about my father, daft about him. It was real true love, something you don't often find. Something I know I shall never attain. Perhaps where he was concerned she didn't know her own mind but did what he wanted. Although they always wanted the same thing, they were always so 'of one' in what they wanted, it was hard to say who had wanted it first. With my father's death, it seemed as though half my mother died, too. She was quite out of her senses for a time, and then she came to center her life on me. But with a mother and son, it is quite another thing from a wife and husband. That is where the trouble lies between my mother and me. We're a different generation, different everything, and so we are bound not to agree. In flashes, my mother sees this as clearly as I do. But then she forgets, I seem to have gone rather far afield from you and your husband. Tell me, now that we can talk, more about the way you feel toward him." Gilbert was all sympathy.

"I wish I knew myself," Betty said. "My feeling are mixed. I miss Jim terribly. I miss him as my husband and as himself. We have lived together so many years, with no quarrels, no strife. I know all his little wants, the things he likes to eat, the way he likes his clean clothes put away in his bureau drawers, and I enjoy fixing everything in the house so that he will be comfortable. And in the same breath I almost hate him. I glory in being alone in my house here in St.-Raphael. I call it my house and feel suddenly free and gay and myself, Elizabeth Moon. That was my name before I was married. Do the French have such a queer name, Moon?"

"No, but I think it is very charming. I wish I had known it before. Elizabeth Moon. It is lovely."

"It is silly, really." Betty laughed. But she looked pleased.

"Ah, Madame. And do you like so much for me to say Elizabeth Moon? You must step carefully." He laughed, too. And quickly he picked up her hands and kissed them. "There. That is to show you, you are not to trust me. And it is to show you that I respect you and admire you and that I enjoy spending the day with you and your children. And to teach you that the woman makes up her mind as much, and maybe more rapidly, than the man. You American women seem to think you have no responsibility. I tell you, the married woman must take all the responsibility when a man and woman sit together in the fields. Did you not know that?"

"But I didn't ask you to kiss my hands," Betty said. She was rattled and did not know what was expected of her. His kisses had been light, quick, one on each hand.

"Yes? You note I respectfully kissed your hands. When I kiss your mouth, then you may be disturbed. But Madame"—nonchalantly, Gilbert picked up a bent piece of grass and broke it off, And when he turned to look at her there might have been a wall between them—" tell me, with your husband, do you plan things consciously, for an effect, when you write your letters?"

"No, I certainly don't. I write what I feel."

"Ah, Madame. But first let me ask you, do you want this divorce which he threatens? I think you should take a big sheet of paper and pencil and jot down just what you want from your husband, just what you get from him, and finally what you expect to get from him. Tabulate the items, one, two, three, list under a big A the spiritual factors, under a big B the physical, and under C the economic. Make a regular copybook outline of your life. Then you can direct your attack by letter with the precision of a military campaign. What about this divorce, do you want it or not?"

"You make me gasp," Betty said. She had not recovered from his sudden kissing of her hands. "How do I know what I want? Yes, yes, I would like a divorce, and yet I know that I wouldn't. How could I? I really love Jim, I have my two children, I could not dream of a divorce. But your mathematical way of looking at life appalls me."

"Oh no, not at all. But now you must settle this problem of divorce, that is from your end. Yes or no. Of course, you always have your husband's attitude to reckon with. How about going back to America? Are you going? If so—"

"No, I'm not."

"You see how easy it is." Gilbert twisted the grass in his hand. "But Madame, let me say a few words. Perhaps none of my business, but you know I think your husband is a much more amusing man than you give him credit for. After all, he is putting up with a good deal, letting his wife stay over here without him. You make him out too dull, too full of business and money matters. You know, if you had been my wife, when you decided to stay over here, I should have taken you by the hair of your head and dragged you along behind me. But then, I'm not your husband, or anyone's, for that matter."

Betty leaned down and whispered in his ear, "You know, I think I rather should have liked it." She was hasty to add, "But don't tell anyone!" She was laughing.

"Most certainly not," Gilbert said severely. "But I do want to tell you my theories about married people. I think *any* couple can live together, and do so with as much happiness as any of us can find. Any man can live happily with any woman, or vice versa.

"You're perfectly absurd. What do you know about it anyway?"

"I tell you, it is theory. That is the best part of theories. You don't have to live them yourself. But I stick to it. Any couple can live together once they've made up their minds to it. But there is a catch. They *both* must make the effort together. Divorce comes where one of them refuses, or both. It is making up the mind. People make up their minds to dive when they are going swimming. The mind once made up, the man dives in easily. It is the same with a man-and-woman relation. Make up your two minds. Dive in together. That is all there is to it. And with your minds made up, you can keep on diving and doing it beautifully together. I think it is a wonderful theory. And think what energy you'd save yourself. Marry someone, and that would be the end of it. But this eternal seeking after happiness, this worry you Americans have whether the marriage is perfect. No marriage is perfect. One in a thousand. But why fuss about it? Jump in, marry, and be done with it."

"I notice you don't practice it yourself," Betty said.

"I have never found anyone who would practice it with me." Gilbert gave her a quick grin.

"So how could I? I am a Diogenes of marriage, eternally hunting for the perfect woman."

"You know, on the impulse, I should like to cry out, 'I am that woman!'" Betty looked at him to see if he thought she was being melodramatic. "You forced me to say that. There was nothing else for me to say." She put it off by appearing coquettish, but there was a hint of seriousness in her tone.

Gilbert looked at her and smiled, but she could not decide whether he liked her playfulness or thought her foolish.

"You know what I wish you would tell me," she said. "It is sheer impertinent curiosity."

"Go ahead." He nodded.

"I wish you would tell me what Suzanne is like. I mean what she really is like. Most French girls have voluptuous mouths."

"What do you mean, voluptuous?"

"That is the only way I can described it. Dozens of French girls. There is something in the way they hold it. It can't be the lipstick they use; girls at home use lipstick, too. But it looks very sensuous to me. Although not at all unpleasantly so. On the contrary, I think it very attractive. But you aren't answering my questions. I want to know why you went with her to begin with. I am being too curious, I can see by your face. I have never seen a real mistress. To read about one is not the same."

"Well now, let's see," Gilbert said, trying to look serious, but he burst out laughing. "Tell me why, but I guess all nice, proper girls are curious about the improper ones. She is not a registered mistress, you know. She is just like you or me. She is very quiet, she is a good cook, she sews beautifully, she never reads anything, she isn't very well educated nor is she interested in improving her mind, she hates to have her hair mussed."

"There, that is more what I mean. What sort of underwear does she use? Oh dear," Betty flushed. "I shouldn't have asked that."

"Why not? She wears lovely underwear. A fine batiste that she makes herself, with tiny tucks and crocheted edging and the tiniest pale pink buttons with buttonholes that are impossible to button, or unbutton, if you must know, and it always looks as though she had just pressed it. My benefit, I suppose. But she is very exquisite about her person."

"How nice. It is female of me to ask such questions, isn't it? I don't want to be vulgar, and I'm almost afraid that you think I am, but you can put it down to female curiosity. And another thing that I think is nice is that you notice and appreciate Suzanne that way. It seems...sweet. Jim makes a point of not noticing what I wear, a typical American man, afraid he might seem effeminate."

"Don't forget to catalogue that item in your outline under the heading 'What to train a husband to do.' I'm so taken with my idea, I must see you carry it out. But the trouble with my ideas is that they don't work out in a practical way. You'll write out my paper outline, and then with a little flesh-and-blood emotion it will fall to pieces on the first tryout. Tell me, Madame, you are so curious about my little Suzanne. Can I, too show curiosity?"

"But of course," Betty said.

"You American women—ah, how to express to you my exact, my precise meaning? You American women with your husbands—I try to generalize for I have seen many American women over here—are you not a trifle cold? No, that is not the word. Reserved, shall we say? Are you not reserved with your husband? The least little afraid to let yourselves go? You speak of the voluptuous French mouth, but is not your American mouth held a little too stiff? With love between human beings, I think the men and the women need to be taught and trained how to love. It is like being taught how to dance, how to sing. The young baby thrush, you know, is taught its song by its parents. And so the human mother must teach the girl. Especially in our present civilization with this concept we have regarding virginity, the woman cannot learn about love from early love affairs as freely as a man can. The French boy learns mostly from experience with prostitutes, although his father tells him, too, and a French girl before she enters marriage is taught by her mother how to make love, so many details, not all at once, but gradually until when the marriage is to occur the young girl is no longer innocent, but she really has learned to play an active part. Now, I understand that this is not at all common with you Americans. That you spring into marriage as though into the heart of a rose, but without any practical guidance ahead of time."

"That is too often true. My own mother tried in a lame, embarrassed sort of way to tell me about intercourse, but she embarrassed me so much the way she talked, and I knew already most of the details from other girls, that I froze her up and would not listen to her."

"You know, that is shocking to us French. And the girl must be trained to make love far more than the boy. From the very nature of her body. I suppose it is the Anglo-Saxon, fanatical religious element you English and Americans have instilled into lovemaking. You look upon it as a sinful pleasure. Whereas how to make love is the very essence of family life."

"How amazing it is to be able to talk to you calmly about such things." Betty sighed. "We Americans can never talk easily. That is, without emotion. It is either a dammed-up flood of sex that breaks over everything, or else there is nothing, as though it didn't exist, talking of everyday things like what shall we have for dinner or whom shall we invite to some party. I don't know why I should expect to have it any different, but—" The tears came to Betty's eyes, and she had to stop to find her handkerchief. "Why I should cry? It is too absurd. My husband loves me, I know he loves me a great deal, and I have always been attracted to him—loved him, if you like—but he is always in such a hurry, just when I feel we are together as one, when everything will be ecstatic, suddenly it is all over, and well, there we are. It is once more the everyday things of life." Betty wiped her eyes and laughed, shrugging her shoulders. "Big confession, true story of an American wife. I suppose a lot of it is my fault, but I think I am tied by my own nature, my background. Of course, it isn't as bad as I make out, or we couldn't have stayed as fond of each other as we have. But because our marriage has not come up to what my young girl's dream was, that, I think, is the reason I am here now. There was a stagnation of everything about my life back home. Restless, I thought perhaps there was something to be learned from life over here, and I simply cannot go back to my former life so soon. I wonder if this is the way most of these notorious American divorces you read of in the papers start. A waywardness between husband and wife, a vague longing that doesn't materialize, and suddenly the two of them find themselves on different roads.

"Tell me, Gilbert, tell me. What do you think is the trouble with Jim and me? Do you really think it is our own fault, that we are afraid, that if we both made up our minds to dive in, we still could make a go of marriage? Or is it hopeless? Am I too cold? Do you really think anything my mother might have trained me to do in the way of lovemaking would have made the slightest bit of difference? If you could see my mother—sensitive, shy, a little brown sparrow of a woman—and yet I know my father adores her and she him. They have had a happy married life, a quiet one. Am I too violent, do I expect the moon, am I spoiled because I cry for it and can't find it? Tell me, tell me." She looked at him hopefully. "No wonder you French call us American wives children. I sound no older than Mary, the way I talk to you. But to talk at all..." The tears came again. "This is absurd, you know."

"But my dear girl, why is it absurd? It is the very center of your life which is off balance. It is very serious. And I can't solve it for you. But I can talk to you about it. And then maybe you'll be able to find the solution. The French, you know, are so hardheaded and practical about emotions. They never strain after moonbeams like the English. You Americans are an English branch. A new one. You have wonderful vigor but no tradition. French people are all tradition. They have pigeonholed and catalogued the last emotion until it is cut and dried. I think that is why the French have a soft spot in their hearts for you impetuous Americans who never do anything the same way twice. And you will talk about any subject with the innocence and openness of children. The English grow stuffy and consider Americans forward. But I insist it is the child in you, and how we French love children. But to go back to you and your husband, what can I to for you? I have been talking like a professor."

"No, you haven't. You have been like an angel. Do you know what you can teach me?"

"What?" Gilbert was amused at her earnest question, but he tried not to show it in his smile.

"You can teach me to make love."

"Oh, you impetuous American. Did I not just say you were like children?"

Betty faltered. "But you are putting the wrong interpretation on what I meant. You offered to help me. Oh, you are going back on your bargain. I meant for you to teach me as a French mother would help her daughter. You asked me yourself."

"Dear child, dear child. Don't get upset. I understand, really I do. Your abrupt demand."

"Hullo, hullo, hullo!" Peter and Mary came tumbling down from the rocks. "What are you two talking about anyway? Are we never going to ride Marquis anymore? Do we have to stay here all day?"

"But come now. What's all this commotion? Of course we are going to drive, and we are waiting for you, Pierre and Marie." Gilbert talked to distract the children from watching their mother dry her eyes. "Let's go at once." He jumped to his feet, and, taking both Betty's hands, he pulled her up. Slipping her arm through his, he patted her hand. "Don't worry," he whispered. "My dear, I shall do what I can, and you must be gay with your children. We shall talk again."

"I want to ride in front and drive," cried Peter.

"Oh, me too, me too!" cried Mary, furious that she hadn't thought of it first.

"You both can. Your mother will sit in the middle. No, Mary had better. The three of you can squeeze onto the board, and I shall walk beside you and direct. All aboard. Come on, Marquis. Speed up there."

They were off, but Marquis had lost his morning pep. He wanted to stand in the shade and chew dry bread. The sun was overhead, and it had grown very hot.

"Oh, I say, this is neat fun," Peter said, sitting up straight to look more impressive. Marquis, however, would hardly move forward. Gilbert touched him with the whip. Marquis trotted for a dozen paces and then once more ambled into a walk. Gilbert snapped the whip in the air, but Marquis walked more slowly.

"He's showing his stubborn donkey traits," Gilbert said, this time hitting Marquis sharply.

"Oh, don't!" cried Mary. "You're cruel." But Marquis seemed to understand that business was meant, and with a toss of his head he fell into a brisk canter. Then suddenly, without warning, they were all thrown forward by Marquis's violent halt. Betty was able to prevent Mary from falling onto Marquis's back, because her legs were not long enough to brace them, but Peter toppled off onto the road and did his best to look dignified, holding a firm grip on the reins.

"What happened?" everyone cried at once.

"Oh, Gilbert, it is your cruel beating of Marquis. He is fainting." Mary cried.

"Why, that is absurd. I hardly touched him." But something was wrong. Marquis had made his impossible stand by spreading his legs, and he was practically on the ground, head down, his legs stretched on either side in a position that was anatomically out of keeping for a hoofed quadruped.

"What in the name of God is the animal doing, anyway?" Gilbert said, annoyed. "It all comes of treating him like a human being."

Mary cried excitedly, "He's dying! He's fainted."

"He certainly is acting queerly, I think he must be sick." Betty jumped out, and they all ran around to look at poor Marquis. And what was the spoiled animal doing? Trying to recover a large hunk of dry bread which he apparently had been sucking on and had dropped in the road. The check rein had prevented him from lowering his head, so he had lowered his body by spreading his legs, and in this ridiculous position he was nosing for the piece of bread. There was not a thing wrong with the little beast. Mary was the first to action, and without fear she ducked under Marquis's head, got the bread, wiped it, and handed it to him. Daintily, he bared his teeth and grasped it. he didn't even wait for them to get in again, and slowly he moved forward as though nothing had happened.

"I tell you, that donkey is more spoiled than a child," Gilbert said when they could get their breath from laughing.

Once more, they all climbed in and settled themselves. Once more, the fields, poppies, and roadside trees moved past majestically. The heat made the horizon trees and hills a blue haze, and little clouds began to creep upward in the sky. They passed a couple of dilapidated farms, none of them in any way comparable with Monsieur Papillon's concentrated, neat acreage.

"Tell me, Pierre," Gilbert said. "I understand things are not going at school just the way they should." Betty had previously told him of a letter she had received from Monsieur Bonnet. "What is it, too much play?"

Peter's life at school had been the opposite of Mary's. Mary had been given none of the cruel teasing that Peter had. The boys and girls in her class were little more than babies, and they looked on Mary as a sort of talking doll. Her big brown eyes and dimples were disarming, and they liked to poke her to hear the strange English words she made. But she was sturdy for her age and used to playing with boys older than herself, so she was quite ready to answer back with a quick hand. But Peter's class was all boys, and young boys are too near the savage not to poke fun at queer customs or anything that differs from the duplication of their on image. Peter had suffered much, he was sensitive, and while he had not been very popular at home—he was not strong enough physically for that—he had always been accepted as one of the gang. Here he was made a butt of, a boy would steal his cap and throw it in the mud by way of insult, he was always *It* in games, and they would talk about him in Provencal, knowing he could not follow, and jeer at his American shoes. But once, with a fistfight, the tide turned. He did not win, but when challenged he fought with such pent-up fury that he roused some admiration, and Jacques, always afterward Peter's chum, began to make friendly advances. It made all the difference. Someone offered him a bit of lunch, boys passed notes to him in class, and at recess he was accepted as one of them. It was at this point that Monsieur Bonnet noted the change, but to him it was adverse. Peter had struggled so hard in class that the master had given him better marks than he deserved, if only for the energy he put into studying. He began to slide downhill, he was inattentive in dictation, he didn't know his verbs, he said Buenos Aires was the capital of Brazil. With his mother, he would recite the next day's lesson without a mistake, but as soon as he got to class the boys went to his head. "I actually caught him looking out of the window in recitation," Monsieur

Bonnet wrote, which seemed to be a terrible crime in a French school-room. "And I must ask you to take immediate action." Betty considered the new friendships more important than a little window-gazing, but it would never do to admit this treason to Monsieur Bonnet, who as full of humor as a dry haystack.

"Please talk to Peter," she had said to Gilbert. "What you say will have far more influence than my frivolous attitude. He needs a man's critical advice."

"I can't help it," Peter answered now. "That old Bonnet man picks on me all the time lately. Everything is my fault. He blamed me for folding a pair of paper spectacles the other day when I didn't even know how to make them. Stood me in the corner for half an hour. You can make sure as soon as recess came, I spent the whole time learning how to fold them. Here's a pair I did, as good as any boy in the class." He took a paper out of his pocket, and it did resemble a pair of automobile goggles, and with a bit of string it looked quite realistic.

"I'll admit, in a foreign school you have certain handicaps which Monsieur Bonnet does not take into consideration," Gilbert said, swallowing his smile. "I understand that you are extremely good—or, rather, that you were before you took to this window-gazing—in arithmetic. As it is impossible to be good all the time, and as I agree with your mother that French boyfriends are as much a part of your education over here as history or geography, why don't you concentrate for the rest of this month on being as good as you know how to be in the one subject of arithmetic? Don't pass a note, don't do anything you know you shouldn't do, and learn your lesson in that one subject perfectly so that Monsieur Bonnet cannot help but admire you. Then relax a little in the other work. Not too much, but enough to have a small amount of pleasure. What do you say to that?"

"I'll try it," cried Peter, who felt attracted to the novelty of having a grown-up permit some fun in class. "You know, Gilbert"—both the children had long since given up the *Monsieur*—" you sure know how a boy feels. I'll work for all I'm worth in arithmetic this next week and see if old Bonnet isn't impressed."

Betty had listened in silence, and her admiration for Gilbert increased. He had not scolded Peter as most grown-ups would have done, nor had he laughed at him. She smiled her appreciation over Peter's head. At the same time she asked herself, *What would Jim have said to Peter*?

The sun was again on their left, for the road had turned and was taking them back toward St.-Raphael.

"To me, this has been the most perfect day in France," Betty exclaimed.

"Why, Mother," Peter reprimanded her. "You said when we were in Paris that you would die happy and that nothing could ever equal the moment when you put your foot down and touched the streets of Paris."

"Besides," Mary interrupted, "how can it be the most perfect day without Daddy here?"

"All your witnesses are against you." Gilbert laughed. "You haven't an argument left to stand on."

"At any rate, it has been near perfection. You'll all have to admit that."

"I wish I could get perfection in my lessons without bothering so much, "Peter sighed. "But I'll try the arithmetic, Gilbert."

"Good for you, Pierre. But one other thing, while we're on the subject of school. Don't be afraid to be wrong. Did you know that is the trouble with most people in this world? They are so afraid they'll be wrong that they won't go ahead and try. That is another one of my theories. I think there should be included in the schoolwork a special course, how to be wrong. Most grown-ups are afraid to be wrong, and so they won't dash ahead. They are afraid they might not do it correctly."

"That is a wonderful theory of yours," Betty said. "Tell me more."

"Better, I'll give you an example. This road is taking us home, but by a different way, and we shall go right by the house where young baby Gilbert lives. Shall we all be afraid to be wrong and not stop in to see him?"

"Oh, let's stop!" Mary cried. I love babies. Don't you, Mummy?"

Betty looked at Gilbert to see if he meant what he said, but he gave no imitation from his expression. He was putting it up to her, and she hesitated. Madame Glisson would not easily forgive this move on Betty's part, and Betty was afraid of the old lady's opinion. More than Madame Glisson, it was against the general opinion in town. Gilbert evidently was doing it on a dare. "We'll go," Betty said finally.

They came to a row of small houses on the edge of town, cheaply built with modern angled stair rails to the porch, an oddly placed chimney, but set up close together with not enough yard space to turn around in. Evidently a real estate deal of the last boom, a community of small shopkeepers and tradesmen, respectably neat, but near the borderline of being poor.

Betty felt great misgivings after she had taken Gilbert's crazy dare. Nor did her misgivings lessen as the donkey cart was pulled up in front of a bright blue house with white painted trimmings. Even though she couldn't see them, she could feel female eyes peering behind curtains from every house in the row. A well-dressed foreign woman, with two well-dressed children sitting in a donkey cart that was painted bright red and yellow and attended by Gilbert Glisson, notorious to all of these households, was anything but inconspicuous. Why hadn't she waited until they were comfortably seated in the shabby little Citroen car? No one but farm people ever rode in donkey carts, and never for pleasure. Betty angrily hardened her face to meet the barrage of unseen eyes as Gilbert handed her out of their chariot.

"You should have brought us here in a circus wagon," she said.

"Afraid?" he smiled

"I'm trying not to be," she said.

They fastened Marquis to a tree trunk, walked up onto the porch, and rang a bell which tinkled cheerfully inside the house.

Mary was anticipating with pleasure the sight of the baby. She had an instinctive sympathy for Gilbert and seemed to know, as though she were a mature grown-up, the things he liked the best. She stood beside him, holding his hand instead of her mother's, while they were waiting for someone to answer the door. Squeezing his hand, she looked up and said, "You are very excited, Gilbert, aren't you? Do you think the baby can walk yet?"

"Why, Mary Barton, you're a goose," Peter said. "You know the baby is only a month old and that babies can't walk at that age. Have you ever known anyone as stupid as Mary is?" Peter asked his mother.

But whether Mary was talking sensibly or not really didn't make the least bit of difference. She had divined Gilbert's nervous excitement, and by saying such a preposterous thing about the baby's walking she had set them all laughing. When Suzanne came to answer the door herself, she found such a lot of merry faces that she, too, smiled easily; otherwise, it would have been an awkward moment.

"But how delightful! What a surprise, what a pleasant surprise," Suzanne cried. "And how kind you are to come, Madame Barton. I can never thank you enough." She took both of Betty's hands instead of formally waiting for an introduction, and then, unaffectedly, she reached up and kissed Gilbert on each cheek, putting her arms around his neck for a moment. "Ah, the children," she exclaimed, leaning down to shake each limp small hand. "My sister, she is not home at the moment, how lucky. But you must come in at once. Little Gilbert, he sleeps, but at once you must come in to see him. Will you be tiptoe quiet?" She put her hand to her lips and nodded at Peter and Mary.

They entered the house as though it were natural that they should call, and Suzanne, without any pretense, led them through the front living room into a small room in back. They all peered in turn, over a dainty bassinette basket at a miniature red-faced little creature lying there sound asleep. It was very touching to Betty to see Gilbert throwing the baby kisses and beaming proudly on him. What pleasure shone in his face.

They all walked back into the front living room and sat down, talking politely of the weather, the donkey, and their picnic.

"And how does he eat, little Gilbert?" Gilbert asked Suzanne, as though he had not been there just that morning, very early.

As Suzanne answered, Betty relaxed. She was accustoming herself to the oddness of the visit. Afterward, she could not recall anything about the house except that it looked like most any house, for she was looking at Suzanne all the time. What surprised her the most was how respectable

Suzanne looked. Her figure was slight, perhaps too thin, but there was a glow in her skin that came from happiness. She was quite pretty. Her hair was marcelled, with the tips of her ears showing, and bangs. Her breasts were very full from the nursing. *It is impossible that she is not his wife and that I am not sitting here in an ordinary house like any house at home among my friends in Merchantville,* Betty kept thinking to herself.

"I really think we should not stay too long," Betty said. It was the proper statement to make.

"Before we go, let me see once more if little Gilbert is not awake," Gilbert pleaded. And, of course, when he came back, he was carrying the baby. Whether he had been awake or not, they would not know, but Betty was sure he had wakened him on purpose. Betty felt the baby was very frail and weak, his little hands seemed to have no strength when they curled around her finger. But Suzanne was also tiny and small-boned. And then, how easily one forgets the size and activity of a small baby." Betty was allowed to hold him for a minute, and he seemed to weigh less than a breath of air. His little gown was beautiful with hand-work. He could not focus his eyes, which were the blue of a kitten's, but his expression was extraordinarily like Gilbert's. Gilbert did not have a baby face, but there was exactly the way he must have looked as a baby, the way the eyes were placed, the shape of the forehead, something in the mouth. The whole had the stamp of Gilbert Glisson. Mary begged and begged to hold the baby, but they would not let her. "In another month, when he is a little older, then perhaps you can," Betty said, handing the baby back to Gilbert. He seemed to know just how to handle him, and the baby settled into his arm.

As they were about to leave, Suzanne was saying, in reference to their picnic, "I had forgotten it was Thursday. The days slip by so fast. How I used to adore Thursdays when I was a child going to school. The nicest day of the whole week. And here it is the last Thursday of the month of November. How the time slips by."

The last Thursday of November! The words rang in Betty's mind like some old theme. *The last Thursday in November, I, president of this nation, hereby proclaim...*How could she, how could she? How was it possible to have forgotten? How had she not known? That she should forget that this was Thanksgiving Day was such a shock to Betty that all the way home she could not forgive herself. It was like forgetting she was an American. Like forgetting who she was, what she was. How would she tell the children? It made her realize how far she had traveled from Merchantville, New Jersey. And the basis of her horror and fear at herself was to know how far she had traveled from Jim, her husband. A divorce was not out of the question.

She waited until they were at home and Gilbert had said good-bye and the children were eating their supper of bread and milk and fruit. Then she told them that today was Thanksgiving Day, and yet what a beautiful day they had had, and she made out that she had intentionally not told them until now so that they would not be disappointed that there was no turkey or pie.

She cried by herself after she had put them to bed, and she was sitting alone darning stockings in the evening.

11

Christmas and New Year's

etty sat and looked at the Christmas tree.

It was a laurel bush she and Gilbert had cut out in the woods and propped unsteadily inside a jardinière. It was decorated with nuts and oranges covered with tinsel paper and hung on strings, a cardboard star and paper angels, homemade. The whole effect was as un-American as a Frenchman could make it.

The children were in raptures when they ran downstairs [why did I think it was a 2 story house?] in their pajamas early that morning. Gilbert had crept in by the back door and was hiding behind the curtains to watch their first surprise. And he was as thrilled as another child. For Betty, the whole performance was playacting. She hid tears and anger.

She missed Jim terribly. At the same time, she was feverishly angry with him. In the past two days she had received two letters, one from Jim himself and one from a friend in Merchantville, and they had neatly divided her emotions. She was crying to herself, *Jim, my beloved Jim, where are you at this Christmastime?* In the same breath with, *Oh, Jim, how could you act so badly and with that unscrupulous Roberta?* If he had chosen another woman, she wouldn't have felt such rage. So she argued with herself.

She recalled each Christmas she and Jim had spent together. They had always made so much of it. Before the children were born they had a tree, trimmed it together, bought each other five-and- dime stocking presents, and made a great mystery and celebration out of their Christmas breakfast. The rest of the day had not mattered, dinner at one or the other's family, friends in, but early morning, awakening to be the first to shout, "Merry Christmas, dear," in bathrobes and slippers, holding hands, they would go down to see the tree and stockings together.

All other mornings in the year might be what they would, but about this one morning they had been fanatical. No one else was ever allowed to spend Christmas Eve in their house. Microscopic maid or brawny Lila were sent off with the excuse that meals were eaten at Grandmothers' houses anyway. Maids, aunts, or cousins were shooed out of the house for that night. It emphasized the unity of family as nothing else did, waking up to feel there was nobody else in the world but Jim, Betty, Peter, and Mary. And it lasted until ten or eleven, with breakfast eaten in single bites separate by billows of gay paper as they unwrapped their presents. Jim filled her stoking so that every present in it was a complete surprise, and she did the same with him. The children, of course, were easy to surprise and assume. There might be a diamond and emerald ring alongside a five-cent horse referring to a family joke. The least present was received and given with total enthusiasm. They usually opened them one at a time in order to enjoy their common pleasure together.

Some years they had said, "Oh, this year let's not bother, it's the children's day," but as Christmastime drew near and one smelled the spicy spruce, fir, and pine in the air and felt that electric touch among people shopping, the spirit of the thing drew them close together, and they would dash to do last-minute feast of brilliant, silly things.

And this year they had a whole ocean between them.

Two weeks previously, Betty had realized the time was coming close, and in halfhearted fashion she had bought some trinkets in the Bon

Marche, a sewing reticule for traveling that had a miniscule pair of scissors inside a thimble for her mother, a pair of French suspenders for her father, a paperback French novel for Aunt Eliza—but she was at her wit's end to find anything for Jim. St.-Raphael had none of the diversity of the five-and-dime at home; she had to consider the question of dutiable goods. She duplicated the suspenders, a necktie, and then she came across some bicycle clips for trouser legs and attached a poem. She did them up and got them off. A couple of days after she had mailed it, a giant package came from home, and this had upset her for several reasons. It showed that Jim had made the herculean effort of Christmas shopping at least a month ahead of time. The size of the box alone was overwhelming. Of course, there were grandmothers, grandfathers, and aunts as well as Jim to contribute, and they were sending presents, above all, to the children. Jim had managed it so that she had no duty or hold-up on the French end. He must have put it on a boat in New York himself, judging from the elaborateness of stamps and papers attached. Would he ever receive hers, and would he have to fuss about customs and duty? Her French baggage master had been as inefficient as he could be, she was sure. She could see Jim's eyebrows go up and hear him mutter, "If this isn't the frog system." Whereas his package had been delivered as though royalty had sent it.

She had torn open a corner of it and read, "Betty from Santa," "Bet from Jim," "A wife from a husband who loves her," "Elizabeth from James," and she had sat down and cried so hard she had blurred the ink on the Betsy one. It was remorse. Terrible homesickness. If only she could have opened her arms and closed them around him. She would have done anything for him at that moment. And she sat down and wrote a letter to that effect. It was a maudlin letter, and she mailed it at once so that she wouldn't have time to reconsider the wild promises she made to him.

And on Christmas Eve she had received the other letter. She should not have been disturbed by it; she was sure it was not written with the intention to upset her. It came from a girl with whom she had grown up in Merchantville and who also was in her class at Smith College. Mildred

Lovell. Mildred had never married, and that meant that Mildred looked on men and husbands with a sentimental-cynical eye. Mildred taught school, she was trim, witty, intelligent, with a tailored smartness regulated by earning her own money and living at home. Betty enjoyed a matinee once or twice a year with her, and it was refreshing to be stirred up by Mildred's New Republic modern- fiction mind. Mildred had spent several vacations in Europe, and that had created a recent bond between them. Mildred was impressed by Betty's year-abroad experiment, and they had exchanged several letters. This last one was chiefly concerned with places in the vicinity of St.-Raphael which Mildred had visited. She gave a delightful account of Aix-en-Provence which made Betty hunt up her Baedecker at once. Betty resolved to take the children to Aix. But there was one paragraph in the letter that troubled her deeply.

She lit a cigarette, a new habit she found relaxing when she was alone—she still could not Smoke in front of the children—and, taking Mildred's letter, she came to the section:

Henderson's Saturday-night Thanksgiving-week party: me invited, though no reason for Irma to put herself out. All married couples and dull—no offense. Half a dozen boring stags, your own wifeless husband counted among them, and the high and handsome exception. But who am I, the humble old maid, to have him look at me. Though I could have told him a lot about his wife with a long letter, and tried, but he only would give a yes, yes. All eyes for Roberta, she monopolizing, as usual. They say she is working fast while the cat's away.

Everybody has seen them everywhere. Jealous? I wouldn't be jealous of that gal if she hooked the Prince of Wales. As you and I know, Roberta would flirt with a pair of pants in a department store window. Your boyish-smile hub is too much the *gentilhomme* to leave a girl ogling the air without answering. Still, I wish he wouldn't mess around with her.

Drinks were everywhere. And the foulest stuff. A thing they call bathtub gin which was mixed with fruit and perfume, and if you held your nose you could gulp it down. Did you know that yours truly has succumbed and sips cocktails on occasion? What else is a lone female to do—at least, that is my alibi. I am only a leaf floating on the stream. You are going to come back to a changed *Etats Unis*, and you must let me know your reaction. It is in the air. I notice it like a doe sniffing danger. A curious wildness. A sort of unprincipled disregard of consequence. The stock market affair is one beautiful example. The ugly rearing head of gangsters another. The indecent degree of drinking and flirting, too—prohibition is doomed or else somebody has got to do something about it. But nobody does. Our common friend Roberta is another splendid example. Your husband looks clean and pure when he drinks, but Roberta is plain leering disgusting, and it is I who ordinarily take the women's part. Ellis is fatter than ever, but he can always hold Roberta by his checkbook.

I tell you these things to show trends. Postwar they are. Degeneration, I feel. Maybe I'm not staying modern enough. Jaundiced eye of old age. The twenty-year watermark approaches too quick. My dear, I tell you this as seen by the cold eye of a friend. You'll hear of it again distorted by some woman's love-of-gossip letter, by a mother-love letter, or maybe smoothed over by a casual husband-love letter. My advice is stay on your own side of the ocean while you have the chance.

And now I want to tell you all about Aix, which is so near to where you are living...

The letter continued in a European tour vein and ended without further reference to Jim or his flirtation.

Betty flicked her cigarette ash into the fire and thought. Mildred was kind. She was sincere. Betty wondered if Mildred knew how to judge a husband dispassionately. Whatever the truth was, Betty felt uneasy and uncertain of herself. Mildred's remark about the letters that would inform Betty about this Roberta mess was prophetic. She had already received them and had not had the sense to know it. One from her mother: "Now, dear, it is high time you came home. Jim is human, you know, and as his wife it is your place by his side." Jim's last three letters each had a sentence—

"had dinner the other night with Bertie and Ellis," "at the Henderson's party, usual crowd, Bertie and Ellis and all the rest of them, good time," and "Roberta has a new permanent," which at the time she had taken for Jim's idea of feminine news in which she would be interested. But now, how dare Jim tell her the fact about Roberta Evan's permanent? And she had been ninny enough to have swallowed all he said about missing her at Christmas, and he would be reading a letter from her that was soupy with sentimentality.

Jealous? Yes, she was jealous. She was angry with jealousy. Or was it pride? Never before had Jim ever looked at another woman. Not the way Mildred described it. And Roberta, of all people. That flighty, stuck-up creature. Jim had always made fun of her airs. Betty couldn't believe Jim could be seriously interested in her. And Jim's financial state was no inducement to Roberta. But whether it was serious on not, whether it was no more than too much drinking, Betty was jealous of that. Jim was insulting her, "messing around" with this woman behind her back. She felt ashamed to have her husband doing the flirting; that was her prerogative as an American wife. Before marrying Ellis Evans, Roberta had been just another girl in Merchantville. It was Ellis who had the family, the background, and who would be extremely wealthy when his father died. He was well-off at present. Jim might have looks and a gay smile, but Roberta knew where the money was.

The whole thing is nothing more than that, Betty assured the fire. *It is a waste of time to give it another thought.* And back her mind would go to Jim. Was he actually seeing this woman? What was the extent of their lovemaking? She stood up and went over to look in the mirror. She looked at herself and said, "Of course, you know, Elizabeth Moon Barton, you can't go off and leave a husband alone. After all, as your mother says, he's only human." It was startling to hear her own voice. With the children asleep and Caterina away, it was absurd of her to stand talking out loud to her own reflection. "But I've got to argue it out with myself," she continued aloud. "Gilbert is right. I've got to take account of things. What am I going to do? What do I want? What are Jim and I going to do? The thing has got to be definite."

It was cold, and she went back to her fire. *What am I going to do?* Forget about Jim and Roberta 'messing around'. Mildred put the whole thing into a trend, a phase, a period in history, and it was an admirable way to look at life. Objective. To get upset just thinking about what Jim was doing necking with that silly Roberta was subjective. To decide what she was going to do and to do it quietly, that was detached and objective. Betty wondered if she had enough detachment within herself to do that. It was, in a way, what she was here in France for, perhaps why she had stayed behind. Originally, way back in the beginning, she had wanted to come to France to learn the language. Then, later, she had wanted it for her and Jim together, and she had the romantic idea that she and Jim could rekindle that first flare of love which seemed to have died down. Jim had refused to understand what she meant; he probably still considered that the only reason she had this crazy idea was just another way to spend money. Mildred's letter was stiffening her will which had been softened by all the Christmas sentiment.

The effect of a Christmas alone in France without other Americans had caused an unlooked- for reaction. She was homesick for America, for American ways, American customs. She looked at the Christmas tree. It was beautiful. How complete it was in itself, how contrary to anything American. She had seen something like it in an early Italian painting It was Mantegna, with foreign fruits twined in green leaves.

It was one of Monsieur Papillon's artificially-trained fruit trees bearing, in jest, artificial fruit. Any American flavor connected with this tree she had to manufacture. It had satisfied the children, but for her it made it more lonely. She had Jim's big box of presents to help her, and the memory of past Christmases, but the French people she met shopping, the climate, the very aroma of Christmastime at home was entirely lacking here. She recalled a Christmas Eve years ago before she was married. She was driving in a car way out in the country, and she had watched the little towns laid out on the white snow, with their windows yellow and the light streaming out across the snow and each house and its Christmas tree lit up red and blue and green, and it seemed as though something held all these little houses together and held her with them, too, and made her happy to be a part of it. It had remained a pleasant picture memory. Tonight it grew significant. How casual the French were toward Christmas. High mass on Christmas Eve and a sort of Sunday to follow. It didn't amount to anything more than that. It was her first taste of homesickness, and she didn't know how to react to the symptoms.

Gilbert had been a help. It was his enthusiasm, not hers, which had made the children happy. How he had worked on that tree, decorated it to have balanced color, form, and line. His angels, which he had drawn with Mary's crayons, needed a Madonna and child decorated with gold leaf and holding a precious pomegranate. She wondered if she had supplied the living Madonna, but Suzanne was better suited with the baby Gilbert. What an unreal day it had been. She shouldn't have allowed Gilbert to stay for breakfast. The breakfast was foreign, too, with hot chocolate and thick slices of crust (that was what French bread amounted to) and butter. He had demurred. It was the children who clamored. But if he hadn't stayed, she was sure she would have cried openly. A Christmas breakfast with Gilbert. Not Jim, Gilbert.

In once of those sweeps of imagination which the mind will take, and which people call daydreaming as though such thoughts were beyond voluntary control, Betty could see Gilbert as her husband. She shied away from the thought and then came back to it. She had as much right to daydream as the next person. She made it logical by the fact that she and he had eaten Christmas breakfast together.

She carried the fancy farther. As a very young girl, when her interest in boys was first budding, she used to lie in bed before going to sleep at night and weave fantastic extravaganzas. The boy she chose for her mate in these chapters of romance was usually composed of the gray eyes of a young teacher at school, the nose of a stranger she had seen on the train, topped by the sleek hair of an uncle, a younger brother of her father. This imaginary husband was dressed like a young man-about-town from the short stories of Richard Harding Davis, with the sterling qualities of Quentin Durwood. His action were as debonair as a Rudyard Kipling subaltern, touched with the playfulness of Barrie, the romance of Sir Lochinvar, and the sadness of Edgar Allen Poe. Any living American boyfriend of hers would have despised him, but to Betty he was perfection. Could it be that Gilbert Glisson was like some of these characters?

That was the trouble with life, it didn't let you carry out the perfect solution to your dream. She adored the way Gilbert looked, his mustache, his full lips, his keen expression with the sophisticated lift of an eyebrow, the laugh wrinkles around his eyes, which were cold and direct and warm all in one. She knew they could be tender, although they never had been for her. She liked the way his cheekbones held the line of his cheek, the bulge of his forehead, the curve of his hand as he held a cigarette. She liked him being just her size, and what a time they would have together with life. They would toss it back and forth between them. She could rise to any mood, any emotion he would demand. She could play up to him with the full sweep of all that she had in her. People would turn to look at them in a café, at the opera. How smart he would look with a cane. What a couple they would make. She would read everything, study all the books she could find to be up on French politics, literature, sculpture, painting, music. They would have a salon in Paris. She would run a wonderful house, learn all the subtleties of French cooking, take a course at the Cordon Bleu. She would dress simply, elegantly. They would go native in the summertime, barefoot on the sands of some simple fishing town, and in the winter no one in Paris would be more sophisticated than they. They wouldn't need a lot of money. Enough would be nice, but things could be managed on next to nothing.

She would give him a child, a boy, or would he prefer a girl this time. She would not stint him in his desires. Oh, it would be easy, no effort, it would be easy. He would believe in her, to the full, to the limit, and she would never let him down. And all the time she would believe in him so that he would perform miracles. That was all that miracles were, anyway. Believing. If she believed in Gilbert and he believed in her, what could they not do together? Anything. Anything together.

Of course, there was Mary and Peter. They could be taken along. The love that she and Gilbert would have for each other would be strong enough to bear taking anything and everything along. And the divorce would be easy, too. Of course, there was Suzanne. And then the dream collapsed. Absurd, that was all.

Peter was a little American boy asleep in his bed upstairs. Mary looked exactly like Jim. And both the children loved their father, James Barton, who was in the automobile business in the United States. You couldn't steamroller Jim no matter how big your dream might be. And there was Madame Glisson, a very determined old French lady, and what about Suzanne and baby Gilbert? Betty had to include them, and she had better not forget Mademoiselle Roule, either. And, lastly, there was Gilbert himself, who had never so much as suggested such a mad dream, even to be her lover. True, he had kissed her hands, but most carelessly, out in a field with a donkey eating grass beside them and her own little American children playing on the rocks overhead. She was a fool, that is what she was, a fool. And she was getting very chilly, the fire was almost out, it was Christmas night. Christmas Eve and Christmas Day were over and past. She needed a big close of common sense and to go to bed.

She could hear her father's voice as he came into the living room at home when she was a young girl. "What, sitting here along? To bed, Elizabeth, my little girl, to bed. Where will your rosy cheeks be if you lose your sleep? Go dream your natural dreams of sleep." And he would rake the fire before her feet and arrange the screen for safety, raking away her warm, young dreams. And he would put his arm around her and kiss her cheek. Of course, she loved him, too, he was her father, but it had been a young girl's love for a parent. Suddenly she could understand her father's love for her. She could see her love for her children. Her father was not humble, subservient, as he had appeared to her fresh youthful bravado. He was aware of his limitations. He had proud, wild dreams when he was young; he had wanted the skies when he had been a young man whom she could never know. He had resigned himself. All he asked as he had kindly stroked her young cheek was to protect and help her. If she were home, that is what he would do for her. It terrified her to think she should want to let him down. And she knew she could not, from that quiet solicitude that she had seen so many times in her father's eyes. He would say to her if he could see her before this fire made of burnt-out briquettes, "Daughter, go to bed, or your roses will fade," and he would pinch her cheek. Not once would he mention her break with Jim.

> Gather ye rosebuds while ye may,
> Old Time is still a-flying;
> And this same flower that smiles today,
> Tomorrow will be dying. (Editor: Poem by Robert Herrick, 17ᵗʰ Century, that inspired Waterhouse painting.)

Betty raked the fire, covered the last coals with ashes, and went to bed. She had another cry before she went to sleep.

"But I'm crying because of the love of my father," she said to herself stubbornly, "not at all because of a lack of love of my husband.

The day after Christmas was pouring, slashing rain. The children were content enough to stay in the house with new toys and no school. Lessons had been methodically assigned for every day of the vacation, which seemed a sacrilege to the American idea of a vacation. *Let them run wild today at least*, Betty thought. *Tomorrow we'll do two day's lesson in one.* Caterina was back again, and Betty decided to do the marketing herself. A brisk walk in the wind would be a tonic. And I need a tonic, Betty said to the mirror as she added lipstick.

Once downtown, she stopped at the Glissons'. They had invited her and the children to a bang-up New Year's dinner, goose and all. The invitation had been given her verbally from Gilbert, and she wanted to thank Madame.

The office door tinkled as it had done for her and Jim the first time they walked in. That was three short months ago, and it might as well be measured by three years. Incredible, the stretching and shrinking of time. There were the same grasses in the vase, the worn brocade love-seat, the map of the countryside thumbtacked over Gilbert's draftsman's table.

"Why, Madame Barton, how delightful." Old Madame Glisson wrinkled her face into a gay smile. "What a day. But all the nicer to see you, as I had expected no one. Gilbert, of course, is out." There was the fraction of hesitation in her voice, as though she had added, *I trust you didn't want to see him, because you can't, and if I tell you beforehand, you can leave at once.*

"Oh, I don't want to see him anyway. I had much rather have the chance to talk with you," Betty said, and she meant it. She was feeling guilty that she had not been to call on Madame more often. "I'll leave my umbrella and this wet coat and rubbers out here." She followed Madame through the passageway. "Oh, how warm and lovely your fire looks." Betty felt she must make conversation fly to avoid pitfalls over Suzanne and the baby, but she needn't have troubled herself. Madame was master of this art. The old lady had missed her calling in the diplomatic service, for the mere mention of any plot and intrigue was an incentive to her greater effort.

"Ah, but Madame Barton, it is I who am at fault, that I have not been to call on you. My doctor is my excuse. He keeps me home. I have lived so that I cannot complain. Is not that so when we are widows?" The bright black eyes smiled at Betty. Betty did not at all like being called a widow but could hardly protest. "But Madame, I keep you standing. Let us sit by this fire. You are cold." She took Betty's hand, and, finding it substantiating her remark, she exclaimed, "Ah, it is true. But quick. Let us come to the warmth."

She took the most comfortable chair, but that was her prerogative as an older woman, and it was one in which she had been previously sitting, as could be seen by her glasses and book on the arm. "I shall let you sit in Gilbert's chair, and that will please you very much, will it not?"

Betty was not sure she should take notice of this remark. There was a feeling when talking with Madame Glisson that everything had a double meaning. There were innuendos that Betty was not quick-witted enough to counter. It was as though Madame had been reading her guilty thoughts. Betty was tempted to say out loud, *Madame, I shall daydream no more. Cease your worries.*

The tinkling of the office doorbell sounded, far way, and almost at once Gilbert walked into the room. "Well, this is a surprise, and a jolly one. What wet weather you choose, Madame Betty."

"I needed the air," she said, smiling and feeling buoyed up by his arrival. And I wanted to tell your mother how I am looking forward to the New Year's dinner. Why, what is the trouble?" she said, catching an exchange of looks between Gilbert and his mother.

Gilbert raised his eyebrows, and his mother imperceptibly shook her head. Heartily, Gilbert said, "We were just going to see if we couldn't postpone it until the following Sunday."

"Oh," Betty said, and she could not keep the disappointment out of her voice. "Of course, of course."

"Don't be foolish," he said. "You don't let me finish. Our very dear friends, the Groses in Aix, have invited us. But wait, listen. This afternoon, as I was driving in the rain, I had the idea. Mother, don't try to interrupt. It would work beautifully. I have known Charles for years, and heaven knows he has asked enough favors of me in our student days. And think what fun it would be to have some children. One should always have children at a New Year's dinner. Charles adores anything American. I tell you, they would all love it, and if anything can make Charles happy, his mother and father are happy, too. And his English is perfect."

Gilbert seemed excited by this idea. Betty watched him as he made a couple of turns around the room. He came back to her chair, and, sitting down on the arm of it, he smiled for her benefit. Betty looked at Madame Glisson, who all this time had also been watching her son but with an expression as though she did not agree with him and was just waiting for him to stop talking.

"I shall write to Charles at once. To Charles and his mother."

"Gilbert, you grow each day more and more impractical. You shall do nothing of the sort. I am going to ask Madame Barton herself and let her show you how it could not be done." Madame Glisson appealed to Betty.

But again Gilbert interrupted. "Nothing of the sort. Let's all have tea, and then we can talk about it comfortably." And he ran out of the room to put the teakettle on the gas stove.

Madame shrugged her shoulders. "My son!" She threw up her hands. "Wait, Madame, until your son grows up. One devotes one's life to one's children, and they will turn into tyrants. I know you would not want to intrude on the Groses' invitation," she added hurriedly in a low voice so that Gilbert could not hear her. "They are old friends we have not seen now for a long time, and when their invitation came for New Year's dinner, I knew that you would not mind having our dinner put off a week. Christmas is, of course, your big celebration. And when we received the Groses' letter yesterday, there was nothing to do but answer at once."

"But of course," Betty readily agreed. She did not believe Madame Glisson had sent off her letter so promptly. However, she answered sweetly, "I would not think of intruding. That is what it would be. How could the children and I go with you? Aix is a long way off, and it would mean staying overnight. It would be impossible."

"What are you two women whispering about?" Gilbert shouted. "Don't think for a moment you have settled anything." He stuck his head into the room. "Are there any cakes, Mama? No? One moment, and I shall run across the street to the *patisserie*." And out he ran.

"Without hat or coat," Madame Glisson said, sighing. "How can an old woman like me ever keep anything together? You will give your promise that you will not go?"

"Of course," Betty said, amused and a little repelled by the old woman's persistence.

Madame got up arrange the tea tray, and Betty helped her. "Do you ever feel death?" Madame asked casually.

"What do you mean?" Betty said, astonished.

"Ah, you have not loved your husband," Madame said, nodding her head. "It is evident enough you do not truly love him now, but you never could have. You may laugh. When there is true love, one is haunted by the fear of death. For death is the only thing that can separate you. I tell you all this because it is not too late to fall in love with your husband. Maybe this separation will teach you how. I have seen it happen. I was favored by heaven. Who can tell? Fate, maybe. All I know is that we loved." She sighed heavily as she took out three silver spoons from their flannel casing. "It seems now as though we loved from the moment our hands touched. It grew, however it started. And with its growth, my fear grew, too. I was obsessed by the fear of death. When my husband left the house in the morning, whenever he went out of my sight, I held that fear hidden within me, with a prayer that death would not separate us. Strange to think of my feeling of long ago. Now that it has already happened, I should be thankful that death waited thirty years, but I begrudge that we could not go together. Indeed, I feel it cannot have happened to me, that it isn't true. But I know it is." Madame's voice was low. She put three saucers on the tray, three cups on the saucers, a spoon beside each cup, the sugar, the little cream pitcher. The veins on her hands were prominent and blue, with splotches of brown on the skin. Her hands moved stiffly. Betty felt the determined effort of this old woman willing herself to make the gestures over and above her intense sorrow with life. Betty could ignore death because she knew nothing about it, but Madame had met death and was living with it.

Gilbert returned, holding a little box, and he turned down the collar of his coat with his free hand. "I ran all the way, Mama," he said. "Not a drop of water could touch me. Only look. Baba au Rhum. One for each. Denise said they were the best."

"They are such a mess to eat, though. We'll need plates and forks," his mother muttered, going back to the cupboard which she had closed.

"Nothing tastes better, though. I detest all this chocolate and paste. Ah, the water boils," he said as the lid popped up and down.

Betty stood watching mother and son. There was not enough to do for her to help. Gilbert winked at her once. He was very good in the kitchen, and with everything ready they formed a line back to the living room and the fire. Betty was allowed to carry the little pasteboard box.

"And now," said Gilbert, "to make arrangements."

"They are all made. I couldn't possibly go, so let's change the subject," Betty said, taking her cue from Madame Glisson.

"Sometimes women exasperate me beyond words," Gilbert said, handing Betty her cup. "And what's more, I'll make a scene if Madame Betty and the children don't go," he continued to his mother as he went back to get his own cup. "Not that I want to be mean, my dear mother, but I merely want my way." He sat down on a footstool between them. "My, this hot tea feels good. I want to tell you all about Charles." This time, he was turning toward Betty. "My mother and father knew the Groses very well as young couples, years ago. Indeed, it went farther than that, for my father and uncle Paul were friends before either married. I called them uncle Paul and Aunt Julie, although we're not related—it goes to show the extent of the intimacy between us. And then Charles and I were in the Sorbonne together when Charles tried to study too hard, had a sort of breakdown which was the beginning of tuberculosis. Since then, we see them every so often. Charles has had a tough time of it, always trying one sanitarium after another. He gets cured, then he gets bored, tries a job, works too hard, and back he has to go. His family worships him and gives him whatever he wants, they're fairly well-off. Papa Gros is in the olive oil business. They are delightful people, French of the French, and so conservative. Charles was in America, went to some sanitarium there, and he is one of the few people I know who really likes and can understand American things; he adores jazz and has dozens of records for the Victrola. Oh, you'd be crazy about him, Betty, and he about you. I can't imagine why I didn't think of all this at once. Too troubled by my own affairs, that was it." he stopped to take a sip of tea.

Betty shrugged her shoulders and looked at Madame Glisson. "What shall we do with him?" she asked. The trip to Aix-en-Provence was just what she needed, she thought, to pick her up out of her doldrums.

"You mean, rather, what shall you and I do with my mother?" Gilbert said, putting his hand on Betty's knee as though it were the most natural thing for him to do. "You know very well you are dying to go yourself."

Betty pushed his hand away. She wished he weren't so careless of affection. She saw Madame Glisson observe her gesture and wondered what that shrewd old lady thought of it.

"Of course, if you're going to be obstinate and unpleasant about it," his mother answered him, "There is no use in my saying anything more. It would just hurt Madame Barton's feelings, which I would not do for the world. I felt that to invite another grown-up and two children to a dinner was a good deal of an imposition, particularly when you don't know who else might be there, and the way you want to do it they can't very well refuse. That is all."

"All the same," Gilbert said, unperturbed, "that is just what I am going to do. It would be only for the dinner. They would stay at some inexpressive little hotel. Couldn't you, Betty?"

"Why don't we leave the children home with Caterina?" Betty said, pleased to have thought of such a solution. "It could be managed and would simpler all around."

"What an idea," Gilbert said.

Betty saw it was a faux pas, and a bad one. "I had only meant—" she said, and was silly enough to blush. They both thought she was trying to push herself, and it certainly would be odd for Gilbert and his mother to arrive with a grass-widow American woman; the only way she was being invited at all was through her children. "I leave it all with your mother," Betty said. "Whatever you want, Madame Glisson, I shall gladly do." That was being virtuous. "I think I really shall have to go. I left the children just to come down to buy some eggs and butter," she said to carry out her virtuousness. "The baba au Rhum was delicious. Many thanks, and please don't let Gilbert be so stubborn, Madame. I would be much happier left at home."

"No indeed, Madame Barton. We shall see what we can arrange." Madame Glisson spoke as though it had been her idea all along.

Betty left immediately, wondering how Gilbert had made his mother give in. She liked things to be done just the way he did them. It was wonderful the way he could manipulate (that was just the word for it) his mother. She wouldn't even dare try to stand up to Madame Glisson for a pin, and yet Gilbert would make his mother contradict herself and be very polite about it. He could wind his mother around his little finger. And did he do that with all women? It was a quality most women loved, Betty told herself, but she didn't want any male dominance in her life. She would dare Jim to try such a method, and at the same moment she smiled to herself. Would Gilbert ever be trying out his domineering maleness on her? And with a little self-conscious laugh, she half hoped he would.

◆ ◆

Yes, they went to Aix, all of them. Gilbert, Madame Glisson, Betty and the children. It took a good deal of arranging, more than Betty felt was worth the effort. But complications increased Gilbert's enthusiasm. The train ride was hilarious with his tomfoolery. Even old Madame Glisson, who could justifiably have been sour, caught the infection of the thing and made herself good company. Betty saw how fond of her one might grow. Express from St.-Raphael to Marseille. And an endless searching wait in the smoky station at Marseille for the local Aix train to be made up. It was an hour late and an hour and a half overdue when they finally stepped off at Aix. They were all dead tired, the children half asleep. "I'll go to bed with the children," Betty said as they left her at her hotel. Madame and Gilbert drove on to the Groses' in the cab.

Consequently, Betty saw nothing of Aix until morning. She had breakfast brought to her room, and Peter and Mary enjoyed the novelty. They took a little walk as soon as they were dressed. Betty was astonished to find how large the town was, and modern. There was no sign of the *Ville Ancienne*. The streets near the hotel were wide, and the houses had a look of Paris. The same effect of pink-gray walls and tracery of black iron balconies, and always the mottled gray trunks of the sycamore trees. They came to a big boulevard with a round center square and a magnificent fountain. They watched it from a distance, plumes of spouting water, giant dolphins and horses. The cars were swift and made a close approach difficult.

"Oh, I want to get over to the water. What a geyser!" Peter cried.

"No, we can't. I don't want to leave the hotel for too long in case Gilbert comes for us." The children romped around, a little out of hand because she had refused them. At the hotel, Gilbert and a tall man were standing, undecided whether to go or stay. The presence of the stranger made both the children stop running and wait for their mother, which made Betty feel pleased as a grown-up, first that her insistence on their return was justified in the children's eyes and second that the children turned publicly to her for protection. It increased the complacence of her smile as she came up to the two men.

Charles Gross did not look a bit like a Frenchman. He was very tall, with intense blue eyes which stared at the person to whom he was talking. His cheeks were red, not hectic but healthy. He held his chest high, as though he needed to catch all the fresh air he could when he breathed. He looked athletic, as though he had never had a day of sickness in his life. He wore knickers, golf stockings, a sport shirt like a little boy's, and a plaid coat that was belted at the back. His handshake was strong, but his hand was moist. That was the only thing about him that Betty could possibly stretch into a symptom of disease. Health was a halo around him, and his manner was healthy, too. He held one hand in his pocket and was smilingly amused at Betty and both of the children.

"It is a great pleasure to meet you, Madame Barton. My curiosity is at last satisfied, after the letters between Gilbert and me. Gilbert here has been trying to described you. But he did not do a very good job." Charles Gros beamed down on Betty, like a big brother. He was like an

American almost. " And how do you like our Aix? Small-town stuff after all your travels, Philadelphia, New York, Paris, what?"

"But I was just thinking how much like Paris it is," Betty said.

"Like Paris!" both men exclaimed, shocked. Charles laughed aloud. "Like Paris!" he repeated. "Paris? Hear that."

"Well," Betty said, a little nettled, "perhaps I should have said French rather than Parisienne. The gray building, the charming iron balconies, they both make me think of the few days I was in Paris. I miss that feeling in the smallness of St.-Raphael with its modernistic villas and its severely plain townhouses. And, too, it is so different from the colorful southern exuberance of Marseille. I still insist there is something of the cool elegance of Paris—that is, what I have seen in five minutes."

"Stick to your guns, Betty," Gilbert said. "You'll have a tough time with a crotchety old Provencal like Charles. Heresy, that's what it is. Comparing aristocratic Aix to commercial Paris. You must tell Papa Gros that one."

"Don't worry," Charles said. "I wouldn't miss the opportunity, and Madame with such a sweet, innocent-girl-look to her. What else have you to say, Madame?"

"Oh, I am thrilled to death to be here in Aix. I was just picturing Paul Cezanne walking up and down these very streets. You must be proud of him. I want to see your museum. You must have so many wonderful painting of his."

Both men exploded again. "Madame, Madame. I didn't dream you had the wit," Gilbert cried. "But save it for Papa Gros."

"I simply can't seem to say the right thing," Betty said. "What is the trouble with that? I never heard of Aix, except in connection with Cezanne."

By this time the tears had come to Charles's eyes. "Don't, Madame, don't. Don't you realize Aix inhabitants are ashamed of Cezanne's painting? It you can keep this up at dinner today, it will be memorable. I long to see Papa's face, that is all I ask." Charles wiped his eyes. "Where did you find her, Gilbert?"

Betty was beginning to feel annoyed. "I think you two are very rude, really I do."

"Please forgive us, please. We are not laughing at you. It is just your delightful Americanism, and Gilbert has told you how I love American things, I'm sure. Forgive the clumsiness on my part." Charles was quite sincere.

Betty was easily mollified.

"How do you like our fountains?" Charles asked by way of making his apology.

Gilbert had stepped ahead to walk with the children, and Charles moved behind Betty to be on the outside of the sidewalk. His manners were excellent but arrogant. Betty had known a couple of wealthy men with the same arrogance, punctilious to the dot in the outward form. Perhaps she felt this because he had laughed at her, although when she looked up at him and met his blue, blue eyes, he expressed a simple, honest sincerity. "I have seen only that big fountain," Betty said after a pause.

"Listen," Charles said. And it did seem as though one could hear water tinkling above the noise of traffic. "We have fountains everywhere in Aix. Come. We'll follow Gilbert. I see he is taking the children over to this one." There was an old, high, square stone basin looking like a horse-watering trough. Water was gushing from a lion's head. The children put their hands in as directed.

"Why, it is warm!" they both exclaimed together.

"Aix is a great retreat for hot baths and therapeutic treatment. It used to be fashionable, and still is among some. Old ladies have come here for years. Perhaps that is why you never heard of Aix in this respect," Charles said, his blue eyes beginning to dance again. "There are more fountains in Aix than any other town in France. Warm. Cold. Some have a superstition attached. You must drop a penny in la Fontaine des Quatres Dauphins, and you will come back."

"Oh, they have that in Rome."

"But this is Aix-en-Provence, not Rome."

"Excuse me," Betty said. She was beginning to get the stubborn flavor of the Aixois who will not stand for any other city taking precedence over Aix.

Charles led them on a long walk. The shopping section, old houses larded with new, by the thermal baths, through the ancient part of town. The Saint-Sauveur cathedral, a short visit inside. And as Charles had said, fountains all the way. Betty liked Aix, she liked it immensely. It had today a Sunday-at-home quality, family people like themselves out for walks. All the shops closed and shuttered. On their return, Betty found the Groses lived in a big old-fashioned apartment, second floor and very near the hotel. They separated to dress for dinner, but Charles insisted he would call for her in half an hour.

"Why bother?"

"It would not be seemly otherwise," Charles said. How proper he was. True to his word, in one half-hour by her watch, the maid announced to Betty that Monsieur Gros was waiting. Betty had dressed the children very carefully, Peter in his best dark blue suit with a stiff collar, Mary in the new dark red silk Grandma Barton had sent her for Christmas. She herself put on a brown velvet afternoon dress. She felt the need to bolster her courage.

The Gros family matched their apartment well. The living room was paneled in dark oak with a dark blue brocade wallpaper, and the furniture was heavy, plush, ornate. There were big dark oil paintings on the walls with scrolls of gold frame, bookcases, ornaments cluttering, vases, paperweights, lamps that were heavy with ironwork, a large Oriental rug, dark blue tapestry draperies at the windows which harmonized with the wallpaper in design. There was much too much in the room. At the same time, it gave you the feeling of comfort. A comfortable home. The sort of place that contradicted itself in the layers of time and thought that had gone to build it up, but which even so, was comfortable enough to return to after a day's work, put on carpet slippers, adjust one's glasses, turn on the light, and sit down to read the evening paper.

"So, this is the American lady and her two children. She looks more like a daughter than a mama." Monsieur Gros was the first to speak. He was a delightful Frenchman, short, stocky, with broad shoulders, hair thinning but still black, sharp blue eyes, a big nose balancing old-fashioned pince-nez gold-rim glasses with a black cord, and an explosive big black mustache. He wore a black coat with braid and tails and striped trousers, and his enormous tie was held by a little pearl stick- pin. Betty loved him.

There also was a married daughter, the first time Betty had known that Charles had a sister. She was gentle and very retiring, and her husband was a slight, pale young man from Marseille who did something or other with cloth. Madame Glisson was very stiff and French and vivacious in black taffeta. Gilbert was also in afternoon clothes. Mary, bless her heart, curtseyed. She had learned it with Mademoiselle Roule. And Peter looked extra clean and brushed. They all turned as the mother came out from another door with a little white frilly apron over her black taffeta. Madame Gros was tall, taller than her husband; she had beautiful brown eyes, graying hair, and a lovely sweet expression with an arched nose. *Family* was written in capitals. Every Sunday family dinner and Thanksgiving and Christmas Betty assumed was consummated in this group. And it was distinctly French.

In a few minutes, they went into the dinning room, and this was in the same heavy, ornate style. To move one of the chairs was a task. The color scheme was a rich red, rich too, in its variety. What Frenchman does not love to juxtapose touches of pink, magenta, crimson, and cerise? Madame Gros placed them all at the table and then fled kitchenward. Her helper was young and inexperienced. Betty found herself between Charles and the quiet son-in-law. Madame Glisson was placed beyond on the other side of the son-in-law and on Monsieur Gros's left. And opposite were the daughter, on her father's right, Mary, Gilbert, Peter, and at the head was Madame Gros's place.

"I love little boys," Madame Gros said when she told Peter he was to sit next to her.

"And I love little girls," Madame Salmon, the daughter, said, taking Mary under her wings. It was the first time Madame Salmon had made a definite statement, and by its positiveness it seemed to contradict her mother. She might have said, You always did love Charles the best.

There was a large plate of hors d'oeuvres with radishes, sliced meats, and little fish and olives which was passed around. Papa Gros was struggling with the cork of a bottle of light red wine. "Let me help," Gilbert said.

"You're too young," Monsieur Gros said as the cork came out. He poured a teaspoonful in his glass, then filled Madame Glisson's glass, and around the table back to his own.

"It is eight minutes after one," Charles said aloud, looking at his watch. "I wager it will be six o'clock before we are finished. What do you say, Mother?" he asked as his mother returned from the kitchen.

"I'm a little worried about the chickens," his mother said, paying no attention to his question.

"But you're always worried about the chickens. Why on earth don't you get a regular cook for New Year's dinner? Then we might have the pleasure of your company."

"No one can cook the way your mother can," Monsieur Gros boomed from his end of the table.

"Tell me, Monsieur Gros, can you still do much hunting?" Madame Glisson asked.

"Oh, yes indeed, yes indeed. I have two dogs. I keep them in a barn, belonging to a friend, since we have moved to the apartment house."

And how is business in Marseille?" Madame Glisson continued, including the son-in-law on her left.

"Oh, so-so, so-so." Monsieur Salmon answered, coming out of the absorption with his dinner for a moment.

"I hear they are having quite a problem with condemned houses there," Gilbert said. "Several falling down, someone getting hurt."

"Oh, yes, yes," Monsieur Gros said before his son-in law had a chance. "Poor section, though, nothing serious. What about this bull-fight that came off up near you, Gilbert? Grasse, wasn't it? shocking thing, mayor should have forbidden it."

"Politics, I suppose. They held it outside Grasse. Made everyone walk a mile on a country road. But a big crowd, I understand, all the same."

"And how do you like school?" Madame Salmon was asking Mary.

Mary smiled shyly and nodded her head.

The little maid came in and cleared away the hors d'oeuvre plates in an unprofessional manner. A hot, clear dark soup was brought in.

"And now," said Monsieur Gros with formality, "you must tell us how you like France." He turned to Betty as though he were a judge asking a witness some revealing question.

"I adore it," Betty said. "Everything about it."

"But what I can't understand," Madame Gros said—she had just come in to eat her soup—" is how you could stay here and let your husband go back alone. To me, it is incredible. Madame Glisson was telling me all about it."

"Come, come. That was nothing to do with it," Monsieur Gros said severely to his wife.

"He has to work to get the money to keep them here. But tell us, Madame Barton, is your prohibition going to last? An amazing thing. It is a situation beyond belief to us French." Betty tried her best to answer this, floundering in French. "And then tell me," Monsieur Gros went on in the same tone," do all Americans who are white and of English descent, as yourself, belong to the Ku Klux Klan?"

This last was more than Betty could cope with. She turned her eyes up to Charles and across the table to Gilbert for help, and she found both of them laughing.

"Tell me," Charles said," don't you have exactly the same sort of family conversation at holiday dinners at your home?"

"I had thought so," Betty said in English, "up until your father's last question. Where did he ever hear of the Ku Klux Klan, anyway? Please tell your father it is an abomination."

Charles repeated Betty's answer to his father and then continued, "Dad's been reading Siegfried's latest, that's all. You mustn't be frightened. My father's excited at having an American to talk to in the flesh. Isn't that what you say in American slang, "in the flesh"? now, Father, you must not scare a poor American lady, alone among all of us French people, by throwing all the economic problems of her country at her at one time. One question should be limited to one course. Prohibition is for the soup. Wouldn't you say that was the fairest way, Gilbert?"

"My dear Charles, whatever you suggest is sure to be the fairest," Gilbert said. Gilbert in this French family setting seemed like another person, formal, remote. The talk was entirely in French, as no one in the Gros family but Charles spoke English.

Betty was up against the long-standing intimacy of French friends. She was able to grasp the superficial, but she knew she was missing the deep exchange carried on beneath the top level of conversation. Monsieur Gross outlined the United States by French impressions: prohibition, Ku Klux Klan, the southern negro, alien immigration, New York skyscrapers. He was secretly delighted by *"le Craque du* Wall Street" but would probably be too polite to say so, and yet would he ever know what America was about?

Madame Gros stunned Betty by saying, "American women sleep without their husbands. When they are together, they use twin beds." And she returned to busy herself with her roast chickens. And in the closed-corporation French family, Gilbert too made her an outsider. He didn't want to, but he had been born to one way of living, she to another.

How could she ever explain America to these people? She pictured the North America autumn, for instance, the brilliant leaves that glowed until they hurt your eyes, the high blue sky, the smell of a fall afternoon. How could she tell them about Thanksgiving, which was just such a dinner as they were eating? They wouldn't believe her, because all Americans were terrible cooks, who bought all their food in delicatessens or ate out of cans. How could she describe Christmas to them, with its fragrant smells of trees, and the Americans who loved home and children? Americans lived in automobiles driving at sixty miles an hour, they had no homes, they all lived in skyscrapers with modern plumbing. American movies depicted an unreal America to these people. How was she to combat such prejudices? How was she to tell them about the beauty and tradition of the Philadelphia Orchestra? Or that there were Americans who walked in the country for the pleasure of walking? Could she ever make these people believe there was a Wissahickon Bird Club and that Merchantville had its own small Merchantville Bird

Club? And what about the pleasure she derived from a winter bird feed-
er where brilliant, cocky little cardinals and chickadees came to eat her
sunflower seeds? Here American cardinals were kept in cages.

Instead, Monsieur Gros asked if she were a member of the Ku Klux
Klan and doubtless believed she was, whatever answer she might give
him. She, who despised and was ashamed of such fanaticism, who de-
tested the beliefs for which the Klan stood and considered them mad
and absolutely un-American, must carry the Ku Klux Klan upon her
shoulders because she was an American. "I do not hold you responsible
for the blood of Marie Antoinette, Monsieur Gros," she wanted to cry,
"but you put the blood of tragic sacrificial negroes on me."

Soup was removed, and there was a baked fish entrée. Monsieur
Gross was passing around the wine again, white this time. Betty felt she
must refuse and wished she could put her gloves in her wine glass like
Madame Bovary. She wondered if people did that today. It seemed like
a very impractical custom, she had no gloves at the table—and her glass
was stained with the wine she had with the first course. She was getting
positively silly.

"No, no, thank you so much," she protested, hoping it would not call
forth a remark on American prohibition. But how could it be helped?

"You are in France, Madame Barton, not America where you have
to drink out of a teacup as a subterfuge." Monsieur Gros giggled. Betty
let it pass.

"Tell me, how is your Radical-Socialist party doing in Aix?" Madame
Glisson inquired. How delightful to have the conversation turned away
from America into such a safe French channel.

"Well enough, well enough. A change is coming, though, as is
indicated in Paris. Last June, you remember, there was a vote of con-
fidence for Poincare shortly after the stabilization of the franc. And
the Radical-Socialists, most of them, voted in favor of Poincare. But
the way things stand today, he will have to face another vote of confi-
dence. Then the Radical-Socialists will swing the other way. That is
how I see it." Monsieur Gros was very solemn in his statement, wiping
his mustache.

"Really. That is extraordinary. Ah, these are troubled times, troubled times." Madame Glisson sighed. "What my husband would have thought of them. He is troubled, I am sure, even in Heaven."

"We are quite as troubled here on earth," Monsieur Gross added practically.

"What are the Radical-Socialists?" Betty asked Charles in an aside.

"They are crazy, if you ask me," Charles said flippantly. "Let me tell you the definition of a gentleman. One who is interested in neither politics nor religion." Charles and Gilbert laughed more heartily than anyone else.

"You define a Radical-Socialist, Gilbert," Charles asked.

"What a thing to ask," Gilbert said, still laughing. He looked around the table. "The Radical-Socialist party in more French than the French," he said slowly, looking at Monsieur Gros, who also was smiling. "It is old-fashioned, conservative on one hand, and very radical on the other. It loves the little grocer, the small shops that sell hats and dresses and deal in paper or coal or olive oil. All Provencal businessmen belong to it because they love the excitement of the radical talk in the café, and then they all go quietly home at night, and the next day they vote more conservatively than some right-centered royalist. Except that they hate the church and are violently anticlerical. Have I answered your question, Madame Barton?" Everyone burst out laughing, they could not help it, although Madame Gros and her daughter stopped sooner than the rest.

"Well, I must say." Betty was laughing because the rest were. "I can't follow that, Monsieur Gilbert. How can they be against the church in a Catholic country?"

"How can they be, indeed," Gilbert continued. "But they are violently opposed to having the priests dabble in politics. And all Radical-Socialists have the most devout of wives and daughters. As witness." He stood up and bowed to Madame Gros and Madame Salmon.

"Don't you be troubled, my dear," Madame Gros said kindly to Betty. "That man down there at the end of the table"—indicating Monsieur Gros—" he is always full of contradictions. Gilbert has hit the nail on the head. But secretly Monsieur Gros, Radical-Socialist that he is, expects me to save his soul."

"And she will, too," Charles said, patting his mother's arm. "And all of our souls, what, Mother? And bodies and minds. Sister Leonie there went to convent school, and Dad was pleased to see her go, it was safe. There's a lovely story about Jaures, who was being heckled at a political meeting. He turned to the man and said, 'My friend, no doubt your wife obeys you, I am less fortunate.' He brought a big laugh, for while Jaures was violently anticlerical, everybody knew his wife was very religious. But really, these French papas like to have their wives go to church a lot, for then they know where they are, out of mischief. Especially if they are pretty. Mama is very pretty, don't you think?"

"Charles, how can you? What will Madame Barton think of me?" But all the same, Madame Gros liked to be made fun of by her son.

"Where are those chickens, Mama?" Monsieur Gros cried. "I want to get at our first bottle of champagne. We shall drink to all Radical-Socialists. And at the same time to the Saint-Sauveur. Now, even the children must have a taste of this, only a taste, it is nothing more than bubbles and water," Monsieur Gros said with a flourish as he unwound the wire holding the cork. "Shall I make the cork hit the ceiling, little Marie? I'll give it to you as a souvenir."

"Is it really champagne?" Mary asked. "Oh, can I have a taste, Mother dear?"

"If it is a tiny, tiny one." Betty nodded. "You may never have the chance again. At least for years and years. I have never tasted champagne."

This seemed to astonish everyone. Quiet Monsieur Salmon could not believe his ears and kept exclaiming, "Think of it. a grown woman and has never tasted champagne."

The chickens came in, three of them, golden brown and of melting tenderness. They were served with tiny white potato balls sprinkled with parsley. Madame Gros carved them. Monsieur Gros was busy with his champagne.

"Mother really hates to relinquish her chickens, even to eat them," Charles said.

"Don't you think I could keep this plate?" Peter piped up. "It is perfectly clean." He had wiped it with his bread. "There seem so many, many plates." They all laughed at Peter, but Madame said no, he must have a clean plate.

"You cannot mix fish and chicken. The chicken must be just so," Madame explained to him.

The children had been very quiet, watching the grown-ups, and yet neither shy nor bored. A great deal was going on at the table, what with the plates of one course retreating and those of the next advancing, and the little kitchen helper was growing red in the face. Madame Gros and Monsieur Gros kept jumping up to oversee the food and the wines. Added to this, overhead, there was a sudden thud which shook the chandelier. It sounded as though someone had dropped a large trunk right over the dinning-room table.

"Oh, those horrible people," Madame Salmon cried. "Are they still here? You should have them put out of the apartment house, Papa."

"What are they doing?" Mary asked.

"Nobody ever knows, Marie," Papa Gros said kindly. "They make the most horrible noises, and one never knows how or why. And now all the glasses are full. Let us drink to your lovely little children, Madame Barton."

"I think is very nice," Peter said. "We must have champagne more often, Mother. I like it better than ginger ale."

The children took a long time to eat. And then came a beautiful tenderloin roast, looking like a fat brown sausage, tied elaborately with string over and around and topped by a line of browned onion crescents. This was sliced an thin as paper and was cooked just enough to leave it red in the center. They had string beans with the roast. And Monsieur Gros opened a bottle of rich burgundy.

"Shall we ever get up from the table?" Betty asked. Such a dinner, as Gilbert had foretold, she had never eaten before.

And then came a salad, served in a giant bowl with oil and vinegar and a light sprinkling of truffles. This was refreshing after the heavy meat. But, as though Madame Gros must impress them further, in she

KATIE BUTTERWORTH

came with a huge chestnut soufflé pudding, which cloyed the palate with its heavy sweetness. Monsieur Gros opened a special champagne for this sweet and gave Peter the cork as his souvenir. They were drugged, glutted with food. Next Madame served cheese and coffee, and Monsieur Gros came in with a tray of tiny glasses and several varieties of liqueur.

If only Betty could remember the order, the taste of all these courses. It had the formality of tradition but was served with the jumble of a family that was intimate and easy. How complete it was and how eternal. One felt that years hence on New Year's Day, Madame Gros would be fussing about her chickens, Monsieur Gros opening his champagne bottles to let the cork hit the ceiling. Long after *les Americans* were forgotten. It was a thing done well for its own self. It needed no outside improvements, no modern inventions. The group seemed to Betty a little smug, self- contained, but that was ungracious of her after these people had been kind enough to admit her to their circle.

She stood up with the rest and realized that however little wine and champagne she had tasted, it was not as easy to stand as to sit. She must be careful to hide her sensations. She waited for Peter and put her arm around his shoulder for support. She felt ashamed and shy of the fact that the wine should affect her. She found herself clenching her hand in her effort to appear normal. It did not occur to her that everyone else was also feeling stimulated. She had a horror of disgracing herself before these respectable, quiet people. Gilbert came up to her and put his hand under her elbow. She smiled at him broadly. How stupid of her not to have sought Gilbert's arm. She called him *Monsieur Gilbert* before these friends of his, but she said *mon Gilbert* to herself.

As though she were mesmerized to do it, she whispered in his ear, "*Mon Gilbert, tu es gentil.*" It seemed to her that she whispered, and then, as though in some bad dream, her voice was a shout.

Gilbert held her arm firmly, and she leaned her body toward him. It seemed the most natural thing in the world. How kind he was, how sweet, and how concerned his eyes were. "*Mon cher,*" she murmured.

Gilbert seemed to be talking in a very loud voice, right in her ear. He needn't shout. "Ah yes, yes indeed, a little fresh air is what you need,

164

Madame Betty. Do you mind if I open the window, Monsieur Gros? This one, I think, would be better. Why don't you play Madame some of your latest American jazz records, Charles? Madame might translate them."

Why did Gilbert talk so loudly? She wanted to tell him she loved him. She looked around and could not seem to locate either Madame Gros or her daughter or the children. Well, let them go. Madame Glisson had been there a moment, and then she was gone too. Good. She could tell Gilbert her innermost thoughts. What if Jim did flirt with Roberta? What of it? The window was open, and she and Gilbert leaned out with the darling little French iron grillwork before them, and she touched it with her hand and said, "How sweet. How French." They looked away down the street through the branches of the syca-more trees, and at the end of a little vista was the big fountain. After a short time or a long time, she wasn't sure which, but it didn't mat-ter, Gilbert turned her around, and she hoped he would put his arms around her, but he didn't. He moved her into a chair, and there were the faces of Monsieur Gros and Charles looking very concerned and the face of Monsieur Salmon with his mouth open and his eyes staring. She must say something, and so in a loud voice she said, "*Je suis chaud*." After all, what else was there to say? Why did the eyes of the men fo-cus on her? Charles gave a snort, Monsieur Gros smiled broadly, and Monsieur Salmon gaped.

"You mean, my dear Madame, '*J'ai chaud*.' It is not correct—or—po-lite—to ever say the other." Gilbert's voice was reproving but quiet.

"But I mean, Je suis chaud," Betty said, and calmly met his gray eyes. He needn't think he could treat her like a child. Or was she wrong? Her mind faltered over the idiom.

"I'll play the jazz," Charles said, inserting a needle, "before Mother comes back. It is perfectly easy to understand. You see, Father, with the prohibition, Madame is not used to drinking. Ordinarily, she is very quiet, very correct. We'll have her right in a jiffy." His voice trailed off, and it sounded like the doctor's voice talking to the nurses when Mary was born. Or was it Peter? There didn't seem to be any smell of ether.

And then came the loud voice of Cliff Edwards singing "The Dressmaker's Daughter." "Oh, I know that one," Betty cried out. "Give me a paper and pencil, and I'll jot down the words in English, and then we can put them into French." With the greatest ease, she sang them along with Cliff Edwards and scribbled down the English words. It took two playings before she had them all. She read the catchy lyrics almost too dramatically for the benefit of Charles and Gilbert, who were the only ones to understand her.

"And now I think I feel very tired," Betty said. "I need to be taken care of." She looked at Monsieur Gros and remembered all she had wanted to tell him about America and the French point of view. "I am going to bed. To bed at once. But before I go, I want to say one thing." She stood up. "I am an American woman, but I won't stand for the Ku Klux Klan. I won't stand for prohibition. I won't stand for—I won't stand. You know, I don't think I can stand up any longer, Gilbert." And Betty passed out.

—␣—

Betty opened her eyes. She gave a start. She was in bed with a cool pillow, the shutters brought together. One of the last things she remembered saying was, *Je suis chaud*, "I am in heat." What a ghastly thing to say at a dinner party. How had she ever confused the idiom, *J'ai chaud*, "I am hot." Yes, she was in bed. It was horrible, it was a nightmare. But now she was awake, she had come to. And with the movement of her head, Madame Glisson was at her side. Where was Gilbert?

"My dear Madame Barton, I hope you are feeling better."

"But what is it? I'm terrified. What has happened? What am I doing here?" Betty felt frantic with fear. "Where are the children?" Her voice grew hysterical.

"They are all right, and so are you," reassured Madame Glisson, smiling. "Be quiet, and I'll tell you the whole story. You see, you became quite ill at the Groses' house. The wine was too much for you, and we decided it was best for you come to your room at the hotel, and that is where you are. I undressed you, and Gilbert and Charles took the children for a little walk. They probably are now back at the Groses' house. You mustn't mind a bit, my dear, you just aren't used to wine. Madame Gros and her daughter think you are a little indisposed. Gilbert managed it beautifully. He and Charles slipped you out of the house, brought you over in a taxi. You were unconscious. Monsieur Gros is such a sweet, understanding man, he told his wife how you had fainted. Madame is not always so kindly. I talked a lot. I explained about your poor husband's business, all the Christmas presents he had sent, how he is coming back on a boat soon to get you— oh, it is quite *comme il faut*. Charles returned very shortly and asked me to come help you get into bed. Madame Gros wished to come too, but I said she had done quite enough with her dinner and you were used to me. Gilbert and I popped you into bed, and he went back to see the children. There now, you see how easy it all was. And how do you feel? Why don't you try sitting up?"

Betty sat up gingerly. Her head ached, but she said, "I feel fine, but how I have disgraced you and Gilbert! How could I do such a thing? Was I horrible to look at? Did I pass out cold, as we say in America?"

"My dear, you did, but you mustn't regret it. Just busy yourself with getting well now. Stand up and walk around." Madame Glisson was a good nurse.

"I feel very queer and nauseated."

"Oh, you've been sick to your stomach all right." Madame Glisson wouldn't let it pass off too smoothly. "I am going to get some black coffee for you." She rang for the maid.

Betty sat in her nightgown and thin kimono and shivered. More with remorse than with a chill. What a terrible thing to have done. How could she have behaved like that? What a chance for the French to raise their eyebrows and say, Oh, a drunken American. What had she said about Gilbert? She wanted to die and leave Aix right then and there. She began to cry weakly.

"Come. Come, none of that." Madame Glisson was back and briskly arranged the coffee and saucer. "Now, sip it with a spoon very slowly. Sit in this chair." Madame laid a blanket over Betty's knees.

"How can I ever, ever face the Groses?"

"You don't have to. Tonight I'll go back to the Groses'. You will be all right. If you are well enough, Gilbert will bring the children over here. You look fine to me. Weak, of course. In the morning, you can come over and pay your respects to Madame Gros."

"Oh, yes," Betty said humbly, feeling like a little girl. "This coffee really is wonderful. The nausea is going. I think I could eat something soon."

"Don't overdo it. After that giant dinner, I wouldn't eat until to-morrow. One thing, before anyone comes, I do want to say. When you were intoxicated, you said some rather foolish things. You talked very wildly when I was alone here with you. Do you remember any of it?"

Betty shook her head, and then she remembered several endearing phrases she had murmured to Gilbert, and she blushed. "Only—only—" she said in a low voice in confusion.

"You apparently recall some of it. This is very hard to express. But Gilbert's life—and mine, too—are quite involved enough without any-thing else. I just want you to realize this. I know I am talking to you as though you were not able to see for yourself. I am very fond of you, and your children are adorable. And you have such a fine, good husband. You must not forget that. I like him so much, and you. You see how it is. Gilbert has done some very foolish things. You know all about them. I don't want anything more foolish. If only I can keep the Groses from finding out about Suzanne and that baby until it is straightened out. I need all my courage at times. An old woman, you know. Gilbert is all I have. Things used to be so easy. Ah, at times it seems as though I would go out of my mind. Mademoiselle Aurelie, such a sweet girl, money, education, all there. And then Gilbert..."

Madame Glisson had Betty in tears again. "Oh, Madame Glisson. If only I could help you, too. I can see how hard it must be for you."

At once Madame Glisson said briskly, "Oh no, not at all. You can do nothing, nothing. It is much better you stay out of it entirely. Madame Gros gives a wonderful dinner, does she not? Yes, yes. When my hus-band was living, I too used to cook like that. It is a great art."

12

Carnival love

"Take it from me, and don't worry. A sick child, even when he is as old as Peter, can look like death, run a temperature up to 102, and scare you into fits, and have nothing more than indigestion. When Peter was a baby, I was in a constant state of worry and would call the doctor at two in the morning, stay up all night myself, and find in the morning it was a new tooth or colic or nobody knew what—the pip. I was wiser when Mary came along. I would give her an enema and go back to bed. My theory is that babies are tougher than grown-ups. They have a resistance far greater then we give them credit for. So don't worry." Betty puffed the smoke from her cigarette, looking at Gilbert to see if her words had any effect.

Gilbert was morose this morning. The baby Gilbert had run a temperature for a day and a half. Gilbert had called in Dr. Bohme, Suzanne and her sister pooh-poohing the idea. Didn't Gilbert trust them as nurses for his precious son? The doctor had been a little condescending—these parents with their firstborns. He had suggested a lighter diet, half milk, then orange juice, and gone away. The baby had been better this morning, but still Gilbert didn't feel right about it. He hadn't wanted to go, but in the end he did.

It was Mardi Gras, carnival week in Nice. He had promised Peter and Mary to take them, and he hated to disappoint them. Betty could have managed, but Gilbert had been going for so many years. Madame Glisson wouldn't budge—get herself in a mob like that? At the last minute, Betty had produced Caterina. "She'll help look after the children," Betty said, "and will make it much easier for me. I can't have a good time if I'm bothering to watch that scamp Mary every minute."

Betty and Gilbert were standing shoulder to shoulder, leaning on the handrail in the corridor of the train. The crowd had been seething at the St.-Raphael station. It was like an American football crowd, excited and carefree, and when the train did pull in, it was all they could do to get on, let alone find seats. Gilbert had pushed his way through and found a little space for each child, and Caterina's black eyes standing guard over her little charges had softened the heart of another peasant, who had given his seat to her. Betty and Gilbert decided the corridor was the easiest place to stand. There was gaiety in the air that was catching.

The weather was cold and, as usual, threatening rain. Betty made the children wear rubbers, and she had put on heavy walking shoes with crepe soles which she had bought in St.-Raphael. She wore a dark blue suit with a topcoat over it and a beret, another French purchase. To make herself look less severe, she had frizzed her bob and put on an extra amount of makeup. A young boy walking past had winked at her and said, "*Comment ça vá, Mamselle*," thinking she was French.

Gilbert noticed it and smiled a little. "You know, you do look French. You've changed a lot since you came." He looked her up and down. "I can't make out whether it is the bobbed hair or the French beret and shoes. But more, there's a difference in your expression. It is very French. I often wonder why we go on speaking English together."

"Do you approve the change?"

"Yes, I like it." His answer was serious.

"Thanks. You know, I am thinking of living over here."

"What do you mean?"

"Well, Jim has to support me and the children somewhere. He might as well do it in France. We can live here much more cheaply."

"But how can that be, with your husband in one place and you in another?"

"Oh, I mean with a separation, or a divorce, if he wants one."

"Betty, you're crazy. What do you want a divorce for? A good husband doesn't grow on every bush. You wouldn't last over here alone a year, you'd be so homesick. Thus far, it's been a holiday excursion. How could you support yourself over here anyway if you got a divorce?"

"Why, Jim would have to support me and the children, of course, pay me alimony."

Gilbert looked at her with a tightening of the mouth and raised eyebrows. "You little American. I was going to say something rude. Why should you get money? What are you, a goddess?" He hunched his shoulders. "Women are rotten. Nothing but prostitutes at heart, the whole bunch of them."

"Is that so? Well, just let me show you a newspaper clipping someone sent me. My perfect husband has been playing around with another woman. Got in an auto accident—in her car, too. Intoxicated was the charge. It doesn't look to me as though he is such a wonderful example of the lonely husband mourning for his wife."

Gilbert read the article, raised his eyes, and looked at Betty. "And so you're going to divorce the man for that."

"Of course not, don't be stupid. It is just another indication, though."

"I should say the poor guy missed you dreadfully. And won't admit it. He's trying out all sorts of suppressed desires just to forget you, that's my guess. If he can get his money straightened out, I should say he would be taking a boat over here one of these days, without telling you beforehand, and you'll find him dying for love of you."

"Nonsense. Let's forget Jim. I want to have a wild, gay time today and forget everything American."

Gilbert looked sarcastic. "Going to pass out?"

"Why bring that up? I suppose that is so I won't think Jim is such a black sheep, compared to my own actions. That dinner at the Groses', the way I acted, makes me blush even now. But in a way, I was a victim of the situation. Jim's action is deliberate. Mine was a ghastly miscalculation, that was all. Why do we have to argue all the time, Gilbert?"

"You seem to be able to do your share," Gilbert answered. Still morose, he watched her. He would never tell her how attractive he found her. Odd the way they came together. It was about time to stop. She had an openness that was honest; he admired that. He could see that she was growing attached to him. The children were his shield; he did delight in them, but they would not always be a protection between them. Better to make a break before anything happened. His mother was a good thermometer, and she was sending all kinds of danger signals. She had been pretty outspoken about his expedition to Nice. Ever since New Year's, she had indicated her disapproval, avoiding Betty with a headache or another engagement, and he had not seen as much of Betty either. He had intercepted the kids on the way home from school twice, taken them for a ride, another time for a walk, and not invited their mother. She was furious over that, he was sly enough to note, and it flattered his vanity. But she hadn't dared to come out in the open and actually fight with him about it. He had been quite deliberate in those visits with the children when he had neglected to include her.

He had seen much more of Suzanne because he had been watching the growth of the child. How a baby kaleidoscoped the years. Day by day, one could watch the growth and change. In the waving of a foot, the focusing of the eyes, one saw the history of the human race unfold.

Suzanne made him laugh. It was as though little Mary had turned into a mother. He was fond of Suzanne, but she had no depth. She was all surface tucks, fresh bonnets, knit wool booties. The baby's nose was hers, no matter how much he looked like his father. What a feature to pick as resembling her, when a baby's nose was nothing but a button and had no character at all for years. It was typical of her to choose a nose that could have no meaning. "*Fais Do-Do*," she sang in her high, light voice. She was a kind little mother. But he had to teach her how to make the formula. It was preordained she couldn't nurse the baby. She had tried, but she had not enough milk to feed a sparrow, the baby had wailed, and he had seen to it that the doctor provided the right food. The baby hardly ever cried now, until his last sickness. Gilbert had taught Suzanne how to sterilize, how to be efficient to the n th degree, and he had shouted until he put the fear of God into her. She had hysterics one day when a hairpin fell into the pan of sterilized bottles. She boiled every last thing over again. He supposed it was foolish of him to worry over this illness. Betty was right that he was overdoing it, but he could not quiet his uneasy fear. It was like a bell clanging away in the back of his mind.

He watched Betty's reflection in the window while she, unconscious of his eyes, powdered her nose. He could see her now clear, now faint, with the sliding landscape as ground for his mirror. She had sturdily nursed her children through many ills. She was game for any emergency. He liked her looking French. It pleased him that it was his doing in a roundabout way. He let his fancy loose a bit. If she were French, if there were no American husband, if there were no Suzanne, if he were younger—and then he laughed.

As though she had heard him thinking, Betty turned her head quickly and looked at him.

"Why do you laugh?" she asked.

"Spying on me, are you?" Gilbert said. "Women are a spying lot."

Betty made a face at him and went back to finish her nose and straighten her beret to a more becoming angle. "Seems to me it is the other way around."

That facial expression of hers was French, too, he thought. "Well, we're coming to Nice," he said aloud. Two men and a woman began to sing. Several compartments took up singing in rivalry.

Nice was big and formal. The gay crowd of the train had scattered. The citizens who walked along the quiet streets were proper and going about their business. As they walked along several streets, Betty felt at once how different it was from cozy, obvious St.-Raphael. There you saw at once the flower shop, the *patisserie*, the post office, the villas, or the boardwalk along the sea, and if there was a big walled-in reserved house, you put it out of your mind as containing people you would never meet, and right next door was an obvious little villa rented by an English spinster with a black dog. Here how different. Streets and streets and streets, and never a soul one would ever recognize or even be introduced to. Nice was a city, St.-Raphael a village. The children's legs ached with all the strangeness.

"I have to go to the bathroom, Mother," was Mary's way of meeting the endlessness of the city.

"Oh, Mary, you would. Well, the only thing to do is find a café. Why didn't you think of it on the train or in the station? Of course, there isn't a café in sight." Betty was put out.

"We need coffee to warm us, or cocoa or something." Gilbert was encouraging. "Wait, and we'll find one soon." He took Mary's hand and squeezed it.

Caterina plodded behind, carrying two umbrellas and a raincoat and looking resigned to anything.

It took another three blocks to find a café, and Betty had to hurry Mary to the rear. Gilbert ordered chocolate for the children, black coffee for Caterina, and two *thé au rhum* for himself and Betty.

"I don't want tea and rum," Betty said. "I want just plain coffee."

"But I've ordered it."

"Well, change it. Is there a law against it?"

Betty certainly had an acid tongue today. Gilbert shouted, "*Garçon. Encore du café, s'il vous plaît.*"

You didn't change the tea and rum," Betty said, on the alert.

"I'll drink them both," Gilbert said easily. "And maybe a third," he added when Betty opened her mouth to say something more. She closed her mouth, and he counted that as score one for himself.

"Betty, *tu oublie que c'est un excursion gai,*" Peter said to his mother. He had taken to calling her Betty lately, and speaking in French even when they were alone, and Mary was following his lead.

Betty smiled at the little boy's gentle reprimand. "Sorry, darling," she said. "I must have climbed out on the wrong side of the bed this morning."

"I should say you did," Mary said.

She made them all laugh, and Gilbert choked over his hot tea. "Say, this is wonderful stuff. I'll let you put this extra rum in your coffee if you just say the word," Gilbert said.

"No thanks," Betty was firm.

"What is a carnival for anyway, Gilbert?" Peter asked.

"That's a hard question, Peter. It's like recess time at school. You've been working hard studying sitting still, and then you're given a little time to run and break loose before you go back to work again. It's a breaking loose in the springtime. Dancing drinking, wildness before things settle down to regular jobs and things. The word is supposed to come from *carnus*, meaning body or flesh, and *levare*, meaning to lighten, to loosen. It is a sort of cutting loose. They have carnival all over the world. Parties, dancing. Down in Italy some of their carnivals get pretty wild. And of course, Nice was a part of Italy before it belonged to France."

Once more they were on their way, and this time they could hear the music and the dull roar of the crowd.

"Oh, look, look! the children cried like puppies straining at the leash. L'Avenue des Palmes was a block away.

"Peter, you walk with Gilbert. Mary, you walk between Caterina and me, and hold my hand," Betty said.

"I will not. I'm the one to go with Gilbert." Mary pouted.

"Mary, if you don't do what I tell you, I'm going to send you right back home with Caterina. And it is perfectly possible to do it."

"I don't care. Gilbert likes me best. I'm his girl. You're not. You're always fighting." Mary flounced.

Ladies, ladies, I beg of you." Gilbert turned to them, laughing before Betty could say more than she meant to.

"I suggest that Mary come with me, as she is the most likely to get lost. Peter, stand by your mother, and Caterina by the umbrella." His voice was mocking and laughing. "And you are all my girls." He then leaned down and whispered something to Mary.

Mary ran back and said, "I'm sorry, Mother," and Betty decided she should stop being so picky and take Mary's apology for what it was worth, even though it was obvious Gilbert had instructed her.

"That's all right, my dear," she said, patting Mary's shoulder. "You've got to be careful with that tongue of yours."

The sidewalk of L'Avenue des Palmes was full up, and over the backs of the crowd they could see the tops of floats moving slowly by. There was a jolly band, people shouted, blue and yellow confetti lay thick on the sidewalk. Mary at once leaned down and scooped up a handful.

"Don't take that, it is dirty," Gilbert said. "We'll buy some fresh. The barkers used to scoop it up and resell it, but the stuff got filthy, so the Board of Health changes the color each day. Here's a man now." The man had a huge market basket of loose confetti with little cornucopia bags filled, fifty centimes each.

"He's a robber, he's a robber," Caterina said, the first time she had spoken for ten minutes. The man grinned and handed Caterina a bag for free. Gilbert had bought two francs' worth. "That is some saving," Caterina sniffed, hardly thanking the man who ogled her for one smile in payment. But she wouldn't give it to him, and he went his way.

"That's the way, treat 'em rough, they like it," Gilbert said in English.

"Do they?" Betty asked.

"Indeed they do." Gilbert tossed her a grin and pushed his way into the crowd, using Mary as a wedge.

The crowd was constantly shifting, some walking alongside the floats, others in costume mingling in the street, and they all soon were able to get in the front row. It was a grand sight. Confetti ankle-deep. The watching crowd as responsive as those marching by. Shouts back and forth from almond-eyed young men to red-mouthed, mascara-eyed girls riding high overhead. Grotesque men with heads like giants on squat little human bodies, scuffing confetti in a froth before them.

The blaring bands that played untiring. Long queues of Harlequins, Pierrots, and Columbines, weaving twisting lines, breaking, resting, starting up out of the sidewalk crowd with no reason but impulse. Fluttering confetti dropped from the sky. Betty was the first victim. She had opened her mouth to call Peter's attention to a float of elephants when a tall masked passerby threw so much confetti at her face that Betty gasped, getting confetti in her mouth. The unknown masker, laughing, pommeled more and more at her until, blind, she stretched out her arms to Caterina for support. The children were delighted.

"Oh, I wish someone would do that to me," Mary cried, laughing. Before she had time to close her mouth, hers was full, too. Gilbert had taken advantage as she turned to laugh at her mother. And then he did the same to Peter, who was laughing at Mary. Then Peter, catching the spirit, showered Gilbert, Caterina, Mary, and his mother. But Mary held her bag tightly.

"Why don't you play, Marie?" Gilbert whispered.

"It is so pretty, I hate to throw it away," Mary whispered back.

"What a silly. I'll buy you all you want."

Betty recalled the Mummers parade in Philadelphia which she had watched a few times with her father. "It has an old tradition and is very fine," she explained. "It was started by local clubs of South Philadelphia, each one entering it as a band of minstrels. The dances, a few running steps with the music, were wonderful. Primitive, dating way back. But is held in the worst weather of the year, freezing cold, slush, snow. A brilliant spectacle in a bleak, cold setting. But I'm just aware that it is a spectacle compared to this. The people watching don't ever join in, which I think is due to northern temperament. Cold northerners compared to hot, intimate southerners." She marveled at the constant good-natured tempo the present crowd could maintain without going bawdy.

Gilbert half listened. "Is that so, is that so?" The two the au Rhum he had drunk were hot inside him. He had felt chilly before, and fearfully depressed. He wished money were easier to acquire. It took more energy than it was worth to take care of the three essentials. Americans annoyed him that way; they complained when there wasn't money for luxuries. This *craque du* Wall Street made him feel better. He wondered if Americans would ever understand the French, and he felt that all Americans were obvious. Frenchmen never needed to leave France, but Americans felt the need to travel anywhere as long as they were moving. They couldn't even stay in one spot in their own country. They were born frontiersmen, moving farther and farther west until they hit the ocean, then turning around and moving back east again. He had read a novel about it once. He felt restless himself. He wondered if Suzanne were keeping little Gilbert properly warm. He ought never to have left her alone with the sick child. "Let's walk along the edge of the street. They won't let you in the street unless you're in costume, but it is getting late, and they aren't as strict when the crowd is great. We'll all get stiff, standing still." He took Mary by the hand; the others followed. It was like walking through an orchard of constantly falling almond blossoms.

Betty walked along behind Gilbert's back. She was trying to make out what was wrong. Probably her expectations had been too great. She and the children had been counting on this day for so long, what the weather would be, what clothes to wear, would they try to take a lunch with them, would she bring Caterina along, which day of the week would they choose, would they ask the teachers to excuse them from school or just take the day off unexplained, how much milk would she have Monsieur Masse leave that morning in consideration of the fact that they would be gone all day. These trivial things had mounted up the way they do when one is going anywhere with children. How easy life had been when she was first married. She powdered, put on her hat, and called, "I'm ready." Nothing depended on her. Wouldn't it be fun to go off with Gilbert like that?

And here she felt she had put her finger on something, for that was just what she had longed to do. To go on this excursion to Nice with Gilbert alone. To want to be with him alone was absurd, but she wanted an absurdity. She demanded an absurdity from him, and he would not play back. She could see the whole thing in a clear outline. She had been attracted to Gilbert when they met, and that attraction had grown with each meeting. And she knew that he was attracted to her. He kept putting the children between them as a barrier. She knew she could make him love her, ever since New Year's in Aix. She had never been so happy in her life, the morning after she had recovered her balance from her social faux pas, and she had felt that it was all going to be very wonderful between her and Gilbert. Just how, she hadn't been sure. That was up to him. There certainly were enough outside interferences, but there had grown up a friendship between her and Gilbert which would ride them over everything like a surfboard over the breakers, like a miracle. And then the miracle had never come off. And for the life of her, she could not make out why. Madame Glisson, of course, was violently opposed to anything like an American divorcee entering her son's life, but Betty couldn't see why that should stop Gilbert when he paid no attention to his mother in other respects.

Gilbert didn't want to play with her. He didn't want to get entangled with her. Was he afraid of Jim? Pretty flimsy. Was Suzanne holding him? That was equally improbable. Betty could never say how hurt she was when Peter and Mary had come back from a ride with Gilbert and she was deliberately left at home. He had told her he could be cruel, but she had not believed it until then. It wasn't cruelty but an insult. Walking along behind him with this singing, hilarious crowd made everything unreal.

She had a new thought. Gilbert was afraid of love. He was afraid of her because he was afraid the love between them would carry him away, and he didn't dare to be carried away. He was afraid to love her because her love would carry them in one leap over the husband, over the mothers, over the children and babies, over everything. She would divorce, marry, adopt. She would move Gilbert, his child, her two children, his mother, the whole of France is she felt like it, to America. They'd make money, and they'd move back to France. She'd do anything she wanted, once she had his love. Madly, she hugged these dream ideas to herself. The carnival had gone to her head.

And as though fate were at work, Gilbert was halted by a crowd in front. He turned to smile at her. A big float with horses approached from behind, and Caterina, fearing that the other had not seen it, grabbed hold of the children. And as though the confusion were not enough, a line of clowns came dancing up, hand in hand, and saw Betty and Gilbert standing near but apart. The line encircled the two of them and drew them away from the children. It happened in a second's time. Betty, frightened for the children, could not see them for the dancing clowns. The clowns swung up close in a circle, chanting as they danced dizzily around, "*Em-bras-sez, em-bras-sez, em-bras-sez.*" The chant beat like a dactylic tom-tom in her ears so that the words had no meaning. She felt as though she were being kidnapped, torn away from her children, and she would have screamed but for the fact that Gilbert's familiar face was there, smiling beside her. His face came very close, his eyes smiling down into hers. She leaned back, a little afraid. His arms were around her. Slowly, he drew her toward him, and, holding her so that she could feel the whole length of his body, even to the bones of his knees against her legs, he gave her a long, full kiss.

Gently, he let her go. When he did, the clowns were gone, and Caterina, Peter, and Mary were standing as though nothing had happened. The street whirled. People, houses, balconies, sycamore trees, confetti, and the sound of music seemed to whirl with the actual objects so that it was impossible to distinguish what one heard from what one saw. Faintly, way up the street, returned the chanting, "*Em-bras-sez, em-bras-sez, em-bras-sez.*"

Gilbert steadied her and said in a matter-of-fact voice, "That is an old custom. Dancing around a couple, singing '*Embrassez.*' They won't let you go until you kiss. And if you don't give the girls a good kiss, they'll keep you in their circle until you do. Do they do that in America?"

"No," Betty said. "They don't." She tried to smooth her hair with a casual hand, and she looked at her hand and found it was trembling. She felt for her purse and hoped no one noticed.

"I think the custom is very quaint. Don't you like it at all?" Gilbert continued pleasantly.

Betty looked at him, her eyes dazed. Was that the way he felt? Pleasant? She knew her breath was coming in gasps and that her cheeks were flaming. She could feel the imprint of his lips on hers as though they were still there. Looking at Gilbert, she saw him watching her with a little mocking smile, and not one hair of his waxed mustache was out of place. She could not find a word to say.

The children did not seem to know what it was all about, for they were all interested in the prancing horses, but Caterina smiled with her black eyes and her catlike expression, and it was impossible to tell what she was thinking.

"Mary legs are awfully tired," Mary said.

"Mary, you are right. What do you say we all have something to eat? I know a fine little restaurant, if you can keep up your courage and walk that far," Gilbert said.

It was a relief to think about food. Betty looked at her watch and was surprised to find it was after two, way past their dinner hour. They set off at a brisk pace, and that was easy as soon as they left the main boulevard. Gilbert seemed to know his way around Nice, and the children did not complain as long as they knew there was to be food at the end of their walk. At last they were inside a neat little restaurant. What a pleasure to sit down and smell the warm solidity of food. It was a family place. Madame was cook, Madame's daughters did everything, Monsieur supervised, and everything was as clean as though it had been scrubbed and boiled. Betty was allowed to take the children out to the kitchen to wash their hands, and everybody spoke in polite exclamation points.

"We must all have napkins," Betty said, sitting down once more.

"Oh, that's too extravagant," Gilbert said, laughing with the prettier of the two daughters, who was spreading the clean cloth. Caterina disapproved, too, looking as though she disapproved of the pretty daughter even more.

"The other day we had an American in here." The pretty daughter spoke to Gilbert, with a nod to include Betty and a cold look to exclude Caterina. "And we all nearly died laughing. He couldn't speak any French, and he ordered straight down the menu by pointing with his finger, and after his *sucre* and *café*, he pointed to *serviette*, and I kept saying, '*Mais, pourquoi, Monsieur, mais pourquoi quand vous etes fini.*' But he continued pointing, so I shrugged my shoulders and brought him his napkin. At first he grew very angry, but when I pointed to the word *serviette* and then to the napkin, he got it through his head and laughed as hard as the rest of us."

Mary and Peter enjoyed this joke. Betty was thinking that they were beginning to look very French, too. "We shall have napkins to begin with," she said crisply to the waitress.

"*Oui, Madame*."

"What about some wine?" Gilbert said. "I would like something special." Now it was Monsieur's turn to step forward, and he described the contents of the house cellar. Gilbert finally settled on a Chateau Neuf du Pape 1918. They all had hot soup and began to feel better.

"And there was another American." The pretty daughter was stimulated by Gilbert's smile when she came to change the plates. "But his French was pretty good, until we had *macreau* on the menu one day. He ordered it for dessert because he thought it was a macarron. Was he surprised when I brought in a nice fried mackerel. But he was a good sport and ate it. We have a lot of Americans here, but they're all queer. You never know what they'll be up to next."

Caterina was like a thundercloud.

"Madame is American," Gilbert said.

"Oh, is she?" the pretty daughter said, taking in Betty all over again. "I thought your wife was English. Madame is American, then. She is very pretty."

And Gilbert let it stand, about the wife. "We were out watching the Mardi Gras." He began talking again as the daughter served each person's *chateaubriand*, which consisted of an individual steak, deep-fried potatoes, and watercress. "And a chain of maskers took Madame and me for lovers, crying '*Embrassez*,' but Madame made me do all the kissing."

"Ah, you should have had me with you, Monsieur," the daughter said, and, frightened by her own boldness, she ran out to the kitchen.

"I really think that was quite unnecessary," Betty said, cold as ice.

Gilbert looked very pleased. "I love to see you mad, Betty, and I do not have the opportunity very often, you are too sweet-tempered." Caterina relaxed her frown.

"You know what, Gilbert," Peter said, digging into the meat Betty had cut for him. "I think you ought to come back to America with us when we go home. We'll miss you fearfully."

"That's a long way off, Peter, but thanks. I never cross bridges until I come to them. Tell me, shall I see a cowboy if I come?"

Peter and Mary laughed. "We've never seen a cowboy except in the circus."

"Oh, go on, I can't believe that. I heard a cowboy song once, very sad and minor key, a sort of *ranz des vaches*."

"What is a *ranz des vaches*?" Peter asked. "Monsieur Bonnet in school the other day was talking about it, and everybody else seemed to know what he meant. I was afraid to ask."

"*Les ranz des vaches*? They are pastoral songs, songs the goatherds sing in Switzerland. They are very sad and sweet. Years ago, when the Swiss were hired soldiers in France, they were forbidden to sing their *ranz des vaches*. It made them so homesick when they heard these songs, some of the soldiers deserted, and some of them committed suicide."

"How too bad," Mary said. "The French should have sent them home anyway."

"Do you get homesick over here, Marie?" Gilbert asked

"No," Mary said. "But I'd like to see my daddy."

"Ah," Gilbert said, and he looked at Betty, but Betty said nothing.

"Did you take the children to the circus when you were in Paris?" Gilbert asked Betty by way of making them all more cheerful.

"I never thought of such a thing."

"You should have, and you must see the *Cirque de Paris* with the Fratellini Brothers. You make your mother promise to take you. Everyone in France sees the circus again and again, grown- ups and children. As soon as I get up to Paris, I always go. My father used to tell me a nice story about how the clowns began. He came from Normandy, you know."

"Oh, tell it to us," Mary said.

"The little daughter of a wandering juggler had a dream. She told her father that she dreamed she saw him with his face painted white and a tall pointed hat and big baggy, white trousers, and he was doing his act before a tremendous audience. Her father was very superstitions and impressed, so he made himself a costume just the way she described it, and he became the first clown."

"Oh, I love clowns, too," Mary said. "I should think you would make a very good clown, Gilbert."

"Well." Gilbert laughed. "I've thought of being a good many things, but never thought of being a clown. Maybe I've missed my calling."

"What do the clowns in the Paris circus do, those brothers you were speaking about?" Peter' asked.

"Well, let's see. They have a few acts they do over and over and over. It is a small circus, one ring, in a house, not in tents like your American ones or our little provincial ones. There is one act I can remember as a tiny boy, and the last time I was in Paris they were still doing it. One clown is going to shave the other clown, and he brings in a huge pail of soap suds and giant razor made of wood, and the soap fluffs up and gets over everything in the ring until finally a couple of people in the audience, they are placed there, get covered with this fluff. You have to see it to get the fun."

"I don't think it is a bit funny," Mary said.

"Oh, I remember another act. You would have liked that, Mary. Preparations are made for the entrance of a great bareback rider, and then there are whispers, and the ringmaster announces that the rider has been hurt. The beautiful horses trots around, and then an old drunken man comes lurching in and gets in the way and falls down and tries to get on the horse and trips and falls, and the ringmaster sneers at him. 'I suppose you think you can ride.' The drunk loses his hat and his coat comes off and his trousers are half falling off, and there is a lot more backtalk between them. And when the drunk is about to strike the ringmaster and the ringmaster calls for help, suddenly the drunk springs out of his terrible clothes, he is in spangled tights, he leaps on the horse and then does wonderful tricks."

"Oh, that is nice. Tell us another."

"What's going to happen to the Mardi Gras? We came to see that. Let's go out again."

The daughters had been hovering around, listening. Even Madame came out of the kitchen to see them off. They seemed to be very much impressed by Gilbert and very curious about the mixed French and American couple and the fact that Caterina accompanied them like a faithful duenna, how exotic. There must be money for that. It had piqued their imagination. The pretty daughter had grown shy and simpering to watch Monsieur helping Madame on with her coat. When people were seated in her natural setting, she could act very bold, but when they arose to move outside and lead their own lives again, then she grew shy before the immensity of their strangeness. The other daughter, who was plain, never said anything; most of her work was in the kitchen.

The mother, however, who was more used to the unusual principally because she had watched it for a longer time, spoke up. "Do tell us, Monsieur, do you and your wife spend the time in this country or in America?"

Gilbert was very merry-eyed as he turned at the door, hat in hand. He let the children and Caterina pass out first, detaining Betty by her elbow. "Oh, my wife and I live in France, that is, for the present," he said, jauntily adjusting his hat.

"Ah, how very fine, how very fine. Well, good luck to you, Monsieur, Madame," they all said together in chorus.

Betty and Gilbert each smiled and said, "Thank you very much, a wonderful dinner. *Au revoir, Messieurs, Mesdames.*"

Gilbert let Caterina continue with the children while he slipped his arm through Betty's, then he took it out and drew her arm through his. "So," he said. "That is better so. And how do you like playing the part of wife?" The dinner and wine seemed to have restored his good spirits. "You know what American really means." He continued squeezing her hand. "It doesn't mean modern machinery or speed or materialism or any of those things most French people lay at the American door. It means romanticism. Every American is a romanticist, this is my new discovery, and you are the most romantic of them all. Nothing practical, just sheer romance."

Caterina, either through discretion or to keep them warm, led the children far ahead.

At last Betty spoke. "I think I am very practical. I was the one who brought Caterina along with us to take care of the children." She could not hide from him her happiness that he was once more gay and friendly. "Oh, Gilbert," she said. "I know you do not approve. I know your mother does not approve, no one approves, but I cannot help but be happy when I am with you. I never in all my life met anyone like you, and I have always dreamed I would meet a man who would be just like you. I should not tell you this, but how can I help it?"

Gilbert looked at her, tried to make a frivolous remark, but Betty forced him to listen.

"I should not see you, I should go away, I should do anything but what I am doing. But I cannot control myself, I cannot go without telling you about it." her voice went on, with a touch of hysteria to it. "What shall I do, what shall I do? I shall do whatever you say."

Gilbert shrugged his shoulders. "You are much too serious about it. Sufficient unto the day. Come on," he cried, catching her hand. "We'll run and run and run. There is nothing like running to cheer up one's spirits." He laughed at her as they ran together. "Don't worry." He whispered to her as they caught up to the children. "Don't worry, my dear, we'll solve it yet."

"You certainly are slow pokes," Mary said. "We thought you were lost."

Caterina beamed on them. "Oh, I can manage the children." They had arrived at that part of the Avenue des Palmes where it meets the promenade in a big circle of streets and a small formal garden. Here the big floats were disgorging their riders, statues coming to life and scrambling down over the wheel guards, stiff-skirted dancing girls mixing with young men in trenchcoats and berets. A bandleader shouted to his orchestra to step up and get instructions for where they should meet in the evening. It was a behind-the-scenes spectacle, catching the actors and actresses in dressing- gown attitude. The mist was turning into rain, and umbrellas popped up like mushrooms. Everyone began to scatter.

"This is a nuisance," Gilbert said as they were forced to open their umbrellas. "I thought we could wander around here and see each float as it unloaded. It won't be any fun if it is going to rain hard. Let's get under shelter somewhere. The Jetee Promenade has a good concert sometimes. That is very near. Would you like to try that?"

Betty hesitated, but the children brightened.

"It is an old-fashioned casino. I think the children might be amused."

"Well," Betty said, "we might see what it is like."

They walked through the formal garden, very wet and bedraggled-looking, and came out on the Promenade Anglais. The sea was hardly visible for the rain, but you could hear the waves swishing up and down with a sucking noise over the pebbled beach.

The Jetee Promenade casino was once famous, but it had long since tarnished into mild respectability. Its remaining distinction was that it was the only casino in Nice that was permitted to be built out over the sea. Its architecture dated back to 1900, and those who frequented it had something a little seedy about them. The dashing smart ones went up to some of the modern palaces where everything was *ultra-moderne* and the dance orchestras played blues. Here a lot of odd- hatted English ladies attended, and genial French papas, full-bosomed French mamas, and children were seen, too. Peter and Mary were not at all out of place.

They checked wet clothes, and entered the dark concert hall, where a dance was in progress. It looked like the formal toe exercises of some Russian ballet girls. Peter and Mary were lost in wonder at the sight. They had been to the theater seldom, and they had seen nothing like this before. They sat with their mouths open, watching everything, not even asking questions. Mary thought they were fairies, and Peter thought he was at last seeing some of this "night life" he had heard the grown-ups talking about. Gilbert tried to hide his boredom and moved restlessly in his seat. He whispered explanations to Mary, who was next to him, but she didn't listen, and the people sitting in front objected to the interruption.

"Would you come out with me and play a little game of *boule*?" he whispered to Betty. "The children would be perfectly safe here with Caterina. The room is just across the hall. I'll explain to her where we'll be."

Betty nodded. They made the arrangement to the annoyance of those in front.

"I can't stand those archaic dances," he said when they were outside. "I thought they'd have some music. They probably will later. Have you done any gambling over here?" he asked her. He acted as though he didn't know quite well all the things she had been doing in France.

"Why do you talk like that?" she said.

He laughed. "To keep you from talking like that."

"Must everything be as impersonal as though we had met for the first time? I swear you're afraid of me."

"Suppose I am. Do you like me the less?"

"No."

"Well, you see, now be a good girl and give me ten, twenty francs, and I'll get you some counters to play *boule*."

Betty opened her purse and handed him two ten-franc notes. That was another minor point she admired about Gilbert, his absolute naturalness with money. All the American men she had known leaned over backward to pay for a woman. After all their married years, Jim still did. If at a restaurant he happened to be short of change and was forced to ask her for some, he took it with the guilt of robbing the innocent female. It was a standard American joke for a man to say, "My wife treated me to the movies," and by way of apology he would justify himself with, "Changed my suit and forgot the wallet accidentally on purpose." All of this when the husband earned the money and had filled his wife's purse. Gilbert, on the other hand, would divide the bill down to the last centime and get the proprietor to make change if it didn't come out even. It gave her the greatest kick to have him say, "Give us your purse, Betty," and he would hunt out for himself the amount, even to looking at the other things like powder and papers. Ist suggested an intimacy in other matters. A few times he'd say, "All out, you've got to pay the whole thing," and that pleased her even more. That gave her power. She had not realized what a compliment he was paying her and the children when he had offered to treat them, the time she'd bobbed her hair. She appreciated now in retrospect.

"I've bought you one-franc counters," he said, coming back. "Twenty for you and five for me."

"Oh, let me give you ten," she said. "I never played the thing in my life."

"Certainly not," he said. "Besides, I shall win more than you do anyway."

"Oh, is that so?"

"You wait and see."

There were half a dozen people playing when they got there, the master of ceremonies calling, "*Faites vos jeux,*" in a bored voice and raking in the counters after each play. No one seemed excited or looked depraved as Betty had expected. The master of ceremonies was a gray- haired man with clipped mustache and dress suit, and with his grayish skin and sad, cultured voice, he resembled the professional gambler more than anyone else. Gilbert assured her in a whisper that he was the only one not allowed to gamble, that he was on a salary and probably had a wife and a couple of children and led a most virtuous private life. The rest of the people looked nondescript. One could have picked them up in a grocery store or waiting for a train in the railroad station. Two English ladies smiled naughtily as each laid her counter on a number and both immediately lost their money.

Gilbert played for red and won. He was handed two extra counters. He played red again and won.

"Oh, I want to play black." Betty was all excited. "That will have to win. Why bother with numbers?" it lost. She changed to red and lost, she returned to black and lost, she stayed on black and won. "It isn't as easy as it looks, is it? Isn't there a queer fascination about it? I've always been taught it was wicked, but it is as innocent as marbles. You either win or lose."

Gilbert smiled at her. "Don't be too philosophical. The people who play here all the time aren't they're as superstitious as businessmen. Or else they have enough to lose and so it doesn't matter." He had begun playing numbers, and twice luck ran his way. He played number nine, won, and then stopped playing for a couple of times to smoke a cigarette. Then he played again, lost again, won, and doubled his bet, won. Trebled his bet and won. He put out the stub of his cigarette and tried not to show how pleased he was.

Betty was outwardly thrilled for him. "Oh, Gilbert, how exciting! Play mine, will you? Oh, please play mine."

"Do you think that yours will bring me more good luck?"

"Yes, I do."

"And suppose they should win. Do I have to give all the winnings to you?" he looked at her if as to say, *You wouldn't dare demand a thing from me.* Or was she reading it into those light gray eyes of his?

"Of course not." And then, as though she was afraid she had been too lenient, she added, "But you've got to give me back the original twenty francs, that's fair."

"Betty, Betty. You tell me I'm afraid of you, and look at you, you're scared to death of me. You're afraid to say 'yes', and you're afraid to sacrifice your ego with a good, strong 'no'. 'Give me back my measly little twenty francs,' you squeak."

"I don't want the twenty francs or anything," she said, "It is all yours."

"That's the way to talk. I like a woman who isn't afraid to give. Most of them are so damn picky, they'll give their souls to any old tramp, but when it comes to somebody they love they'll hold back the twenty francs, or something else just as silly."

"Oh, Gilbert, do you really mean that?"

"Do I mean what?"

"Do you mean that you think I love you?"

"You told me you did once, but I didn't say you told me you loved me."

"But I do, I do. I can't help it."

"You know, Betty, you should stick to *boule*. You mean, and told you, and you told me, and you did, and I didn't, and let's each go over to the bar and drink a whiskey sour, and then go back and play the twenty francs, and then we can see what will happen."

"I'll do anything you say, Gilbert, but I can't drink a whiskey sour. I feel completely drunk as it is."

"Wait until I get through with you."

Gilbert drank his whiskey sour, and Betty watched him, and they walked back to the *boule* table.

"Which shall I play, nine or eleven?" he asked her.

"Nine," she said.

He put the twenty counters on nine, and it won. He asked her again, nine or eleven?

"Eleven," she said.

He put all the counters he held on eleven, and it won. To Betty, it seemed as though he mesmerized her and then that he turned and mesmerized the revolving wheel. The ball jumped lazily at the end from one number to another. It almost stopped at twenty-six, skipped to nineteen, and slowly rolled to the next number, four, twenty-one, two, skipped again to the red thirty-six, and then, as though Gilbert's willpower made it move, it gave, a tiny jump and rested at eleven. It was unbelievable, but there it stood. With a weary smile, the master of ceremonies handed over the counters. Gilbert took them in both hands. He went over to the booth. "Do you want it all in cash?" the man asked. "Yes, please," Gilbert said. He took the notes and led Betty over to a settee. They counted them out in her lap. There was the equivalent of twenty-five dollars.

"Are you satisfied to stop?" Gilbert asked.

"Oh, isn't it too thrilling?" Betty said.

"Most of this is yours, you know."

"No, it isn't. It's all yours. That was the bargain."

Gilbert grinned. "*C'est de l'argent pour le sport.* We'll spend it together."

The gambler spirit infected the two of them, the spirit of adventure. They had amused themselves with thirty francs, and now they held in their hands more than six hundred francs. It was fantastic, and because the money was fantastic and at the same time very real and solid in their hands, it seemed as though they could do fantastic things with it. But in a real, solid way. It lifted the quiet, dull routine of work which earns money which in turn is pushed over the counter to pay for protective shoes and necessary bread and warming coal, and by the flick of a number it changed all of this into a shining aurora. The shining aurora might not last, but the money was very real. And the spirit of adventure that went with it, was that real or tawdry? Would it last? But what did that matter? The substance of adventure was the glow, the missing heartbeat. As for what happened to the lost heartbeat, that was beside the point. At least, that was what Betty thought as she sat beside Gilbert on the Louis XVI settee.

She had been thinking for some time that anything might happen, but seeing the money spread out in Gilbert's hands, she knew it could happen. It was silly of her to be moved by the sight of this gambling money. People had been gambling for years. American people were noted for gambling for gold, when by some fluke a man with one coat to his back was made a millionaire and the man panning gold next to him would be lucky if he owned two coats before he died. Over and over again, it happened in America. One man settling down on a narrow strip of land in what was to be New York City and another man moving to a tract of land in Texas. They were all flukes. As far as Betty was concerned, she had lived the regular, uneventful, and calm life lived about her. The things she thought were just like the things other women thought; she had felt smothered by the flow of quiet, dull routine; and she had stretched her arms to start up the flow of life into herself and her husband. Through several flukes, she had met and grown to know Gilbert. Here they sat with this money which didn't belong to them, which had no value, and yet which the world looked upon as theirs to have and spend.

"How extraordinary," Betty said. "How extraordinary you are, too. How amazing everything is."

"Not at all," Gilbert said, sorting the notes into two equal piles. "This is yours, and this is mine," he continued, taking out his wallet and carefully inserting the bills. "And it all goes to show you what the world is like. Money is so important, but money is nothing more than pieces of paper. You can work all your life, and that's what you have, paper, nothing more. As for me, I'm the most ordinary of small-town Frenchmen. Everyone is extraordinary, you know, as soon as you get close to them. Look at Caterina over there. If you were to know the whole of her life, you probably wouldn't believe it possible for her to do some of the things she does, and yet look how quietly she leads the children, and she can be trusted as a very good and faithful nurse."

Betty looked up to see the children coming toward her. There was an intermission, and Caterina had come out to find them.

"Well, how did you like the dancing?" Gilbert said.

"Oh, I want to be a dancer when I grow up, Mother," Mary cried.

"You can't be," Peter interrupted, "unless you're born into it or you're Russian. That's what Caterina said."

"Will you do something for me, Peter and Mary?" Gilbert said, putting an arm around Peter and making room for Mary to sit beside him. "Will you lend me your mother for the evening?"

"Why?" said both children together. "Why should we?"

"I'll tell you why. It is something extra especial. You see, your mother and I played a game called boule, and we won a lot of money, and me want the fun of pending it together, and I have invited your mother to play with me this evening, although I haven't told her yet. It is a surprise, but she can't go unless you children will be generous and lend her to me."

Betty felt the blood rush to her face, and when the children looked at her, she could not say a word.

"Would you like to go out with Gilbert?" Mary asked.

Betty nodded her head.

"What would happen to us?" said Peter.

"Oh, I should take wonderful care of you," Caterina said, all smiles. "You need not worry for a moment, Madame. Not for one moment. The children will be safer with me than if you were along."

Betty moved among them as if she were in her sleep, walking, talking, doing things beyond her control. They all had something to eat, they went to the railroad station and arranged about the tickets. The train came in, Caterina still assuring them that no one needed to worry. She was given the house key. Gilbert had brought each child a tiny present which they were to open on the train. He received permission to enter the train to be sure they found seats. The early train was half empty, and Betty looked up at the train window to see the faces of Peter and Mary smiling out at her. They took it as quiet an adventure for themselves, traveling alone with Caterina. Actually, there was not a particle of danger. It could have happened and had happened a dozen times at home. A moment later, Gilbert was jumping off as the trainman closed the door. Slowly the train moved by, they waved their hands, and she was alone on the station platform with Gilbert. He was smiling at her and holding her hands.

"You still think I am afraid of you," he said.

"No," she said.

"And you must not be afraid," he whispered. "I shall take care of you and return you safe. Even though this is a carnival night, everything is excused then."

They walked. They walked for miles over the city. The rain had stopped. There was a mist in the air, but the wind began to dry things up. It was only about six, but with the winter clouds it was dark. They walked. They went through beautiful residential sections. Lawns, gates, fences, hedges. Glimpses of big estate houses. They walked by city houses in blocks, apartments. They went to the old part of the city and saw the market. They sat on one of the tables which tomorrow would be filled with colorful fruits and vegetables.

"Suppose it is a fish table," Gilbert said. "I think I smell fish."

"I don't care," Betty said, "if it is fishy fish with scales." His arms was around her waist, and he had just kissed her. Shyly, she had returned his kiss.

They climbed off the wooden table and explored the old section of the city. The streets were stairs, up and up they went, round and round. The gutters had refuse, and the corners of houses smelled of urine. Betty would have been afraid for her life alone, but with Gilbert she led a charmed life. What would hurt them? They passed drunken men, and the men let them pass without even an extra glance.

"That is because you look French, and a special kind of French. They know the girls with the frizzed bobs, the berets, the sensible shoes. They've seen hundreds of them, nice girls too, working girls, pretty, with a young man, but the kind who know how to cook and clean as well as sit in a café. Let's stop here and get something to drink."

They went into one of those cheap little bistros working men frequent, with only enough room for three or four tables and a long zinc bar, one man tending it. they sat down in a corner beside each other. Gilbert ordered a beer for her, she had consented to drink that, and a whiskey, in honor of her country, for himself. But they were all out of whiskey, not enough call for it there, so he changed to a Pernod. They brought him water in a glass, and when he poured it into the goblet it changed to a milky, translucent green. He let her taste it.

"It makes me think of when I was a little girl and used to buy a penny licorice stick. It is very nice."

He wanted to get her a Pernod, but she stuck to her beer. He lit a cigarette, and they took turns smoking the same cigarette. He put his arm around her again.

"Are you all right?"

She nodded. "Do you know what?" she said suddenly. "We're speaking nothing but French."

People came in, went out, but they meant nothing to either of them. They were a separate unit in themselves. It was amusing to watch people but not necessary. Other people were so much atmosphere. They finished their drinks, went out, and began walking again. This time, they returned to the promenade and went way up the far end around the big cliff, called Rauba Capia because the wind blows so hard around it that it steals your hat. It was too cold, so they retraced their steps, walking close for warmth, her arm through his, their hands in his big pocket. They began the ascent along woodsy paths up the big Castle Hill with its gardens.

"It is beautiful in the daytime, all sorts of flowers and unusual shrubs and trees. It is one of the sights of Nice and a heavenly view at the top," Gilbert explained.

"It is beautiful," she said. "Just look at the rose. Isn't it exquisite?" This made them laugh because they couldn't see a thing. It was ink black, and Betty stumbled over a root. "I'm sure there are bears in here."

'I guess we had better give it up for another time." This was the first reference to the future which had been made. They let it pass.

Back on city streets it seemed more cozy. They came across a little café where there was dancing . They went in and danced. It made them warm again, it was cold out, they had a beer apiece.

"That's what I'll drink if that is what you want," he said.

They told each other stories of when they were children. Gilbert described his father, tall with a pointed beard, and how he used to take him and his mother on a Sunday excursion to a place outside Paris called Robinson's and how they ate their dinner way up in a tree. The waiter had to trudge up and down narrow stairs that were built around the tall trees, and at the end of each flight there was a small platform built among the branches with a table. He had liked to climb to the top platform if the table was vacant, and the waiter brought their dinner to them, course by course. Afterward, Gilbert was allowed a donkey ride through the woods, and his father would go with him, and his legs were so long they almost touched the ground, but his mother sat in the woods and watched them go by.

"Oh, you should have seen me on Sundays, button boots and long black stockings and a white pique dress with Hamburg lace, and a hat that was scalloped and the crown buttoned onto the brim. I was so good. We rode in a horse and carriage and had picnics," she said.

"I remember when I was a young man in the Lycee and I used to pass a girl with a long curling feather in her hat. I never dared to speak to her, but I used to meet her every morning," he said.

"Oh, I shall never forget my first kiss. I was about eight, and the boy next door kissed me in the hammock, and my mother saw us and whisked me into the house and wouldn't explain a word. I didn't know what was the trouble. I used to play Indians with him, and when he was chasing me my dog thought it was real and ran out and bit his leg, and what a to-do that was. They got a doctor to cauterize his leg, and poor Trip was in disgrace and had to be sent away. Our families were very cool toward each other after that."

They were walking again. They were back in the marketplace. "Which one is our table?" Betty said.

"We'll have to find the fishiest one."

"You know, I have simply got to find a *lavabo*. I don't know why I didn't think of it in that café. What shall I do? French towns were never built for ladies, and the men have conveniences every two blocks. It isn't fair."

"The best thing I can suggest is for you to go right here. I'll stand watch."

With many giggles, Betty tried to hide behind a table and felt the whole of Nice was watching her.

Walking again. "It must be fearfully late. What time it is?" Betty started t look at her watch, but Gilbert covered her wrist with his hand.

"No watches tonight. Time doesn't count. Whatever you want to do, we'll do. If you're tired, we'll sit down. If you're hungry, we'll eat."

"I think I am hungry," Betty said. "We've eaten a dozen times today, it seems, but even so. How do you feel?"

"I think we should eat, too. Let's find the grandest place we can. We can pay for it."

They set out to find it. It took a long time. Betty was getting exhausted. She would have taken any restaurant, the first. But Gilbert didn't like this one, another was too quiet, the next not expensive-looking. Betty was drooping fast. "I've got to stop soon," she wailed, but he was indifferent. At last they came to one that satisfied him. It was very grand and expensive. Inside an elegant waiter in a suit which equaled that of his patrons led them to a table. He seemed uncertain where to place them, for their clothes did not jibe with the rest of the setting. There were not many seated, it may have been early, but she could not tell. She didn't dare look at her watch. The waiter finally hid them behind some palms. "I don't think we should have come here," Betty said.

"We aren't dressed right,"

"You're a silly bourgeois. What do the clothes matter? We have the money, haven't we? Good money. And we're going to have a good dinner, too. You run down to the ladies room and Powder your nose and comb your hair, and you'll feel better."

"Oh, I can't go by all those tables again."

"Go on with you." And with Gilbert's eyes to sustain her, she made her way out and downstairs. It did help. She washed her hands and fixed up her face in all the elegance she found. She gave the woman attendant a two-franc piece and got the door held for her with a smile.

Gilbert certainly did enjoy that dinner. Gradually, Betty began to relax into enjoyment, too. It was served with all the finesse the French can put into food, which can turn an ordinary meal into a pleasurable pastime. A fine dinner beautifully combines the esthetic with the practical, and this all Frenchmen dearly love. Frenchmen can find more amusement in this than in all of theater, vaudeville, or cinema. It lacked the family richness of Madame Gros's New Year's dinner, but it was supplemented by the grand formality of the restaurant plus the French waiter who never intrudes in a tete-a-tete but with a subtle flourish can increase the intimacy for Monsieur and Madame. Gilbert's national characteristic never showed to better advantage. For a patron to know his wines is essential to any French waiter, and Gilbert knew all the wines, and the dates too. Their waiter was no *garçon* but Monsieur Jacques, and he recognized in Gilbert a gentlemanly partner who would pass the ball back and forth and who knew all the rules of the game. Soup was chosen with dignity, and the wine was the subject of a debate between cabinet ministers. Their attire, which had at first misled Monsieur Jacques, was put aside. It was not mentioned except by the bending of a shoulder, the whispered concern, the Madame in a draft, was Madame comfortable, could Madame's coat be arranged just so over the back of her chair. All went to show his respect. As Gilbert reached over and put his hand over Betty's while the discussion of soup and wine was under way, Monsieur Jacques knew they were lovers. And what Frenchman can resist a pair of lovers? Gilbert and Betty floated through the dinner. An elegant lorgnette was raised in their direction. Monsieur Jacques treated them like his children, all but tying their napkins under their chins. It was fun, there was no doubt about it. Gilbert had slipped Monsieur Jacques a ten-franc note while Betty was downstairs. At the same time, he had whispered that he wanted the dinner just right for Madame, who was timid, but Betty did not know any of this.

There was a gravy, and Gilbert scribbled a little note to the chef to compliment him on his gravy, and on Monsieur Jacques's return, he brought back the thanks of the chef. There were artichokes which were a meal in themselves for size and color and delicacy. There were crepes suzettes which involved a little table being wheeled forward by a *garçon*, and Monsieur Jacques lit the alcohol lamp and flashed copper pans, bowls of batter, a dash of *rhum*, the sprinkled sugar, and by a magician's turn of the wrist that concoction was rolled and steaming on their plates. The whole dining room was watching. They ended with a cheese that had been raised in cellars and ripened for the particular benefit of lovers. Americans are liable to sneer over the fuss that is created out of nothing but soup, meat, and dessert, pointing with scorn to the premature tip which will have to be increased with interest at the end, but the whole thing is a game. The usual American prefers to rush his dinner and pay ten dollars flat for his seat in the opera or the leg display of the vaudeville, but the Frenchman will play the game of dinner for three hour straight. You can't just sit and eat; you have a part to play whether you happen to be sitting down or standing up.

Gilbert's conversation sparkled in counterpoint with the progress of dinner. Betty wanted to laugh, to cry, and her eyes sparkled in answer. He kissed her hand once. He fed her a taste of his main dish, which was something with rabbit and gravy, while hers was built up from a beef foundation. He held it on his own fork across the table to her, and there was so much merry kindness on his eyes that she could not resist. She felt completely his in that moment. It was light, gay, and happy. Under the table, he had captured one of her feet between his, their knees touched, and their legs rested side by side, and to Betty it seemed sweet. He told her that they were not to think of time, and she would not. She would laugh with him in the now. She merely tasted the wine with her lips; she would not repeat that terrible sensation she had experienced at the Groses' house, and Gilbert respected her wish and only poured her a thimbleful for sociability.

"I think you are awfully good not to force me to drink with you," she said. "You could. You know I shall do whatever you want. I am pleasurably drunk just to be with you this way, and you are kind enough to know it." Her manner was humble.

"My dear, my dear. Don't talk to me like that. It makes me feel I have caught a little rabbit in a trap. I have given you my promise, I will not harm you. On the other hand, you must be more willful, more spiteful toward me. You had better watch out. If you are too grateful, I may lose my head with feeling my own power, and show you some *gallique* cruelty."

"I'll risk it."

Bravely they moved through dinner. Gilbert bravely paid the bill. It seemed like a great deal of money to give away when they had been counting their francs with such care. Gilbert did not show any regret; Betty did for a second as she saw the notes lying on Monsieur Jacques's little round silver tray. Grandly, Gilbert left the tip, and Betty could not help but think that it would be more than enough to buy the week's food for them at home. As she pulled on her gloves and smoothed the fingers, her hand and arm involuntarily drew back as though the thoughts of her subconscious had come up to the surface to control her gesture. Hurriedly, her mind said, What am I doing? But Gilbert had taken her coat from Monsieur Jacques with a nod of thanks, and Gilbert's hands as he held it by the collar brushed against her neck. The touch was a caress. Yes, Gilbert was sweet. She turned to let her eyes meet his.

Outside in the dark, she again became frightened. "Oh Gilbert she cried, and clung to his arm. He crossed his two hands with hers and they walked along as though they were skating.

"You're a scared cat. Shame on you. I thought you were grown up. You're scared cat." He laughed at her.

"No, I'm not afraid," she told him. "I'm afraid of the other people, the other things. I'm not afraid of you and me. You can never know how careful everything has been for me in life, how even it has been. It is as though I had been kept all my life in cotton wool, as though I were some sort of rare china that might break. You read such terrible stories in newspapers. They happen to people I never met, but reading about them makes me wonder if we can be different."

"You read about the violent ones, you don't read about the quiet ones. There are hundreds and millions of them. The love life of people is a curious thing. Few of us, men or women, experience it only as the church teaches us in the one and perfect way, only in monogamous marriage." He talked on and on in her ear, he told her a joke and made her laugh.

"Well," he said, suddenly sharply. "Shall we take the train back to St.-Raphael?" His manner was harsh and cold; he stood away from her.

She looked at him in amazement. He might have said that they would take the next boat out to sea and jump into the cold Mediterranean. "But Gilbert," she faltered. "I love you. You cannot talk to me like that, and you know I'm getting exhausted. It's been a long day, sustained on excitement. Can't we sit down somewhere?"

Then she saw that he was teasing her, that he liked to watch her being upset by his change of voice. "Betty dear, I love you," he whispered in her ear. "Will you stay with me, here, and early in the morning we'll take the train back? At four or five, this carnival nights is ours. I think it is our due. Tomorrow we can talk about the practical, not tonight. It has grown between us, and we should be allowed to taste the pleasure of it. I cannot see that it will hurt anyone else particularly. I promise to protect you, there'll be no babies. It is up to you and me. Will you come with me?"

"Yes," she said

They found a very quiet place on a side street called L'Hotel Georges. Madame was very gracious, showing them their room. It could have been unpleasant, but it was not. It was easy, quick, matter-of-fact. Gilbert explained that they would have to take an early train out of Nice. Madame helped them look up the timetable, the night girl would call them, and a cab was ordered. Gilbert paid in advance to save time in the morning. The fact that they had no baggage and that it was odd to be arriving late and leaving early did not trouble Madame in the least. "I hope you will be comfortable," she said.

They were alone, and it was as natural as though nothing were new or strange. They pretended they were an old married couple taking a little vacation in Nice, that this was their last night, and that tomorrow they would be returning to Paris and their everyday work and life. Gilbert had a government job, Betty ran a small apartment beautifully on nothing, and they had all the comforts of life. They talked as though it were all on the stage. They even mimicked a quarrel over why Betty sewed his buttons on so tight and why she never spent money for new hats but insisted on making over her old ones. They planned about buying season tickets for the concerts that year. Suddenly, Betty burst into tears, and Gilbert comforted her with all the tenderness he possessed. They lay in each other's arms, and he cajoled and whispered and comforted and fooled with her until she was herself again.

Gilbert made love to her gently, slowly, pacing himself to meet her distress. Betty tried in vain to control her terror. Again she burst into tears, again he comforted her, and then without effort her fears left her and she was able to let her emotions ride high and free. She hoped she would be able to keep up her ecstasy to meet his, but just as she should have risen to the climax of their love, she became tense and afraid. Quietly, she lay in his arms and stroked his face. "I'm not much good as a lover." She spoke with tears in her eyes. "Am I?"

"Real lovemaking takes a lot of practice," he said kindly. "You can't force it, but this was very nice."

"Oh, Gilbert, I love you, I can never bear to leave you, and all the time I keep thinking of the other people. Of all the responsibilities that lie between us."

"You mean, my dear, you have suddenly recalled your husband."
She nodded her head.

He smiled at her, but she saw his smile as coming from a long way off. They had been as one all the evening, but now that he was satisfied he grew remote. "That's a good sign in a wife, shows she doesn't take this carnival madness too seriously." He pulled a pillow behind his head.

"Why do you keep talking about 'too serious'? You've said that a dozen times this evening. In nothing ever to be serious in your mind? Well, let me tell you, I'm dead in earnest. I love you, and that is serious. I cannot live without you, if you want another serious admission, and some way or other we are going to live together happily ever after. Some way or other we're going to get married. I have known for some time that I love you, I adore you, and tonight you have shown that you love me. What more do we want?"

"A good deal. A lot of money, for one thing." He turned his head to beam at her. "First, I want to finish my definition of a carnival which I was trying to describe to Peter at lunch. Carnivals are as old as the hills, spring festivals. Roman saturnalia. The thing has a religious character, a spring fertility of crops and animals and man. It goes way back beyond any Christian religion. Although the time chosen for this Mardi Gras festival is limited by the Christian Lent. Much license is overlooked. There is some small town in Italy that still allows the men to lay aside all convention, the women all modesty, without losing their reputation. And when it is all over they go back to their respective husbands and wives as though nothing had happened. The same is true in some place in India—Assam, I think—and you and I are a beautiful example of it. we'll return to the ordinary, but it has been wonderful while it lasted."

"Oh, keep quiet." Betty's voice was taut. "You talk and talk. What good does that do? There is love between us, and that means the beginning and the end. The means will work itself out. I am ready to renounce the whole world for you. I am gong to marry you."

"My dear girl, you're flattering, I must admit. I told you, you were a romanticist. It wouldn't work, it couldn't work. What has marriage got to do with us? Marriage isn't love. Marriage should promote love. Marriage is a congenial business contract between a man and a woman, setting up their worldly goods—money, dowry, and house. It is the coronation of a small king and queen in their home kingdom, and their subjects are the children. It has to do with property and law. It was nothing to do with love, at least in the beginning. If the woman does her part of the bargain and the man does his part, then you have a handsome thing, a happy marriage, and it happens once in a blue moon. It could happen every time if people wanted it to. It is why you Americans fail at it so often. You begin on romantic love, which is to begin on the wrong foot. You don't begin your dinner with dessert, do you? Be as romantic as you want afterward, but begin by being analytical and practical."

"And I suppose you expect me to go back to Jim after this?" Betty could think of nothing but the personal.

"Of course I do. He is an ideal husband, and after this you should settle down and make him a model wife. If I had the time and energy, I could, in about six weeks, give you a diploma with the highest honors for a true and loving wife. As it is, you'll have to do it yourself. I think you have it in you to make a glorious wife, if you would open your eyes."

"What in the name of God am I going to do with you?" Betty began to laugh hysterically.

"Here we are as good as married, in my way of thinking, and you talk about my being a model wife for Jim. You're crazy. All I have to do is get a divorce and marry you."

"Did you say all? My dear girl, give yourself to me physically a thousand times, but you're no good to me as a wife. What do you think I'm managing, a harem? It would be better for me to marry Suzanne, and I believe it is you who urged me to, if I must marry someone. Your husband will go on supporting you after you are married to me? And what about your children?"

"I can't help it." Betty began to sob. "Gilbert, I love you, I adore and love you, that is all I can say."

"Come here." He held out his arms. She hid her head in them. He smoothed her hair, her face, he kissed her tears dry. Voluptuously, he handled her body, making love to her. She could not resist, she did not want to, she only wanted him near her. Their lovemaking grew wilder, more unrestrained; he arranged for their protection.

But again, at the second when she should have given her soul and body to him, she failed. She was left alone swinging in space, her mind frozen in a cloud.

Gilbert was warm, relaxed, laughing beside her, and she hated him with a fury of passion unspent. Her anger left her, and she lay back. Gilbert grew matter-of-fact, lit a cigarette. His indifference made her feel sorry for herself. She tried to be playful, but in the middle of it he fell asleep.

Betty lay with her mind a barbed tormentor. She covered the years of her life. She had classed herself with the great lovers of history, but she had failed. It was hard on her female pride. She was no du Barry, and she had thought she was.

She tried to force her mind to make plans for the future with Gilbert, but she could not seem to straddle the point that she had failed to meet him in love. Gilbert lay asleep beside her, his face content, his arm thrown across her in protection, but his arm could not protect her mind. She thought of slipping out from under his kind hand, dressing, running out into the night. What good would it do her to run? She had herself with her . . . herself which had failed in love.

Never had she felt more alone. It was the loneliness of looking up at the stars and realizing that one's ego is a speck of dust on the edge of the universe.

She fell asleep with cosmic dust and the universe and the decision of her life lost in troubled dreams.

There was the actual awakening, cramped, her neck was broken, she jumped to feel the cold floor. A hurrying of numb, sleep-laden muscles to get into their clothes, dashes of cold water on their faces, currying a comb through the hair, hat. Last look for forgotten things, running downstairs, the cold gray street, the cab standing in clear morning light. Rattled to pieces as they were driven to the station. Thoughts and tongues were as numb as the muscles, running up the station steps with only a minute to jump onto the puffing train. The train began to move before they could find an empty compartment.

The ride was long, sleep filled their eyes, there was little to be said. Betty had thought they would talk again and settle everything; they settled nothing. Reality was growing big and real. The figures of Madame Glisson, Suzanne, Peter, Mary, the baby Gilbert were growing bigger every minute. Even Mademoiselle Roule was in the picture. But the one who sat between them was Jim. He was Betty's lawful husband, and he was there with them more real than in body. He kept them from talking. He was present when Betty said, "Isn't it stuffy?" and when Gilbert said, "It's too cold to open the window." Betty could see Jim's hands, his gestures, his eyes, hear the timbre of this voice, watch the manner in which he smoked a cigarette, how he turned his head when he wanted to call her attention to something he was reading in the paper, how he looked when he was brushed and sleek for a party, how he looked tousled in bed. She recognized him by his walk at a distance and by the crow's feet of his eyes in a close-up. She could positively smell the essence of Jim's body, Jim's clothes.

She looked at Gilbert sitting beside her as they were being a rushed past rocky hill and parasol pine tree, and she said to herself, *Who is this man?* And she shivered in the morning chill. *It's the morning light*, she answered herself. *It's this terrible waking up without any hot coffee to start you going.* "It's the early morning." She found she had said the words out loud.

Gilbert gave her once of those quick, brilliant smiles of his which began with his mouth and ended in his eyes and which did not need words to explain. No wonder his mother loves him, no wonder Suzanne got pregnant, Betty thought, and then she stopped, horrified to have had such a thought. Was she going to let these other people intrude between her and Gilbert forever?

"You'll make it," he said. The train approached St.-Raphael, and how it arrived in that short time Betty could never know.

"I'll make what?" she said, not having the remotest idea what he meant.

"You'll make it," he repeated, and he smiled because still she didn't understand. "You know, for a flash I could see Mary in you—little Mary—it was very nice."

"What shall I make?" she doggedly said over again.

"I was using what I thought was an Americanism..."You'll make the grade. Isn't that the correct usage? You're a very good sport and all the rest of it, my dear, and I wish you all the luck and all the rest of it, and there is the train sliding into St.-Raphael. And now, my dear, you and I no longer know each other, for everyone in town, beginning with the station master, knows me. So I shall kiss you here and now, and when we get off the train, you will walk one way and I shall walk the other, and we shall not speak. *Adieu*, my dear, *adieu*."

He kissed her tenderly, and she was very grateful.

The cold air met them in the deserted station, but resolutely they turned their backs on each other for the sake of her reputation. She was thankful for the wonderful kiss he had given her with which to warm herself as she walked to her house.

13

Jim returns to France

Caterina was standing in the open door when Betty walked in on that cold, numb morning.

"Ah, Madame. It has been a wonderful experience. It has been too wonderful. I have a hot drink for you. Come to the fire and warm your hands, and then you will rest. Drink this herb tea. Don't try to think."

Betty looked at her in astonishment but instinctively did as she was told. Later she went up to her room and flung herself down on the bed. She must have slept, for she woke to see the bright sun. Someone had covered her with a quilt. Peter's delicate little face and Mary's brown eyes were waiting for her to open her eyes, they were all dressed; they had had breakfast and were ready to start off to school. When Betty came downstairs, there was Caterina drinking a cup of coffee and with a cup all steaming full waiting for Betty.

"Madame, I want to tell you something," Caterina began at once. "When I got off the train last night, I met one of the sisters at the hospital, and she told me that Monsieur Gilbert's baby was taken very sick after we left yesterday. So sick the doctor was alarmed and moved the baby to the hospital."

"But how terrible!" Betty cried, putting down coffee. "I must go at once to Gilbert. There'll be something that I can do."

"Just a minute, Madame, just minute. Monsieur Masse was here very early with the milk. I knew we would need bread, butter, and eggs, and I asked him to make inquiries before his delivery. He has just been here and gone. He went to the hospital, and he found out that Monsieur Gilbert was there with the baby. He is the only one allowed in. Madame Suzanne is in hysterics, and they will not let her inside because the baby is far too ill. They say there is little hope, the sisters, but they don't want to despair. They have given Monsieur Gilbert a bed, and he is to be served his meals there so that he need not leave the child."

"I must go to him, I must go to him at once!" Betty cried. "He will need me."

"You see, Madame, the child is very, very ill. No one else is allowed in, he cannot be disturbed. Not even Madame Suzanne. Monsieur Masse will return in an hour and tell us if there is any news. The last wish Monsieur Gilbert would have would be for you to create a disturbance at the hospital. All must be very quiet and calm, and you could not help but be upset. Monsieur Masse will come back in an hour. He has promised me." On and on went Caterina's soft voice.

Until finally Betty took another sip of coffee and said, "That is true. It might be better so. In an hour I could go. I would not want to create a disturbance."

It was three hours before Monsieur Masse came, but Betty did nothing because she constantly expected his return. She paced the garden. She helped Caterina with the beds. She went down to the promenade, but she gave Caterina her solemn promise she would not attempt to go any farther. Back and forth, and her mind unraveled last night's cloth, thread by thread, as she walked. How terribly Gilbert must feel, that he should have been making love while little Gilbert was hot with rising fever. How terrible that she had permitted it. How wonderful it had been. It was terrible and wonderful all in the same breath. Could they have done anything, if they had come home? The child would have been ill in either case, and Gilbert could have done no more then the doctor and the sisters. But that would not prevent him from recrimination. The child would get well. He would *have* to get well. Hadn't she seen Peter with hot dry skin and eyes that were over-bright with fever? Children could call up a temperature that raised the hair on your head and in no time they would sleep and recover. This child would recover. Children did not die; they were tough like Peter and Mary. Love. Yes, how she loved Gilbert. Her love for him would save his child, would heal and make him well. There was strength in willing a thing. She willed that Gilbert should love her, and he did, and she willed that the child would get well, and he would grow well. Already the fever was falling. She would will it to happen, and it would. Her love would turn over the world. Gilbert need not think he could turn aside the flood of her love with the absurd dams he built with convention and custom. He might use these weak arguments on a French girl, but for an American they were nothing. Anything was possible if you wanted it enough.

Back and forth she walked. She stopped to look at the girofleurs and gave them a brief cultivation and left the rake beside the walk. She couldn't concentrate on gardening. She reviewed all the things they had done together the night before—scraps of conversation. The face of a girl in the bistro, the smell of the market tables, the elegant restaurant, when Gilbert had first kissed her with the dancing clowns crying *"Embrassez."* The love he gave her, that terrible sensation of waking and hurry in a cold room. All this time the baby was sick, turning his hot little head; the sisters with giant coiffes were bending over his crib and rustling in the night. And Gilbert was there now, watching for the flicker of a change that might come. Did he give Betty a thought? Did he review any of the past night with her? Was his remorse too great, or did his mind halt for a second over some pleasurable incident and a half-smile come to his face at the thought? He must have one such flash of pleasure, and for that flash in his mind she clasped her hands and thanked heaven she had given him all she had to give. She would not change one moment of it, she would never regret one second, if only he would give her one smile in his mind.

She had left the promenade and was walking back to the house when Monsieur Masse came pedaling slowly up on his wheel. He was puffing with exertion as he came to a stop and took his pipe out of his mouth and walked the wheel. Caterina came running from the house, the wind catching her apron as she ran. "*Alors, alors,*" she cried.

"They do not know. They think it was something to do with the brain. It is very serious. No one can come in or out. Monsieur Gilbert is very tired. He rests on a cot in the room."

"Oh," said Betty, thinking of Gilbert tired, lying on a cot. "Oh, what is there to do? Should I go to Suzanne? Should I go to Madame Glisson? What can I do? Why don't I write him a note? That is it, I shall write a note."

"It must not disturb him," Caterina said, looking as though she would like to write it herself.

"Oh no, I shall write. Why didn't I think of it before?"

She raced into the house and dashed off, "Darling, I think only of you and little Gilbert. What can I do? Only tell me. Forever, your Betty." She sealed it, for she knew Caterina's sharp eyes would have no compunctions. Then she decided to write notes to his mother and to Suzanne. It made her feel very busy and useful. She wrote each a proper sweet page of "I do hope," "I am so distressed," "Please call on me if there is anything I can do to help," and with these she felt the flap of the envelope unsealed and with a small tip gave them to Monsieur Masse.

The children came home for lunch, and there was the bustle of food and talk of school. Betty wanted to walk back with Peter, but Caterina had some fool story that she had to go out on business, and by the time it was straightened out, Peter had gone, and Caterina had skipped out and left Betty with lunch dishes and Mary to look after. Somehow she got through the afternoon and dinner, and when the children were in bed, she flung on her coat and hat and ran out of the house. Caterina would have to stay with the children. Caterina was becoming a nuisance and altogether too forward. In the dark, Betty walked rapidly to the hospital, where she took several turns up and down, trying to decide which was Gilbert's window. There were a number of low nightlights. Wouldn't a miracle happen and let Gilbert come out the door for a breath of fresh air? She prayed fervently for this to happen, but it didn't. The hospital was located in the old section of town, and it was very quiet. A group of men came down the road, singing, and she went down a side street to avoid meeting them. She wished she dared to call on Suzanne, but it was too late. She walked back to the hospital, but nothing happened. A doctor's car drove up, and the doctor went in a side entrance. Sadly, she went home by way of Gilbert's house. The shop had its shutter pulled down, and it looked dark and deserted. She started to ring, changed her mind, and walked home on the trot to warm her feet.

Caterina was waiting, bent over the fire, and gave one of her catlike smiles which said, I told you couldn't see him.

Finally, Betty went to bed and couldn't sleep. She turned the light on and off a dozen times, and the minutes crawled. Toward morning, she fell into a heavy sleep to be awakened by Caterina tiptoeing into the room. She could see the light coming up in the sky through the half-open shutters. It was early.

"Madame, Monsieur Masse is here. I wanted to tell you when the children would not be with you. The child is dead."

Betty took it without a change. "And Monsieur Gilbert?" she said. "How is he?"

"That Monsieur Masse did not know. But we can imagine. Poor soul."

Betty got up at once and dressed. She helped the children get dressed for school, was in the way of Caterina who usually prepared breakfast, but Caterina did not complain. Betty said she was going to walk with Peter and Mary up to school. She was dressed in plain dark blue. She made a mask of herself, covering up every trace of emotion. She just didn't think. She left Peter at his school, kissed him, walked with Mary, saw her safely in the door, and then she was free. She went to the hospital and inquired at the office for Monsieur Gilbert.

"Monsieur Gilbert in not here now," the sister told her.

Betty half ran to Suzanne's. The blinds were closed, and there was no car in front. Timidly, she rang the bell, and Suzanne's sister opened the door. "I wondered," Betty stammered. "Can I see Madame Suzanne for a moment? I have just heard, I only wanted to say how terrible it is. Is there nothing I can do?"

The woman looked sad, weary. "My sister is ill. There is nothing to be done."

"Will you tell her Madame Barton called? I am so sorry. And will you tell Madame Suzanne if there is anything I can do..."

"There is nothing. She is too ill to be talked to. Your note came. She can see that," the hard voice said without a change of expression. Slowly, the door shut on *"Au revoir, Madame."*

Betty wished she had never rung. What had made her come to this house when Gilbert's car was not outside? What a horrible woman the sister was. Poor little Suzanne. The baby was all that held Gilbert to her, and now that tie was gone. Gilbert would be kind to Suzanne, but he would never... The thought of Gilbert was too much for Betty; tears choked her thoughts. She pressed her hands until the nails hurt. She must not break down in front of Madame Glisson, the last place where she could find Gilbert. She braced her shoulders for the ordeal. To meet him in front of his mother would be like meeting him I front of the whole town.

Betty arranged her face in her little pocket mirror. Was it only thirty hours ago that she had done the same thing in Nice? Thirty years. No lipstick or rouge this time. A dab of powder on her nose. She stiffened herself and walked quickly to the office. The shutter was still pulled down over his shop window; no car was in front. Betty's heart sank. But that might not mean Gilbert was not home. She rang at the back when the shutters were down. She walked into the hallway. No one came, and she rang again. A door opened in back, and Madame Glisson came.

"Ah, Madame Barton." Her voice was weary. "Come in. I cannot ask you to stay, but at least come in for a moment."

Betty followed her without a word.

"I suppose you have heard the news. Yes, of course, it is a blessing. That is the only way I can see it. It does solve so much. Gilbert. He was here a moment. Gone. Walking, God knows where. I could not keep him. It was like having a crazy man. Let him walk and sleep and pass the time, and then time will heal it for him. You want to see my son. Unless he comes to you—I cannot prevent that—but you must not see him, Madame Barton. You know that, I know that, we all do. These things grow, they come to a head, they pass. I can only ask you to be the lady I know you are and not annoy my son. It is, of course, ridiculous. You haven't heard when your husband returns? No? Well, the sooner the better, and he will. It will have to work out that way, of course. Hard when you're young, but you're not too young. You've lived enough to know. We have to face these things. Gilbert's whole future would be jeopardized. Out of the question, naturally. This Suzanne thing can now run its course. It will only be a matter of weeks. A few months, and he'll forget her name. The child, of course, that will take him some time.

"You told me before you have never met death," Madame said, a little more kindly. She talked of it as though death were a person to meet on the street.

Betty shook her head.

"When you have a dear one die, then you know about death. Death is one with life. There is no margin between. But Gilbert will forget. He'll forget before the year is out. She sighed and looked at Betty. "What are your plans, Madame Barton? You must have plans, you know."

"I haven't any plans," Betty said. "I only wanted to see Gilbert, that is all."

"But Madame Barton, I understand very well. Indeed, there is only one thing that I do not understand. That is, having such a wonderful husband as you have, why should you find the need to wander? You say it is not my business, but dear Madame, you have made it my business. Now, I must tell you something. My son, Gilbert, was here for a moment this morning, and as he was going out the door he said, 'Mother, if Betty comes here, and she will, tell her that I cannot see her. At least, not for the present.' You see, Madame, I wanted tell you as gently as I could. I know that you are very fond on my son, too fond, and yet those were his words. You probably will not want to believe them. But I can do no more for you." Madame Glisson put out her hands as though she wanted Betty to leave.

Betty stood up. Her face was set. "I don't know, I must admit, whether or not to believe you. But there is no use in my staying, is there?" She did not want to break down in front of the old lady. She nodded good-bye.

Madame said, "Good-bye, Madame. Time will help you, too. Someday you'll feel more kindly toward me. You must not act foolishly now. Good-bye, my dear." Quietly, she closed the door.

Betty walked out onto the street and stopped to find a handkerchief, she could not see for the tears. She was standing by the florist, and she stopped to look up into the brilliance of the color. It never ceased to be a surprise to her that a tiny town like St.-Raphael could maintain a shop that surpassed anything she had ever seen elsewhere. The cyclamens, the calla lilies, the anemones, the primroses. How beautiful they were. What violets. Flowers were beauty. They were love. They represented what she thought about Gilbert. He never, never could have said he did not want to see her. His mother had made it up to get rid of her. She was convinced of it. He would come to see her and lay his head in her lap. Perhaps he was there now, looking for her. She must hurry back. Why had she ever left the house? How terrible if he should come and not find her waiting for him? She would run all the way, and then, glancing again at the flowers, she decided to take one minute more to send him flowers. She would order arms full.

She went into the shop and ordered them. She wanted them loose, dark-streaked anemones, violets, white carnations, little yellow primroses. She had a big box filled with their dewy fragrance. Nervously, she wrote a card: "To my beloved. My thoughts are with you." There was the problem of where to send it. Finally, she decided on the hospital. The kind sisters would see to it that it was delivered. Luckily, the card had an envelope which could be sealed. The inquisitive eyes of the little sales-girl, who stood with her high heels inside the big black wooden sabots, did their best not to miss anything. Betty kept her eyes lowered, paid for the flowers, and hurried home.

No Gilbert. Caterina was desolate, but Monsieur had not called. Betty began to suspect Caterina of lying, too. The whole French world was in league to keep her and Gilbert apart.

The day passed, the night passed. Betty stared at the sunrise through the shutter; she had slept in snatches. It seemed as though she had never slept. She got up and dressed the wooden figure of her body. The children made her keep a routine. Caterina fed her. Life must go on. The day dragged through its course. It was Thursday, and the children were home all day. She helped them with their lessons. Caterina suggested a walk. Betty refused, but the children pleaded, and she consented to go if they left a note pinned to the door for Gilbert, telling him just where they would be. They followed a dirt road which led them to the hills in back. Passing a brook, they saw blue pervanche growing, giant periwinkles as blue as the deepest sky. Betty had never seen them before. They found romarin with its sweet little lavender flowers. The pretty leaves of the laurier tin and the beautiful myrtle. Caterina called it *erba-daou-lagui* in Provencal, and she said it was a symbol of happy lovers. Betty broke off some sprigs and hid them in her pocket.

Betty insisted that they return before the children were ready. She began to fear that they would miss Gilbert. For a moment as they approached the house, she thought he had been there. The note was gone. But Mary found it blown over the side of the porch and folded tightly as they had left it. there were no marks from the wheels of his car or other signs of his having been there, although Betty's hope persisted.

In the evening, she sat up until midnight with a bright fire burning and the kettle ready on the gas stove for tea. But he never came. She had a hard time keeping a awake, but when she finally did go to bed, sleep left her.

Another day. Her body was growing sick with her mind, but the children were noisy, laughing, making their demands. She decided when they were off for school that she would go back to bed, but Caterina pooh-poohed it as nonsense.

"We'll go for a little walk, Madame. The air, it will revive you."

Caterina led her into town, under the railroad bridge, by the old part, and out along a road Betty had never followed. With a bend, they came in sight of the cemetery. Betty's eyes lighted upon it. "Why," she said, "he will have to bury the child."

Caterina nodded. Slowly, they went in through the big heavy iron gates which stood open expectantly. Caterina crossed herself and bent her knee. She was carrying her beads as though this had been her intention all along. It was another world. There was little green. It did not dominate as it does in American graveyards. Stone, gray stones, placed close; the surrounding walls were high. The walks were fine gray pebbles. Nearly all the graves were decorated with lavender and gray bead flowers, there were hundreds of these artificial decorations, which seemed strange with the abundance of living flowers, and they were made in every conceivable form. The eye was bombarded with these dots of gray and lavender. Only in the English section, and this comprised a surprisingly large space, was there green ivy and a few faded bunches of real flowers. They came to a small, freshly dug hole, and they knew this was where the baby would be buried. Caterina said a prayer, and Betty stood staring down into the opening of dark, wet earth. Slowly, they walked out side and started back.

Caterina put her arm through Betty's and held it there. Betty looked up and saw the procession coming toward them. She was turned to stone herself as she looked and watched it pass. There were two small choir boys with long black skirts and white lace surplices. One carried a box on a pillow. The other swung an incense holder. The road was muddy, and sometimes their feet splashed. A light rain had begun to fall. Behind them came the priest in his long straight robe, carrying a Bible in his hand. The small white casket was laid on a black hearse drawn by two black horses. One would have been enough for such a small burden. Suzanne followed on foot, dressed in black with a long black veil, and her sister walked beside her. There were three other strange women in black. And among them stalked Gilbert, his head bare in the rain; he literally stalked. He was in black and carried in his hand a black hat. He did not see any of the people around him; at least, he paid no attention to them, as though they were not there. Betty knew he did not see her. Several people were standing and watching beside the road for the funeral to go by. Gilbert looked years older, his face gray, lined, his mouth hard. Betty drew into herself every particle of Gilbert that she could in the short time that he approached, was apposite to her, and walked by. One trouser leg was spattered with mud. His eyes seemed to be focused on the white casket. There were flowers on the casket. Some of them she hoped were her flowers.

Betty wanted to hold out her arms to Gilbert, to tell him how she longed to comfort him. He did not know that she was there. She and Caterina turned and watched the little procession plod on and through the iron gates. It was gone. Caterina pressed her arm, and they walked home.

She had seen Gilbert. She could almost have touched his hand. With a few steps, she could have. But what a tragic Gilbert. Why could she not comfort him? Did he not want her? He would, he must return to her. He would have to; he was hers. She would wait until the stars fell. She would love him, heal him, soothe him, minister to him. But that white, drawn face of his planted a doubts in her mind. How far away he seemed. As though he had died, too, there was something horrible about it. Like one those dreams in which one sees the inevitable about to happen but cannot move a muscle to prevent it.

One day took the place of another day. Was if four days since their night of love together? Was it six days? It was hard for her to remember. She and Gilbert were living in the same town together, but they did not meet. Was it fate? Or was Gilbert trying so hard from his end, and Caterina from her end, to keep them apart? God knew she herself tried every conceivable means to bring them together. She spent hour after hour at night reviewing the various ways that they would meet. But the children and Caterina were omnipresent, and she could never seem to carry out her plans. She was like a sleepwalker who has insane desires but lets herself be led like a child. Of course, Madame Glisson and Suzanne were doing all in their power to restrain Gilbert. Betty comforted herself with this, but all the time her brain told her that if Gilbert wanted to, he would come to her. She needed sleep, she longed for sleep, but she could only sleep in nightmare snatches. She asked Caterina if there were not some drug she could take to make her sleep, but Caterina shrugged and said she didn't know. Betty could only think of triple bromide and didn't know the French for it. "Why don't we go to the doctor and get a prescription?" she suggested.

"Go to the doctor, and have the doctor and his wife gossiping all over town? I guess not. We'll not go one step to the doctor," Caterina had answered.

Betty looked at her and thought about it. Gossip? Did people gossip? Perhaps it was better to let well enough alone, but God knew she'd like to sleep. She wanted to talk, too. She thirsted to talk to someone about Gilbert. That was dangerous.

Caterina never left her. Sometimes all four of them walked over to school together and let the breakfast dishes stand. Then, when Peter and Mary were in school, Caterina would lead her on long walks. They came to know the roads for miles around. Caterina was foxy. They went past Gilbert's shop either when it was closed and shuttered or at lunchtime when no one was in the streets, or she would lead Betty home by some back road, avoiding the center of town altogether.

Anyone would think (Betty argued with herself) *that I was a crazy woman and Caterina was my keeper. I might just as well be. Perhaps I am insane and don't know it. How shocked Gilbert would be to know that I've lost my mind for his sake and wouldn't recognize him if I met him.*

She wrote Gilbert a letter. She waited a week, but she never received an answer. There may have been reasons why. He may not have got the letter, his mother could have seen it first and torn it up, and Betty would not put it by Caterina to have intercepted any answer. So Betty came to a decision. She was going to see Gilbert. She laid her plans carefully, waiting until the children were asleep and Caterina herself was preparing for bed. Her coat and hat were ready, and she slipped out the back door. She half ran all the way into town. At Gilbert's door, she stood to get her breath, and then she boldly rang the bell. She rang it for a long time. He could not fail to be home this time, but she prayed desperately that he would be. At last there was a door opened in back, and someone was coming through the hall. She held her breath, but from the slowness of the step she knew it was Madame Glisson.

Betty was ready meet her. "I am sorry to disturb you at this hour, but, Madame, it is very important. I must, it is imperative that I see your son."

Madame Glisson was in her nightgown with a coat thrown over her shoulders, her hair was done up in curl papers, and she looked very old, wrinkled, and delicate. Betty expected her to shout, I have told you before you cannot see my son. Go away. But gently she took Betty's hands. "My dear," she said. "Come inside." Slowly, she led Betty through the dark hall into the apartment. It was evident that Gilbert was not there. Madame made Betty sit with her on the couch. She kept smoothing Betty's hand as she held it in her lap. "I'll tell you what I've done. I have sent Gilbert to Paris for a time. I had a little money put aside, and I insisted that he go. I like you, Madame Barton, I like you a lot. I admire you, too. But you haven't much sense. You say you are over here to learn new ways. Learn one of our French secrets to a happy marriage: namely, fall in love with your own husband. The pair of you have all the makings of the happiest of couples. As far as Gilbert goes, he is so impractical, it would never work. Another requisite to a happy marriage is money. You may think you don't need a lot, but you need money when you have children. Gilbert hasn't any. Your husband has lost a lot, but in no time he'll make it back again. You have loved each other before, and it will all come back again. But with Gilbert, it is madness, it is what we call an infatuation, and an infatuation will pass. An infatuation can be real one minute, and a few days later it will be so changed you will not recognize it."

"And you have sent Gilbert away to Paris," Betty said, the first she had spoken.

"You see—that distresses you. For you know there will be a change. An infatuation is not strong enough to withstand a change."

Betty looked around the room, and she could feel Gilbert in every object. His books, a half- empty package of his cigarettes, a coat of his hanging on the rack on the back of the door. He was part of the old Norman furniture, part of the neatly piled briquettes of coal. She was trying to get used to the idea of his being in Paris. What would he do there? He could so easily have said good-bye to her. Would she have ever let him go?

"It does upset me," she finally said. "I had never dreamed he would or could go away Without coming to me."

"I think you should return to America, Madame Barton."

"Not now," Betty said. "Or should I say, not yet."

"Ah, Madame, how can I show you? Gilbert has gone from your life. He was a flash, with you a minute, gone the next. He won't return. Can't you see he has not said 'good-bye', and when he returns he will not return to say 'hello'? The thing was like that." Madame held her thumb and forefinger and blew on them. "*Pouff*. And over with. He is fond of you, friends, but no more. It is cold in here. you must go."

"I suppose I shall have to," Betty said, standing. She was glad she had not shown Madame the weakness of tears. But she wanted to cling to all the things in the room that looked like her beloved. Were they ashes, grown cold? She shivered.

"You should not be out alone, unprotected," Madame said. "You look sick. You need your husband, Madame, to take care of you."

"I can manage alone," Betty answered.

Walking home alone in the dark, she tried to think, but she was incapable of it. It was as though all sensation had gone numb. *Gilbert was in Paris.* It made no impression on her mind other than the words as she said them to herself. *Gilbert has gone to Paris. He's gone.* They sounded like a sentence from her school primer when she was learning to read. Wooden. She didn't react one way or the other. She just accepted them as statements. Noun, verb, preposition, noun. Somebody might get excited by such a sentence, but she couldn't. She might as well say to herself, *Corn is selling at fifty cents a bushel.* Somebody might look upon that as life and death, a fortune wiped out, a matter of feeding his children or starving to death. But what did it mean to her? And that Gilbert had gone off to Paris and left without a good-bye meant to her no more. What was going to happen to her now? Could his going away be final? Never, never, she thought passionately. She was thoroughly inconsistent.

She walked along the lonesome, poorly lighted promenade without fear. If she had met the roughest sort of person, she would have tossed him aside. No one could molest her, no one could hurt her, no one could touch her. When she walked up on the porch, she found Caterina positively wringing her hands.

"Oh, Madame, Madame! What a relief to see you back. I have worried so. I have been torn whether to leave the children alone to run out to find you, and I have died a thousand deaths with worry. Oh, Madame, are you all right? You have been to his house, have you not? You've found he has gone. Ah, my poor little Madame Betty, my poor little one, how you must suffer. What shall I do, what can I do?"

"Nothing," Betty said coldly. "Caterina, you're acting like a fool. Go to bed. That is where I am going." And she went without another word and slept heavily the whole night, the first time since the night of the carnival. She awoke in the same numb, unthinking state, but her body was refreshed.

Let's go for a walk up in the hills," she volunteered herself after breakfast. "We'll let the housework go hang." She listened to Peter's and Mary's enthusiasm and troubles at breakfast as though these were the only things that interested her. After a two-hour hike, they returned to be house to cook elaborate food. Betty then decided they would clean house. She scrubbed floors herself, wisped down the walls, cleaned all the shelves in the china closet. When night came and Caterina was ready to drop with fatigue, Betty laughed scornfully. "Going back on me, are you?

You're not that weak. Read to me, Caterina, read while I sew." Betty cut out a dress for herself and basted it, her needle running in and out like a shuttle. They sat there, Caterina's head dropping to her chest every five minutes to be brought to with a jump by Betty's sharp command, "Go on and read, girl. I have to be amused."

This went on day after day. It would be one, two, and three before they would retire and up bright and early at six. Betty finished her dress and started on Mary's wardrobe. Two new dresses, hems let down, darning stockings, patching Peter's trousers. She knit a sweater for Mary. She was like a mechanical toy that is wound up too tight and doesn't know how to stop. She would cook enough food for six people and then barely taste a mouthful herself. The children and Caterina grew fat on it, but Betty seemed to lose a pound a day. Her eyes looked hot and over bright.

There was madness in her cleaning. They washed draperies, blankets, linens. They scrubbed, scoured, cleaned everything that wouldn't melt or spoil by washing or rubbing. "I thought the French were demon cleaners," Caterina said, the Italian coming out in her. "But you're worse than all of France."

"I'll clean your soul before I'm through with you." Betty laughed.

Caterina was sure Madame was running a fever. *I've got to do something desperate*, Caterina thought. *The children cannot help, they do not seem to notice that their mother is wasting away, but children don't see things like that.* She wanted to go to Madame Glisson or Mademoiselle Roule, but she hesitated. No one came to call but old Monsieur Masse, and he and Caterina would whisper away in the kitchen. He, too, noticed the change in Madame Barton.

Finally, Caterina did the desperate thing. She didn't tell Betty until the children were in bed and Betty was seated in front on the fire ready for her night's sewing. Betty said sharply, "Come on and read, Caterina. Or are you pretending to want to go to sleep again? *Le Rouge et le Noir*. We'll finish it soon. It was recommended to me by his mother, you know. On purpose, I see now. Do all Frenchmen desert their mistresses? And then get hung? I can see he is going to get hung. What shall we read when we've hung him?"

Without warning, Caterina spoke. "Madame, I have taken a liberty. I have cabled Monsieur Barton to come."

Betty turned to look at Caterina, not registering what the girl had said. She looked at her while the idea took effect.

Caterina repeated her statement in her soft voice. "He has received it by now." She added.

Betty began to react. She called Caterina a great many rude names. She stood up and walked rapidly around the room, returning to the couch. "How dare you?" she kept repeating. When she had quieted down, she had the curiosity to add, "What did you say to him?"

Caterina looked into the fire. "I took the liberty of saying, '*Venez vite. Madame malade. Caterina.*'

"But that's a lie," Betty shouted. "I'm not sick at all."

"That's a question," Caterina said placidly. "Some might say you were sick, very sick, lovesick. I didn't say what kind of 'sick' you were. I think he should be here soon, don't you?"

"Jim here?" Betty said. Busily, she began to picture Jim in Merchantville receiving the telegram. Would he be concerned because she was ill? Would he at once begin packing his bag, making arrangements for his boat? Or would he go and see Roberta? Would they whisper possibilities and plans for the future? The scenes blurred, but vividly she could see the staircase in her father's house—halfway down there was one step that was a little lighter than the rest, and it squeaked when you stepped on it, and she could see herself in her nightgown creeping downstairs when she heard her father's hearty voice call out, "Hello, darling," to Betty's mother. He had just come home from a trip, and Betty was supposed to be in bed, but the squeaking stair betrayed her, and she was discovered in her secret descent, and her father cried. "Hello, Bettikins," and, running up the stairs two at a time, he had caught her in his arms, and she, between fright and pleasure, had not had time to run back to bed. She would like to see her father's face again. She adored her father. Transferring this childish memory of her father to Jim, she looked up and saw Jim standing in the doorway with his arms held wide. He dropped his bag, he tossed aside his hat, his arms were held out for her. She could see him as clearly as though he were actually there. How familiar he was. He was symbolic as he stood with his arms held wide, a symbol for what was safe, what was known, a protection, a pillar, a tower. She knew him completely. Was it for this she had come to France, to see her husband standing familiarly in the doorway, his arms held open for her?

She turned to find Caterina watching her closely. Caterina always gave the impression of someone looking through a crack in a door. Betty felt her thoughts were being spied on, and she grew confused. "I think you have taken a liberty, Caterina," Betty said stiffly. "You had no right to do such a thing."

"But what was I to do, Madam?" Caterina said with her hands and shoulders. "Someone had to do something. You can't deny it. And quick," she added, as though she had just thought of it.

"Caterina, what shall I do if he does come? You don't half understand what you have done. He'll write; he won't come. Do you really think he'll come?"

"But of course he will."

"But I'm not ready for him," Betty said, and then she thought what a foolish remark that was.

"You are not to tell the children," she added quickly, "until we know for sure. No use getting them all upset."

"Oh, never, Madame. I would not think of such a thing. Wait for that until Monsieur Jim is here in the house."

Betty felt a shiver to hear Caterina speak of Jim's arrival with such finality. How would they meet? Was it fear she felt, or the pleasure of expectation? She could not seem to picture Jim and Gilbert fighting a duel over her, the melodramatic outcome of a Stendhalian book, but that did not happen in real twentieth-century life. It was what ought to happen, she consoled herself.

For the first time since she and Gilbert had kissed each other; that last, long, desperate kiss on the train as it was easing into the St.-Raphael railroad station, she admitted to herself that Gilbert was no longer actually by her side. It was a sensation of drowning. Fiercely, she held his image close, but the water was clouding. Gilbert was all, Gilbert was everything. That night they had had together proved it, but there was a sickening in her throat that made her struggle to breathe again the sweet air of his breath upon her cheek. He had not come to her. She had to face that. He had not tried to come to her, once. He had passed her on the muddy road with his eyes on the little white coffin of his child, and he had not even known that he was passing her by. He had not turned his head to see her standing there. She began to wonder if she had been standing there or if she had dreamed that she was there. The death of his child was a terrible dream, and she must struggle to regain her consciousness and make it all a lie. He would come to her, he would have to come to her, because he loved her and she loved him.. He had not come, however. That was the fact she could not dodge any more than she could dodge a cold, hard boulder lying in her path. It bruised her hands, but she could beat her hands on its cold, ungiving surface. He had not come; he had not written a word to her. He no longer knew of her existence. Some of her flowers lay on his child's coffin, and he must know that she had sent them. He did not want to see her. That was the fact she had been trying not to say to herself.

＜ ～

A cablegram arrived: "Coming, Jim." That was all. It was enough. The children were not at home when it was brought to the door, and Betty stood turning it over and over as though Jim might have written something else in the corner, and she didn't want to miss it. *Coming, Jim, coming, Jim*, the words repeated. Jim was coming, Jim was coming. She nodded her head to the man who brought it and handed him some change she had in her apron pocket without even counting it. The man told his wife that evening that the American lady who rented a villa from the Countess was queer in the head. "Coming, Jim," Betty said to Caterina, who was prodding clothes into the wash boiler, and she handed her the slip of paper. "One reason it isn't real," Betty continued, "is that the French print everything on such thin paper. As though they didn't believe in cablegram, such flimsy stuff. I suppose it is another form of American extravagance to expect a solid, thick piece of paper. Why print it on paper at all, is what I say, going the French one better. Just let it come over the air like radio." Betty did look a little lightheaded, and her eyes didn't focus properly when she was talking. She looked as though she were always listening for something she couldn't quite hear.

Caterina, however, wiped the soapsuds from her hands and beamed. "Thank heaven," she said solemnly. "That is settled." And she went back to the wash, singing an Italian song she knew as a child. To her, the paper was as solid as Monsieur Jim's own hearty voice. "And if Monsieur Jim says he is coming, he will come." Caterina beamed into the steaming, bubbling sheets.

He did, too. Before they knew it. A week went by, and he was there.

He threw open the front door as though he had been in the habit of throwing it open all these past sad weeks. The house was filled with him in a minute.

The children were delirious. It was too much for them, and they ran and screamed and threw their little bodies about, always returning to "Daddy, Daddy, Daddy," as though he were a big magnet and they helpless nails. Mary and Peter, too, looked as though they had a sudden fever, their cheeks like poppies, their eyes shining. Betty had done nothing to prepare them.

Here was Jim in the house. He dominated the house, his hat on one chair, his coat on another, bags all over the place, and Jim himself as big and tall as the Woolworth Building, his voice booming out and his shoes clumping on the tile floor.

Caterina actually lost her head, she all but danced. She clapped her hands, she ran with no purpose, she exclaimed with pleasure just for the very masculine smell that pervaded the house. And when she peeped into the room where Jim was, she made little cooing noises and stood with her hands held together in front of her, her head on one side and her black eyes saying all the things her mouth could not. She was no good at all in getting dinner ready, and the dinner half cooked on the stove was in great danger of being burned.

"What has got into everyone?" Betty said when she had let Jim kiss her and she had given him a quick little dab of a kiss in return. "You

might think no one had ever seen you before, the way they are all carrying on about you, and you don't look a bit different." She gave a self-
conscious little laugh, and then her eyes seemed to wander around the
room, hunting for something. "You should have let us know, Jim, the
boat and train and all. 'Coming, Jim,' is all we had to go on, and how
in the world could we go to meet you on that? Why didn't you telegraph
from Paris? I hope we have enough for dinner, although Caterina was
sure you came in on the Bremen."

"I did," Jim said, rubbing his hands. "My God, it hasn't changed a
bit."

Caterina ran into the room at the mention of her name, laughed at
nothing, clapped her hands together, and ran back to the kitchen.

"I'm so happy, I'm so happy, I'm so happy," Mary sang as loudly as she
could, and she flung herself at her daddy for another bear hug.

"What sort of a trip did you have over, Dad" Peter said in a very
grown-up voice. Then he went over in the corner and stood on his head,
his latest accomplishment.

Husband and wife did nothing but avoid each other's eyes, thankful for all these minor interruptions so that they wouldn't have to
come to terms. Betty sat on the arm of a chair, winding a dish towel
around her arm, her apron still on, and with a toe balancing her so
that she could run out to the kitchen in a minute. Jim lit a cigarette,
took two puffs, and threw it into the fireplace. He kept striding about
the room, and when he looked at Betty it was in quick darts, avoiding
her eyes, and the children who kept rushing him were enough of an
excuse. Betty looked at him sharply every time he looked away. She
noted an old suit but very neatly pressed, a fancy flashy shirt, and a
couple of lines along his cheek which she could swear were new. He
seemed tired around the eyes, but who isn't after a long train ride?
He hadn't met her squarely yet, and this pleased her. She felt she was
the stronger of the two.

Dinner came to their rescue. Caterina brought it in as self-consciously as though Jim had come to see *her*. "I am eating in the kitchen to
give you more family privacy," she said in mincing French.

"Don't be an idiot, Caterina," Betty said. "Bring in another plate and sit with us as you always have." Betty translated for Jim, "Caterina says that she won't eat with us as she has always done. She wants us to be intimate, she says. Isn't she absurd?"

Jim gave Betty a quick look, to see if he should laugh. He was obviously ill at ease. "See you're serving wine these days," he said, putting out his fourth cigarette.

"Oh, yes," Betty said. "Don't you approve? I rather like a little with dinner." Her voice sounded very affected, but what could she do about it?

"Gilbert taught her," Mary said brightly. "Even we get tastes when he comes to dinner."

Betty opened her mouth but could say nothing.

"Oh," said Jim with the same guarded casualness. "I had almost forgot him. You haven't mentioned him in your letters lately. How is Glisson these days? Business terrible as usual?"

"He's not here now." Betty spoke rapidly. "He's in Paris. That child of his, you know, he died. Upset him pretty badly. I was talking to his mother the other day. He almost had a breakdown. She made him take the trip to get away." She felt she had explained it very well. She took up a spoonful of soup, and she looked up to find Jim's eyes full upon her. His eyes were staring at her face. They were brown eyes, not light gray.

"God, Bet, you look terrible. What is it, what's happened to you?"

Caterina came into the room like a mouse, holding her full soup plate in her hands, clutching her napkin and silverware. She slipped into a chair at the far end of the table, trying not to interrupt Jim.

Jim turned to look at her and continued, "I got Caterina's cable that you were sick, and, of course, I came without a question. But, God, what is it?" You look as though you'd seen ghosts. You must have lost twenty-five pounds."

"Ten," Betty said, wishing the blood would not rush up to her face.

Jim continued to stare at her.

"Mother's not sick," Peter said. "She can't sleep, that's all."

"That's all, eh?" Jim said.

"We have not seen Gilbert since the carnival," Mary said in her clear, high French. "And I think Betty misses him." She had forgot that her father was not accustomed to French.

Rapidly, Caterina outtalked Mary's French. Caterina, of course, could speak only in French.

"Ah, Monsieur, we cannot tell what has been the trouble with Madame. A malady, a melancholia, a disease that cannot find a name. I tell her she needs her husband, and then he will cure all her troubles at once. She does not need a doctor to tell her that. It is what all we women need. Husbands are the tonic for our ills." Caterina pursed out her underlip, and her black eyes twinkled, and everyone tried to forget the topic of Gilbert. Betty felt they had all stood too near a big crack in the earth. If she tried to stop Mary from talking about Gilbert, it would only make her worse. *What a child.* Mary, Betty could not help but think, might well be saying to herself, *What a mother.*

The rest of dinner was fairly mild. They talked a lot about America, now in English, now in French. The children used either language. Betty wanted to include Caterina. Parents, grandparents, houses, weather, Jim's trip across, his train ride. Jim was curiously silent on the stock market and his garage. He would only give a shrug for each. Betty wondered if it were in consideration of her, that he didn't want to bore her or that his worries were deep-seated. In either event, he hardly mentioned them. He seemed quieter, his voice was lower, he was too sober, too serious. Every time she looked up, she found him staring at her face.

The dinner was very good. It had been prepared with an eye to his coming. She and Caterina had looked up trains and concluded he might arrive on this one. She had told Caterina she could not bear the physical strain of meeting him at the station. She had refused to tell the children about the possibility. In truth, until he walked in the door, she had not really believed that he would come. He had seemed like one of the ghosts he accused her of seeing. But his body was no ghost. It was more real than all the American slang, baseball games, Saturday Evening Post, Uncle Sam cartoons, and Hudson cars rolled into one. Jim did not sit in a room without everyone else knowing it. Her mind had told her this, but she had expected a negative wave of repulsion on her part at seeing him. She was in love with Gilbert. Jim was no longer hers except on paper, and she expected to feel great distaste when she met him. But she didn't at all. She could not say what she felt with the tension of meeting him, but there was not a trace of drawing away. A couple of times she had raised her eyes to his face, and the sensation had come upon her, *Lord, it is good to see him*.

"Well, now," Jim said, folding up his napkin and turning to Mary and Peter. "How about helping me get unpacked?" They knew at once by his expression that there were presents.

"Oh, Daddy, we'd love to," Mary said, wanting to be polite but unable to restrain a skip.

"Which do you think we'd better open first?" Peter said solemnly, implying there was no use wasting time on the wrong bag.

"Let's try this one," Jim said. He entered their game beautifully. They unstrapped it together, and on top lay several packages in white paper. "You'll have to help me sort these out," Jim said when the children hung back. "Mary, call Caterina in from the kitchen. Peter, this is for Mother, and Peter, you give this to Mary. Mary, here, you give this to Peter." Jim then sat back to watch them all open their things. Mary had a child's typewriter, to help her to read and write her letters. Peter had a pair of roller skates which he had been asking for. Caterina had a very gaudy string of pearls beads with pin and earrings to match. And Betty had one of those pure luxury little bedjackets with quilting and eiderdown.

"Oh, Jim," Betty said. "You shouldn't have given me this. It is far too extravagant."

"Couldn't help it, dear, but that isn't the point. Do you like it?"

"I adore it." It was on the tip of her tongue to add, "Why didn't you get the children small, lightweight presents? It all has to be packed again to go home, and as it is, we've collected enough extra to fill two more trunks." But she saved herself in time. It wasn't logical to talk about packing trunks when she was preparing to spend her life in France. Nor was it ethical to accept presents from the man you were going to divorce.

I'm nervous, she comforted herself, *and I don't know what I'm doing.* She looked at the fragile but warm bit of fluff in her lap. It looked French, the sort of thing she could imagine Gilbert picking out for her in one of his carnival moods. Gilbert never had given her a present like this, but if he had the money he would, she staunchly told herself. "Did you really pick it out all by yourself? Somehow it doesn't look like you," she said. She could not resist the barb.

He was standing beside her chair. As she looked up, he met her eyes without flinching.

"And would you be jealous if another woman had helped me buy it?" he said.

She was the first to drop her eyes. "I don't know. I don't think so." Why should she be jealous of what Jim did?

"I'll tell you who helped me pick it out. An unknown salesgirl in Wanamaker's. I went to the women's lingerie department, and I told the girl, 'I want something for a lady who is sick and who lives in a cold house.' I didn't tell her the lady was my wife, because she would have wasted time on something practical. 'It can't cost over twenty dollars, and it has to be guaranteed made in the U.S.A. I have four hours before my boat sails in New York. What have you got?' And she brought out this. 'Wrap it,' I said. 'Charge it. And I'll take it with me.' And the other things were bought in much the same way. I caught that boat by split-seconds."

"You and your America." Betty laughed. "You're much too good to us. You should try being mean to us once in a while, we'd appreciate you more." Unconsciously, she was giving him some of Gilbert's philosophy.

"Is that what you are trying out on me?" Jim said quickly. "It happens that I'm very fond of you already." He turned from her to busy himself with the children, helping Mary insert a sheet of paper and hunt for the letters to spell her name. The racket of roller skates on a French tile floors was enough to drown out the boldest of conversations.

The gift of the bed jacket upset her. She didn't want to accept it, but by opening it she already had. Jim was generous, and too kind. His story of the salesgirl was disarming. Were wives so terrible? Did they always have to have practical gifts? Had he changed since he had been back in America alone? Was it Roberta's influence, or had she forgot what he was like? She felt very unsure of herself with him, as though she must feel her way.

Far more important than a decision on what she was to do with this filmy bed jacket was what she was going to do with Jim. She had forbidden herself any thinking on the subject before his arrival. It had been a protective inertia. She had been banking everything on Gilbert and what move he would make, and Gilbert had not lifted a finger, had indeed run away. It left her at a deadlock with the wind and herself. She put her hands out to grasp Gilbert, and they had met nothing. That moment with Gilbert was as real as anything she had ever experienced in life, she told herself, but it was as though she had dreamed the reality. With the night, he had vanished. She had eased the lack by walks in the hills, breathing in the pine air, gazing at flowers of the southern foreign climate, learning new names and seeing their habitats, the lush blue pervanche growing by a brook and wiry pungent thyme clinging to rocky ground. Things like these seemed to be all she could take hold of in the last six weeks. She and Caterina had found a short-stemmed violet, the first of the spring season, and it had smelled as sweet as the hothouse ones at home. It had helped her a lot to find that violet and to smell its fragrance. But still, she could not face the fact that Gilbert was gone. He had talked about leaving her if one can talk about leaving without staying, but his words had passed her by. She held tight to the idea that he was going to come back, while her reason was beginning to tell her he never would.

There was Jim sitting quietly in a chair. Jim was real; she could touch him. Her hand fell into the feathery warmth of his gift. His body was big, seated in the chair, the curve of his arm strong as he bent over to tighten Peter's skate strap. He was familiar, he brought with him waves of familiar objects. She pictured on her dressing table in their bedroom two glass vials shaped like a man and a woman resting side by side on a matching glass tray. The man held a delicate cologne water strangely called Sweet Hay, the woman, a heavy essence of perfume, La Nuit. Jim had bought it for her when he came back from the war in France. It was one of the first presents he had ever given her, and before they were married it had been the cause of a sentimental game between them.

"Mr. Man and Miss Paris," they had nicknamed them. Jim used to snuffle behind her ears and Whisper, "Oh, so it's Mr. Man tonight is it? Trying to make me jealous, are you? I'll put Miss Paris on my handkerchief and get even with you." He never had, because it was effeminate in his mind for a man to use perfume. Or if she had used Miss Paris, he would say, "Oh-ho. Trying to vamp me, are you? Parisian allure. Bedtime stuff." Years ago, she had used up the original perfumes, and the game was somehow forgotten, but she always kept the empty bottles on her dresser. She had left them at home as they were too difficult to pack.

"Do you remember Mr. Man and Miss Paris?" she asked him, without giving him a hint.

"No, I must say I don't," he said bluntly. "Who are they?"

"Oh, nothing," she said. She stood up and tossed the bed jacket onto her chair. Jim never remembered things like that. A foolish standard to hold a man to, but Gilbert would have remembered as much and more than she could about things that happened between the two of them.

She watched Peter and Mary with their father, and she recalled them with Gilbert. Which man it was did not concern them. Children were self-centered little animals. "Well, I guess it's time to get these kids to bed," she said in her best schoolmarm manner, which was a mild attempt to show female power.

Jim did not recognize it as that, but it irritated him. It always seemed as soon as he could enjoy his children, a household must come between him and them. He could not believe that Betty stooped to doing it consciously. "Suppose I help," he said unexpectedly.

At home, he seldom lifted a finger toward the routine care of the children. "Not my job," he defended himself.

"Well, if you like," Betty said, letting the exasperation show in her voice. She was guiltily aware that if Gilbert had offered his aid she could not have concealed her joy. The children, however, instead of their usual protests, were the first to start upstairs, all because their father was coming along. "Oh, Daddy," Mary said, holding his hand to her cheek. "How good you smell. I love, love, love you."

"Only because I smell good," Jim said, laughing.

"You smell ten times better than Gilbert," Mary said. "Than anybody else in the world except Mother." Her remark hardly eased the tension between her mother and father.

"And does Gilbert help put you to bed?" Jim said, forcing his laugh.

"No," Mary said. "He hasn't yet."

"He did too. New Year's, when we stayed at Aix. Don't you remember? Mother was sick," Peter said.

"I hadn't heard that one," Jim said. He was facetious. "You seem to have been sick a lot."

"I'll tell you about it later," Betty said coldly. There was no use having a scene in front of the children, and she could see one was coming.

The children made a wonderful cover. They had been the cause of bringing up the difficult subject of Gilbert, but they were also something to hide behind to avoid Jim's direct questions. It wasn't avoiding, it was putting off. That was the thing she did best lately. She had put off and put off until she hadn't the remotest idea what she thought or what she was going to do. If she was going to divorce Jim and marry Gilbert, she must make the leap soon. She must do it tonight. But to do this, she must know that Gilbert was behind her ready to take her hand, and Gilbert had turned into a shadow. The children talked about him as though he were still in the present and might return any minute. She needed the bolster, and she liked to hear Mary come out directly with his name. It was the way she should be talking herself. Warily, she watched Jim untying a knot in Mary's shoe string. What was going on in his mind? What would he accuse her of? She had a counterattack in Roberta and his meanderings with her. Would his actions with Roberta match up against hers with Gilbert? How much would she tell him about Gilbert? Make a clean breast of the whole thing and then say, "Well, when do you want a divorce?" Wasn't that fairest to both of them? She would put the divorce up to Jim, and that would salve her conscience.

When she rehearsed in her mind this meeting with Jim, she had always pictured herself saying, "Jim, I want a divorce," and then going on to tell him why. That was no longer possible without Gilbert standing ready in the back room. She would reverse the question and ask him when he wanted a divorce. He would want it when he knew all that had happened. He was too moral, too puritanical an American not to. What she would do with herself after that, she would toss out to sea and let the gods answer. She wanted the children, of course. She had always been a scrupulously careful mother, no court could deny that. How and where she should live, she could not even remotely decide. France was losing the glamour it had had now that Gilbert was fading. Jim brought with him a restless longing to see America again. There had been lonely spells when she ached for home. Maybe she could get a job in Philadelphia.

"Say, Bet, I'm having the living room, dining room, and front hall repapered before you get home. I meant to tell you."

"You're doing what?" Betty's voice overpitched itself. Jim had brought her back out of her thoughts with a thud.

"I have a sample of it here. It's cheap and good-looking. Picked it out myself. But I want your OK on it. I told Billings I'd drop him a card the first night I was here, so he could begin work at once."

"Why didn't you get Miss Spencer to decide? Doesn't she still remind you of birthdays and other anniversaries?" Betty tossed this over her shoulders as she went to get the kids clean pajamas.

"Miss Spencer? Oh, didn't I tell you? Had to let her go a month ago. The place is a mess without her, too. Boy, do I miss that girl. I have to type all the stuff evenings, and you know me with the two-finger hunt-and-find system." He laughed awkwardly.

"You didn't tell me," Betty said, coming back. "That's tough. I'm awfully sorry. Let's see your wallpaper." She was foolish enough to have thought, Maybe I can do the typing when we get back. "The paper really looks very smart, but I must say your two policies of saving money and spending money contradict themselves."

"Miss Spencer's salary came under office expenses, the wallpaper is house, and we really have been saving money on the house with you living here and me at Mother's, and I've paid Mother for my food, too. No telephone, no milk, gas electricity, water, coal. Boy, those things add up. And you should see the paper. The whole house needs doing over, but I'm only doing where it shows the worst. It leaked in the northeast corner, and the stuff is practically hanging off the wall. Had the leak attended to, naturally. We haven't had new paper since we were married. Didn't realize how dirty it was until I went in there just before I sailed. It looks ungodly. And besides, Billings needs the work. The guy is about starving to death."

Betty listened in silence to these comments of her husband's. They brought back America to her with the full volume of an orchestra. It was her American life, her house, the house she had lived in ever since she went into it as a bride. She knew Billings, too, and his wife and five children, through her work in public health. She could see Jim eating breakfast at his mother's. She could see him letting himself into the empty house shrouded in dust covers and thinking of her sick over in France and his children. "Go ahead, write Billing tonight. I don't see why you didn't go ahead anyway. You've chosen a paper that's perfectly plain, looks about like the one that's on there now."

"Yeah? Wouldn't you have been sore? I never would have heard the end of it, me choosing the paper without consulting you."

Betty had counted on retaining Caterina all evening. She had grown to depend on Caterina to such an extent this last month that it did not seem at all odd to her to have Caterina sit with a husband and wife on the first evening they had been together in more than six months. Caterina and she had sat together before a fire fox six weeks of evenings, and Caterina could still be useful to her as a buffer against Jim. But when the last good-night kisses had all been given and she and Jim came downstairs, Caterina was standing in the hall with her hat and coat on, ready to go out.

"I want to see my sister," Caterina explained to Jim over Betty's head. "You see, sir, with Madame Betty sick this way, I have not been able to go out a single evening. I was afraid to leave her alone." This last was added in a whisper as though Betty were not supposed to hear it.

Betty was about to protest that that was absurd, but Jim whispered back, "Is that so, really?" And they both nodded their heads like doctors talking over some case.

"Oh, yes, sir, it was terrible. A couple of times"—here Caterina's face grew unmistakably terrified—" I stayed up all night. I thought Madame would…" And Caterina plunged her clenched hand to her heart as though she were stabbing herself, she reeled backward in realistic pantomime, and then she opened her eyes to see if Jim understood her meaning.

"My God," Jim said. "*C'est terrible, terrible*."

"Oh, yes, yes," Caterina went on without a pause of breath. "We can laugh now." She laughed high. " And Madame can deny it, but that was the time Madame did not know what she was doing, she was—" Caterina nodded her head rapidly, winked, and twirled her finger around, tapping her forehead. Jim's eyes were bulging in sympathy. Neither one paid the slightest attention to Betty, who was doing her best to deny these exaggerated statements. Caterina's sly eyes moved over Betty's face, and she smiled back at Jim. "I want to go out tonight to see my sister."

"Well, well, you go right ahead," Jim said heartily. "Stay out all night. Madame and I have a lot to talk over." He put an arm of protection around Betty, and with his free hand he dived into a pocket. "Here, Caterina. Take this and enjoy yourself. You and your sister have a party." He handed her two ten-franc notes.

Caterina was a sunburst of smiles, and without stopping to put the money in her bag, she ran out crying, "*Merci, merci beaucoup. Le beau Monsieur Jim, merci*."

"Well, the nerve of that woman," Betty said, all her anger rushing to her voice at once. "You shouldn't have given her money, and if you had to give her some, ten francs was five too much, and Caterina hasn't got a sister."

"I would have given her a hundred francs to have alone, my dear," Jim said gallantly, and he led her into the living room, where Caterina had built a huge blazing fire, and he closed the door.

"Now, let's have it," he said when they were seated. "I get a cablegram, come quick, that you're ill. I come, and the kids say right out you haven't been sick, but you look like something the cat dragged in, haggard, lost ten pounds you admit yourself, there are mysterious references to this French guy, Gilbert. Damn Glisson, I say. You are friendly and hostile to me by turns. Now Caterina comes out that you tried to kill yourself, that you've been cuckoo, and nobody's seen this Frenchman for a month which seems to correspond to the length of time you've been off your head. Now, let's have the whole thing and straight."

"Oh, is that so, is that so?" Betty was standing up to him, her eyes snapping. "You think you can judge me like one of your children. Accuse me of this and that, knock me around, and go perfectly free yourself. Would you mind telling me what has been going on between you and Roberta? I get all hinds of stories about you and Roberta here, Roberta and you there. I've even had a newspaper clipping when you were hauled into court for reckless driving, and who was your companion? None other than our dear friend Roberta. Well, I'll let you set the date. It's up to you. I'm the gentleman, and I'll waive my rights to yours. When do you want the divorce?" Her voice was tense with hysteria.

"A divorce?" Jim stared at her, his mouth open. "Bet, my darling, my beloved. What have I done to you? I should never have talked to you the way I have. Caterina has only just finished telling me you've been off your head, and God knows you look it. You need kindness and love and care, and I'm a brute to you. My dear, my darling, I'll do anything, anything you want. Whatever you want, you can have. I love you, do you understand? I love you. That is all that counts. I should never have left you. God, you look near death, and I accuse you of things. Don't talk, please don't talk. Bet, my darling dear."

He tried to take hold of her, but she pushed him off. "When do you want your divorce?" she cried, her voice a scream. She looked at him as though she didn't know who he was.

"But my darling, who wants a divorce? I come in here, not knowing a thing that's happened, and find you like a death head. I'm all upset myself. I demand an explanation, but I don't want to hear a thing. I don't care what you've done or what you haven't done. As for Roberta, that is the most utter nonsense, old ladies' tales. I was lonely as hell without you, didn't know I loved you so much until I didn't have you, my whole business shot to pieces, and I must admit I have been drinking a lot. Roberta will flirt with anything, you know that. She drinks all the time now, she and Ellis never live together, she says he's some pervert. God knows, she'll talk to anyone, though, as long as they'll drink with her. That time I got held up was all her fault. She was driving, it was her car, and I was damn fool enough to take the blame. Roberta's an awful tramp. She's gone downhill fast. She means less to me than a woman you'd see on the streets. I swear it, on my heart, Bet dear. All this time, I have kept thinking, why did I let you stay over here alone, when can I ever get over to you with my damn business the way it is? I haven't known where to turn some days. I've been crazy. Your letters have grown less and less, nothing in them about yourself. When this cable came, I felt, Jesus, the girl has needed me for the weeks and hasn't told me, to hell with business, money or no, I just slammed a shirt in my bag and came. Your dad's lent me money, I'm head over heels in debt to the bank, but to hell with everything but you. Honest, Bet, won't you believe me, dear?"

Betty listened to this long speech. Her fury had spent itself. She stared at Jim as if to say, *Who is this man?* He talked of love and wives and women. There was a familiar warmth to his voice, and it was an anesthetic to her reasoning. "Gilbert," she began slowly, her eyes on the fire. When she looked at Jim, she could not think. Her tongue felt thick. "Gilbert has gone to Paris," she said with an effort.

"But my dear, let's leave him there. It is an excellent place for him," Jim's voice was low, cajoling. "I promise you, I won't talk against your Gilbert, for I know that you love all that is French."

Betty nodded her head slowly at this. "I love France," she said.

"Of course you love France, and you love your children, Peter and Mary." Some guardian angel inspired Jim to add, "And can't you learn to love your husband, too?"

A childish smile came to Betty's face. A smile of recognition at having heard it before.

"Madame Glisson said that when she told me that Gilbert had gone to Paris. 'And you, Madame'— these were her words— 'And you, Madame, must learn our French secret to happiness. Fall in love with your own husband.'" Betty looked vacantly at Jim and gave him a polite smile.

"Madame Glisson is a wise old lady, isn't she?"

"I suppose she is." Betty sighed heavily. When she spoke, each word was separate, unhinged from the rest of the sentence.

"Bet dear, sit down," he said, and gently took her hand and led her to the couch. She let him seat her. He sat on the footstool, and, with his arms around her body, he laid his head in her lap. He could not restrain his tears which fell on her hands. *She doesn't recognize me*, he thought. *She's going off her head*. And he tried to think what was the right thing to do. *Quiet, she needs quiet, rest. God keep me from making a false move*. As he held her, *I mustn't hold her tight*, he thought. One of her hands moved, and she began stroking his head.

"I wanted Gilbert to come to me," her voice said. "I wanted him to come and to lay his head in my lap. He never did, and now it is you."

Did she know who he was?

"You are crying," her voice said. "If I could cry, it would help so much."

"Oh, Bet dear, I will help you, I will help you. Only trust me."

"And what will you do?"

"I'll take care of you. I'll love you all over again as though we had never loved each other before. We shall have a new honeymoon. We'll start all over again. We haven't seen enough of each other these last years. It's been too mechanical, too dull, too used to each other. I accepted everything and gave you nothing fresh. We'll pretend it is ten years ago, and you and I are just meeting. After the war, only this time, instead of leaving France to find you, I come to France to find you. We'll really live the whirl in France, the whirl we've talked about all these years. Wait, wait." His voice was getting excited in spite of himself. He shouldn't excite her. He tried to quiet his voice. "When I was crossing Paris to the Gare de Lyon to get my train down here, the taxi was held up by traffic opposite a perfume shop, and I could look in the window. I shouted to the guy and made him turn around and take me back to the shop. You want me to show you why?"

"Oh, yes." Betty seemed curious, as Jim hoped she would be.

"I'll show you. I wanted to give you this when we were alone, you and me." He got up and fished around in one of his bags and brought her a little package. He sat on the stool at her feet to watch her open it. Her eyes seemed to him less vacant as they were centered on untying the paper.

She pulled aside the paper, lifted the lid of the box, and there were the same little glass figures holding the same perfume he had brought to her from France after the war. "Oh, Jim, my dear," Betty said, and her voice was quick and clear and normal.

"And, so you like it." Jim was as tickled as one of the children. "Say, you know what? That is what you were talking about a little while ago when you asked me about Mr. Man and Miss Paris. By Jove. You know, I tried all the way down here to think of those silly names and couldn't, and here you asked me right out and I didn't catch on. Funny your asking me that."

"Funny," Betty repeated. She was still shaky, but she seemed to know who he was. Jim felt this, but it was hard for him to realize what had taken place. For a minute there, he was sure she was going off her head, but now that her voice was normal again, he began to wonder if he hadn't imagined it. She gave him a little half-smile which had intelligent recognition behind it. The smile had come into her eyes, too. There had been no smile in her eyes before, just vacancy. *What a queer thing the mind is*, he thought, looking up at her. And how wonderful it is to see my wife smiling at me.

"Mr. Man and Miss Paris," he said, looking down at the glass figures in her lap. "It was a long time ago when I gave you the first ones. What happened to them, anyway?"

"They are on my dresser at home."

"You've kept them all these years?"

"Of course."

"I think I'll give you a new set every ten years," Jim said, carried away by his success.

"Oh, no, please don't," Betty said, and her eyes grew troubled. "I could never go through this again." She stared over his head into the fire. "Jim, Jim, what are we doing here, you and I? I had thought we would never be together again."

All the haggard, drawn quality had returned to her face. Alarmed, Jim watched her. He was realizing it was not as simple as he would like it to be, this getting reacquainted with his wife. He was beginning to see how far apart they had gone. He was never one to think of these things himself. He needed to see the flames with his own eyes before he would admit there was a fire, but the sight of Betty's face was sad enough to make him know that a catastrophe had occurred. Was he going to be strong enough to pick up the pieces for her and help her to fit them together? The long days on the boat had lent him the impetus to think about such things. He had always pushed aside any responsibility in human relation by remarking, "Oh, forget it. A good night's sleep will settle anything," but as monotonous day followed monotonous night on the ship, he had done a lot of thinking.

When it was first suggested, he had bundled her extensive European trip into the phrase "Bet's crazy idea," thinking that summed it up, and then with the stock market crash, he had been complacent, "Well, that's over with, Bet's crazy idea," until she had fired her one shot, "I'm not coming home with you." To Jim, that was revolution. He had gone alone, angry, resentful, but he hadn't realized what had happened until he got back to America. He had lost his wife. That was what had happened, and not until it was too late did he find he should have grabbed her and pulled her home with him. And then, with the busy commonplaces of American life about him, he had let it slide, slide downhill, without looking at the bottom of the hill to see that there was no wife waiting for him. Caterina's cablegram was the shock he needed. *My wife is sick, my wife is alone, my wife needs me.* Why he hadn't seen the same need without this outside stimulus he couldn't tell. But it was the same way with a fire. He must see it with his own eyes, and he must feel the shock with his own body, and only then, would he move.

How was he ever to tell Betty all these things? Would she care if he did? Wasn't this Frenchman, with his clever instincts and his sensitive knowing ahead of time what to do, the man for her? Wouldn't it be better to let Bet go with him and lead the romantic mental life she so hankered after? Would he ever be able to satisfy Betty again? He knew how to play poker, but he didn't know how to play chess. *And she despises poker*. He sighed.

"Jim, Jim," Betty was saying, looking down into his face. For all this time, he had been staring at her and forgot that he was doing it. "Can't you forgive me, Jim? Is it so hard? Am I so terrible?"

"But, my dear, don't talk like that. All I want to do is to protect and care for you."

"Jim, I'm not worth protecting. I must tell you everything I have done. Every single thing. And then, let you decide what you want to do." Betty was earnest.

Jim had been stalling, not knowing what in the world he was to do or say. He did know that Betty was not strong enough for another emotional crisis, and he wondered if either of them was. Quickly, he laid his hands over hers and over the little perfume bottles. "Wait," he said. "Will you do that?" he wished suddenly that he were wise and trained like a doctor. Unconsciously, he was kind, and that perhaps was enough.

"But," Betty began.

"Don't tell me anything tonight. Tomorrow, the next day, the day after. When you feel you want to, but not tonight."

"Why?" Betty said slowly.

"Well, for one thing, I've done an awful lot of thinking, away from you. Back at home there, alone. It's been different, all this money mess, but it's not that. It's you and me. I've been lonely, terribly lonely. All these other people, there are so many of them, they're so busy. Things they do take all their time, they took all our time. It is still going on without us, whether we're there or not. But I can't stand it without you. I can't tell you, Bet, how I've missed you. I've come over here, Bet, to find you. That's all I've come for." He looked at her for a full minute, and he seemed to be through talking. Betty started to speak, but he interrupted her. "You know, Bet, I've got a crazy idea. It's just come to me. Tell me what you think of it. do you want to hear it?"

"Yes," she said.

"I want to take you off with me somewhere. Just you and me. Italy, maybe, I've always Thought I'd like to go to Italy. Do you think we could trust Caterina with the kids? For a week or a few days. I don't suppose it ever could work out, but, boy, I'd like to do that. Second honeymoon sort of thing." Jim smiled at her.

"Oh, Jim," Betty said, her eyes filling with tears.

He thought that she did not want to go, that she didn't want him. He stood up stiffly. He had been sitting in the same position a long time. "No use your holding this." He reached down and took the perfume from her lap. Idly, he looked at it, and, taking the little man and woman out of the box, he set them on the mantelpiece, one on each side of Betty's traveling clock.

"Don't leave me," Betty whispered, bending toward him, reaching out to touch his coat.

He sat on the couch beside her and put his arm around her. She needed comfort, he could see, but more than that he did not dare to hope for. Still, he must not hurry her. They sat there for a long time. He had lost his place of vantage with the firelight full on her face.

"Are you sure you don't care for Roberta one bit?" Betty said suddenly.

This way the healthiest sign she had shown yet, and Jim burst out laughing. It was wonderful to him to laugh, with his arm around Bet, and he squeezed her tighter. " Betty, you must still love me a little if you are such a goose as all that. Roberta doesn't matter to me more than that"—he broke a match in his fingers—" and if ever there was a dumb girl, she's it. I suppose that is why I went out with her, just because she is so dumb. I always have thought she was pretty terrible, and I still do. The only good thing that came out of it was that she bought her new car off me, and she made Ellis buy his, and that at least means good hard money for us. It is the only sensible thing she ever did."

"Not being sensible doesn't mean a woman isn't attractive."

"Bet, darling, I tell you, I loathe the woman." He looked down to find Betty smiling into the fire. "and I'm crazy about you. I adore you. To me, you're the swellest gal I ever met."

Betty nodded her head, smiling, but she wouldn't look at him. "Go on," she said, with the hint of a lift in her voice.

"What do you mean, go on?"

"Do you have to stop there?"

"Bet." Betty took her chin and turned her face to his.

"Do you think we could try that French formula?" she whispered.

"Bet, darling, do you mean you would like to take that trip to Italy with me?"

"Do we have to wait for Italy?" she said.

He caught her up in his arms and carried her upstairs to bed.

14

Ending

To meet, after an affair of the heart is over, is one of the most difficult things in the world to do. Betty did so without wanting to face Gilbert's eyes. Jim stood even straighter than usual. Gilbert could not prevent a smile. The responsibility that had been forced upon him was happily placed on another's shoulders and, what was even better, on the right shoulders. Gilbert could afford a smile.

It was in front of the casino on a pale spring morning with a languid warmth in the air.

If Betty had had to take the initiative, she wondered if she would not have tried to sidestep it and walk by with head averted. But the two men shook hands enthusiastically.

"Boy, this is fine," Jim was saying heartily. "We were wanting to see you. Settle business and all that sort of thing. How are you, Glisson? Looking fit. How was Paris? My wife heard you had spent a month there."

Then it was Betty's turn to hold out her hand and try to meet Gilbert's eyes. It was a shock to find them familiar. Idealizing the situation in her own mind, she had thought to have forgotten the Frenchman—she called him "the Frenchman" now. And here she was looking directly into the light gray eyes of Gilbert Glisson, the Gilbert to whom she had given love, the Gilbert whom she had considered marrying and living with the rest of her life. "I have forgotten him completely," she had told Jim so many times that she was under the impression she had. And there he was holding her hand, smiling that gentle, sarcastic smile of his, and she had forgot nothing. Every moment she had ever spent with him came up to her until their total was like a mounting wave which was surrounding and overwhelming her with its sweet flow.

Steadily, she held out her hand, and her voice was steady, too, as she pronounced the words, "*Eh bien, Monsieur Gilbert, et comment ca va. Il y a long temps.*" Her voice was held steady by a willpower she did not know she possessed, and she listened to her own voice, fascinated by its steadiness. She was like a man who knows he is drunk and who is very proud because he can carry a tray full of glasses into a room and set it down successfully without mishap.

"But come now. Tell me, how are the children?" Gilbert said. His voice was the most natural of the three.

"They were right behind us. They must have stopped for something." It was much easier talking about the children. How clever of Gilbert to have thought about them. "How is your mother? And Madame Suzanne?" Betty felt her voice was unbreakable in its inflection. She did not know she was capable of such magnificent stage play.

"Madame Suzanne?" Gilbert exclaimed, as though she had mentioned a name of which he had never heard. "I haven't the remotest idea."

"Ah, so you drop us all, one by one," Betty said gaily.

"I have only been back from Paris twenty-four hours," Gilbert said, and his apology was like honey to her pride. "You should be more familiar with St.-Raphael than I," he said, trying to turn the responsibility off onto her shoulders.

"Not at all. We are the greater strangers. We have only been in town the hours." She looked at her watch. "A trip to Italy," she laughed, but her laugh was quick and high.

"Yes, we went to Rome," Jim said, and his voice calmed the nervous excitement Betty could feel rising up inside her throat. "We had intended doing Florence, Venice, and all the rest, but we began and ended in Rome. A wonderful city." Jim looked at Betty and smiled broadly, and she gave him a dart of response.

"Indeed," Gilbert answered him, trying to hide his intuitive curiosity. He could see the passing of unspoken words between husband and wife, current of emotion of which he was the ignorant outsider. It rather piqued him. "Why should you have such a liking for Rome? I have always found it antiquely heavy, without half the beauty of Florence. Why didn't you tell me you were going to Italy? I could have mapped out a tour for you that would have given you the essence of Italian art without the slightest muddle, and saved you money into the bargain."

"Why didn't we indeed!" Betty voiced her exasperation.

Gilbert flicked her one of those enchanting smiles of his, appreciating his own absurd question, and continued, "But no, really, and of course your never went to Ravenna. No one ever goes to Ravenna, and yet it has the beginnings of everything. All the architecture of our Christian faith seems to have a sample left in Ravenna. It shows so beautifully the Eastern influence that westerners look at askance today. There they are, though, and we label them Byzantine and 'perfect type of mosaic art,' and we look very complacent and smug about it. Ravenna shows it all, and you really hardly need to look at anything else after that. Just to gaze on that blue heaven in the tomb of the Galla Placidia is enough to take the breath out of any one of us moderns."

Betty watched Jim as Gilbert talked. She wanted to observe the effect of the Frenchman's extravagant statements on her husband, but Jim only showed a bland affability. Betty tried not to listen to his voice.

"Whatever did you do in Rome?" Gilbert's voice was turned toward her, and Betty lost her poise.

"Rome?" she stammered, as though she had never heard the name before.

A light came into Gilbert's eyes as he saw her falter.

"Oh, we looked Rome over," Jim's voice rolled out, "but spent most . of our time up in the Sabine Hills. A pretty spot."

"Indeed," said Gilbert. He could see the man had regained his wife, and he wanted to cry, *Bravo, old man, I helped prepare the way*, but that would be crass. Although it was no more than human to relish the fact that he still could upset Betty, he was genuinely pleased to see that she had returned to the arms of her husband, but that did not prevent his pleasure in knowing that she had not forgot their might in Nice. Safely, he could enjoy the regret that his affair with this American lady had been ephemeral. As he had won her over she had the fire of love within her. Curious how men and women acted, barbarians, animals at heart, and yet they could stand talking like this with their clothes, their nationalities, their mannerisms, their culture, their layers and layers of civilization wrapped around them. And all the time there was the wolf, the tiger, the barnyard fowl peeking out of their eyes. Gilbert, while his thoughts were rushing over his mind like the torrent of a waterfall charging over the rocks in its course, was saying, "Ah, yes, the Sabine Hills in the springtime. Tivoli is a veritable love nest." He beamed on Betty and Jim as though to give them his blessing.

Betty was delighted. In a moment, she knew that Gilbert had understood the full flavor of her reunion with her husband and that he had but divined the words they had said and the scene where they had made it up. She was proud she had returned so properly to her husband, and she was fired with the sentiment that this Frenchman for one night had been in love with her. It made her feel more valuable as a woman. There was sentimental sorrow in the look she gave Gilbert, the look a wife can give to a former suitor whom she has left lovelorn and a bachelor. She should have known better than to have allowed herself the tiniest scrap of complacent regret.

In a flash, Gilbert had caught her look, and from the way his eyes were dancing she knew he was laughing at her. This hurt. "You may be amused to know, Betty, that only today my troth is announced to Aurelie Roule."

"What!" Betty said, and her exclamation was more like a cry of *So soon you can be unfaithful to me.*

"Yes. My mother and I went up to her house last evening. Just after my train came in."

"Your mother and you!" Betty's voice was incredulous. Betty could see a long line of American young men going to propose to their girls, each one accompanied by his mother. Is struck her as terribly funny.

"But why not my mother?" Who else should I take? She is in the seventh heaven, too. You would think it was she who was the fiancée . I imagine it well satisfied her."

Betty's eyes widened. Well satisfied! Who was he to say who was satisfied, other than himself? The conceit of the man; indeed, he was like the old French proverb, giving away an artichoke leaf to every woman, with only a small heart of an artichoke left. Shallow. Flirting with everyone. And what made it more poignant was that she, Betty, was no exception. He used to tell her how he despised the very girl to whom he was now announcing his engagement. One could not help wondering what sort of marriage it would turn out to be. With no love to begin it, at least there was none on his side, would his theories work? Betty felt very doubtful. He had told her so many times that any marriage would work provided both parties were willing, that starting out with nothing more than a man and a woman, a marriage could be developed which contained love and full understanding. He certainly was putting his theories into practice with a vengeance, choosing Aurelie Roule of whom he had made so much fun. Betty was glad he wasn't to be her husband, getting one girl pregnant, making love to another, and marrying a third, all in less than a year's time. She was glad to have her own comfortable, constant husband on whom she could depend.

Gilbert looked at her with his merry, gray eyes, and in an instant she could see herself walking arm in arm Gilbert through the streets of

Nice. What fun one had wherever he went, how gay he was, how jolly, never was one bored. He was the most delightful, lovable person she had ever known in her life. She loathed herself for having such a thought. Her eyes fell before his look. "What has happened to the children?" she said, hoping to cover her emotions from her husband and from this man.

The children came running as in answer. Betty felt as though she had just been saved from drowning. They made a great fuss over Gilbert, and he over them. Too much for both Jim's and Betty's liking, but who can make one's children accountable for one's likes and dislikes? One looks upon them as part of one's own identity, like a little finger that is jumping and skipping about but nonetheless obedient, and then one finds they are wooden Pinocchios, pulling their own strings and working themselves into contortions far removed from what one wants.

"Why, Gilbert Glisson, wherever have you been hiding yourself?" Mary exclaimed, for all the world like a little sophisticated woman.

"You might at least have written us a letter when you were in Paris. Our daddy did every day he was in Italy," Peter added.

"But then, you see, I am not your daddy," Gilbert said with a quirk that was not quite nice.

"Are you coming to visit us in America?" Mary asked. "You once said you would."

"Not now, Marie. Much as I would like to."

Betty decided Mary would have them in deep water again if she didn't watch out. It was dangerous making small talk with Gilbert. Chemical reactions were too recent to be predictable, and an innocuous formula might blow up in their faces before any one of them had the presence of mind to stop it. she slipped her arm through Jim's, in case either one of the men might wish to misinterpret her sympathies. Perhaps, too she wanted the extra strength to protect herself from those over-keen, gray eyes of Gilbert's. She was hunting in her mind for the right phrase to bring the meeting to a close.

Again Jim spoke for her. "Well, Glisson, glad to have seen you. We're leaving in a few days when we get this boat business settled. Back via Paree and a last gay whirl. Our lease is up the sixteenth of May. What about that inventory?"

Mention of the inventory made them all laugh.

"Ah, yes, the inventory. I guess my mother had better attend to that. I'll speak to her about it." Gilbert sighed. Was he afraid to come to their house by himself? "But we must have some sort of celebration before you go, for the sake of the children, and Aurelie." He added her name as though he had for the moment forgotten her.

"Yes indeed," Jim said heartily, not giving Betty a chance to voice her opinion, and starting to lead her away. "We shall see you soon." He put on his hat to terminate their meeting.

The children clung to Gilbert, Mary especially. He held their shoulders and gave them each a kiss. Betty took one last long look at Gilbert, his beret in his hand, and she marveled at how she had sickened for him, how she had let him mean so much to her, and how now he was nothing but a Frenchman they had met on the promenade. Well, it was over with. She must not look back.

─ ⌒ ─

The weather their last few days in St.-Raphael was superb. The time was filled with packing trunks and handshaking. Madame Glisson came to take the inventory, but her son did not accompany her. It was business-like and pleasant. They met Gilbert several times but with no further chance for conversation. They went to call on Aurelie Roule. After all, she was Mary's teacher, and it was the correct thing to do, and they found her like a full-blown rose for color, size, and smiles. Betty only hoped she would not favor the beautiful Mediterranean cystus roses which bloomed for but a day. Monsieur Masse shook hands with them so frequently, it was like an obsession.

Caterina was worse than an obsession. She was like jelly the children have spilled. You couldn't touch a thing in the house without having Caterina there first, sticky and clinging. You would go to pick up something you had dropped, say a towel, and there was Caterina already lifting up one end of it. Privacy was not included in Caterina's vocabu-lary. She peered into the bedrooms at any hour, and if Betty scolded her, Caterina looked pious with hands folded on her stomach.

"Soon enough, and you won't be bothered with me. Soon enough, you will have no one to take care of you. And dear God knows whether you'll ever keep the covers on the children at night and they'll die of *le rhume*," she would darkly forebode. She never had approved of the inno-vation of open windows, and this was her excuse for closing them tight.

"Monsieur Jim and I can keep the blankets over them and over our-selves, thank you," Betty answered, half angry. Caterina would even pop her head into their room because she felt "a terrible draft."

When the packing began, Caterina was at her worst. Betty felt she ought to do it herself, and then she would be able to know where every-thing was packed. Traveling with two children is at best a strain on lo-cating the essentials when needed. Caterina would stand silently by the trunks, with downcast eyes, always a bad sign, and the minute Betty was called away, she would rearrange everything to her own way of thinking.

"Caterina, that truck of Peter's simply has to go in the trunk," Betty would say when she found it in a suitcase. "He won't need it until he gets home, and the trunk is going in the hold."

Caterina's hands would writhe. "What goes into the hold of a ship never comes out. A sailor boyfriend of mine told me you couldn't trust the hold of a ship."

"Caterina, don't be absurd."

"It's better for him to carry it in his own hands. Then he'll know where it is. I wouldn't trust a ship's hold anywhere at any time," she muttered. "And if you think you're going to put any of Monsieur Jim's clothes in that trunk!" she threatened, walking out of earshot.

Betty was repeating the conversation to Jim that evening after the children were in bed.

"The trouble with you is," Jim consoled her, "you don't understand Caterina's psychology. She doesn't feel comfortable unless she can take hold of a thing with her own hands or see it with her own eyes. She probably keeps her money between her mattresses, which isn't such a bad idea. If I had known Caterina a year ago, and if I had asked her advice, she would have told me it was the only safe place, and if had followed her advice, we would have all our money today. It's a big if, of course. Yes, the mattress could be the best place."

Betty began to laugh. "And you're going right back home and put all your money in the bank."

"That's exactly what I'll do. Although I won't ever again make fun of the mattress and stocking philosophy of investing money. But Bet, my darling, I'd rather have you then all the money in the world, and if it will make you happier, we'll keep our money hidden in a mattress, that is, some of it. But really and truly, darling, I solemnly swear I won't let money and business matter so much. Now that I've lost them both, I can be much more careless about them. It is when I nearly lost you that I realized what was the most important thing. Bet, dear, we'll be together as we have never been before, and nothing in Merchantville can pry us apart."

"Oh, Jim, I don't want to monopolize you, but I do want you to go on looking at things the way you do now."

    — —

The day came for them to leave St.-Raphael. For Betty and the children, there was as much emotion connected with it as though they were leaving their own home. Jim tried to look sad, but he wasn't very successful. "The way you people carry on, anyone would think you'd lived in France for six years instead of six months," he teased them.

"But Daddy, it does almost seem like six years," Mary said. She had celebrated her sixth birthday in March. "When I think of leaving my beautiful Mamselle Roule, I have to crush the sobs in my heart." Mary spoke entirely in French, and her phrases were apt to have a Midian extravagance. "And as for *mon Gilbert*, it is cruelty to leave him behind." Mary knew that something had happened regarding Gilbert. Vaguely she resented it.

"Well, he's going to marry your Mamselle Roule, isn't he?" Peter said. He and Monsieur Bonnet had never hit it off very well, and he was always trying to pick a fights with Mary on the issue of her precious teacher.

"That is my only consolation. But I wish we could stay for the wedding." Mary always was a precocious child.

"That would just be perfect," Jim said sarcastically, over Mary's head, grinning at Betty.

Betty made a face at Jim.

"Well, at any rate. I've given them a wedding present," Mary said.

"What did you give them?" Betty asked quickly. She was too used to Mary's bombshells.

Mary saw she was trapped. She shouldn't have talked until they were on the boat, when nothing could be done about it. Now they might try to get the present back again. Grown-ups were so stupid. It was Peter who had egged her on to boast too soon. "It was nothing," Mary said sulkily, on the defensive. "You never use it anyway. It was just some perfume."

"What perfume?" Betty said, guessing at once.

"Oh, just some you had left behind in a drawer." Mary refused to be sorry. "It made a darling wedding present. The bottles were a little man and woman.

"Why, Mary Barton," Peter said, horrified. He saw his mother's face go red with anger.

Betty could hardly control her voice. "Jim, Jim" she repeated, and the tears came. "What shall I do? What shall I do? How could I have forgot to pack it? I could swear I packed it! Yet Mary says I left it behind in the bureau drawer."

"But my dear, there are more where it came from. I'll buy you a dozen when we get to Paris." It really was funny the way that little devil Mary had her own ingenious method of troublemaking.

"But Jim, whatever shall I do?" Betty was unconsoled.

"Nothing, my dear. The train leaves in an hour."

"I can never forgive myself for my negligence, and I adored it, that perfume. It idealized you and me together."

Mary was bewildered. She expected a terrible scolding. Of course, there wasn't time to be sent to her room, her usual punishment; they were leaving too soon for that. There was time enough for a spanking, but her mother ignored her, and her tears were for Mary's father. Her mother never cried, and it was a distressing sight. In addition, Mary was still more confused to learn that it was her father who had given her mother the perfume. "I'm sorry, Mother," Mary said quickly. "You see, I had been thinking about what I could give Mamselle for a present, and I happened to be in your room two days ago, and Caterina was making the beds and fussing with the bags as usual, and I saw her take the perfume out of your suitcase and put it away back in your bureau drawer."

"You saw her take the perfume out of the suitcase," Betty cried. "Are you sure you saw her take it out of the suitcase?"

"Well, I just told you," Mary said, exasperated. *Grown-ups simply never believed a word you said.* "And then Caterina said Gilbert gave you these because they were French and that he had brought them to you from Paris, and she didn't want you to keep them, and I mustn't say a word, and I promised. Then afterward I had the wonderful idea of giving them to Mamselle for a wedding present. I didn't have any allowance left to buy her one, and besides, I never could save enough to buy such a fine one. These were really new, there was only the tiniest bit of perfume used. So I filled the bottles up even with water, and you see I had to work in a hurry, and perfume is strong enough to stand it, and then I tied it up and took it to school, and Mamselle went into ecstasies, and she kissed me in front of everybody." Mary closed her eyes for a moment, remembering. "I was going to tell her, if there was any question from Gilbert about where I got it, that Daddy bought it on his way because he was in Paris, too."

"You seem to have thought of everything," Jim said, dying to laugh at the wicked duplicity of his daughter.

But for Betty there was nothing funny about it. "Then I did put it in the suitcase, and I didn't forget you, my darling, did I? And you love me still," Betty said in all earnestness.

"My dear, my foolish sweet dear. You are such a goose." And Jim gave Betty ten kisses in a row.

Mary kept gazing in astonishment that her crime was going scot-free.

Betty regretted the loss of the present, but that was nothing to her distress at thinking she'd forgot to pack it. Such stupidity. However many times Jim assured her that she was morbidly sensitive about things that to him didn't matter, her conscience would not let her rest. *You are a wicked woman*, it would cry at her on the slightest provocation. There was a certain pleasure in pitying herself.

Their trunks and bags had been taken to the station earlier. It was time for them to leave. Betty looked back at the house with a sigh. Her days in France were over. She held Jim's arm very close. Caterina went with them, and one would think it was to a funeral. She had draped her hat with a long black chiffon veil, and her face was long enough to have lost a dozen husbands.

"Monsieur Jim," she would wail if anyone so much as looked at her, and she kept clutching Peter or Mary to her as though they were her own children being torn from her side.

"But Caterina," Peter consoled her, "we'll write you postcards, and in French too—pictures of the Statue of Liberty and the skyscrapers in New York and Independence Hall in Philadelphia. That is very near us, you know. I have been to Independence Hall. That is where George Washington and Lafayette met. Lafayette was French." Peter was beginning to study the rudiments of history and was more proud of than exact with his facts.

"Ah," Caterina said, pricking her ears at anything French. "And you have met him too?"

"Of course not. He's dead," Peter said crushingly. "Even Mary knows that."

"Oh, yes, he is dead," Mary chirped, amazed to hear praise from her brother and quite vague about why she received it.

At the word dead, Caterina shuddered, opening her eyes in terror as though some ghost might jump at her. She crossed herself and cried, "We must hurry, hurry, we may miss the train."

"If we miss it, we'll take one tomorrow," Jim said to tease her. "Here's some money for a *Journal*. Stop at the corner and buy one—no, two, *deux*. One New York *Herald-Tribune*. One *L'Eclaireur*. Madame must have her

L'Eclaireur pour le dernier fois. Madame and I shall go to Monsieur Masse to say *au revoir.* You take Peter and Mary *avec vous.* Meet you at the station."

Again Caterina's eyes widened. She opened her mouth, but she didn't say anything.

"Doesn't dare to," Jim said, chuckling to Betty. "These peasants and their trains. I bet Caterina would have had us down there last night to make sure to catch the train."

Betty and Jim took shortcut down a back street, but for Caterina and the children there was no other way than along the main street past Gilbert's office. The shutters were closed. Caterina all but ran them by.

"How queer," Mary said. Nothing ever escaped her little bright eyes. "And there's a card. What does it say?"

Caterina was strong and yanked the children past, muttering as she ran faster. "It is nothing. They've gone off on a trip. Why be so nosy? That is all, they are closed for the day. Hurry. Dépêche-toi, we may miss the train."

"Oh, we forgot les journaux. "Peter stopped. "Come back. We shall have time."

"Ah, too late, too late, too late," Caterina cried, hurrying again. Then, she changed he tone.

"Oh, *mes beaux enfants*! Wait until you are on the train before you tell your daddy that I forgot. Be good, what? He will be angry, and I do not want him angry this last time. Ah, I know you will do this for your poor old Caterina. Here is the money, Peter, you give it to him when the train starts."

They knew their father would be cross and might even make them miss the train, and so for Caterina they took the money and said nothing. Quickly they forgot, too, in the excitement of the train arrival. Monsieur Masse accompanied their mother and father. There were the bags to be found. The position to take on the platform, the handshakes, the kisses, Caterina's sobs. The train itself hissing and clanging above them, the shouts and running of many feet.

Inside their compartment, they all pressed to the window for more hand waving. Poor Caterina and Monsieur Masse were brokenhearted.

But they beamed through their sadness. Jim had placed a hundred-franc note in the handshake he had given each, and the effect was like a rosy glow on their skin.

The train pulled out. St.-Raphael was no more.

Life revolved in the minute compass of making oneself comfortable, arranging the eternal bags of travel to the tune of the clattering wheels of the train.

"Where's the paper?" Jim asked.

"Your paper?" Mary said, looking to Peter.

"Here's your money," Peter said stoutly. "Caterina forgot."

"On purpose," Jim fumed. "Never have I known the like of that woman. For some obscure reason, in her silly brain, she just wanted to forget. Bet, I can't stand her any longer. You'll have to fire her."

This made them all laugh, as they were leaving Caterina far behind them. It made Betty, Peter, and Mary almost cry. Their St.-Raphael days in their dear villa were over, and their French days were numbered. Other people would be going in and out the narrow gate. Other faces would look up at their parasol pine. Caterina, who had bossed them like her own children, would be tyrant to some other family. And Mademoiselle Roule. The *patisseries*, the beautiful *plage*. And their Gilbert? He had deserted them at the end, but now that the whole scene was retreating, he took his proper place in the center, and they would only remember his friendship. What a wonderful play- fellow he was.

Betty, in her grown-up realism, added *had been*. He was card-indexed in her past, a pleasant memory. For a second, she let her mind think about him, wishing she could peep in on him with Mademoiselle Roule, how they would act together, where they would be married, where they would live. It was comforting to know he was in her own past and could disturb her no more.

She looked up to meet the affectionate eyes of her husband, smiling to read her thoughts. Her thoughts flew out the window, she opened her arms to Jim, and cried, "Oh, my dear, my very dear, do you still love me, for I love you with all my heart!"

— —

"Just to fool Caterina, I'm going to buy my paper here," Jim said when they stopped at Marseille. The children were sure he'd be left behind, but he insisted on getting off. They were leaning out the window when he came back waving a paper in each hand.

"I've a good mind to sent Caterina a postcard, 'Bought papers in spite of you.' She doesn't deserve the silk stocking I promised her. Here, my dear." He dropped *L'Eclaireur* in her lap.

"It'll be the last copy you'll get. Read it carefully."

"Oh, Jim, how silly. I only used to get it for the movies. It is such a dull local thing." It was on the tip of her tongue to say that Gilbert used to make her get it—" nothing like a newspaper to sharpen up your French," he would quote. She checked herself in time, her new resolution, never to quote him again.

She watched the scenery for same time, never dreaming she was holding a bomb spread out in her lap. Aimlessly, she glanced through it, amused to read of local doing, to see familiar names in print. What was this headline? "*Le Drame Passionnel de Saint-Raphael*." How did St.-Raphael get in the paper? Front page?

The style was florid and, unlike American journalism, did not disclose the main facts in the first paragraph. She raced through a sad love affair, many quarrels, and turned the page all out of breath to find out who was the young lady who had shot her lover with a resolver.

She was hunting for the continuation when her eyes was caught by the smiling face of Gilbert Glisson.

The picture was an inch by an inch and a quarter, but she recognized it as a reprint from a snapshot she herself had taken. It was shortly after the donkey ride. He had driven over one day when the children were in school, and he had taken her up in the hills in back of town. He was making blueprints of the property his company held, and he wanted to check up on certain measurement. She had taken some knitting to do while he worked, and in her bag had been her pocket Kodak. When he had finished they walked to see the view, and before they got into the car she had begged him to let her take his picture. She remembered saying, "I must have something to remember you by." She did not realize how soon she would need it.

Laughing, he had stood beside his car, one foot on the running board, his hand in his pocket, his arm leaning on the door. She had captured the nonchalance, the amusement, the essence of the man. Snapshots often catch this quality which a professional picture misses. How many times in the past months she had devoured this picture, trying to make it breathe again. The smile in that picture had at the moment been only for her. She had had two copies made, one for herself and one she had given him. This must be his.

At this point, her mind began to comprehend why his picture was printed in L'Eclaireur. There was another picture of a house with the caption, "The house that produced the drama." Gilbert, then, was the man in the drama. The house was Suzanne's.

As though she were drinking some horrible medicine, she gulped down the story: the young widow murderess, Suzanne David; the esteemed architect, Gilbert Glisson, who enjoyed a solid reputation and was beloved by all who knew him; the sad love affair, the many quarrels; the final break; his engagement to Mademoiselle Aurelie Roule; his last return to the widow's house to remove some belongings; the revolver in the top drawer. Supposedly there had been a terrible quarrel. Neighbors heard a shot, the police were called. The murderess was removed to the house of arrest in Draguignan. The murdered man died of hemorrhages. He had dragged himself to the kitchen door, where the police had found him. The body was removed to the hospital for an autopsy. The doctor pronounced death by violence, the bullet having entered the occipital bone at the base of the skull. The mother of the victim, Madame Glisson, overwhelmed..."

Betty could read no farther. Her throat had a curious sensation, as though someone were cutting of her breath. Her lips had been slightly parted as she read, and her mouth was too dry to swallow.

She felt the train closing in on her. It was slower, more drawn out than fainting. Her ears beat with the sensation one gets just before going under ether. She wanted to cry out, but her voice made no sound. She wanted to run, but she sat quietly. She looked down to find her hands folding up the paper in its original creases.

She looked out the window. Suddenly, she saw Gilbert parking his car. It was in front of Suzanne's house. He slammed the door and walked up to the house. Did he have a premonition what his fate was to be? Did he look up at the house, expecting Suzanne to be smiling at the window? Or did he think as his feet crunched the gravel, Well, this is the last time I visit this house, never dreaming that his life was at an end. Or did he think of nothing more then the thread that was on his sleeve and picking it off? It was the thread of his life. What things had he left at her house? Were they worth his life? What did they say when they met? Did Suzanne crouch behind the door? Was her heart sick with the loss of her baby, sick to death now with the prospect of losing her man? Did she mean to shoot herself when she had fired at her dear one? No one would know just what happened. The 'how' or the 'why'. Gilbert could not. Suzanne's story would be colored by the glazed eyes of her lover and the warm sticky spot that widened on her kitchen floor. Betty could know the story as well as anyone, better than a jury or judge ever would. Yet she could but surmise.

Gilbert was not dead. He was alive as she had always known him. He was laughing, talking, walking around, getting in his car, whirling off with the dust rising up behind him. He was turning into her drive, charging through the narrow gate with the devil behind him, swerving and stopping with a jerk of the handbrake under the parasol pine. The dust sifted up through its branches and over the car and his head like a modernistic halo. All of a piece, he sprang out and was beside her. The coordination of his body always surprised her. She was used to her husband's long, lanky movements, but Gilbert was short, and when he moved all of him seemed to move too. He looked at her and laughed with those light gray eyes of his, and he swung Mary high up onto his shoulder. His strength surprised her. Whatever he did surprised her. That was part of his fascination. In the house was a fire, they drank tea, he moved about restless like a cat. He lit a cigarette. He called out a joke to Caterina in the kitchen. He talked, gesticulating. He picked up a stocking she had darned and laid on her knee, inspected her cross-stitches, grimaced at her, and placed it back on her knee. She shrank from his touch, and she longed to have him near her and touching her.

The train lurched, and Betty's eyes widened. Never again would Gilbert spring out of his car. He was lying behind the kitchen door where he had dragged himself. There was blood on the floor behind his head; he would never move. Lying dead on Suzanne's floor, no tears could make him come alive; he was dead. To lie forever on the kitchen floor in Suzanne's house. They could carry away his stiff body. They could scrub the floor. But there he would lie, the spot dark and wide.

Jim was refolding his paper when he happened to look over the top and saw Betty's face. He dropped his paper and leaned over and took her hands. "My dear, my dear, are you ill? What is the trouble? Tell me quick."

Betty looked at him, eyes pleading. How could she tell him? "I, I need some air. Let's go out. Let's go out in the corridor."

The children were absorbed in the scenery, one on each side of the window. They weren't paying any attention to their mother and father.

Jim led her outside, and, leaning on the rail, she tried to tell him. "It still seems too warm. I feel I may faint," she stammered.

Jim pulled the window down, and Betty sniffed in the air. She put her hands on the edge of the window. She was still holding the journal.

How could she tell Jim? She didn't care how generous he was, he could not prevent the thought, That Frenchman is well out of the way. He would be kind, of course, solicitous of her welfare, but he had never thought highly of Gilbert. It sickened her that there might be any criticism of this man whom she had once loved. Her hand moved on the window edge, her fingers opened a fraction. The paper was torn from her grasp, and it was gone as though it had never been. Her eyes looked at her empty hands, and then they turned to look at Jim's face.

Jim showed not a flicker of what she had done. He hadn't even seen it. His expression was complete concern for her. "My dear Bet," he said. "You feel better, don't you? The color is back a little in your cheeks. You looked like death a minute ago."

She sighed, "Yes," and she wondered how they stood beside each other without communicating their thoughts. "I think I am better." She sighed again. How horrible to die like that. Shot. Murdered. How could that girl have done it? To murder the man she loved.

Betty tried to think how she could tell Jim. Wouldn't be better to do it? The words would not come. "You'd better close the window. It's against the rules, you know." What if he should say, *Well, what can you expect with people like that*? She could not bear to have him think it.

"Let's go back," she said, hiding deeper her horrible secret.

She forced herself to talk to Jim of incidentals, to play with the children. There was lunch to get out, towns to attract their eyes. There was the food to interest their bodies. She had brought along a game of Authors, crayons, and papers. Yet all through the day, there were terrifying glimpses of what lay on that fateful kitchen floor. Caterina had known; she had tried to keep them from knowing. What must Madame Glisson be going through? Poor, poor Mademoiselle Roule, with her name Mamselle sealed for life. And Suzanne, ah Suzanne! She would not, could not be sane, with her heart crucified. That widening spot on her kitchen floor. Betty's throat muscles grew taut; her eyes ached.

The trip was eternity, an ordeal of endurance. The children took naps. The day dragged on. Men and women sat in their compartment and left. Up the length of France their train carried them.

— —

At long last, the train bore them into the lovely city of Paris. It was May.

When the weather is cold and the endless rain is slashing down, Paris is exciting. In May there is a degree of mellowness that cannot be surpassed by any other city in the world. It glows from the walls of the houses, gray and ancient as they are. It shines in people's faces. In the gardens and the sidewalk cafes, it is so intense it affects the heart of everyone. Paris in May. Yes, there is no place in the world quite like it.

— ❧ —

They had been living in Paris a week. Their days were taking on a patterns that gave them the sensation of always having lived in this same manner. Their hotel was quiet and cheap, and the lady who ran it was solicitous of their welfare. She solved for them the problem of children in the city, and this is an overwhelming one when a family is visiting. Children abhor impermanence. They like to do the same thing over and over. The adult pace for absorbing new sights exhausts them.

Therefore, Peter and Mary were jumping with happiness when each morning at precisely ten o'clock, a tidy nursemaid named Lola called for them.

None of this picture-gallery tour with lunch anywhere. Lola carried a string bag for rubbers, an umbrella, and a camp stool—why pay a penny for a chair to sit on when you could carry your own—and she led the children to the Luxembourg Gardens which were just down the street. They had lunch at a family creamery, where Lola berated Mary for not finishing her spinach. At three, Lola returned them to the hotel as happily satiated as they had been full of anticipation when they started out. And each evening, she sat in the hotel bedroom while Monsieur and Madame did the night life of Paris. This allowed Betty and Jim periods of day and night freedom, larded with a family dinner and brief sightseeing keyed to the children's interests.

The joys of that garden. There they could play with the freedom of their own backyard. To outward appearance, it was French freedom, which is to say relaxation with care, with supervision. They played ball, but never out of bounds. They dug in the sand, but in one spot, never on the walk. They looked at the meticulous flower beds, safe behind their fences. They played boats in the round pond, with gloves on. They were not allowed to play croquet, but they could watch. This honor of croquet was reserved for old men with beards who played with canny skill.

Jim became proficient in the art of sightseeing. In addition to his Baedecker, he bought a small flat red Guilman's "Plan de Paris par Arrondissement." With this he felt he could conquer the Bastille. He conducted their trips by bus or the Nord-Sud like a Parisian instead of the regulation American in a taxi. It was adventurous, but Jim brought them safely out in the Bois de Boulogne to wander under the chestnuts, the Cluny Museum, Gobelin Tapestries, St. Cloud for the horse races, Fontainbleu, or the Musee Jacquemart-Andre. "Name your place," Jim would cry out before they started.

Jim was arrogant. He could never seem to get enough of looking at Betty as they wandered down a gallery or dashed off to a horse race or danced in the Bal Bullier. "I love you," he whispered a hundred times a day. Openly, he put his arm around her waist as they leaned on the old wall overlooking the Siene and watched the timeless fishermen who must have been fishing for centuries, catching perhaps the same fish, or never catching one.

Betty sighed, but he seemed not to notice. Jim could be dense when he wanted to be. Why hadn't she told him at once? When their love was the most perfect, the face of Gilbert rose to haunt her. It clutched at her breath. They would be eating filet of sole in Marguery's, and Gilbert murdered on the floor would turn her food to ashes. She would stare at Jim, but never once did he change the expression in his loving eyes, She was now in a quandary whether to ever tell him, and how she hated to hold a secret between then. She struggled to answer his love and forget the horrible vision, but sometimes at night she would break from a dream in which she was drowning.

Briskly one morning, after the children had gone, Jim said, "Pere LaChaise today. They say it is an amazing cemetery and well worth the morbidness that goes with it."

"Pere LaChaise Cemetery," Betty echoed. A cemetery, memories of the St.-Raphael cemetery she and Caterina had visited the day of the baby's funeral. How long ago. Strange that Jim should want to take me to a cemetery. As Caterina did. It wasn't strange, but it seemed so to her. They would be burying Gilbert. Would they send his body to Paris to lie beside his father, or would it be near his son? But she had buried Gilbert in agony that long month when he had never come to her. When she had looked for him and longed for him, he had died for her, torturing her with his absence which was like death up on those windy, rock-strewn hills.

It was a long trip and required a change of subways. "Reamur-Sebastopol," Jim reminded her as he settled behind his usual paper. Like a dutiful wife, she watched for the station and saw the coming and going of the subway people intent on their own doings.

"One of the most popular monuments in here"—Jim began quoting the Baedecker as soon as they got off at Pere LaChaise—" is the gothic one erected to Abelard and Heloise, the famous Medieval lovers. They say it's not authentic, however."

"Oh, not authentic, but they are together."

"Yes." Jim beamed at her. "But I'd prefer to be together alive than dead. Wouldn't you?" He pulled her arm through his.

"Yes, I would, Jim." Her voice faltered. "I've got to tell—"

"There's one I want to see particularly." Jim ignored her remark. "It's to the Dead. A man named Bartholome did it, double star, so it must be good."

"Double star?" she questioned. What as effort to follow what he was saying, and she wanted to so much. Double starred! Ill-stared, rather. To be murdered and drag oneself to the kitchen door to die. How could Suzanne have shot him? It was impossible to love a man and shoot him. Inhuman. "No human woman would murder a man she loved." Unconsciously, she had spoken the last sentence out loud.

"My dear, you must learn how to forget." Jim's kind voice was in her ear. "I'm here to show you."

"Jim, what do you mean? Do you know? How do you know?"

"My dear. Naturally, I bought another L'Eclaireur as soon as I saw you toss that one out the window. Do you think I'm that dense?"

She looked down at the gravel walk, for she had thought he was.

He led her up the gently rising slope of the Avenue Principale bordered on each side with giant cypresses. They paused at Alfred de Musset, the poet's weeping willow tree, and read the little poem he had written himself. They passed generals, painters, bronze figures, until at the end they came to the Monument to the Dead

It was very impressive.

Betty read, "*Sur ceux qui habitaient le pays de l'ombre de la Mort une Lumiere resplendit.* Jim, do you think that's true?" she pressed his arm. "Jim, why didn't you tell me you knew Gilbert was murdered? I thought I was hiding my sorrow from you."

"Translate it for me, my dear. My French isn't equal to it," Jim said evenly.

Betty translated almost literally. "'On those who dwell in the country of the shadow of Death, a light shines.' I wonder if Gilbert has a light shining on him. Perhaps he is the smiling man who has just gone through the door. I frighten you, don't I?" Betty said, looking at Jim, who was considerably troubled by her fantasy.

As she stood there beside her living husband in this unreal atmosphere of death, a curious thing began to happen. Her hysteria began to disappear. She felt she was adjusting herself to the facts. Clarifying them. Could it be that it was because she was sharing them with Jim? This person Suzanne, that man Gilbert Glisson, they were the carved limestone figures. An angel was lifting the tombstone from his grave. He would arise, and a light would shine upon him. But as far as she was concerned, he was turned to stone. Forever.

Illogically, she wanted to throw her arms around her husband's neck. He and she were alive. They loved each other. They would go on loving and living together. To murder was not in Jim or in her. Not in a thousand years would either of them murder.

"Oh, Jim, how kind you are," was all she said.

"And you, my dear, how lovely."

They went off, happily, arms entwined, to go back to the hotel, and to America.

Notes By The Editor

The editor is the author's son, Francis M. Butterworth, who recently brought these pages to life long after the manuscript was completed in the early 1930s. He copy edited the entire manuscript and produced the finished book. He thanks you for reading this book, asks that you write a review at the listing on the Amazon site and to 'like us' at Saugus Books on Face Book where his and other Katie Butterworth books are listed.

The title may seem odd to the modern reader, but it was a term at the time that meant to describe a duplicitous person particularly one who is unfaithful to a loved one. The 'artichoke heart' metaphor was used more recently by writer/director Joseph L. Mankiewicz in his award-winning movie *All About Eve* (1950) when the main character (an aging Broadway star) played by Bette Davis said in a sarcastic voice: "Remind me to tell you about the time I once looked into the heart of an artichoke". She was referring to her seemingly duplicitous boyfriend (played by Gary Merrill) chatting up her young understudy (played by Anne Baxter) with a story about looking into the wrong end of a camera viewfinder. See the quote from Chapter 14: ". . . he was like the old French proverb, giving away an artichoke leaf to every woman, with only a small heart of an artichoke left. Shallow. Flirting with everyone. And what made it more poignant was that she, Betty, was no exception."

Throughout the book, places mentioned in France are real. Indeed, it can be a travel guide. If you are traveling, be sure to follow up on them. For example in Chapter 8 (**Pierre de la Fée**) is an actual place almost as remarkable as Stonehenge (https://en.wikipedia.org/wiki/Draguignan#/media/File:Draguignan_Pierre_de_la_fee.JPG). This, in my view is Katie Butterworth's finest chapter: the writing particularly the dialogue is superb.

Also Katie was a student of botany, and all the myriad flowers and shrubs her character, Betty, sees are actual flowers one can find in Provence.

Finally, the *S.S. Minnekahda*, the ship the book's characters sailed on, is a real ship that made one of its last crossings about the time this novel was being created. It was part of group of transatlantic steamships of The Atlantic Transport Line covered in a book by the same name *The Atlantic Transport Line 1881-1931* authored by Jonathan Kinghorn (2012). The company was a casualty of the Great Depression.

www.ingramcontent.com/pod-product-compliance
Lightning Source LLC
Chambersburg PA
CBHW070324260626
47160CB00003B/944